THE
Annie
Dillard

READER

THE Annie Dillard
READER

HarperCollins*Publishers*

Some of these uncollected poems have appeared in *Field, Georgia Review*, and *Ontario Review*. The short story "The Living" first appeared, in a different form, in *Harper's*. "The Book of Luke" first appeared in *Antaeus* and in *Incarnation*.

HarperCollins books may be purchased for educational, business, or sales promotional use. For information, please write: Special Markets Department, HarperCollins Publishers, Inc., 10 East 53rd Street, New York, NY 10022.

FIRST EDITION

Designed by Nancy Singer

Library of Congress Cataloging-in-Publication Data
Dillard, Annie.
   [Selections. 1994]
   The Annie Dillard reader / by Annie Dillard. — 1st ed.
      p.   cm.
   ISBN 0-06-017158-8
   I. Title.
PS3554.I298A6   1994
818'.5409—dc20   94-19482

94 95 96 97 98 ❖/HC 10 9 8 7 6 5 4 3 2 1

for Rosy

CONTENTS

AUTHOR'S NOTE

Here is a selection from some of my books. There are many chapters from *Pilgrim at Tinker Creek* and *An American Childhood*. *Holy the Firm* appears in its entirety, and revised. In 1978 *Harper's* published a short story called "The Living," the characters of which, and their story, became the core of the 1992 novel *The Living*. It appears here in a third form, as a new and changed short story. There are a few poems, old and new, one uncollected essay, and some narratives from my sole book of essays, *Teaching a Stone to Talk*.

TOTAL ECLIPSE

I

IT HAD BEEN LIKE DYING, that sliding down the mountain pass. It had been like the death of someone, irrational, that sliding down the mountain pass and into the region of dread. It was like slipping into fever, or falling down that hole in sleep from which you wake yourself whimpering. We had crossed the mountains that day, and now we were in a strange place—a hotel in central Washington, in a town near Yakima. The eclipse we had traveled here to see would occur early the next morning.

I lay in bed. My husband, Gary, was reading beside me. I lay in bed and looked at the painting on the hotel-room wall. It was a print of a detailed and lifelike painting of a smiling clown's head, made out of vegetables. It was a painting of the sort that you do not intend to look at and that, alas, you never forget. Some tasteless fate presses it upon you; it becomes part of the complex interior junk you carry with you wherever you go. Two years have passed since the total eclipse of which I write. During those years I have forgotten, I assume, a great many things I wanted to remember—but I have not forgotten that clown painting or its lunatic setting in the old hotel.

The clown was bald. Actually, he wore a clown's tight rubber wig, painted white; this stretched over the top of his skull, which was a cabbage. His hair was bunches of baby carrots. Inset in his white clown makeup, and in his cabbage skull, were his small and laughing human eyes. The clown's glance was like the glance of Rembrandt in some of the self-portraits: lively, knowing, deep, and loving. The crinkled shadows around his eyes were string beans. His eyebrows were parsley. Each of his ears was a broad bean. His thin, joyful lips were red chili peppers; between his lips were wet rows of human teeth and a suggestion of a real tongue. The clown print was framed in gilt and glassed.

To put ourselves in the path of the total eclipse, that day we had driven five hours inland from the Washington coast, where we lived. When we tried to cross the Cascades range, an avalanche had blocked the pass.

A slope's worth of snow blocked the road; traffic backed up. Had the avalanche buried any cars that morning? We could not learn. This highway was the only winter road over the mountains. We waited as highway crews bulldozed a passage through the avalanche. With two-by-fours and walls of plyboard, they erected a one-way, roofed tunnel through the avalanche. We drove through the avalanche tunnel, crossed the pass, and descended several thousand feet into central Washington and the broad Yakima valley, about which we knew only that it was orchard country. As we lost altitude, the snows disappeared; our ears popped; the trees changed, and in the trees were strange birds. I watched the landscape innocently, like a fool, like a diver in the rapture of the deep who plays on the bottom while his air runs out.

The hotel lobby was a dark, derelict room, narrow as a corridor, and seemingly without air. We waited on a couch while the manager vanished upstairs to do something unknown to our room. Beside us, on an overstuffed chair, absolutely motionless, was a platinum-blond woman in her forties, wearing a black silk dress and a strand of pearls. Her long legs were crossed; she supported her head on her fist. At the dim far end of the room, their backs toward us, sat six bald old men in their shirtsleeves, around a loud television. Two of them seemed asleep. They were drunks. "Number six!" cried the man on television, "Number six!"

On the broad lobby desk was a ten-gallon aquarium, lighted and bubbling, that contained one large fish; the fish tilted up and down in its water. Against the long opposite wall sang a live canary in its cage. Beneath the cage, among spilled millet seeds on the carpet, were a decorated child's sand bucket and matching sand shovel.

Now the alarm was set for six. I lay awake remembering an article I had read downstairs in the lobby, in an engineering magazine. The article was about gold mining.

In South Africa, in India, and in South Dakota, the gold mines extend so deeply into the earth's crust that they are hot. The rock walls burn the miners' hands. The companies have to air-condition the mines; if the air conditioners break, the miners die. The elevators in the mine shafts run very slowly, down, and up, so the miners' ears will not pop in their skulls. When the miners return to the surface, their faces are deathly pale.

Early the next morning we checked out. It was February 26, 1979, a Monday morning. We would drive out of town, find a hilltop, watch the eclipse, and then drive back over the mountains and home to the coast. How familiar things are here; how adept we are; how smoothly and professionally we check out! I had forgotten the clown's smiling head and the hotel lobby as if they had never existed. Gary put the car in gear and off we went, as off we have gone to a hundred other adventures.

It was before dawn when we found a highway out of town and drove into the unfamiliar countryside. By the growing light we could see a band of cirrostratus clouds in the sky. Later the rising sun would clear these clouds before the eclipse began. We drove at random until we came to a range of unfenced hills. We pulled off the highway, bundled up, and climbed one of these hills.

II

The hill was five hundred feet high. Long winter-killed grass covered it, as high as our knees. We climbed and rested, sweating in the cold; we passed clumps of bundled people on the hillside who were setting up telescopes and fiddling with cameras. The top of the hill stuck up in the middle of the sky. We tightened our scarves and looked around.

East of us rose another hill like ours. Between the hills, far below, was the highway that threaded south into the valley. This was the Yakima valley; I had never seen it before. It is justly famous for its beauty, like every planted valley. It extended south into the horizon, a distant dream of a valley, a Shangri-la. All its hundreds of low, golden slopes bore orchards. Among the orchards were towns, and roads, and plowed and fallow fields. Through the valley wandered a thin, shining river; from the river extended fine, frozen irrigation ditches. Distance blurred and blued the sight, so that the whole valley looked like a thickness or sediment at the bottom of the sky. Directly behind us was more sky, and empty lowlands blued by distance, and Mount Adams. Mount Adams was an enormous, snow-covered volcanic cone rising flat, like so much scenery.

Now the sun was up. We could not see it; but the sky behind the band of clouds was yellow, and, far down the valley, some hillside orchards had lighted up. More people were parking near the highway and climbing the hills. It was the West. All of us rugged individualists were wearing knit caps and blue nylon parkas. People were climbing the nearby hills and setting up shop in clumps among the dead grasses. It looked as though we had all gathered on hilltops to pray for the world on its last day. It looked as though we had all crawled out of spaceships and were preparing to assault the valley below. It looked as though we were scattered on hilltops at dawn to sacrifice virgins, make rain, set stone stelae in a ring. There was no place out of the wind. The straw grasses banged our legs.

Up in the sky where we stood, the air was lusterless yellow. To the west the sky was blue. Now the sun cleared the clouds. We cast rough shadows on the blowing grass; freezing, we waved our arms. Near the sun, the sky was bright and colorless. There was nothing to see.

It began with no ado. It was odd that such a well-advertised public event should have no starting gun, no overture, no introductory speaker. I should have known right then that I was out of my depth. Without pause or preamble, silent as orbits, a piece of the sun went away. We looked at it through welders' goggles. A piece of the sun was missing; in its place we saw empty sky.

I had seen a partial eclipse in 1970. A partial eclipse is very interesting. It bears almost no relation to a total eclipse. Seeing a partial eclipse bears the same relation to seeing a total eclipse as kissing a man does to marrying him, or as flying in an airplane does to falling out of an airplane. Although the one experience precedes the other, it in no way prepares you for it. During a partial eclipse the sky does not darken—not even when 94 percent of the sun is hidden. Nor does the sun, seen colorless through protective devices, seem terribly strange. We have all seen a sliver of light in the sky; we have all seen the crescent moon by day. However, during a partial eclipse the air does indeed get cold, precisely as if someone were standing between you and the fire. And blackbirds do fly back to their roosts. I had seen a partial eclipse before, and here was another.

What you see in an eclipse is entirely different from what you know. It is especially different for those of us whose grasp of astronomy is so frail that, given a flashlight, a grapefruit, two oranges, and fifteen years, we still could not figure out which way to set the clocks for daylight saving time. Usually it is a bit of a trick to keep your knowledge from blinding you. But during an eclipse it is easy. What you see is much more convincing than any wild-eyed theory you may know.

You may read that the moon has something to do with eclipses. I have never seen the moon yet. You do not see the moon. So near the sun, it is as completely invisible as the stars are by day. What you see before your eyes is the sun going through phases. It gets narrower and narrower, as the waning moon does, and, like the ordinary moon, it travels alone in the simple sky. The sky is of course background. It does not appear to eat the sun; it is far behind the sun. The sun simply shaves away; gradually, you see less sun and more sky.

The sky's blue was deepening, but there was no darkness. The sun was a wide crescent, like a segment of tangerine. The wind freshened and blew steadily over the hill. The eastern hill across the highway grew dusky and sharp. The towns and orchards in the valley to the south were dissolving into the blue light. Only the thin river held a trickle of sun.

Now the sky to the west deepened to indigo, a color never seen. A dark sky usually loses color. This was a saturated, deep indigo, up in the air. Stuck up into that unworldly sky was the cone of Mount Adams, and the alpenglow was upon it. The alpenglow is that red light of sunset which holds out on snowy mountaintops long after the valleys and tablelands are dimmed. "Look at Mount Adams," I said, and that was the last sane moment I remember.

I turned back to the sun. It was going. The sun was going, and the world was wrong. The grasses were wrong; they were platinum. Their every detail of stem, head, and blade shone lightless and artificially distinct as an art photographer's platinum print. This color has never been seen on earth. The hues were metallic; their finish was matte. The hillside was a nineteenth-century tinted photograph from which the tints had faded. All the people you see in the photograph, distinct and detailed as their faces look, are now dead. The sky was navy blue. My hands were silver. All the distant hills' grasses were finespun metal that the wind laid down. I was watching a faded color print of a movie filmed in the Middle Ages; I was standing in it, by some mistake. I was standing in a movie of hillside grasses filmed in the Middle Ages. I missed my own century, the people I knew, and the real light of day.

I looked at Gary. He was in the film. Everything was lost. He was a platinum print, a dead artist's version of life. I saw on his skull the darkness of night mixed with the colors of day. My mind was going out; my eyes were receding the way galaxies recede to the rim of space. Gary was light-years away, gesturing inside a circle of darkness, down the wrong end of a telescope. He smiled as if he saw me; the stringy crinkles around his eyes moved. The sight of him, familiar and wrong, was something I was remembering from centuries hence, from the other side of death: yes, *that* is the way he used to look, when we were living. When it was our generation's turn to be alive. I could not hear him; the wind was too loud. Behind him the sun was going. We had all started down a chute of time. At first it was pleasant;

now there was no stopping it. Gary was chuting away across space, moving and talking and catching my eye, chuting down the long corridor of separation. The skin on his face moved like thin bronze plating that would peel.

The grass at our feet was wild barley. It was the wild einkorn wheat that grew on the hilly flanks of the Zagros Mountains, above the Euphrates valley, above the valley of the river we called *River*. We harvested the grass with stone sickles, I remember. We found the grasses on the hillsides; we built our shelter beside them and cut them down. That is how he used to look then, that one, moving and living and catching my eye, with the sky so dark behind him, and the wind blowing. God save our life.

From all the hills came screams. A piece of sky beside the crescent sun was detaching. It was a loosened circle of evening sky, suddenly lighted from the back. It was an abrupt black body out of nowhere; it was a flat disk; it was almost over the sun. That is when there were screams. At once this disk of sky slid over the sun like a lid. The sky snapped over the sun like a lens cover. The hatch in the brain slammed. Abruptly it was dark night, on the land and in the sky. In the night sky was a tiny ring of light. The hole where the sun belongs is very small. A thin ring of light marked its place. There was no sound. The eyes dried, the arteries drained, the lungs hushed. There was no world. We were the world's dead people rotating and orbiting around and around, embedded in the planet's crust, while the earth rolled down. Our minds were light-years distant, forgetful of almost everything. Only an extraordinary act of will could recall to us our former, living selves and our contexts in matter and time. We had, it seems, loved the planet and loved our lives, but could no longer remember the way of them. We got the light wrong. In the sky was something that should not be there. In the black sky was a ring of light. It was a thin ring, an old, thin silver wedding band, an old, worn ring. It was an old wedding band in the sky, or a morsel of bone. There were stars. It was all over.

III

It is now that the temptation is strongest to leave these regions. We have seen enough; let's go. Why burn our hands any more than we have to? But two years have passed; the price of gold has risen. I return to the same buried alluvial beds and pick through the strata again.

I saw, early in the morning, the sun diminish against a backdrop of sky. I saw a circular piece of that sky appear, suddenly detached, blackened, and backlighted; from nowhere it came and overlapped the sun. It did not look like the moon. It was enormous and black. If I had not read that it was the moon, I could have seen the sight a hundred times and never thought of the moon once. (If, however, I had not read that it was the moon—if, like most of the world's people throughout time, I had simply glanced up and seen this thing—then I doubtless would not have speculated much, but would have, like Emperor Louis of Bavaria in 840, simply died of fright on the spot.) It did not look like a dragon, although it looked more like a dragon than the moon. It looked like a lens cover, or the lid of a pot. It materialized out of thin air—black, and flat, and sliding, outlined in flame.

Seeing this black body was like seeing a mushroom cloud. The heart screeched. The meaning of the sight overwhelmed its fascination. It obliterated meaning itself. If you were to glance out one day and see a row of mushroom clouds rising on the horizon, you would know at once that what you were seeing, remarkable as it was, was intrinsically not worth remarking. No use running to tell anyone. Significant as it was, it did not matter a whit. For what is significance? It is significance for people. No people, no significance. This is all I have to tell you.

In the deeps are the violence and terror of which psychology has warned us. But if you ride these monsters deeper down, if you drop with them farther over the world's rim, you find what our sciences cannot locate or name, the substrate, the ocean or matrix or ether that buoys the rest, that gives goodness its power for good, and evil its power for evil, the unified field: our complex and inexplicable caring for each other, and for our life together here. This is given. It is not learned.

The world that lay under darkness and stillness following the closing of the lid was not the world we know. The event was over. Its devastation lay round about us. The clamoring mind and heart stilled, almost indifferent, certainly disembodied, frail, and exhausted. The hills were hushed, obliterated. Up in the sky, like a crater from some distant cataclysm, was a hollow ring.

You have seen photographs of the sun taken during a total eclipse. The corona fills the print. All of those photographs were taken through telescopes. The lenses of telescopes and cameras can no more cover the breadth and scale of the visual array than language can cover the breadth and simultaneity of internal experience. Lenses enlarge the sight, omit its context, and make of it a pretty and sensible picture, like something on a Christmas card. I assure you, if you send any shepherds a Christmas card on which is printed a three-by-three photograph of the angel of the Lord, the glory of the Lord, and a multitude of the heavenly host, they will not be sore afraid. More fearsome things can come in envelopes. More moving photographs than those of the sun's corona can appear in magazines. But I pray you will never see anything more awful in the sky.

You see the wide world swaddled in darkness; you see a vast breadth of hilly land, and an enormous, distant, blackened valley; you see towns' lights, a river's path, and blurred portions of your hat and scarf; you see your husband's face looking like an early black-and-white film; and you see a sprawl of black sky and blue sky together, with unfamiliar stars in it, some barely visible bands of cloud, and, over there, a small white ring. The ring is as small as one goose in a flock of migrating geese—if you happen to notice a flock of migrating geese. It is one 360th part of the visible sky. The sun we see is less than half the diameter of a dime held at arm's length.

The Ring Nebula, in the constellation Lyra, looks, through binoculars, like a smoke ring. It is a star in the process of exploding. Light from its explosion first reached the earth in 1054; it was a supernova then, and so bright it shone in the daytime. Now it is not so bright, but it is still exploding. It expands at the rate of seventy million miles a day. It is interesting to look through binoculars at something expanding seventy million miles a day. It does not budge. Its apparent size does not increase. Photographs of the Ring Nebula taken fifteen years ago seem identical to photographs of it taken yesterday. Some lichens are similar. Botanists have measured some ordinary lichens twice, at fifty-year intervals, without detecting any growth at all. And yet their cells divide; they live.

The small ring of light was like these things—like a ridiculous lichen up in the sky, like a perfectly still explosion 5,000 light-years away: it was interesting, and lovely, and in witless motion, and it had nothing to do with anything.

It had nothing to do with anything. The sun was too small, and too cold, and too far away, to keep the world alive. The white ring was not enough. It was feeble and worthless. It was as useless as a memory; it was as off kilter and hollow and wretched as a memory.

When you try your hardest to recall someone's face, or the look of a place, you see in your mind's eye some vague and terrible sight such as this. It is dark; it is insubstantial; it is all wrong.

The white ring and the saturated darkness made the earth and the sky look as they must look in the memories of the careless dead. What I saw, what I seemed to be standing in, was all the wrecked light that the memories of the dead could shed upon the living world. We had all died in our boots on the hilltops of Yakima and were alone in eternity. Empty space stoppered our eyes and mouths; we cared for nothing. We remembered our living days wrong. With great effort we had remembered some sort of circular light in the sky—but only the outline. Oh, and then the orchard trees withered, the ground froze, the glaciers slid down the valleys and overlapped the towns. If there had ever been people on earth, nobody knew it. The dead had forgotten those they had loved. The dead were parted one from the other and could no longer remember the faces and lands they had loved in the light. They seemed to stand on darkened hilltops, looking down.

IV

We teach our children one thing only, as we were taught: to wake up. We teach our children to look alive there, to join by words and activities the life of human culture on the planet's crust. As adults we are almost all adept at waking up. We have so mastered the transition, we have forgotten we ever learned it. Yet it is a transition we make a hundred times a day, as, like so many will-less dolphins, we plunge and surface, lapse and emerge. We live half our waking lives and all of our sleeping lives in some private, useless, and insensible waters we never mention or recall. Useless, I say. Valueless, I might add—until someone hauls the wealth up to the surface and into the wide-awake city, in a form that people can use.

I do not know how we got to the restaurant. Like Roethke, "I take my waking slow." Gradually I seemed more or less alive, and already forgetful. It was now almost nine in the morning. It was the day of a solar eclipse in central Washington, and a fine adventure for everyone. The sky was clear; there was a fresh breeze out of the north.

The restaurant was a roadside place with tables and booths. The other eclipse-watchers were there. From our booth we could see their cars' California license plates, their University of Washington parking stickers. Inside the restaurant we were all eating eggs or waffles; people were fairly shouting and exchanging enthusiasms, like fans after a World Series game. Did you see . . . ? Did you see . . . ? Then somebody said something that knocked me for a loop.

A college student, a boy in a blue parka who carried a Hasselblad, said to us, "Did you see that little white ring? It looked like a Life Saver. It looked like a Life Saver up in the sky."

And so it did. The boy spoke well. He was a walking alarm clock. I myself had at that time no access to such a term. He could write a sentence, and I could not. I grabbed that Life Saver and rode it to the surface. And I had to laugh. I had been dumbstruck on the Euphrates River, I had been dead and gone and grieving, all over the sight of something that, if you could claw your way up to that level, you would grant looked very much like a Life Saver. It was good to be back among people so clever; it was good to have all the world's words at the mind's disposal, so the mind could begin its task. All those things for which we have no words are lost. The mind—the culture—has two little tools, grammar and lexicon: a decorated sand bucket and a matching shovel. With these we bluster about the continents and do all the world's work. With these we try to save our very lives.

There are a few more things to tell from this level, the level of the restaurant. One is the old joke about breakfast. "It can never be satisfied, the mind, never." Wallace Stevens wrote that, and in the long run he was right. The mind wants to live forever, or to learn a very good reason why not. The mind wants the world to return its love, or its awareness; the mind wants to know all the world, and all eternity, and God. The mind's sidekick, however, will settle for two eggs over easy.

The dear, stupid body is as easily satisfied as a spaniel. And, incredibly, the simple spaniel can lure the brawling mind to its dish. It is everlastingly funny that the proud, metaphysically ambitious, clamoring mind will hush if you give it an egg.

Further: while the mind reels in deep space, while the mind grieves or fears or exults, the workaday senses, in ignorance or idiocy, like so many computer terminals printing out market prices while the world blows up, still transcribe their little data and transmit them to the warehouse in the skull. Later, under the tranquilizing influence of fried eggs, the mind can sort through these data. The restaurant was a halfway house, a decompression chamber. There I remembered a few things more.

The deepest, and most terrifying, was this: I have said that I heard screams. (I have since read that screaming, with hysteria, is a common reaction even to expected total eclipses.) People on all the hillsides, including, I think, myself, screamed when the black body of the moon detached from the sky and rolled over the sun. But something else was happening at that same instant, and it was this, I believe, that made us scream.

The second before the sun went out, we saw a wall of dark shadow come speeding at us. We no sooner saw it than it was upon us, like thunder. It roared up the valley. It slammed our hill and knocked us out. It was the monstrous swift shadow cone of the moon. I have since read that this wave of shadow moves 1,800 miles an hour. Language can give no sense of this sort of speed—1,800 miles an hour. It was 195 miles wide. No end was in sight—you saw only the edge. It rolled at you across the land at 1,800 miles an hour, hauling darkness like plague behind it. Seeing it, and knowing it was coming straight for you, was like feeling a slug of anesthetic shoot up your arm. If you think very fast, you may have time to think: Soon it will hit my brain. You can feel the deadness race up your arm; you can feel the appalling, inhuman speed of your own blood. We saw the wall of shadow coming, and screamed before it hit.

This was the universe about which we have read so much and never before felt: the universe as a clockwork of loose spheres flung at stupefying, unauthorized speeds. How could anything moving so fast not crash, not veer from its orbit amok like a car out of control on a turn?

Less than two minutes later, when the sun emerged, the trailing edge of the shadow cone sped away. It coursed down our hill and raced eastward over the plain, faster than the eye could believe; it swept over the plain and dropped over the planet's rim in a twinkling. It had clobbered us, and now it roared away. We blinked in the light. It was as though an enormous, loping god in the sky had reached down and slapped the earth's face.

Something else, something more ordinary, came back to me along about the third cup of coffee. During the moments of totality, it was so dark that drivers on the highway below turned on their cars' headlights. We could see the highway's route as a strand of lights. It was bumper-to-bumper down there. It was eight-fifteen in the morning, Monday morning, and people were driving into Yakima to work. That it was as dark as night, and eerie as hell, an hour after dawn apparently meant that in order to *see* to drive to work, people had to use their headlights. Four or five cars pulled off the road. The rest, in a line at least five miles long, drove to town. The highway ran between hills; the people could not have seen any of the eclipsed sun at all. Yakima will have another total eclipse in 2019. Perhaps, in 2019, businesses will give their employees an hour off.

From the restaurant we drove back to the coast. The highway crossing the Cascades range was open. We drove over the mountain like old pros. We joined our places on the planet's thin crust; it held. For the time being, we were home free.

Early that morning at six, when we had checked out, the six bald men were sitting on folding chairs in the dim hotel lobby. The television was on. Most of them were awake. You might drown in your own spittle, God knows, at any time; you might wake up dead in a small hotel, a cabbage head watching TV while snows pile up in the passes, watching TV while the chili peppers smile and the moon passes over the sun and nothing changes and nothing is learned because you have lost your bucket and shovel and no longer care. What if you regain the surface and open your sack and find, instead of treasure, a beast, which jumps at you? Or you may not come back at all. The winches may jam, the scaffolding buckle, the air-conditioning collapse. You may glance up one day and see by your headlamp the canary keeled over in its cage. You may reach into a cranny for pearls and touch a moray eel. You yank on your rope; it is too late.

Apparently people share a sense of these hazards, for when the total eclipse ended, an odd thing happened.

When the sun appeared as a blinding bead on the ring's side, the eclipse was over. The black lens cover appeared again, backlighted, and slid away. At once the yellow light made the sky blue again; the black lid dissolved and vanished. The real world began there. I remember now: we all hurried away. We were born and bored at a stroke. We rushed down the hill. We found our car; we saw the other people streaming down the hillsides; we joined the highway traffic and drove away.

We never looked back. It was a general vamoose, and an odd one, for when we left the hill, the sun was still partially eclipsed—a sight rare enough, and one that, in itself, we would probably have driven five hours to see. But enough is enough. One turns at last even from glory itself with a sigh of relief. From the depths of mystery, and even from the heights of splendor, we bounce back and hurry for the latitudes of home.

1982

AN EXPEDITION
TO THE POLE

I

THERE IS A SINGING GROUP in this Catholic church today, a singing group that calls itself Wildflowers. The lead is a tall, square-jawed teenaged boy, buoyant and glad to be here. He carries a guitar; he plucks out a little bluesy riff and hits some chords. With him are the rest of the Wildflowers. There is an old woman, wonderfully determined; she has long orange hair and is dressed country-and-western style. A long embroidered strap around her neck slings a big western guitar low over her pelvis. Beside her stand a frail, withdrawn fourteen-year-old boy, and a large Chinese man in his twenties, who seems to want to enjoy himself but is not quite sure how to. He looks around wildly as he sings, and shuffles his feet. There is also a very tall teenaged girl, presumably the lead singer's girlfriend; she is delicate of feature, half serene and half petrified, a wispy soprano. They straggle out in front of the altar and teach us a brand-new hymn.

It all seems a pity at first, for I have overcome a fiercely anti-Catholic upbringing in order to attend Mass simply and solely to escape Protestant guitars. Why am I here? Who gave these nice Catholics guitars? Why are they not mumbling in Latin and performing superstitious rituals? What is the Pope thinking of?

But nobody said things were going to be easy. A taste for the sublime is a greed like any other, after all; why begrudge the churches their secularism now, when from the general table is rising a general song? Besides, in a way I do not pretend to understand, these people—all the people in all the ludicrous churches—have access to the land.

The Land

The Pole of Relative Inaccessibility is "that imaginary point on the Arctic Ocean farthest from land in any direction." It is a navigator's paper point, contrived to console Arctic explorers who, after Peary and Henson reached the North Pole in 1909, had nowhere special to go. There is a Pole of Relative Inaccessibility on the Antarctic continent, also; it is that point of land farthest from salt water in any direction.

The Absolute is the Pole of Relative Inaccessibility located in metaphysics. After all, one of the few things we know about the Absolute is that it is relatively inaccessible. It is that point of spirit farthest from every accessible point of spirit in all directions. Like the others, it is a Pole of the Most Trouble. It is also—I take this as given—the Pole of great price.

The People

It is the second Sunday in Advent. For a year I have been attending Mass at this Catholic church. Every Sunday for a year I have run away from home and joined the circus as a dancing bear. We dancing bears have dressed ourselves in buttoned clothes; we mince around the rings on two feet. Today we were restless; we kept dropping onto our forepaws.

No one, least of all the organist, could find the opening hymn. Then no one knew it. Then no one could sing anyway.

There was no sermon, only announcements.

The priest proudly introduced the rascally acolyte who was going to light the two Advent candles. As we all could plainly see, the rascally acolyte had already lighted them.

During the long intercessory prayer, the priest always reads "intentions" from the parishioners. These are slips of paper, dropped into a box before the service begins, on which people have written their private concerns, requesting our public prayers. The priest reads them, one by one, and we respond on cue. "For a baby safely delivered on November twentieth," the priest intoned, "we pray to the Lord." We all responded, "Lord, hear our prayer." Suddenly the priest broke in and confided to our bowed heads, "That's the baby we've been praying for the past two months! The woman just kept getting more and more pregnant!" How often, how shockingly often, have I exhausted myself in church from the effort to keep from laughing out loud? I often laugh all the way home. Then the priest read the next intention: "For my son, that he may forgive his father. We pray to the Lord." "Lord, hear our prayer," we responded, chastened.

A high school stage play is more polished than this service we have been rehearsing since the year one. In two thousand years, we have not worked out the kinks. We positively glorify them. Week after week we witness the same miracle: that God is so mighty he can stifle his own laughter. Week after week, we witness the same miracle: that God, for reasons unfathomable, refrains from blowing our dancing bear act to smithereens. Week after week Christ washes the disciples' dirty feet, handles their very toes, and repeats, It is all right—believe it or not—to be people.

Who can believe it?

During Communion, the priest handed me a wafer that proved to be stuck to five other wafers. I waited while he tore the clump into rags of wafer, resisting the impulse to help. Directly to my left, and all through Communion, a woman was banging out the theme from *The Sound of Music* on a piano.

The Land

Nineteenth-century explorers set the pattern for polar expeditions. Elaborately provisioned ships set out for high latitudes. Soon they encounter the pack ice and equinoctial storms. Ice coats the deck, spars, and rigging; the masts and hull shudder; the sea freezes around the rudder and then fastens on the ship. Early sailors try ramming, sawing, or blasting the ice ahead of the ship before they give up and settle in for the winter. In the nineteenth century, this being "beset" in the pack often killed polar crews; later explorers expected it and learned, finally, to put it to use. Sometimes officers and men move directly onto the pack ice for safety; they drive tent stakes into the ice and pile wooden boxes about for tables and chairs.

Sooner or later, the survivors of that winter or the next, or a select polar party, sets off over the pack ice on foot. Depending on circumstances, they are looking either for a Pole or, more likely, for help. They carry supplies, including boats, on sledges, which they "man-haul" on ropes fastened to shoulder harnesses. South Polar expeditions usually begin from a base camp established on shore. In either case, the terrain is so rough, and the men so weakened by scurvy, that the group makes only a few miles a day. Sometimes they find an island on which to live or starve the next winter; sometimes they turn back to safety, stumble onto some outpost of civilization, or are rescued by another expedition; very often, when warm weather comes and the pack ice splits into floes, they drift and tent on a floe, or hop from floe to floe, until the final floe lands, splits, or melts.

In 1847, according to Arctic historian L. P. Kirwan, the American ship *Polaris* "was struck by an enormous floe. And just as stores, records, clothing, equipment, were being flung from the reeling ship, she was swept away through the Arctic twilight, with most, but not all, of her crew on board. Those left behind drifted for thirteen hundred miles on an ice-floe until they were rescued, starving and dazed, off the coast of Labrador."

Polar explorers werc chosen, as astronauts are today, from the clamoring, competitive ranks of the sturdy, skilled, and sane. Many of the British leaders, in particular, were men of astonishing personal dignity. Reading their accounts of life *in extremis,* one is struck by their unending formality toward each other. When Scott's Captain Oates sacrificed himself on the Antarctic peninsula because his ruined feet were slowing the march, he stepped outside the tent one night to freeze himself in a blizzard, saying to the others, "I am just going outside and may be some time."

Even in the privacy of their journals and diaries, polar explorers maintain a fine reserve. In his journal, Ernest Shackleton described his feelings upon seeing, for the first time in human history, the Antarctic continent beyond the mountains ringing the Ross Ice Shelf: "We watched the new mountains rise from the great unknown that lay ahead of us," he wrote, "with feelings of keen curiosity, not unmingled with awe." One wonders, after reading a great many such firsthand accounts, if polar explorers were not somehow chosen for the empty and solemn splendor of their prose styles—or even if some eminent Victorians, examining their own prose styles, realized, perhaps dismayed, that from the look of it, they would have to go in for polar exploration. Salomon Andrée, the doomed Swedish balloonist, was dying of starvation on an Arctic island when he confided in his diary, with almost his dying breath, "Our provisions must soon and richly be supplemented, if we are to have any prospect of being able to hold out for a time."

The People

The new Episcopalian and Catholic liturgies include a segment called "passing the peace." Many things can go wrong here. I know of one congregation in New York that fired its priest because he insisted on their passing the peace—which involves nothing more than shaking hands with your neighbors in the pew. The men and women of this small congregation had limits to their endurance; passing the peace was beyond their limits. They could not endure shaking hands with people against whom they bore lifelong grudges. They fired the priest and found a new one, sympathetic to their needs.

The rubric for passing the peace requires that one shake hands with whoever is handy and say, "Peace be with you." The other responds, "Peace be with *you*." Every rare once in a while, someone responds simply "Peace." Today I was sitting beside two teenaged lugs with small mustaches. When it came time to pass the peace, I shook hands with one of the lugs and said, "Peace be with you," and he said, *"Yeah."*

The Technology: The Franklin Expedition

The Franklin expedition was the turning point in Arctic exploration. The expedition itself accomplished nothing, and all its members died. But the expedition's failure to return, and the mystery of its whereabouts, attracted so much publicity in Europe and the United States that thirty ships set out looking for traces of the ships and men; these search parties explored and mapped the Arctic for the first time, found the Northwest Passage that Franklin had sought, and developed a technology adapted to Arctic conditions, a technology capable of bringing explorers back alive. The technology of the Franklin expedition, by contrast, was adapted only to conditions in the Royal Navy officers' clubs in England. The Franklin expedition stood on its dignity.

In 1845, Sir John Franklin and 138 officers and men embarked from England to find the Northwest Passage across the high Canadian Arctic to the Pacific Ocean. They sailed in two three-masted barques. Each sailing vessel carried an auxiliary steam engine and a twelve-day supply of coal for the entire projected two or three years' voyage. Instead of additional coal, according to L. P. Kirwan, each ship made room for a 1,200-volume library, "a hand-organ, playing fifty tunes," china place settings for officers and men, cut-glass wine goblets, and sterling silver flatware. The officers' sterling silver knives, forks, and spoons were particularly interesting. The silver was of ornate Victorian design, very heavy at the handles and richly patterned. Engraved on the handles were the individual officers' initials and family crests. The expedition carried no special clothing for the Arctic, only the uniforms of Her Majesty's Navy.

The ships set out in high style, amid enormous glory and fanfare. Franklin uttered his utterance: "The highest object of my desire is faithfully to perform my duty." Two months later a British whaling captain met the two barques in Lancaster Sound, near Baffin Island; he reported back to England on the high spirits of officers and men. He was the last European to see any of them alive.

Years later, civilization learned that many groups of Inuit—Eskimos—had hazarded across tableaux involving various still-living or dead members of the Franklin expedition. Some had glimpsed, for instance, men pushing and pulling a wooden boat across the ice. Some had found, at a place called Starvation

Cove, this boat, or a similar one, and the remains of the thirty-five men who had been dragging it. At Terror Bay the Inuit found a tent on the ice, and in it, thirty bodies. At Simpson Strait some Inuit had seen a very odd sight: the pack ice pierced by the three protruding wooden masts of a barque.

For twenty years, search parties recovered skeletons from all over the frozen sea. Franklin himself—it was learned after twelve years—had died aboard ship. Franklin dead, the ships frozen into the pack winter after winter, their supplies exhausted, the remaining officers and men had decided to walk to help. They outfitted themselves from ships' stores for the journey; their bodies were found with those supplies they had chosen to carry. Accompanying one clump of frozen bodies, for instance, which incidentally showed evidence of cannibalism, were place settings of sterling silver flatware engraved with officers' initials and family crests. A search party found, on the ice far from the ships, a letter clip, and a piece of the very backgammon board that Lady Jane Franklin had given her husband as a parting gift.

Another search party found two skeletons in a boat on a sledge. They had hauled the boat sixty-five miles. With the two skeletons were some chocolate, some guns, some tea, and a great deal of table silver. Many miles south of these two was another skeleton, alone. This was a frozen officer. In his pocket he had, according to Kirwan, "a parody of a sea-shanty." The skeleton was in uniform: trousers and jacket "of fine blue cloth . . . edged with silk braid, with sleeves slashed and bearing five covered buttons each. Over this uniform the dead man had worn a blue greatcoat, with a black silk neckerchief." That was the Franklin expedition.

Sir Robert Falcon Scott, who died on the Antarctic peninsula, was never able to bring himself to use dogs, let alone feed them to each other or eat them. Instead he struggled with English ponies, for which he carried hay. Scott felt that eating dogs was inhumane; he also felt, as he himself wrote, that when men reach a Pole unaided, their journey has "a fine conception" and "the conquest is more nobly and splendidly won." It is this loftiness of sentiment, this purity, this dignity and self-control,

that makes Scott's farewell letters—found under his body—
such moving documents.

Less moving are documents from successful polar expeditions. Their leaders relied on native technology, which, as every
book ever written about the Inuit puts it, was "adapted to harsh
conditions."

Roald Amundsen, who returned in triumph from the South
Pole, traveled Inuit style; he made good speed using sleds and
feeding dogs to dogs on a schedule. Robert E. Peary and
Matthew Henson reached the North Pole in the company of four
Inuit. Throughout the Peary expedition, the Inuit drove the dog
teams, built igloos, and supplied seal and walrus clothing.

There is no such thing as a solitary polar explorer, fine as the
conception is.

The People

I have been attending Catholic Mass for only a year. Before that,
the handiest church was Congregational. Week after week I
climbed the long steps to that little church, entered, and took a
seat with some few of my neighbors. Week after week I was
moved by the pitiableness of the bare linoleum-floored sacristy,
which no flowers could cheer or soften, by the terrible singing I
so loved, by the fatigued Bible readings, the lagging emptiness
and dilution of the liturgy, the horrifying vacuity of the sermon,
and by the fog of dreary senselessness pervading the whole,
which existed alongside, and probably caused, the wonder of
the fact that we came; we returned; we showed up; week after
week, we went through with it.

Once while we were reciting the Gloria, a farmer's wife—
whom I knew slightly—and I exchanged a sudden, triumphant
glance.

Recently I returned to that Congregational church for an
ecumenical service. A Catholic priest and the minister served
grape juice Communion.

Both the priest and the minister were professionals, were
old hands. They bungled with dignity and aplomb. Both were at

ease and awed; both were half confident and controlled and half bewildered and whispering. I could hear them: "Where is it?" "Haven't you got it?" "I thought *you* had it!"

The priest, new to me, was in his sixties. He was tall; he wore his weariness loosely, standing upright and controlling his breath. When he knelt at the altar, and when he rose from kneeling, his knees cracked. It was a fine church music, this sound of his cracking knees.

The Land

Polar explorers—one gathers from their accounts—sought at the Poles something of the sublime. Simplicity and purity attracted them; they set out to perform clear tasks in uncontaminated lands. The land's austerity held them. They praised the land's spare beauty as if it were a moral or a spiritual quality: "icy halls of cold sublimity," "lofty peaks perfectly covered with eternal snow." Fridtjof Nansen referred to "the great adventure of the ice, deep and pure as infinity . . . the eternal round of the universe and its eternal death." Everywhere polar prose evokes these absolutes, these ideas of "eternity" and "perfection," as if they were some perfectly visible part of the landscape.

They went, I say, partly in search of the sublime, and they found it the only way it can be found, here or there—around the edges, tucked into the corners of the days. For they were people—all of them, even the British—and despite the purity of their conceptions, they man-hauled their humanity to the Poles.

They man-hauled their frail flesh to the Poles, and encountered conditions so difficult that, for instance, it commonly took members of Scott's South Polar party several hours each morning to put on their boots. Day and night they did miserable, niggling, and often fatal battle with frostbitten toes, diarrhea, bleeding gums, hunger, weakness, mental confusion, and despair.

They man-hauled their sweet human absurdity to the Poles. When Robert E. Peary and Matthew Henson reached the North Pole in 1909, Peary planted there in the frozen ocean, according to L. P. Kirwan, the flag of the Dekes: "the colours of the Delta Kappa Epsilon Fraternity at Bowdoin College, of which Peary was an alumnus."

Polar explorers must adapt to conditions. They must adapt, on the one hand, to severe physical limitations; they must adapt, on the other hand—like the rest of us—to ordinary emotional limitations. The hard part is in finding a workable compromise. If you are Peary and have planned your every move down to the last jot and tittle, you can perhaps get away with carrying a Deke flag to the North Pole, if it will make you feel good. After eighteen years' preparation, why not feel a little good? If you are an officer with the Franklin expedition and do not know what you are doing or where you are, but think you cannot eat food except from sterling silver tableware, you cannot get away with it. Wherever we go, there seems to be only one business at hand—that of finding workable compromises between the sublimity of our ideas and the absurdity of the fact of us.

They made allowances for their emotional needs. Overwintering expedition ships commonly carried, in addition to sufficient fuel, equipment for the publication of weekly newspapers. The brave polar men sat cooling their heels *in medias* nowhere, reading in cold type their own and their bunkmates' gossip, in such weeklies as Parry's *Winter Chronicle and North Georgia Gazette*, Nansen's *Framsjaa*, or Scott's *South Polar Times* and *The Blizzard*. Polar explorers also amused themselves with theatrical productions. If one had been frozen into the pack ice off Ross Island near Antarctica, aboard Scott's ship *Discovery*, one midwinter night in 1902, one could have seen the only performance of *Ticket of Leave, a screaming comedy in one act*. Similarly, if, in the dead of winter, 1819, one had been a member of young Edward Parry's expedition frozen into the pack ice in the high Arctic, one could have caught the first of a series of fortnightly plays, an uproarious success called *Miss in Her Teens*. According to Kirwan, "'This,' Parry dryly remarked, 'afforded to the men such a fund of amusement as fully to justify the expectations we had formed of the utility of theatrical entertainments.'" And you yourself, Royal Navy Commander Edward Parry, were you not yourself the least bit amused? Or at twenty-nine years old did you still try to stand on your dignity?

God does not demand that we give up our personal dignity, that we throw in our lot with random people, that we lose ourselves and turn from all that is not him. God needs nothing, asks nothing, and demands nothing, like the stars. It is a life with God that demands these things.

Experience has taught the race that if knowledge of God is the end, then these habits of life are not the means but the condition in which the means operates. You do not have to do these things; not at all. God does not, I regret to report, give a hoot. You do not have to do these things—unless you want to know God. They work on you, not on him.

You do not have to sit outside in the dark. If, however, you want to look at the stars, you will find that darkness is necessary. But the stars neither require nor demand it.

The Technology

It is a matter for computation: How far can one walk carrying how much silver? The computer balks at the problem; there are too many unknowns. The computer puts its own questions: Who is this "one"? What degree of stamina may we calculate for? Under what conditions does this one propose to walk, at what latitudes? With how many companions, how much aid?

The People

The Mass has been building to this point, to the solemn saying of those few hushed phrases known as the Sanctus. We have confessed, in a low, distinct murmur, our sins; we have become the people broken, and then the people made whole by our reluctant assent to the priest's proclamation of God's mercy. Now, as usual, we will, in the stillest voice, stunned, repeat the Sanctus, repeat why it is that we have come:

Holy, holy, holy Lord,
God of power and might,
heaven and earth are full of your glory . . .

It is here, if ever, that one loses oneself at sea. Here one's eyes roll up, and the sun rolls overhead, and the floe rolls underfoot, and the scene of unrelieved ice and sea rolls over the planet's Pole and over the world's rim, wide and unseen.

Now, just as we are dissolved in our privacy and about to utter the words of the Sanctus, the lead singer of Wildflowers bursts onstage from the wings. I raise my head. He is taking enormous, enthusiastic strides and pumping his guitar's neck up and down. Drooping after him come the orange-haired country-and-western-style woman; the soprano, who, to shorten herself, carries her neck forward like a horse; the withdrawn boy; and the Chinese man, who is holding a tambourine as if it had stuck by some defect to his fingers and he has resolved to forget about it. These array themselves in a clump downstage right. The priest is nowhere in sight.

Alas, alack, oh brother, we are going to have to *sing* the Sanctus. There is, of course, nothing new about singing the Sanctus. The lead singer smiles disarmingly. There is a new arrangement. He hits a chord with the flat of his hand. The Chinese man with sudden vigor bangs the tambourine and looks at his hands, startled. They run us through the Sanctus three or four times. The words are altered a bit to fit the strong upbeat rhythm:

> Heaven and earth
> (Heaven and earth earth earth earth earth)
> Are full (full full full)
> Of your glory . . .

Must I join this song? May I keep only my silver? My backgammon board, I agree, is a frivolity. I relinquish it. I will leave it right here on the ice. But my silver? My family crest? One knife, one fork, one spoon, to carry beneath the glance of heaven and back? I have lugged it around for years; I am, I say, superlatively strong. Don't laugh. I am superlatively strong! Don't laugh; you'll make *me* laugh. The answer is no. We are singing the Sanctus, it seems, and they are passing the plate. I would rather, I think, undergo the famous dark night of the soul than encounter in church the dread hootenanny—but these purely personal preferences are of no account, and maladaptive to boot. They are passing the plate and I toss in my schooling; I toss in my rank in the Royal Navy, my erroneous and incomplete charts, my pious refusal to eat sled dogs, my watch, my keys, and my shoes. I was looking for bigger game, not little moral lessons, but who can argue with conditions?

"Heaven and earth earth earth earth earth," we sing. The withdrawn boy turns his head toward a man in front of me, who must be his father. Unaccountably, the enormous teenaged soprano catches my eye, exultant. A low shudder or shock crosses our floe. We have split from the pack; we have crossed the Arctic Circle, and the current has us.

The Land

We are clumped on an ice floe drifting over the black polar sea. Heaven and earth are full of our terrible singing. Overhead we see a blurred, colorless brightness; at our feet we see the dulled, swift ice and recrystallized snow. The sea is black and green; a hundred thousand floes and bergs float in the water and spin and scatter in the current around us everywhere as far as we can see. The wind is cool, moist, and scented with salt.

I am wearing, I discover, the uniform of a Keystone Kop. I examine my hat: a black cardboard constable's hat with a white felt star stapled to the band above the brim. My dark Keystone Kop jacket is nicely belted, and there is a tin badge on my chest. A holster around my hips carries a popgun with a cork on a string, and a red roll of caps. My feet are bare, but I feel no cold. I am skating around on the ice, and singing, and bumping into people who, because the ice is slippery, bump into other people. "Excuse me!" I keep saying, "I beg your pardon—woops there!"

When a crack develops in our floe and opens at my feet, I jump across it—skillfully, I think—but my jump pushes my side of the floe away, and I wind up leaping full tilt into the water. The Chinese man extends a hand to pull me out, but alas, he slips and I drag him in. The Chinese man and I are treading water, singing, and collecting a bit of a crowd. It takes a troupe of circus clowns to get us both out. I check my uniform at once and learn that my rather flattering hat is intact, my trousers virtually unwrinkled, but my roll of caps is wet. The Chinese man is fine; we thank the clowns.

This troupe of circus clowns, I hear, is poorly paid. They are invested in bright, loose garments; they are a bunch of spontaneous, unskilled, oversized children; they joke and bump into people. At one end of the floe, ten of them—red, yellow, and blue—are trying to climb up on each other to make a human pyramid. It is a wonderfully funny sight, because they have put the four smallest clowns on the bottom, and the biggest, fattest clown is trying to climb to the top. The rest of the clowns are doing gymnastics; they tumble on the ice and flip cheerfully in midair. Their crucifixes fly from their ruffled necks as they flip, and hit them on their bald heads as they land. Our floe is smaller now, and we seem to have drifted into a faster bit of current. Repeatedly we ram little icebergs, which rock as we hit them. Some of them tilt clear over like punching bags; they bounce back with great splashes, and water streams down their blue sides as they rise. The country-and-western-style woman is fending off some of the larger bergs with a broom. The lugs with the mustaches have found, or brought, a Frisbee, and a game is developing down the middle of our floe. Near the Frisbee game, a bunch of people including myself and some clowns are running. We fling ourselves down on the ice, shoulders first, and skid long distances like pucks.

Now the music ceases and we take our seats in the pews. A baby is going to be baptized. Overhead the sky is brightening; I do not know if this means we have drifted farther north or all night.

The People

The baby's name is Oswaldo; he is a very thin baby, who looks to be about one. He never utters a peep; he looks grim, and stiff as a planked shad. His parents—his father carrying him—and his godparents, the priest, and two acolytes, are standing on the ice between the first row of pews and the linoleum-floored sacristy. I am resting my bare feet on the velvet prie-dieu—to keep those feet from playing on the ice during the ceremony.

Oswaldo is half Filipino. His mother is Filipino. She has a wide mouth with much lipstick, and wide eyes; she wears a tight black skirt and stiletto heels. The father looks like Ozzie Nelson. He has marcelled yellow hair, a bland, meek face, and a big, meek nose. He is wearing a brown leather flight jacket. The godparents are both Filipinos, one of whom, in a pastel denim jumpsuit, keeps mugging for the Instamatic camera that another family member is shooting from the aisle.

The baby has a little red scar below one eye. He is wearing a long white lace baptismal gown, blue tennis shoes with white rubber toes, and red socks.

The priest anoints the baby's head with oil. He addresses to the parents several articles of faith: "Do you believe in God, the Father Almighty, creator of Heaven and earth?" "Yes, we believe."

The priest repeats a gesture he says was Christ's, explaining that it symbolically opens the infant's five senses to the knowledge of God. Uttering a formal prayer, he lays his hand loosely over Oswaldo's face and touches in rapid succession his eyes, ears, nose, and mouth. The baby blinks. The priest, whose voice is sometimes lost in the ruff at his neck, or blown away by the wind, is formal and gentle in his bearing; he knows the kid is cute, but he is not going to sentimentalize the sacrament.

Since our floe spins, we in the pews see the broken floes and tilting bergs, the clogged, calm polar sea, and the variously lighted sky and water's rim, shift and revolve enormously behind the group standing around the baby. Once I think I see a yellowish polar bear spurting out of the water as smoothly as if climbing were falling. I see the bear splash and flow onto a distant floeberg, which tilts out of sight.

Now the acolytes bring a pitcher, a basin, and a linen towel. The father tilts the rigid baby over the basin; the priest pours water from the pitcher over the baby's scalp; the mother sops the baby with the linen towel and wraps it over his head, so that he looks, proudly, as though he has just been made a swami.

To conclude, the priest brings out a candle, for the purpose, I think, of pledging everybody to Christian fellowship with Oswaldo. Actually, I do not know what it is for; I am not listening. I am watching the hands at the candlestick. Each of the principals wraps a hand around the brass candlestick: the two acolytes with their small, pale hands at its base, the two families—Oswaldo's and his godparents'—with their varicolored hands in a row, and the priest at the top, as though he has just won the bat toss at baseball. The baby rides high in his father's arms, pointing his heels in his tennis shoes, silent, wanting down. His father holds him firmly with one hand and holds the candlestick beside his wife's hand with the other. The priest and the seated members of Wildflowers start clapping then—a round of applause for everybody here on the ice!—so we clap.

II

Months have passed; years have passed. Whatever ground we gained has slipped away. New obstacles arise, and faintness of heart, and dread.

The Land

Polar explorers commonly die of hypothermia, starvation, scurvy, or dysentery; less commonly they contract typhoid fever (as Stefansson did), vitamin A poisoning from polar bear liver, or carbon monoxide poisoning from incomplete combustion inside tents sealed by snow. Very commonly, as a prelude to these deaths, polar explorers lose the use of their feet; their frozen toes detach when they remove their socks.

Particularly vivid was the death of a certain Mr. Joseph Green, the astronomer on Sir James Cook's first voyage to high latitudes. He took sick aboard ship. One night, "in a fit of the phrensy," as a contemporary newspaper reported, he rose from his bunk and "put his legs out of the portholes, which was the occasion of his death."

Vitus Bering, shipwrecked in 1741 on Bering Island, was found years later preserved in snow. An autopsy showed he had

had many lice, he had scurvy, and had died of a "rectal fistula which forced gas gangrene into his tissues."

The bodies of various members of the Sir John Franklin expedition of 1845 were found over the course of twenty years, by thirty search expeditions, in assorted bizarre postures scattered over the ice of Victoria Strait, Beechey Island, and King William Island.

Sir Robert Falcon Scott reached the South Pole on January 18, 1912, only to discover a flag that Roald Amundsen had planted there a month earlier. Scott's body, and the bodies of two of his companions, turned up on the Ross Ice Shelf, eleven miles south of one of their own supply depots. The bodies were in sleeping bags. His journals and farewell letters indicated that the other two had died first. Scott's torso was well out of his sleeping bag, and he had opened wide the collar of his parka, exposing his skin.

Never found were the bodies of Henry Hudson, his young son, and four men, whom mutineers in 1611 had lowered from their ship in a dinghy, in Hudson's Bay, without food or equipment. Never found were the bodies of Sir John Franklin himself, or of Amundsen and seventeen other men who set out for the Arctic in search of a disastrous Italian expedition, or the bodies of Scott's men Evans and Oates. Never found were most of the drowned crew of the United States ship *Polaris* or the body of her commander, who died sledging on the ice.

Of the United States Greely expedition to the North Pole, all men died but six. Greely himself, one of the six survivors, was found "on his hands and knees with long hair in pigtails." Of the United States De Long expedition to the North Pole in the *Jeannette*, all men died but two. Of the *Jeannette* herself and her equipment, nothing was found until three years after she sank, when, on a beach on the other side of the polar basin, a Greenlander discovered a pair of yellow oilskin breeches stamped *Jeannette*.

The People

Why do we people in churches seem like cheerful, brainless tourists on a packaged tour of the Absolute?

The tourists are having coffee and doughnuts on Deck C. Presumably, someone is minding the ship, correcting the course, avoiding icebergs and shoals, fueling the engines, watching the radar screen, noting weather reports radioed in from shore. No one would dream of asking the tourists to do these things. Alas, among the tourists on Deck C, drinking coffee and eating doughnuts, we find the captain, and all the ship's officers, and all the ship's crew. The officers chat; they swear; they wink a bit at slightly raw jokes, just like regular people. The crew members have funny accents. The wind seems to be picking up.

On the whole, I do not find Christians, outside of the catacombs, sufficiently sensible of conditions. Does anyone have the foggiest idea what sort of power we so blithely invoke? Or, as I suspect, does no one believe a word of it? The churches are children playing on the floor with their chemistry sets, mixing up a batch of TNT to kill a Sunday morning. It is madness to wear ladies' straw hats and velvet hats to church; we should all be wearing crash helmets. Ushers should issue life preservers and signal flares; they should lash us to our pews. For the sleeping god may wake someday and take offense, or the waking god may draw us out to where we can never return.

The eighteenth-century Hasidic Jews had more sense, and more belief. One Hasidic slaughterer, whose work required invoking the Lord, bade a tearful farewell to his wife and children every morning before he set out for the slaughterhouse. He felt, every morning, that he would never see any of them again. For every day, as he himself stood with his knife in his hand, the words of his prayer carried him into danger. After he called on God, God might notice and destroy him before he had time to utter the rest, "Have mercy."

Another Hasid, a rabbi, refused to promise a friend to visit him the next day: "How can you ask me to make such a promise? This evening I must pray and recite 'Hear, O Israel.' When I say these words, my soul goes out to the utmost rim of life. . . . Perhaps I shall not die this time either, but how can I now promise to do something at a time after the prayer?"

Assorted Wildlife

INSECTS

I like insects for their stupidity. A paper wasp—*Polistes*—is fumbling at the stained-glass window on my right. I saw the same sight in the same spot last Sunday: Pssst! Idiot! Sweetheart! Go around by the door! I hope we seem as endearingly stupid to God—bumbling down into lamps, running half-wit across the floor, banging for days at the hinge of an opened door. I hope so. It does not seem likely.

PENGUINS

According to visitors, Antarctic penguins are ... adorable. They are tame! They are funny!

Tourists in Antarctica are mostly women of a certain age. They step from the cruise ship's rubber Zodiacs wearing bright ship's-issue parkas; they stalk around on the gravel and squint into the ice glare; they exclaim over the penguins, whom they find tame, funny, and adorable; they take snapshots of each other with the penguins, and look around cheerfully for something else to look around at.

The penguins are adorable, and the wasp at the stained-glass window is adorable, because in each case their impersonations of human dignity so evidently fail. What are the chances that God finds our failed impersonation of human dignity adorable? Or is he fooled? What odds do you give me?

III

The Land

Several years ago I visited the high Arctic and saw it: the Arctic Ocean, the Beaufort Sea. The place was Barter Island, inside the Arctic Circle, in the Alaskan Arctic north of the North Slope. I stood on the island's ocean shore and saw what there was to see: a pile of colorless stripes. Through binoculars I could see a bigger pile of colorless stripes.

It seemed reasonable to call the colorless stripe overhead "sky," and reasonable to call the colorless stripe at my feet "ice," for I could see where it began. I could distinguish, that is, my shoes, and the black gravel shore, and the nearby frozen ice the wind had smashed ashore. It was this mess of ice—ice breccia, pressure ridges, and standing floes, ice sheets upright, tilted, frozen together and jammed—that extended out to the horizon. No matter how hard I blinked, I could not put a name to any of the other stripes. Which was the horizon? Was I seeing land, or water, or their reflections in low clouds? Was I seeing the famous "water sky," the "frost smoke," or the "ice blink"?

In his old age, James McNeill Whistler used to walk down to the Atlantic shore carrying a few thin planks and his paints. On the planks he painted, day after day, in broad, blurred washes representing sky, water, and shore, three blurry light-filled stripes. These are late Whistlers; I like them very much. In the high Arctic I thought of them, for I seemed to be standing in one of them. If I loosed my eyes from my shoes, the gravel at my feet, or the chaos of ice at the shore, I saw what newborn babies must see: nothing but senseless variations of light on the retinas. The world was a color-field painting wrapped around me at an unknown distance; I hesitated to take a step.

There was, in short, no recognizable three-dimensional space in the Arctic. There was also no time. The sun never set, but neither did it appear. The dim round-the-clock light changed haphazardly when the lid of cloud thickened or thinned. Circumstances made the eating of meals random or impossible. I slept when I was tired. When I woke I walked out into the colorless stripes and the revolving winds, where atmosphere mingled with distance, and where land, ice, and light blurred into a dreamy, freezing vapor that, lacking anything else to do with the stuff, I breathed. Now and then a white bird materialized out of the vapor and screamed. It was, in short, what one might, searching for words, call a beautiful land; it was more beautiful still when the sky cleared and the ice shone in the dark water.

The Technology

It is for the Pole of Relative Inaccessibility I am searching, and
have been searching, in the mountains and along the seacoasts for
years. The aim of this expedition is, as Pope Gregory put it in his
time, "To attain to somewhat of the unencompassed light, by
stealth, and scantily." How often have I mounted this same expedition, has my absurd barque set out half-caulked for the Pole?

The Land

"These incidents are *true*," I read in an 1880 British history of
Arctic exploration. "These incidents are *true*,—the storm, the
drifting ice-raft, the falling berg, the sinking ship, the breaking
up of the great frozen floe: these scenes are *real*,—the vast
plains of ice, the ridged hummocks, the bird-thronged cliff, the
far-stretching glacier."

Polar exploration is no longer the fashion it was during the
time of the Franklin expedition, when beachgoers at Brighton
thronged to panoramas of Arctic wastes painted in shopwin-
dows, and when many thousands of Londoners jammed the
Vauxhall pleasure gardens to see a diorama of polar seas. Our
attention is elsewhere now, but the light-soaked land still exists;
I have seen it.

The Technology

In the nineteenth century, a man deduced Antarctica.

During that time, no one on earth knew for certain whether
there was any austral landmass at all, although the American
Charles Wilkes claimed to have seen it. Some geographers and
explorers speculated that there was no land, only a frozen
Antarctic Ocean; others posited two large islands in the vicinity
of the Pole. That there is one continent was not in fact settled
until 1935.

In 1893, one John Murray presented to the Royal Geographic
Society a deduction of the Antarctic continent. His expedition's
ship, the *Challenger*, had never come within sight of any such
continent. His deduction proceeded entirely from dredgings

and soundings. In his presentation he posited a large, single continent, a speculative map of which he furnished. He described accurately the unknown continent's topology: its central plateau with its permanent high-pressure system, its enormous glacier facing the Southern Ocean, its volcanic ranges at one coast and, at another coast, its lowland ranges and hills. He was correct.

Deduction, then, is possible—though no longer fashionable. There are many possible techniques for the exploration of high latitudes. There is, for example, such a thing as a drift expedition.

When that pair of yellow oilskin breeches belonging to the lost crew of the *Jeannette* turned up after three years in Greenland, having been lost north of central Russia, Norwegian explorer Fridtjof Nansen was interested. On the basis of these breeches' travels he plotted the probable direction of the current in the polar basin. Then he mounted a drift expedition: in 1893 he drove his ship, the *Fram*, deliberately into the pack ice and settled in to wait while the current moved north and, he hoped, across the Pole. For almost two years, he and a crew of twelve lived aboard ship as frozen ocean carried them. Nansen wrote in his diary, "I long to return to life . . . the years are passing here . . . Oh! at times this inactivity crushes one's very soul; one's life seems as dark as the winter night outside; there is sunlight upon no other part of it except the past and the far, far distant future. I feel as if I *must* break through this deadness."

The current did not carry them over the Pole, so Nansen and one companion set out one spring with dog sledges and kayaks to reach the Pole on foot. Conditions were too rough on the ice, however, so after reaching a record northern latitude, the two turned south toward land, wintering together finally in a stone hut on Franz Josef Land and living on polar bear meat. The following spring they returned, after almost three years, to civilization.

Nansen's was the first of several drift expeditions. During World War I, members of a Canadian Arctic expedition camped on an ice floe seven miles by fifteen miles; they drifted for six months over four hundred miles in the Beaufort Sea. In 1937, an airplane deposited a Soviet drift expedition on an ice floe near the North Pole. These four Soviet scientists drifted for nine months while their floe, colliding with grounded ice, repeatedly split into ever smaller pieces.

The Land

I have, I say, set out again.

The days tumble with meanings. The corners heap up with poetry; whole unfilled systems litter the ice.

The Technology

A certain Lieutenant Maxwell, a member of Vitus Bering's second polar expedition, wrote: "You never feel safe when you have to navigate in waters which are completely blank."

Cartographers call blank spaces on a map "sleeping beauties."

On our charts I see the symbol for shoals and beside it the letters "P.D." My neighbor in the pew, a lug with a mustache who has experience of navigational charts and who knows how to take a celestial fix, tells me that the initials stand for "Position Doubtful."

The Land

To learn the precise location of a Pole, choose a clear, dark night to begin. Locate by ordinary navigation the Pole's position within an area of several square yards. Then arrange on the ice in that area a series of loaded cameras. Aim the cameras at the sky's zenith; leave their shutters open. Develop the film. The film from that camera located precisely at the Pole will show the night's revolving stars as perfectly circular concentric rings.

The Technology

I have a taste for solitude, and silence, and for what Plotinus called "the fight of the alone to the Alone." I have a taste for solitude. Sir John Franklin had, apparently, a taste for backgammon. Is either of these appropriate to conditions?

You quit your house and country, quit your ship, and quit your companions in the tent, saying, "I am just going outside and may be some time." The light on the far side of the blizzard lures you. You walk, and one day you enter the spread heart of silence, where lands dissolve and seas become vapor and ices sublime under unknown stars. This is the end of the Via Negativa, the lightless edge where the slopes of knowledge dwindle, and love for its own sake, lacking an object, begins.

The Land

I have put on silence and waiting. I have quit my ship and set out on foot over the polar ice. I carry chronometer and sextant, tent, stove and fuel, meat and fat. For water I melt the pack ice in hatchet-hacked chips; frozen salt water is fresh. I sleep when I can walk no longer. I walk on a compass bearing toward geographical north.

I walk in emptiness; I hear my breath. I see my hand and compass, see the ice so wide it arcs, see the planet's peak curving and its low atmosphere held fast on the dive. The years are passing here. I am walking, light as any handful of aurora; I am light as sails, a pile of colorless stripes; I cry "heaven and earth indistinguishable!" and the current underfoot carries me and I walk.

The blizzard is like a curtain; I enter it. The blown snow heaps in my eyes. There is nothing to see or to know. I wait in the tent, myself adrift and emptied, for weeks while the storm unwinds. One day it is over, and I pick up my tent and walk. The storm has scoured the air; the clouds have lifted; the sun rolls round the sky like a fish in a round bowl, like a pebble rolled in a tub, like a swimmer, or a melody flung and repeating, repeating enormously overhead on all sides.

My name is Silence. Silence is my bivouac, and my supper sipped from bowls. I robe myself mornings in loose strings of stones. My eyes are stones; a chip from the pack ice fills my mouth. My skull is a polar basin; my brain pan grows glaciers, and icebergs, and grease ice, and floes. The years are passing here.

Far ahead is open water. I do not know what season it is, know how long I have walked into the silence like a tunnel widening before me, into the horizon's spread arms, which widen like water. I walk to the pack ice edge, to the rim that calves its floes into the black-and-green water; I stand at the edge and look ahead. A scurf of candle ice on the water's skin as far as I can see scratches the sea and crumbles whenever a lump of ice or snow bobs or floats through it. The floes are thick in the water, some of them large as lands. By my side is passing a flat pan of floe from which someone extends an oar. I hold the oar's blade and jump. I land on the long floe.

No one speaks. Here, at the bow of the floe, the bright clowns have staked themselves to the ice. With tent stakes and ropes they have lashed their wrists and ankles to the floe on which they lie stretched and silent, face up. Among the clowns, and similarly staked, are many boys and girls, some women, and a few men from various countries. One of the men is Nansen, the Norwegian explorer who drifted. One of the women repeatedly opens and closes her fists. One of the clowns has opened his neck ruffle, exposing his skin. For many hours I pass among these staked people, intending to return later and take my place.

Farther along I see that the tall priest is here, the priest who served grape juice Communion at an ecumenical service many years ago, in another country. He is very old. Alone on a wind-streaked patch of snow he kneels, stands, and kneels, and stands, and kneels. Not far from him, at the floe's side, sitting on a packing crate, is the deducer John Murray. He lowers a plumb bob overboard and pays out the line. He is wearing the antique fur hat of a Doctor of Reason, such as Erasmus wears in his portrait; it is understood that were he ever to return and present his findings, he would be ridiculed, for his hat. Scott's Captain Oates is here; he has no feet. It is he who stepped outside his tent, to save his friends. Now on his dignity he stands and mans the sheet of a square linen sail; he has stepped the wooden mast on a hillock amidships.

From the floe's stern I think I hear music; I set out, but it takes me several sleeps to get there. I am no longer using the tent. Each time I wake, I study the floe and the ocean horizon for signs—signs of the pack ice that we left behind, or of open water, or land, or any weather. Nothing changes; there is only the green sea and the floating ice, and the black sea in the distance speckled by bergs, and a steady wind astern, which smells of unknown mineral salts, some ocean floor.

At last I reach the floe's broad stern, its enormous trailing coast, its throngs, its many cooking fires. There are children carrying babies, and men and women painting their skins and trying to catch their reflections in the water to leeward. Near the water's edge there is a wooden upright piano, and a bench with a telephone book on it. A woman is sitting on the telephone book and banging out the Sanctus on the keys. The wind is picking up. I am singing at the top of my lungs, for a lark.

Many clowns are here; one of them is passing out Girl Scout cookies, all of which are stuck together. Recently, I learn, Sir John Franklin and crew have boarded this floe, and so have the crews of the lost *Polaris* and the *Jeannette*. The men, whose antique uniforms are causing envious glances, are hungry. Some of them start roughhousing with the rascally acolyte. One crewman carries the boy on his back along the edge to the piano, where he abandons him for a clump of cookies and a seat on the bench beside the short pianist, whose bare feet, perhaps on account of the telephone book, cannot reach the pedals. She starts playing "The Sound of Music." "You know any Bach?" I say to the lady at the piano, whose legs seem to be highly involved with those of the hungry crewman; "You know any Mozart? Or maybe 'How Great Thou Art'?" A skeletal officer wearing a black silk neckerchief has located Admiral Peary, recognizable from afar by the curious flag he holds. Peary and the officer together are planning a talent show and skits. When they approach me, I volunteer to sing "Antonio Spangonio, That Bum Toreador" and/or to read a piece of short fiction; they say they will let me know later.

Christ, under the illusion that we are all penguins, is crouched down, posing for snapshots. He crouches, in his robe, between the lead singer of Wildflowers, who is joyfully trying to determine the best angle at which to hold his guitar for the camera, and the farmer's wife, who keeps her eyes on her painted toenails until a naval officer with a silk scarf says "Cheese." The country-and-western woman, singing, succeeds in pressing a cookie upon the baby Oswaldo. The baby Oswaldo is standing in his lace gown and blue tennis shoes in the center of a circle of explorers, confounding them.

In my hand I discover a tambourine. Ahead as far as the brittle horizon, I see icebergs among the floes. I see tabular bergs and floebergs and dark cracks in the water between them. Low overhead on the underside of the thickening cloud cover are dark colorless stripes reflecting pools of open water in the distance. I am banging on the tambourine, and singing whatever the piano player plays; now it is "On Top of Old Smokey." I am banging the tambourine and belting the song so loudly that people are edging away. But how can any of us tone it down? For we are nearing the Pole.

1982

CONTEMPORARY
PROSE STYLES

WE HEAR MANY COMPLAINTS ABOUT contemporary fiction—that its characters are flat and its stories are dull—but we hear no complaints about prose style. For in fact, prose styles have been one of the great strengths of Western fiction throughout this century. Prose style in fiction is like surface handling in painting. No matter how much people complain that contemporary works say little, no one denies that they say it very well.

Contemporary prose styles have two overlapping strands. One is what we might call for the moment plain, the other fancy.

SHOOTING THE AGATE

Many contemporary prose styles derive from the mainstream of traditional fine writing. Fine writing, like painterly painting, has always been with us. We will, I hope, never cease to admire it. The great prose stylists of the recent past, until Flaubert, were fine writers to a man. A surprising number of these—those I think of first, in fact—wrote nonfiction: Robert Burton, Sir Thomas Browne, Samuel Johnson, Thomas de Quincey, Thomas Macaulay, Ralph Waldo Emerson, Henry Thoreau, John Ruskin, William James, Sir James Frazer.

Who were the grand stylists of eighteenth- and nineteenth-century fiction? There is the lovely Turgenev and the brilliant Gorky, if we are to believe their translators; Melville had a rare strength; Hardy can be magnificent, and so can Dickens. But we do not think of any of these, except Turgenev, as great stylists—although we wrong Dickens not to. Who else? Stendhal? Chateaubriand? I think fine writing in fictional prose comes into its own only with the modernists: first with James, and with

Proust, Faulkner, Beckett, Woolf, Kafka, and the lavish Joyce of the novels.

This is an elaborated, painterly prose. It raids the world for materials to build sentences. It fabricates a semi-opaque weft of language. It is a spendthrift prose, and a prose of means. It is dense in objects that pester the senses. It hauls in visual imagery of every sort; it strews metaphors about, and bald similes, and allusions to every realm. It does not shy from adjectives, nor even from adverbs. It traffics in parallel structures and repetitions; it indulges in assonance and alliteration. Here is a splendid sentence from Ruskin:

> Every alteration of the features of nature has its origin either in powerless indolence or blind audacity, in the folly which forgets, or in the insolence which desecrates, works which it is the pride of angels to know, and their privilege to love.

The sentences of this prose may be very long, heavily punctuated throughout, and welded with semicolons. Its lexicon is enormously wide, its spheres of reference global. We think of it as decorous, but actually it is not. Those old men in frock coats were after power, and power they got, by going for the throat. (Far more decorous is plain writing, the prose of Hemingway, Cather, Chekhov, and other stylists in shirts, who carefully limit their descriptions to matters at hand and who produce a prose purified by its submission to the world.) There is nothing decorous about calling attention to yourself:

> The world is a Dancer; it is a Rosary; it is a Torrent; it is a Boat; a Mist; a Spider's Snare; it is what you will; and the metaphor will hold. . . . Must I call the heaven and the earth a maypole and country fair with booths, or an anthill, or an old coat, in order to give you the shock of pleasure which the imagination loves and the sense of spiritual greatness? (Emerson, *Journals*)

Fine writing, with its elaborated imagery and powerful rhythms, has the beauty of both complexity and grandeur. It also has as its distinction a magnificent power to penetrate. It can penetrate precisely because, and only because, it lays no claims to precision. It is an energy. It sacrifices perfect control to the ambition to mean. It can pile object upon object to build a tower from which to breach the sky; it can enter with courage or bravura those fearsome realms where the end products of art meet the end products of thought, and where perfect clarity is not possible. Fine writing is not a mirror, not a window, not a document, not a surgical tool. It is an artifact and an achievement; it is at once an exploratory craft and the planet it attains; it is a testimony to the possibility of the beauty and penetration of written language.

Clearly we are in the presence of a paradox here. How can prose be said to penetrate and dazzle? How can it call attention to itself, waving its arms, while performing metaphysics behind its back? But this is what all art does, or at least all art that conceives of the center of things as insubstantial: as mental or spiritual. Fine prose in this sense is like Shakespeare's dramatic poetry, or Milton's epic poetry, or even Homer's. If you scratch an event, you get an idea. Fine writing does not actually penetrate the world of familiar things so much as it penetrates what, for lack of a better term, we might call the universe or even the realm of ideas. That is, this language does not penetrate things so much as it bears them away with it.

Shakespeare does not analyze Lear, or enter Lear. There was no Lear. Had there been a Lear, we could only say that Shakespeare transmogrified Lear. Lear, like Melville's whale, is an aesthetic or epistemological probe by means of which the artist analyzes the universe. When you really penetrate the world of things, as I understand the world of things, you encounter idea. And art, especially poetry and twentieth-century painting and fiction, objectifies idea on its own surface, by imitating thereon, in bits of world, the complex way that bits of mind cohere.

In twentieth-century painting, the art of mind and the art of surface go together. When painters abandoned narrative deep space, their canvases became abstract and intellectualized.

Similarly, with its multiple metaphors and colliding images, an embellished language actually abstracts the world's objects. Such language wrests objects from their familiar contexts. We do not enter deep space; we do not enter rounded characters; we contemplate them as objects. And when an artist both powerfully "realizes" his objects, rendering them in full material detail, and simultaneously "abstracts" them, rendering them under the aspect of eternity, then we may say that he penetrates these objects not to their specific, material hearts, but, as it were, out the other side, to their generalized forms, their created capacity to mean. He runs them through and hauls them off to heaven. Shakespeare does it with Lear; Cézanne does it with Mont Saint Victoire. Paradoxically, an artist does all this on the surface, by the studied application of materials. He tacks his objects to the sky, either by baring their flattening forms, as Cézanne does, or, as Shakespeare does, by spiriting the objects out of the world with a hundred flights of language never heard.

Two subspecies of fine writing are particularly suited to postmodernist ends. One is a prose style so intimate, and so often used in the first person, that it is actually a voice. The voice appears in Europe throughout this century, and particularly between the wars. One could argue that it appeared in Eastern Europe and worked its way westward. It is the voice of a crank narrator. You hear it a bit in Gogol and in Dostoyevsky; you hear it especially in Kafka; you hear it in Elias Canetti, Witold Gombrowicz, Knut Hamsun, in Beckett, and in Nabokov (*Despair, Pale Fire*).

This crank narrator is an enraged petty clerk, or a starveling, or a genius, or a monomaniac, or any sort of crazy. His is not an especially adult voice. He specializes in mood shifts. His voice is poetic, bellicose, and resigned. It deals in ironies, self-deprecations, arrogances, apologies, aggressions, whinings, obscenities, lyricisms, abrupt silences, flights of transcendence, and tantrums. This tone's energy depends, of course, on the rapid juxtaposition of these disparate moods— particularly a lyric mood interrupted by a note of aggrievement. Samuel Beckett has written three great novels using this one trick. The fact of the sky, in particular, seems to call forth the essence of this prose style. In *Molloy,* Beckett writes, "The sky was that horrible colour which heralds dawn." In *Ferdydurke,* Gombrowicz writes, "The sky, suspended in the heights, was light, fresh, pale, and sarcastic."

The crank narrator is a character outside bourgeois European culture; so is his creator. These writers either derive from peripheral countries, or are Jewish, or émigré, or are in some other way denied social access to mainstream European culture. One could easily argue that this culture itself disintegrated early in the century, and now everyone is adrift: this would account for the curiously contemporary sound of the voice. You may recognize the following as an imitation of Woody Allen, but it is not:

> Unparalleled cunning, great honesty of thought, and intelligence sharpened to a degree will be required to enable man to escape from his stiff exterior and succeed in better reconciling order with disorder, form with the formless, maturity with eternal and sacred immaturity. In the meantime, tell me which you prefer, red peppers or fresh cucumbers?

This is another passage from Gombrowicz's *Ferdydurke,* which appeared in Poland in 1937 and caused a scandal. Now everyone has caught the sound of this sort of mood-shifting prose. It has moved from the provinces and ghettos of Eastern Europe to New York City; now graduate students in writing and comedians can reel it out like yard goods.

The voice of the crank narrator is modernist in its distance, irony, and alienation; it is a mood composed of many shifting moods. Another subspecies of fine writing is even more contemporary. I have no name for this. It is a dense extreme of fine writing.

This prose repeats a fiction's narrative collage in a prose collage. Word by word, sentence by sentence, paragraph by paragraph, it proceeds by the same leaping transitions and bizarre juxtapositions of voice, diction, and image as the fiction as a whole does. It may use the present tense: he walks, he remembers his father, his father is running. This flattens time and lends a floating, objectlike quality to the narrative. (Oddly, the eighteenth-century novelists used the present tense for immediacy. Now we have learned to use it for distance.) This prose is, above all, a wrought verbal surface. It changes subjects as often as it changes moods; it presents an array of all the world's objects moving so fast they spin. It whirls us on a tour of language. It does not pause to examine any object; the verbal surface is itself the object.

William Gaddis and Denis Johnson use this prose in fiction. Anne Carson and Albert Goldbarth use it in vivid narrative essays. Mark Strand and W. S. Merwin use it in lyrics short as poems—as Rimbaud did in *Illuminations*. This prose is a shifting and refracting language surface whose subject matter is largely its own technique. The world, flattened and fragmented, becomes for the reader a vivid and ironic memory in chips and dots. Such works are objects composed of glittering language cemented by reference. The partly abstracted language surface is like a paint surface that replaces deep space. No sentimentality interferes with formal development. The pleasure such prose affords to the senses, and its attraction to the mind, may be considerable.

A very self-conscious, hammering prose is difficult to sustain over the length of a novel. Even if the writer can keep hammering, the reader may balk at being hammered. A fiction writer does well to unify dense prose with a voice. An English writer, Nik Cohn, wrote a novel using such an opaque voice. *Arfur,* published in the seventies, combined the rhythms of a rarefied New Orleans jazz slang with the vocabulary of pinball (!) to make a brilliant piece of fine writing. Cohn refers to "a very mosey style of walk, adopted off the riverboats, known as shooting the agate." "Willie the Pleaser," he writes alliteratively, "he was a cheat without equal, and he taught me many strokes, how to flare, how to float, how to flick from the elbow, so that I became an expert in all the paths of subterfuge."

Since Dorothy Richardson, stream-of-consciousness convention has provided a handy narrative occasion for technical collages—like *Ulysses*, like *The Sound and the Fury*, Henry Roth's *Call it Sleep*, and Tillie Olsen's "Hey Sailor, What Ship?" These and many others are rich and broken cubist surfaces. Their very intimacy, on the other hand, makes them anathema to those postmodernist writers who prefer to handle characters from great authorial distance, as if with tongs. For Borges and Nabokov, who despised Freud, stream-of-consciousness prose is suspect for its perilous proximity to matters subconscious, which in turn is entirely contaminated by the enthusiastic attention of amateurs.

There are abuses. In the nineteenth century, fancy-writing abuses ran to the pious sublime, and in our own, to the private ridiculous. Here is a fragment from Beckett's *How It Is:*

> my life a voice without quaqua on all sides wordscraps then nothing then again more words more scraps the same ill-spoken ill-heard then nothing vast stretch of time then in me in the vault bone-white if there were light bits and scraps ten seconds fifteen seconds ill-heard ill-murmured ill-heard ill-recorded my whole life a gibberish garbled six-fold.

Or do you prefer this? It is William Burroughs, writing in *A Distant Hand Lifted:*

> You/and   I/sad   old/broken   film/knife/cough/it   lands in/cough/present   time/long   cough/decoding   arrest/wasn't it?::::::cough/immediacy/cough/empty   arteries   must   tell you/cough/"adios"/who   else?/cough/drew   Sept.   17,   1899 over New York???

Sometimes too-dense fine writing is simply a psychological tic on the writer's part. The prose of the first thirty pages of Nabokov's *Ada* is a barrage of language released from occasion. It is a breastwork of puns and cryptic allusions which effectively defend the novel's contents from the reader's interest, until Nabokov is good and ready. The opening of Cormac McCarthy's excellent *Blood Meridian* and his *Suttree* are similarly obscure.

So, for that matter, is the opening of *War and Peace*—but not because of its prose. Many great writers accidentally release and reveal a certain amount of self-consciousness, anxiety, or even hostility as they settle in, or resign themselves, to the task.

Fine writing is still with us. Density, even lushness, and formal diction, forceful rhythms, dramatically fused imagery, and a degree of metaphorical splendor—these qualities still obtain. Henry James launched the century with a splash: *The Ambassadors*, *The Wings of the Dove*, *The Golden Bowl*. It is hard to see why writers write anything else after James, and readers read anyone else, but literature persists.

Here in the generalized category of fine writing belong the brittle sarcasms of Nabokov, and his much-wrought tendernesses, and especially his cryptographs—those challenges to literary criticism and parodies of its finds that are such red herrings to young writers, who must endlessly be relieved of the notion that the critic's role is to "find the hidden meanings" and the writer's role is to hide them, like Easter eggs. Here also belong the poignant lyricisms of Beckett, the embroideries of Gabriel García Márquez, the surrealisms of Italo Calvino, and the polished turns of Milan Kundera. Traditional in their elegances are E. M. Forster, the Ford Madox Ford of *The Good Soldier*, and Richard Hughes, Anthony Powell, Joyce Cary, Edna O'Brien, the D. M. Thomas of *The White Hotel*, Julian Barnes, and Graham Swift. In this country, grand stylists like E. L. Doctorow, Lee Smith, William Kennedy, Marilynne Robinson, Louis Begley, Denis Johnson, John Updike, and William Gass continue to expand the territory of fine writing.

Penetration may no longer be the fine writer's intention. A fine writer may now, as in the eighteenth century, be ironic or playful as well as sincere. He may brandish his wealth of beauties in a traditional way, as a traditional painterly painter handles paint: to describe beautifully and suggestively, to engage us, to fashion a world in depth. Or he may go abstract, and raid the world for fleeting images from which to fashion a moody expressionistic surface. This is Gass: "The sun looks, through the mist, like a plum on the tree of heaven, or a bruise on the slope of your belly. Which? The grass crawls with frost."

CALLING A SPADE A SPADE

Other twentieth-century writers avoid fine writing. Borges, interestingly, disclaimed his early story "The Circular Ruins" for its lush prose. Fine writing does indeed draw attention to a work's surface, and in that it furthers modernist aims. But at the same time it is pleasing, emotional, and engaging, like quondam beautiful effects with paint. It is literary. It is always vulnerable to the charge of sacrificing accuracy, or even integrity, to the more unfashionable value, beauty. For these reasons it may be, in the name of purity, jettisoned.

With Flaubert a new value for prose styles emerges. Prose must not be elaborate, at risk of being lacy. Instead it should be, as the cliché goes, "honed to a bladelike edge." This is a new sort of beauty in prose. Verbal dazzle, after all, is almost universally attractive; nineteenth-century Europeans admired it enormously. It takes a sophisticated ear, even a jaded ear, to appreciate the beauty and integrity of a careful simplicity. I am thinking here of the prose of Flaubert, Chekhov, Turgenev, Willa Cather, Sherwood Anderson, Hemingway, Paul Horgan, Wright Morris, Henry Green, and Borges.

This prose is, above all, clean. It is sparing in its use of adjectives and adverbs; it avoids relative clauses and fancy punctuation; it forswears exotic lexicons and attention-getting verbs; it eschews splendid metaphors and cultured allusions. Instead it follows the dictum of William Carlos Williams: "no ideas but in things."

Plain writing is by no means easy writing. The mot juste is an intellectual achievement. There is nothing relaxed about the pace of this prose; it is as restricted and taut as the pace of lyric poetry. The short sentences of plain prose have a good deal of blank space around them, as lines of lyric poetry do, and even as the abrupt utterances of Beckett characters do. They erupt against a backdrop of silence. These sentences are—in an extreme form of plain writing—objects themselves, objects that invite inspection and flaunt their simplicity. One could even, if one were cynical, accuse such plain sentences of the snobbery

of Bauhaus design, or of high-tech furnishings, or of the unob-
trusive dress suit: one could accuse them of ostentation. But I
anticipate a theoretical flaw I have never encountered in fact. As
it is actually used, this prose has one supreme function, which is
not to call attention to itself, but to refer to the world.

This prose is not an end in itself but a means. It is, then, a
useful prose. Each writer of course uses it in a different way.
Borges uses it straightforwardly, and as invisibly as he can, to
think, to handle bare ideas with control: "Hume denied the
existence of an absolute space, in which each thing has its
place; I deny the existence of one single time, in which all
events are linked." Robbe-Grillet uses it coldly and dryly, to
alienate, to describe, and to lend his descriptions the illusion of
scientific accuracy. His prose is a perceptual tool: ". . . the
square in the far left-hand corner of the table corresponds to
the base of a copper lamp now standing at the right-hand corner: a square base about an inch high . . . " Hemingway uses it
as a ten-foot pole, to distance himself from events; he also uses
it as chopsticks, to handle strong emotions without, in theory,
becoming sticky: "On the other hand his father had the finest
pair of eyes he had ever seen and Nick had loved him very
much and for a long time." (This flatness may be ludicrous.
Hemingway once wrote, and discarded, the sentence, "Paris is
a nice town.")

Writers like Flaubert, Chekhov, Turgenev, Cather, and Knut
Hamsun use this prose for many purposes: not only to control
emotion, but also to build an imaginative world whose parts
seem solidly actual and lighted, and to name the multiple
aspects of experience one by one, with distance, and also with
tenderness and respect. Wright Morris is a careful writer of
unadorned prose. He wrote, "The father talks to his son. The
son listens and watches his father eat soup."

This prose is craftsmanlike. It possesses beauty and power
without syntactical complexity. Because of its simplicity, writers
use this prose to handle children, as Joy Williams does often in
her stories in *Taking Care*. These children see the lives around
them with mocking irony. Philosophically, they stick to facts, as
though they believed that where we cannot be certain, we

should be silent. The effect is deadpan: "There is Jane and there is Jackson and there is David. There is the dog."

Many Western writers (like Jim Harrison), many if not most Scandinavian writers (like Knut Hamsun, Pär Lagerkvist, and F. E. Sillanpää), and other writers of scenes rural (like Flannery O'Connor in the South and John Berger in France) use plain prose to handle characters who do not belong in a drawing room, but are not merely picturesque rustics like Hardy's. Plain prose follows such characters intimately, lovingly, even a little ironically, and always with respect. It is a perfected prose of surpassing delicacy, control, and power. It honors the world because the characters honor the world. Listen to these adjectives:

> Floyd Warner kept a calendar on which he jotted what sort of day it was, every day of the year. Windy, overcast, drizzly, rain, clear and cool, clear and warm, and all through October he put simply, *Dandy*. Practically every day was dandy, and that had been true over the years. (Wright Morris, *Fire Sermon*)

This prose is a kind of literary vernacular. It possesses the virtues of beauty, clarity, and strength without embellishment.

In England, Henry Green also writes very often from the minds of people who are not formally educated and who know the world and love it on its merits. Green's prose is sometimes stylized to the point of self-consciousness. It is so plain it distracts as much as any fancy writing. Almost any experimental writing is fine writing; Green's is experimental plain writing. At its quirkiest, it omits articles for the sake of concision, and sounds like Tonto: "Mr. Cragan smoked pipe, already room was blurred by smoke from it." The warped purity of such sentences in *Living* achieves a watercolor lyricism: "Just then Mr. Dupret in sleep, died, in sleep." "What happened of her. What did her come to?"

Plain prose is almost requisite for handling violent or emotional scenes without eliciting dismay or nausea in the reader. We have long since tired of imitation fine writing, of bad fine writing, of the overwritten straining prose that we find not only in unskilled and youthful literature but also in junk fiction—and we tire of it especially in the wringingly emotional and violent scenes of which failed literature and junk are made. So unless he is William Faulkner, a serious writer of this century has little other recourse than to plain writing for violent and emotional scenes. If a writer wants to play safe, he will underwrite drama. Plain prose affords distance; it permits scenes to be effective on their narrative virtues, not on the overwrought insistence of their author's prose. The central love scene of Anthony Powell's twelve-volume "A Dance to the Music of Time" ends unforgettably: "I took her in my arms."

There is something about plain writing that smacks of moral goodness. Interestingly, many writers turn to it more and more as they get older. (The exception is Joyce, whose writing gets steadily fancier and worse as he ages.) There is a modesty to it. Paul Horgan uses it in his "Richard" trilogy, a series of novels that take the form of autobiography. Henry Green uses it in his autobiography; Graham Greene uses it in his autobiography. It is a mature prose. It honors the world. It is courteous. Its credo might be that of French entomologist J. Henri Fabre: "Lucidity is the sovereign politeness of the writer. I do my best to achieve it." Part of its politeness to readers is based on respect; this prose credits readers with feeling and intelligence. It does not explain events in all their ramifications; it does not color a scene emotionally.

This prose is humble. It calls attention not to itself but to the world. It is intimate with character; it is sympathetic and may be democratic. It submits to the world; it is honest. It praises the world by seeing it. It seems even to *believe* in the world it honors with so much careful attention. In the nineteenth century, readers liked their prose syntactically baroque and morally elevating. Each bit of world was a chip off the old sublime, and tended distressingly, in the prose that described it, to ascend to heaven before we got to know it.

Nothing so fair, so pure, and at the same time so large, as a lake, perchance, lies on the surface of the earth. Sky water.

It needs no fence. Nations come and go without defiling it. It is a mirror which no stone can crack, whose quicksilver will never wear off, whose gilding Nature continually repairs . . . (*Walden*)

Our reaction to such ebullience is of course to reverse it. We have modern tastes and like writing that is precise and uncluttered. We are agnostic or materialist and like writing fastened to the world of things. This plain prose represents literature's new morality. It honors each thing one by one, without metaphor. No angelic systems need be dragged in by the hair to sprinkle upon objects a borrowed splendor. Instead, each of the world's unique objects is the site of its own truth and goodness. Each thing is its own context for meaning. Its virtue is its stubborn uniqueness, in its resistance to generalization, and even in its resistance to our final knowledge of it. The most general trend we know is speciation.

Plain prose can be polished to transparency without losing strength. At its best, its form follows its function so accurately that its very purity and hard-won simplicity excite our admiration almost in spite of themselves. It does not err on the side of exuberance. It does, in theory, win through to material "things as they are"—things seen without bias or motive. That can be its epistemological claim. Aesthetically it can claim control, purity, and the dignity of material essences. And it can claim the just precision of a tool, the spareness of bone, the clarity of light. Do not confuse these claims with the clichés of contemporary craftsmen in materials who labor to help you understand that a wooden spoon may have integrity, a wooden apple barrel may have dignity, a wooden bench simple functional beauty, so that you labor in turn to find some kindling and a match. There is nothing clichéd about clear prose yet. For all its virtues, fine writing may be a mere pyrotechnic display, dazzling and done. And plain writing is not a pyrotechnic display, but a lamp.

I have contrasted these two categories of written prose as if they were opposites—and indeed they are. They are ends of a spectrum. If we put radically experimental prose together with dense and shifting prose collage at one end of the spectrum, we must put at the other end a plain, humble prose that points to the world. It is a broad spectrum. It extends clear from the art end of art to the life end of art. Naturally, most writers of this century, including the historical modernists themselves, write a prose that falls somewhere in the middle of the spectrum—just as the stories and novels themselves do. The prose, that is, points to a world we can enter, a world of emotional depth analogous to Renaissance painting's deep space; the prose, insofar as it refers, is invisible. Simultaneously, this prose builds a complex patterned, and semi-opaque, technical surface.

If we call very opaque modernist prose a painted sphere, and plain prose a clear windowpane, then we will see that these are extremes; most literary prose belongs somewhere in the middle. Or if we call fancy experimental prose "poetry" and plain prose "science," then again we will see that most prose falls somewhere in the middle. In this middle ground we have contemporaries writing complex modernist fiction using straightforward prose. We have writers using dislocated prose to tell stories of intimacy and depth. We have most frequently writers of traditional literature modified by this century's concerns, who use a beautiful and strong literary prose that may be flat, tough, or shifting. This prose is at once perfectly clean and capable of stunning elegance.

Robert Stone, like Tolstoy, usually keeps his prose plain, but it is a plain fact that it is sometimes a beautiful world. Here is how it was in an unnamed Central American country, coming into the *finca* landings at night:

> The boat would slow and ease toward the bank until the searching spotlight over the wheelhouse picked up the vehicle and the waiting men together with a thousand spinning moths, their bright wings flashing a thousand colors in the glare. Into this well of light, the Indian deckhands would toss the starboard hawsers . . . (*A Flag for Sunrise*)

You know how a puppy, when you point off in one direction for him, looks at your hand. It is hard to train him not to. The modernist arts in this century have gone to a great deal of trouble to *untrain* us readers, to force us to look at the hand. Contemporary modernist fine prose says, Look at my hand. Plain prose says, Look over there. But these are matters of emphasis. So long as words refer, the literary arts will continue to do two things at once, just as all representational painting does two things at once. They point to the world with a hand. So long as you write literature, you cannot unhinge the world from the words, nor the words from the page.

The very finest works of art do both things at once extremely well. Cézanne's still lifes and landscapes, for instance, depict. They push the paint surface into a modified simulation of deep space; the meadow tilts back toward the mountain. At the same time they pull deep space up toward the surface of the picture plane; the mountain looms flat against the canvas. The paintings' greatness depends on this spatial tension. Now look at Shakespeare. Who could say where the greater power of *King Lear* resides? Do we enter it as an emotional world of enlarged sympathies wherein we lose ourselves? Or do we admire it more as an artifice of theater and language?

Finally, it is interesting to note Robbe-Grillet's notion (which I think is accurate) that a writer thinks of a future novel first as "a way of writing." The narrative, he says, "what will happen in the book[,] comes afterward, as though secreted by the style itself." One does not "choose" a prose, or a handling of paint, as a fitting tool for a given task, the way one chooses a $\frac{5}{16}$ wrench to open a $\frac{5}{16}$ bolt. Rather—and rather creepily—the prose "secretes" the book. The book is a side effect of the prose, as our vision is a side effect of our seeing. Prose is a kind of cognitive tool, which secretes its objects—as though a set of tools were to create the very engines it could enter, as though a wielded wrench, like a waved soap-bubble wand, were to emit a trail of fitted bolts in its wake.

1982

THE LIVING

SOMETIME IN THE MIDDLE OF a December night in 1892, in the town of Whatcom on the north coast of Washington State, a man called Clare lay asleep with his wife in their bed. He was a tall, thin man forty-two years old. He slept like a baby. He slept facing the window, facing west toward the water; his wife slept on her belly between him and the window. His sleep was a great falling, a free and confident drop into nowhere.

At some time during that night, at some time before he woke for the day, the man's two eyes opened. The eyes' lids rose; the man's head lifted an inch from the pillow. His eyes moved together as though they were pointing at the nest of wife's hair on the mattress, or at the sea tide far beyond the window, swelling under the brightening sky. The man's two eyes moved, but only reflexively. The head dropped; the man slept on.

The Nooksack River was born of a drip in a cirque at the tongue of a glacier hung on a western rampart of Mount Shuksan. The drip froze into an icicle which dropped into a small pool; a runnel from the pool threaded a high valley out of the cirque and through the mountains, adding seep to melt and swelling so fast that a mile from its source a man needed one-piece rubber waders and a stout stick to cross it. This was the Nooksack River. It ducked into the forest, chuted between foothills, and fell asleep on the Nooksack plain.

The plain spread from the foothills to Gooseberry Point, the Lummi Indian reservation that bounded Bellingham Bay. The plain spread smoothly, without shadow, because the river had rolled over and over in its sleep, or dreamily swished its heavy tail, and flattened everywhere the land. Emigrants who knew farming looked for river silt under the fir forest, and found it; it made a likely loam, lightened by sand. They cleared the woods with oxen to farm it, sold the logs, grazed cattle around the stumps, and planted peas.

In this way the town of Whatcom had grown up in the 1880s, and continued to grow. The settlers built the town on the shore of Bellingham Bay, north of Puget Sound. The settlers hoped to have a share in greatness as the town's fortunes rose; they hoped Whatcom would become the chief Pacific port. But the port aspect failed. Bellingham Bay was not a sheltered harbor, and it silted up. At low tide the mudflats extended out to the railroad trestle that crossed the bay. Still, the long wharf was good for fishing boats in season, and by and by a spur of the railroad came.

I

On that December night in 1892, Beal Obenchain stood in the mud of Bellingham Bay. He bounced on his big boot toes, stepped aside, and watched the saltwater mud fill his boot-toe dents. The tide was going out; it was a black neap tide that barely moistened the mudflats. From these mudflats, in the frequent depressions and panics that racked the Puget Sound towns, people scratched up inferior clams—horse clams, bent-nose and jack clams. The town's children waded here in summer evenings' high tides. It was the children who, the previous summer, found the top of the head of a "Hindoo" who jumped or was pushed from the Great Northern Railroad trestle that spanned the bay in a wide curve. Digging revealed that beneath the Hindoo's head was the rest of him; his body stood buried upright in the mud. When things dropped from the trestle, they tended to accumulate on the mudflats, or wash up on the beach: so also did lost octopus traps, scuttled boats, and broken boom logs on a westerly.

There was an old shark carcass on the beach; Obenchain had passed it on his way to the open flats. The carcass represented a shark that had once been eighteen feet long; the living creature fouled in a fisherman's gill net and drowned. The fisherman had displayed the shark on the town wharf till the carcass exploded and stank; then he towed it out to sea and cut it loose. An autumn floodtide dragged it back shoreward and lodged it, disintegrating and crawling with crabs, against the trestle pilings. The crabs were yellow Dungeness crabs; they ate the flesh in their clattering fashion, by squatting over it and lowering what looked like arms from their mouths and passing bites directly into what looked like their stomachs. At last the fisherman had enclosed what was left of the shark in his ruined net and towed it south to the mudflat; he beached his boat on the flood tide and man-hauled the mess up the beach. There, on round stones under a sandstone cliff, the shark had solidified, barely bothered by shade-chilled flies. The sun and the freeze dried and blackened it; rain ran down it; the northerly wind turned it to stone.

The fisherman's net rotted at once and his manila line became a ridge of shreds, but the black shark carcass under the cliff ceased changing. It looked like a creosoted log, or a lava tube, or a vein of coal, or a sewer pipe. It was one of many obstructions on the upper beach that a man had to crawl over or walk wetly around. The others were all dead Douglas firs whose spiked trunks jutted out from the crumbled cliffside and pointed seaward like artillery.

It was December. It was December all day and dark as the center of earth. Solid cloud pressed over the land and water like a granite slab. For three weeks, no one from the town had seen Mount Baker or any mountain in the east, or the moon overhead, or the sun. This morning the sun had in fact appeared fuzzily on the far side of a fog, but then the granite clouds had sealed the sky again. By noon, no one could see even the western islands. Walking on the mud below the beach, Beal Obenchain could barely make out the old wharf and its bent pilings, where nine months ago he had tied and drowned a Chinaman at low tide. He could barely make out the trestle behind the old wharf; he saw the dark bulge where the trestle flew out from the woods on the cliff, and the dark streak of its curved flight over the bay. A figure was moving along the trestle's walkway, out to sea. It was raining a little, and stopping a little, as it did all winter, as if the sky were a cold cave ceiling that dripped.

It was four-thirty, after sunset. The colorless light came from nowhere and dimmed, and the blue dark, like a purse seine, was drawing close. Obenchain stood in the center of an ever-decreasing circle. He chewed a salty strand of bull kelp and spat the bits on the mud. He could still see, halfway out of the bay where the current still ran, a dozen drenched cormorants, motionless in silhouette, which rode a tide-caught log, but he could no longer see the raft of black brant sucking eelgrass under the trestle. He could see humped eelgrass in the mud by the water, and he could see black pools and channels of standing water everywhere splitting the flats; the shining darkness of the water carved the dull darkness of the mud into lobes.

A thought had taken deep root in his mind; absently, he removed his high-crowned derby and combed his hair over his temples. There were gaudy patches of oil film visible at his feet. Whenever something died beneath the surface, its decay released a film of iridescent oils, blue and yellow, on the mud. Near one of these oil slicks, Obenchain found a lady's comb. Everywhere he walked he saw big wormholes in the mud. There were bloodworms under there, bloodworms as fragile as egg yolks. If a man touched one while he was digging, it broke and spilled cold blood into the hole. There were lugworms under there, too; they always stretched and never broke.

Now Obenchain awoke from his thought and discovered his pants' leg was soaked; a horse clam had squirted a load of water on him. He quit the mud then, and moved to the black eelgrass humps, where he trod on hidden skeleton shrimps, sea urchins, and snails. The rain picked up. The mudflat stank of cold live mud, fish parts, and fog. He was getting cold.

Beal Obenchain was tall and stout, twenty-eight years old. His long head seemed to flow directly into his neck, for thick muscles covered a small jaw. He had come to the mudflat to think. He had killed a man near here last year, and was just deciding not to kill another. He and an itinerant Wyoming miner had killed an ugly Chinaman by lashing him to a piling under the old wharf one midnight; they left him to drown when the tide came in.

They had knifed a purple starfish, which was in the way, and pried it from the old wharf piling in sections. They stripped the struggling Chinaman, who had, so far as they could make out, a particular dread of the big crabs that would roll in with the water. Obenchain himself had become weepy, and recited a psalm from his childhood. They gagged the man and bound his wrists and lashed him to the piling with a rolling hitch. The Wyoming miner said, "I've had enough," and walked off to the north. Obenchain glanced after the miner and let him go.

As a final gesture, on the mudflat halfway between the Chinaman and the low-tide water, Obenchain had left a lighted lantern, so the Chinaman could study the tide for the first three hours as it rose, until it tipped the lantern and washed it out. After that, he would perforce imagine the water until it touched his feet. Then he could feel the water, and measure its rise against his skin. Obenchain departed, and no one from the town saw anything.

The least singular aspect of the Chinaman's death for Obenchain was its possible consequence on the temporal plane. Obenchain knew that he was not afraid of the town. He was an intellectual, and the townspeople were laborers or sharpers. They were laborers or sharpers with pretensions, who never left the life of sensation but only refined its objects: when they had a little land, or a ten-year-old name, they switched in their boots from beer to sherry, and got them a Lummi Indian man to cut their wood. Respectable people were those who avoided outcry. Obenchain was more than respectable; he was a natural aristocrat, self-made, whose high skull scraped the sky.

He was a stranded mystic, an embodiment of reason's directing will, who alone understood the Chinaman's luck in sacrificing his body for this experiment on his mind. Above all, Obenchain knew himself to be a man of science, a man who had access to metagnostical structures, a man of methods conceived in purity, who knew secrets.

It was by the simplest, most worldly wisdom, too, that he knew that if the powers that be were to deny him their forces, and people tried to trap him, he could always use his mastery of the powers that are. If the sluggish and greedy laborers of the town should stir against him, he was smart enough to keep the sheriff flattered by losing at chess—and if that failed, he was loose enough to move.

Obenchain had no ties on earth. He had rowed into Whatcom from one of the outer islands when he was fourteen; he rowed up and down the tides for two days and a night. He sold his boat to a childless couple he found back of the beach, who boarded him free while he went to school. He held the fawning couple in contempt; he read Byron in the shed. When he was sixteen he built himself a room in a hollow cedar stump near the railroad right-of-way in the woods south of town. He lived there still, in the cedar stump near the tracks. He raided fishtraps for cash, or worked clearing trees; he adopted, fed, and petted mice; paid no taxes; he rolled blanket stiffs he found alone by the tracks. Bored, he invented games with dice and with cards; he bet on bad weather; he whistled; he made a spectacle of himself near the tracks when the passenger coach passed. He sent for translations of recent books from France. He baked bread, cinnamon rolls, and pies. He had killed a man near here last spring, and had just decided not to kill another.

Obenchain could no longer make out the high trestle, or the dull waterline. He recrossed the mudflat in a drenching dark and gained the beach, where stones ground loudly underfoot. Obenchain thought he needed to walk in order to think, or in order to quiet his thoughts. He had not thought well on the mudflat, but he had not been wholly bored. His own actions often surprised him; his feelings and deeds overtook him like seizures, like storms of inspiration. Now he knew what he would do.

The man he resolved not to kill was Clare Fishburn, who taught domestic arts in the high school shop. Obenchain had drawn his name that day from a bucket of names, still uncertain then whether he would go through with it. The way in which he had now decided not to kill Clare Fishburn was by threatening to kill him and doing nothing. He would let his victim live as best he could in the knowledge that he was at any moment to die.

You simply tell a man, any man, that you are going to kill him. Then—assuming he believes you enough to watch his every step but not quite enough to run away or kill you first—then you take pains not to kill him and instead watch what he does, stuck alive on your bayonet and flailing. Killing the Chinaman had afforded less interest and spectacle than Obenchain hoped it would. When you kill a man directly, on no matter how gradual a tide, you do not, he discovered, actually take his life. You merely end his life; you do not take it. His life force is not added to yours, nor do his guardian spirits flock to you; these forces perish, and nobody profits by them. You take as yours, bluntly, only his carcass if you want it, which is of no value or intrigue to any save to hungry crabs and his wife.

If, however, you make a man believe that you will arrange for his dying at any moment, then you can, in effect, possess his life. He enters the circumference of your personal power. It was as easy as eating striped candy. For how could that man perform the least or the greatest act with his whole heart? You would give him, like bondsmen, self-consciousness and uncertainty, and they would deliver him unto you where you sat. How could such a man eat a plate of food or lie with his wife or take two steps in a row without thinking the very thoughts you bade him think? You would own this man—he would own Clare Fishburn—without lifting a finger. His every action and thought would be in some sense under your control. You would pipe and he would dance.

Obenchain followed the beach south. His eye sought the line of forest on the headland, but its black silhouette was lost in the black sky, as if the sky had abolished it. Life is mind, Obenchain thought, and mind in some unguessable way operates in words. In his very breath was power. You tell a man his life is in your hands, and, miraculously, his life is in your hands. You own him insofar as he believes you. You own him as God owns a man, to the degree of his faith.

There was no light, human or inhuman, up or down the beach, or out on the invisible islands, or up in the forest, or anywhere on earth or in heaven, except a chill and fantastical sheen on the unstable dark of the sea. What, Obenchain speculated, would become of this man's former, heedless life? To what category of being belongs a dead life whose body lives on? Obenchain had known Clare Fishburn four years ago, in the high school shop. Professor Fishburn, as people called him, directed the high school manual-training course. At that time he had a wife who was expecting, a dead-end job, a house on a hill, and a head full of nothing. Should someone hold a funeral for this dead life? Clare's body would live long after Clare's real life was over. This was the dead opposite of murder; it was birth, or conception. Obenchain thought—and sentimental tears rose in his eyes—that in many long years, when the body called Clare Fishburn should die of natural causes, he, Obenchain, would attend the funeral apparently as a townsman but in fact as the father of a dead only son.

He would call on Clare Fishburn after supper. Now he was bound for his house in the forest—the roofed-over hollow cedar stump. He could light a bucketful of folded papers in the stove, fire up some wet alder, and dry his trousers.

He passed the dripping shark carcass and distinguished, among the multiple textures of blackness, the dull path through trees up the sandstone cliff. The mudflat held more light than the land; the forest blotted it out. When he gained the clifftop, Obenchain walked south, seeing nothing, and felt with his feet for the tracks.

Clare Fishburn, with a spoon in one hand and a daughter in the other, ate apple pudding. He was at home, in the tall house on Lambert Street. He wore a gabardine vest and a blue shirt. He leaned in and out of the lamplight; he was telling a story in the dining room, between the kitchen and the front parlor, and he was waving his spoon. "It was almighty fine," he said, about an initiation prank his lodge had played. "It was really woolly." His nose was long, his forehead was long, and his jaw was long. He was so loose-jointed, tall, and shambly, that even sitting he resembled the stick doll that dances on a slat. His lively motions kept the effect constant; he shifted his legs, jerked his arms, swiveled his neck.

His wife, June, listened, smiling, without looking at him; instead, as if against her will, she followed his apple-pudding spoon as it wagged over the blue tablecloth, as it wagged over Mabel's fair head and good dress, and over Clare's own shirt-front. June was short and round-headed, thin. Under her green apron she wore a pinch-waisted dress of blotchy dark linsey-woolsey, ribboned in rows and creased at random. She had grown up in Baltimore; her father was a senator.

Clare's mother, Ada, was clearing the table. Ada was no taller standing than Clare sitting. On top of her head was a small white roll of hair, the size of a corn dodger. Her bow-shaped mouth and expressive, keen eyes had made her striking in her youth. Now age had pulled down her round face and narrowed it, taken half her teeth, and thinned the brows on her clear fore-head, so her eyes looked even bigger and blacker than they had when she was young, when they blazed out from a bonnet deep as a bucket.

"Come sit down," Clare told her. "You look baked."

"If there are any more lodge initiations to tell," Ada said, "you will spill not only the pudding, but the child as well."

Mabel slid lower on Clare's lap. She was an India-rubbery-looking person even when awake. Her moist child's face shifted from one half-formed expression to another; even while she climbed things, even while she marched boisterously about the house, she retained a limp, sleepy look. She had fine, reddish hair and skin pale as putty; her round limbs looked jointless and unmuscled. She was a jot shy of four years old—born on Christmas. If she heard her father's exalted voice at all, it was through a bright fog of sleep.

On the back porch the door banged, and banged again: old Ada was throwing salmon scraps to the dog, the dog that had been crying pitiably since sunset, as though it had never in the length of its life so much as seen a morsel of food, yet knew, with its dying breath, that there was such a thing, inexplicably denied to it of all creatures alone.

Clare met June's ironic gaze. Her high brows outlined the rim of bone under which her eyes were deep as wells. He loved to know her opinion of things. There was not a bill in the House of Representatives or a bulb in the garden of which he did not consider his wife's probable opinion before he framed his own, if any. Now she was looking at him in the precise way she had; he did not know why. He gave Mabel a squeeze and shifted his legs.

They were running late. Clare himself had begun fixing the pudding long after dark. He peeled the newspapers from the apples in their carton and chopped them—red-and-white Kings, green-and-white Gravensteins—into a yellow bowl. He shunted the stove's heat into its oven, where eventually the king salmon baked, split by its stuffing, and five brown potatoes baked, and the dark pudding frothed down the sides of the yellow bowl. Now it was after eleven. Old Ada was shuffling her feet; he and June were starting to stare, and the child was asleep, her loose mouth tidily shut. His must be a slatted sort of lap, Clare thought, but Mabel had a way of softening to fit any occasion, as though she had no bones. The skin on her hands was hot; her hair gave off a sour steam as she slept.

Clare scraped hardened brown sugar and butter from the yellow bowl's side; he offered it to June, who smiled her ironic smile, and ate it himself. He meant to pick up some sherry; he wished they had a boat. They could get a rowboat, at least, for Mabel. Tomorrow he would surprise June with an electric sewing machine. He made only sixty dollars a month teaching shop and science at the high school, but he recently sold some building lots he had bought with June's legacy two years ago, and realized a 400 percent return. The way business was swelling and his investments were boiling up, he fancied getting a horse and carriage—a high-seated victoria, and a certain beautiful, freckled mare with a high, long action, which Jim O'Shippy might sell. They could build a carriage house by the cowshed.

Clare grew up with the boisterous new country and boasted of its youth; he shared its glory's rise as its trees fell. His family had crossed the plains in an emigrant train of wagons, and joined in a raw settlement on Bellingham Bay. He saw the firs rise straight from the water's edge a hundred feet without branching, and he cricked his neck to see their tops another hundred feet higher. He saw Puget Sound and the Strait of Juan de Fuca, where Pacific water, deep and sheltered, made an inland sea. He saw the settlement called Whatcom spring up urgent to do business by cutting, floating, milling, and selling fir timber. Capitalizers drew into town and plunked down money. Their bold enterprises platted building lots, chopped trails through the forest, and flung out wharves.

Now Whatcom County spread from the glaciated North Cascades to the inland sea. The state of Washington was three years old, bigger than all New England, and the coming magnificence of its Puget Sound harbors was plain to any man. Clare felt himself as immortal as the nation whose destiny, as he put it to himself, he shared; no moss grew under his feet. His was the first generation to rise in this wilderness, and some magnificence lay in store for it, and some unnameable heroism would be his. He would achieve, he would do, succor, conquer, succeed.

He would enclose the front porch, extend another porch beyond it over the lilacs, and root more lilacs farther out. He and June would add to the family. They could pick up some beachfront land in the islands this summer, roll up a cabin, build a rowboat or buy a sloop, tour the islands, maybe keep bees.

June lifted Mabel from Clare's lap, balanced her on her legs, and led her upstairs. Ada soused the dishes. Clare sat at the dining-room table, alone. His vest hung open. Honor had come to him, and distinction, in a modest way, as it had come to the expanding town. He had served as county clerk, as city assessor. When he won the county clerkship, he passed out cigars. He purchased a topper. He knew that June regarded these honorable posts as thankless.

There was sawdust, fine as powder, on his bare neck and sleeves. His thick dark hair rose every which way, and added two inches to his already exaggerated height. He disdained to comb, ever, this hair, for his mother had combed it too much when he was a boy. Every morning he parted his hair with his fingers and pressed it down. By day he put on and took off his bicycle cap a hundred times, and by evening his hair stuck up.

Clare could see, reflected in the dark window across the table, the yellow gas lamp floating and globular like a planet or star. Beneath it, and also floating over the outside dark, were reflections from the kitchen window behind him—which contained again, golden, the gas lamp, and his wife's round head in motion—and Mabel near and spread pale along the darkness, and a cluster of vaporous teacups on the table, and a cold bottle of milk.

Clare heard the doorbell and walked through the parlor to answer it, surprised, thinking, "It must be midnight."

The big man, whom Clare recognized, ducked under the doorway to enter. He pushed into the parlor, blinked in the lamplight, and stopped abruptly in the middle of the room. The dark parlor furniture shrank; did Clare himself so occupy a room? Under his curved hat brim, Obenchain's soft eyes looked muddy about the skin. Clare had no idea what Obenchain would do.

He offered him some tea. "I'm sorry we're plumb out of sherry." As Clare spoke he shooed the yellow cat from the fringed sofa and picked up a doll, a painted doll, which had been standing on a flowered cushion. Clare started to seat himself to put his guest at ease, but rose again, uncertain, and stepped forward. He had seen a long-barreled revolver tucked in Obenchain's pants.

"What do you want?"

Obenchain told him. He said, looking sideways at Clare and then idly at the tops of the lace parlor curtains, "I am going to kill you . . . as it happens." Both men stood in the decorated parlor, their arms tense at their sides. Obenchain, coiled in his loose stained clothes, pressed his jaws together. Clare held himself still.

"I am going to kill you, shortly . . . for my own reasons . . . with which you need not concern yourself." His voice was a pressured baritone; it filled the small, still parlor the way the brocade-draped organ's noise filled it when June pumped it and played, panting, and her shoes knocked on the pedals and the whining notes swelled.

". . . concern yourself," Clare thought.

Obenchain's white forehead rumpled. "You might view it in this light: you have not much longer to live." When he lifted his head, Clare saw that his eyes, set close in the moist skin, were glassy; they caught the lamplight and reflected it in gleams. Clare had never been truly fond of the fellow.

"What are you saying, man?"

"I have considered it a part of . . . justice to impart this knowledge to you."

Obenchain was earnest, frightened, and arrogant; he rarely looked at Clare. The men were standing within a foot of each other. Clare crossed his arms. He wondered if Obenchain always packed a revolver. He heard June climbing the back stairs.

"I was going to mend this doll's head," he thought. He understood that Obenchain did not expect him to speak or respond in any way; his role was to listen until the speech wore itself out. "The topic of justice," Obenchain said, "has long interested me."

He raised his thin hands upward, to the height of his shoulders. "Your life, Mr. . . . Fishburn, is in my hands." His lips spread, and he looked, Clare thought, right tickled with himself. The man read too much. Everyone knew that.

Clare tried to concentrate on what Obenchain was saying; he wanted to learn his place in this scheme. He could not, however, follow it. ". . . always by your side," he was saying, "waking and sleeping, early and late." His dark lips were askew, and his voice was urgent.

"It need not, of course, have been you, but it . . . was you, delivered up to me this evening, you"—Obenchain's voice surged and fell, his high-crowned derby bobbed—"whose life I hereby . . . take." Clare could see only that Obenchain believed himself. He was uttering a creed. Clare hoped to get him out of the house—mighty carefully—so he could think, or sleep on it. How long had it been since he had faced someone his own height? Obenchain was burly and wide—twice the man Clare was. Obenchain's agitated face seemed to loom above him

closely, as if the moon had inched up on the earth, causing people who noticed it near on the horizon to look away, embarrassed.

Obenchain broke off. He held himself in control. Was this
the young man Clare knew from the high school shop, Beal
Obenchain who finished his work early—he made his bird-
house, cookie cutter, bookshelf, doorbell—and read books in a
corner, licking his fingertips? Now with his head cocked back he
was examining Clare as if he were an unusual binding on a
book. He flashed his wide smile and confided, "I picked your
name at random from a . . . cedar bucket."

Clare wondered what June would say. Would he tell her?
The weather would be clearing any day now; it would be a
shame, if Obenchain killed him, to miss a fine northeaster,
when he had waited so long, without grousing, for a clear day.
What would the sheriff say? He had seen Obenchain and the
sheriff together in the Lone Joe Saloon, playing chess. Perhaps
the new doctor could declare Obenchain unfit, and send him
away. A weariness overcame Clare, and intolerance, and a wish
to sleep by his wife in their bed.

"You will excuse me now," he said. "I was just going
upstairs." Clare was ready to turn his back on him and start
mounting the stairs. If Obenchain drew his revolver, he would
hear it, and kick back with full force.

Obenchain, however, was leaving. He had never taken off
his hat. He found the door and was ducking out, and saying
cordially, "Forgive the lateness of the occasion. One must
strike . . . "

Clare closed the door. He heard Obenchain's heavy tread
descend the steps.

He had been so young, ever since he could remember—so
young, and so full of ideas.

Clare extinguished the dining-room lamp and the parlor
lamp; he smelled the heavy coal oil. He found a doll in his hand.
He replaced it on the sofa. He fetched a log from the back porch
and jammed it into the stove.

Obenchain sounded as if he meant to kill him that very

night, or on Christmas tomorrow, or the next day. What about the sewing machine? Ada knew where he had hidden it in the cowshed. Who would show his pupils the three acids in brown bottles and their properties, or how to run the ripsaw? He had planned these projects for the dark of winter. One of his classes had yet to cover electromagnetism, a "daisy topic," as he put it to himself, which he purely enjoyed.

In another eight years he and June would own this house. They could own it now—June could own it if he got himself killed—but the capital was doing more good on the loose. Their money was no longer tied to real estate; prices were going up so fast that professionals had taken over, and Clare had withdrawn. June possessed a legacy of $35,000, to which he had just added another two or so thousands from the land sale. He had tucked it in a spread of "copper-bottomed," solid things—bank certificates, the gas company, national railroads—for which prudence he was now grateful.

The Lummi Indians called him Sma-Hahl-Ton, the long one. He was taller than all the men in the settlement when he was just fourteen. He was so thin, Iron Mike said, "you couldn't hit him with a handful of dried peas." He himself told people he took his bath in a shotgun barrel. He could hold his own, though, and did. He flew out and gave thrashings and tannings to other boys when he felt he had to, a bang on the nose here and there with heedless gaiety. He was, in the words of Iron Mike, "a fine broth of a boy."

He enrolled halfheartedly at the Goshen Normal School and qualified himself as a schoolteacher in science. He met June the following September, when he was thirty-five; he was building a house. She roused and flashed wonderfully easy, and the skin on her face colored up. Her dark eyes struck around alertly. She spoke so softly a man could hardly hear her, and so sharply he could be sorry he tried. Her physique was scaled down. A Maryland lady, gently reared, she possessed five or six accomplishments, more than any woman he ever saw. Her stranger's glance included him in some particular joke, the details of which he had been eager to learn. He delighted, in those days, in the startling fixity of her opinions; he taught her, bit by bit, what she needed to know about the country.

When he married, Clare set his net and it held. Good things accumulated; their life grew and spread. Languid Mabel arrived, and a son who did not live. He and June had added a front porch to the house, and a cowshed; they had dug a garden, to which they added a new row every year. Chance had added to them an aggrieved terrier and a bobtail cat. When his stepfather died, his mother came; she and June ran the house. They bought an organ for the parlor, on which June banged out ballads and hymns so fiercely her hair came down and her face flushed up. He planted cottonwoods front and back, and a row of poplars. In the shop he fashioned cherry frames for two watercolor prints of Niagara Falls; June hung the pictures in the kitchen. He refinished the chairs; he made windfall-apple cider; he painted the house blue. Every spring he vowed to quit teaching school, and every summer he missed his pupils and searched for them on the streets. Every month June reminded him to pay the mortgage.

Everything was his idea of a good time. He would do any favor for anyone who asked. He never answered letters. Once he walked fifteen miles to save half a bit on twenty pounds of potatoes. He never deliberately told a lie, and he never happened to keep a promise. June told him one night that when she met him, he looked like "a boy burnt out from playing," and said she loved him for his undiscriminating enthusiasm for all things equally, for snow or no snow, and for whatever he was doing at any moment, for planing a plank or reading the paper. He told people he hated schedules, appointments, finances— anything fussy or detailed. He enjoyed enjoyment. It was fine to have a drink, and almighty fine to have a family, and damned fine to have it rain the day he said he would fix the roof. He was a high-school physical science and manual-training teacher.

He sought deeds and found tasks. He was a giant in joy, racing and thoughtless, suggestible, a bountiful child. He whistled in bed every morning and fell asleep every night after tea. He took his sweet time. He was late for work and late for supper. His wife laughed at his jokes; his mother waited on him; his daughter rode on his shoulders and bounced her heels in his heart.

As soon as he blew out the parlor lamp, the yellow cat cried at the door. Clare opened the door to let it out. He looked into the night.

Obenchain was still there. He was standing still as a boulder in the mud lot below the house, barely visible in silhouette against the distant water. He was facing the house, a wrathful shouldered hump in a hat. Clare did not know if Obenchain could see him; the house was dark.

"Go away," Clare called out. "Go home. Go away!"

Clare lay in bed under the cold window. His sharp feet poked the blankets up; his sharp nose poked into the air. When June asked what Obenchain had said, he answered that he only wanted to use the old steam lathe at the shop. When June asked who he was shouting at, Clare said it was a stray cat hissing at their cat. These were just about the first cold-blooded lies he ever told her. Now she was asleep. Clare knew Obenchain had no reason to wish him dead. Obenchain liked reasons; he had a bucketful of reasons for everything he did, which he would explain to anyone who could understand them.

Obenchain understood his own reasons, however, and Obenchain believed himself. He was unpredictable, he was perhaps drunk, or having a spell of nervous excitement, or cold-out crazy; he was perhaps acting on someone else's orders—but for all that, he was not kidding; he was earnest. Clare had seen his meager eyebrows draw together in a bulge under his hat brim, from the effort of explaining; he saw the incongruous, imploring smile. Clare's life had become important to Obenchain. And so, even while he lay in bed that first night, Clare began the process of believing him. Who was he not to believe Obenchain, when Obenchain believed himself? People do what they believe they will do. If a man believes he will plant peonies, Clare thought, then he will probably plant peonies, and he will not if he does not believe. If a man believes that your death fits his plans, however obscure, then your death fits his plans, how-

ever obscure, and he is the one with the gun. Clare could try to
kill him first, or he could take his family and leave, or he could
try to get him locked up. For how long? What would Obenchain
do? When?

In the high school shop, Obenchain would do anything.
Once he shouted suddenly, addressing the class. He knew what
power turned the big saws; he knew the limits of cold chisels,
the ontology of gases, the secrets of numbers on the rule. The
sweat on his white forehead shone in the basement windows'
light. People swindled him, he confided to Clare, whispering;
they tried to take advantage of his honesty. His mind was quick
and his hands were sure. One-fifth of Clare's students failed
manual training; Obenchain led the class. Sometimes he wandered away, wounded, when Clare was talking to him. He
loomed over the schoolboys, head and shoulders. He quit his
first term of algebra; he could not stick it. Clare found him once
in the hall standing still, with his jaws open like a seal. His lips
stretched down like the lips on a cedar mask. His pants were
wet; his eyes were wide and astonished; his skin was red and
wet with tears.

Obenchain mastered his nervous weakness, Clare knew,
more every year. His vehemence took on the force of coher-
ence, the force of a large and balanced battery of ideas aimed at
a single point. He possessed skills. Once at the livery stable
Clare had seen Obenchain pinch the eyelid of a skittery horse,
to hold it still for haltering; he seemed to have the eyelid by his
fingernails. The tormenting trick worked; the horse held its
very breath. Obenchain was erratic, but his wrath and distrust
were steady. Most people were afraid of him. Respectable families multiplied in the town, and the south-side roughs and crimi-
nals—hoboes and cardsharks, old buffalo hunters, train robbers,
bounty hunters, deserters, and murderers—had diminished in
numbers and notice, while ordinary hermits abounded. People
said that Obenchain could read Greek. They said he was a
genius who would make the town famous. They said a falling
tree had cracked his head when he was a boy on the island, and
one of its branches jabbed into his brain. They said he ate
cloudberries, which are poisonous; they said he ate soap. They

said he swam in the bay at night trailing eelgrass, and lay stark naked on the rocks. They said he had a hand in tying the Chinese fellow under the old wharf at low tide. People said every sort of thing.

Clare was looking at the window beside the bed; it revealed nothing and reflected nothing, for the sky and house were dark. June, he wanted to think: June with her deep-arched eyes, and limp Mabel, and his straddle-legged mother, carrying on in the house without him, as if he were late forever, and they were holding dinner. For a moment he saw June and Mabel stiff and blurred and bewildered. He could not, however, keep them in mind. If he died now, his life would have been a brief, passing thing like a hard shower. If he died later, having done more, it would be no different.

Clare liked "to keep abreast," he said, "of what is afoot." Just knowing all the news was a job. Every day things happened. Today he had raced through a full day; he always did. He knew he blazed with health and abounded in the goodwill of men. He was what his mother called a crackerjack, and all possibility. He lived at gale force; he moved between activities at railway speed; he had to. Everybody did. The town of Whatcom was "a comer," as people said. Its new high school was "a hummer." Now, as streamers of colored fog began to advance on the black clearness of Clare's thoughts, he found he could not recollect why he had been so all-fired busy all these years, congratulating himself, like everyone else; no wonder people were so astonished to die.

Every night, Mabel centered herself on her feather bed to sleep, and never extended a finger or toe, for she believed herself to be surrounded by sharks and black death. She was right. She was surrounded by sharks and black death. He used to know that too, when he was a boy, but it had slipped his mind.

II

Spring came to Puget Sound and to the Nooksack plain and the mountains. The earth rolled belly-up to the light, and the light battered it. Clare Fishburn was still alive, was still walking abroad in the daylight where everything changes, and holding tight to the nights as they rolled.

Spring came to the northern coast, and the daylight widened. Daylight stuck a wedge into darkness and split it open like a log. Winter was lost and irretrievable before Clare caught up with it. He had thought the seasons were longer. He had thought he was younger. Now things were unhinged and floating away. Every day, people moved from their houses. Every hour, the sea ducks of winter vanished from the water, the harlequin ducks and the brant. The trees were going. All winter Clare had learned his own trees' hard branches, how they grew and twigged: the lilac bush by the porch with the sky behind it, the alder saplings, the cottonwood in the yard. Now those dark lines were vanishing into leaf and disappearing before his eyes. The strong roads softened under his bicycle tires. Through the parlor window he saw the snow on the ridge diminish and disappear.

Every day was a day in which Clare expected to die. When he woke one Sunday morning in the last week of March, he regarded his sleeping wife gravely. Her head lay lightly on the mattress and smoothly, flush, as a clam rests on its shell. There was perfection and composure in her small face. He admired the supple and irrigated quality of her skin; it took a shine to the coming day. Light masses shone on her cheek and brow, and passed subtly to shadow in the soft, expressive hollow over her eyes. He had looked at June's face so often, for so long, that he half believed it was his own face.

He was aware that common wisdom counseled that love was a malady that blinded lovers' eyes like acid. Love's skewed sight made hard features appear harmonious, and sinners appear saints, and cowards appear heroes. Clare was by no means an original thinker, but on this one point he had recently reached an opposing view: that lovers alone see what is real. When he courted June he thought it a privilege to wash dishes with her in river sand. He thought it a privilege to hold her cutaway coat, to look at Mount Baker from her side; he thought it a privilege to hear her family's stories over tea and watch her eyebrows rise and fall. Now, he knew it was.

At breakfast Clare considered his mother. She was perky in the mornings, as if the day might offer her something. She had been just twenty when she and Clare's father had crossed the plains in a wagon train from Illinois. Now she was shrinking perceptibly, and her skin was softening for death. Her dark skirt was shiny at the seat; her bun of white hair was no bigger than a button. Her skull was starting to show, yellow, through her forehead. He could not remember how she looked when she was young. She was strong, too, and able; she could split a cedar shake bolt with a tenpenny nail. It was a trick everyone had seen. He had not done right by her, and now there was nothing he could do. He could let her talk to him more.

His mother believed, Clare thought, that dead people left here for somewhere else. She would be happy to leave plates. Now he would die first. He would go and prepare a place for her, if there were places to be had. If there were places to be had, he would set a table for her, and bid her sit and eat. But there would be no tables, and no plates, and strictly nothing to eat. It was hard to imagine a place without any sort of plates.

He looked at his own chipped plate. He had eaten his breakfast and was not dead yet. A month ago he had decided not to think any further about being poisoned at home. Obenchain had talked about killing Clare specifically, as though pinpointing him alone in the mobs of the living demanded a precision that attracted him. He would not want to risk killing June, or Ada, or Mabel, by mistake. Or would he? Would he take them all by some neighbor's doctored pie? Obenchain would do anything. But of thinking of poison there was no end. Everything tasted good.

He felt under his jacket for his sidearm, a new double-action Colt Lightning. June saw the movement, and caught his eye. He touched her, covering her hand with his, but she rose then and slipped away to the kitchen. Was he too sentimental for her? He carried his plate to the sink, following her, and laid his hand over the waist of her basque. She turned to him, confused, and took his plate. He saw her embarrassed frown.

There was a wagging patch of light on the wall above the sink; the lilac bushes outside the dining room wagged too. The planet wagged on; the man who planted those lilacs was dead. And time, for Clare, had sprung a leak.

For he was on his way, it seemed; he was a man already exited. To these familiar people in the kitchen, time was a secure globe in which they rode protected from one end of things to the other. June stacked the clean dishes and hung the towel by the stove. Old Ada fetched a tray from the pantry and headed out back toward the cellar. Mabel, now four, sat on the kitchen floor in the peculiar way she liked to sit, with her back straight and her legs pointing every which way, as though they were broken or popped at the hip. Her red braid hung limp on her neck. She was wearing an undershirt and sateen bloomers. She was scratching the cat with a fork. The cat cringed and made no move to leave.

"Quit your fooling," Mabel said to the cat. "You make my tail ache."

Clare could see the dark at the edge of the plain. He felt a hole in the wall behind him; things rushed out of that hole. He was running low on air. Yesterday he had imagined and seen the long horizon of water and islands begin to tilt and upend. On the low side a gap appeared, and water and islands and houses and all the world's contents slid into the gap and blew away.

Possibly everyone now dead considered his own death as a freak accident, a mistake. Some bad luck caused it. Every enterprising man jack of them, and every sunlit vigorous woman and child, too, who had seemed so alive and pleased, was cold as a meat hook, and new chattering people trampled their bones unregarding, and rubbed their hands together and got to work improving their prospects till their own feet slipped and they went under themselves, protesting. Clare no longer felt any flat and bounded horizon encircling him at a distance. Every place was a tilting edge. "And I will wipe Jerusalem as a man wipeth a dish, wiping it, and turning it upside down." Time was a hook in his mouth. Time was reeling him in jawfirst; it was reeling him in, headlong and breathless, to a shore he had not known was there.

Now something crashed. Clare saw Mabel fly out of the pantry, crying. She had dropped something. June and Mabel had been carrying armloads of jars past him, he realized. Mabel had just dropped a loaded tray of plum preserves. He saw every glass jar smashed on the pantry floor. Now she had run away. This alarmingly bright and self-sure little Mabel, of whom Clare usually lived in some awe, was crying too hard to help clean up her mess. June and Ada passed Clare and crowded into the pantry carrying rags and a bucket. Clare ordinarily considered Mabel a human marvel, and her accomplishments miraculous. She hung out over the stairs to make an entrance, wagging her stockinged legs like a pendulum. She lettered her name, opened umbrellas, and erupted forth to give precisely articulated opinions on household matters, which startled Clare as much as if the cat had spoken. She possessed a queer, manly chuckle, which arose from her smooth depths at apparent random. If anyone asked her, "How are you?" she replied, looking away, in a stolid, thrillingly low voice, "Good."

He found her crying on the parlor sofa, twisted up and half dressed. She was too old and too big to pick up. Clare picked her up.

He picked her up and bore her from station to station around the parlor. Its dark wallpaper repeated a ribboned bouquet of pale flowers, over and over. Absurdly he pointed Mabel's face toward each window in turn, as though she were an infant still and might see some bright sight over his shoulder to distract her. He pointed her at the organ, its lacy carved front, its many ivory-ringed plugs. She cried wetly on his neck; he smelled her familiar, sour hair. What had he done with his life? He had been arranging things and putting things to rights, so he could get started.

Beyond the window's lace curtain the lilac bush in the yard seemed real enough, and the sky's gray light seemed handmade for the moment's heat like any fire. This was, however, a year among years, and him dying early. The whole illumined, moving scene would play on in his absence, would continue to tumble into the future, extending the swath of the lighted and known, moving as a planet moves with its clouds attached, its waves all breaking at once on its thousand shores, and its people walking willfully to market or to home, followed by dogs. He had thought he had more time.

Clare carried Mabel outside to the porch and toted her around as he did formerly, when the porch was new and so was Mabel. When had she grown so big and heavy? She kept slipping inside her sateen bloomers; he hoisted her up. She hushed her crying. Now, Clare knew, she held herself still so Clare would not notice her and set her down. He noticed her, but he wanted to carry her on the porch a while longer. How had he got to be forty-two? What had he meant to do with those years?

He would be one ancestor of Mabel's grandchildren, at best three strangers away. They would be careless, wretched, ignorant great-grandchildren, badly behaved, who would swing on swings in the bright sunlight of those future days without a care in their cruel, cussed hearts, and who would never have heard mentioned one Clare Fishburn of Whatcom, Washington, who was once a prominent figure in a local way and considered, by some, to have possessed promise, vigor, and enterprise, who might even have attained high office . . . or who, he concluded to himself, at any rate loved his life and his urgent times with all his strength. He looked down the hill across the vacant lot where Obenchain had stood. The wind blew from the southwest. Loops of Mabel's hair wrapped against his face. She hid her bare arms in his coat. Cloud parts were leaving the sky. Sea ducks were leaving the water. The morning high tides of winter were gone. Night after night, Orion dived unseen to the west behind the clouds and died young. The wood stems of lilac bush by the door were banging together. Those blunt stems would be gone soon, broken into lilacs. How does a man learn to die when the experts are mum?

It seemed to Clare this morning that he had consumed his life. He had played false and, perfectly pleased, fell for a sham. He followed the news; he floated like a sea duck with the crowd. The momentum of activity and accumulation lulled him. The Whatcom *Bugle Call* and the Seattle *Post-Intelligencer* endorsed it as real, this sheer witless motion and change. The minister, the biggest men in town, the most pious women, and everyone he knew except his mother endorsed it as real; they followed the news. He had gone along. He had burrowed into the whirling scheme of things; he had hitched himself to the high school men, to the growing town and the mighty nation and its sensations, events, and shared opinions. He had lost the fight with vainglory, and the fight with ignorance, for what he now guessed must be the usual reason: he had not known there was a fight on.

Clare set Mabel down; she idled into the house to dress for church. He felt the blood returning deep in his arms. He paced by the porch rail, looking out. The sea was yellow and swollen. White clouds blew and stretched under the leaden cloud cover. The cottonwood in the front yard looked dried out. He could feel the planet spinning ever faster, and bearing him into the darkness with it, flung. These were the only days. "The harvest is past," Clare thought, "the summer is ended, and we are not saved."

There was not time enough to honor all he wanted to honor; it was difficult even to see it. The seasons pitched and heaved a man from rail to rail, from weather side to lee side and back, and a lunatic hogged the helm. Shall these bones remember?

It had been three months since Obenchain told Clare he was going to kill him. During January, February, and most of March, Clare had watched his own increasing detachment. Throughout his life before Obenchain's threat, he awakened some mornings and perceived that things were easy and pleasant, and some mornings, by contrast, he fancied that things were fixed and dreary, and these moods reversed from hour to hour, wherever they started. Now things seemed, for the first time, simply big, all day. He had begun to view his own Lambert Street—the scraped hillside before him, its elaborate houses, its few poplars and cottonwoods—altered into an abstraction and revealed as a piffling accident, as a certain street in a certain town. Whatcom was a town among thousands of towns—the town in which most of his haphazard life had elapsed. His own time was a time among times. This bright year, this new 1893 with its shifting winds and great, specific clouds, this raw-edged winter with its stiff mud and gray seas—this was one year.

Clare leaned against the cold porch rail. He saw beneath him the lower hill with its houses; he saw the growing business district, and the dull sea spreading beyond it under thick skies. The railroad trestle curved across the bay in a pencil line from south to north. This was his town, and in his way Clare had helped build it, as he had helped break its wilderness as a boy.

Mabel came out to the porch and twirled dully, like a hanged man, in her new Easter dress—something white and ruffled, with red braid. She had a stiff straw hat pinned flat on her head; someone had blacked her shoes—and she did look an angel. Clare told her she was "the ant's ankles." Pleased, she perked up, plucked at her bloomers, and said she was going down the street to display her glory to her cousin Nesta. Clare watched her flit down the steps, her black-stockinged legs apparently boneless.

He had begun to wonder where, in this series of accidents, the accidental part left off. Could he as readily have been an actor, or a lawyer, as a high school teacher, when he had felt himself so profoundly and for so long to be a high school teacher? Would he do just as well as some other sort of fellow altogether? Was June only one of many women he might have married? Might he just as readily be living on some other street, in some grievous town in Wisconsin he had never heard of, with some other woman—a woman he did not know? This was a grim thought. He disliked strange women.

A fresh, stiffening wind blew up through the lot below. A sheet of water gleamed behind the plunging precipice of the town. The colorless sea and the colorless sky were batting the dead light back and forth. What Clare really wanted to know was this: Would he ever see June again?

It was a novel, uncomfortable question, linked in his mind with the shed church he attended as a boy, and with his mother's floppy Bible, whose assigned chapters he had memorized perforce. He knew that forty years ago in the west they used to say, "Ain't no law west of Saint Louis, and no God west of Fort Smith." But now God had been planted in the west for two generations—God, women, and railroad trains. Towns welcomed churches for their civilizing influence and noble architecture. One of Clare's favorite stories was about Chief Seattle. Chief Seattle had heard much about a common heavenly father who had come down to earth to live among people and save them. Chief Seattle remarked, "We never saw him," and Clare repeated this to general hilarity in the hotel bar and in the Lone Joe Saloon. Chief Seattle said, "We never saw him." Would there be something he and his friends could do together, like old times?

Clare moved inside. His father had died many years ago in what people called a freak accident; he had not seen a hair of him since. From time to time he dreamed of him standing mute in his overalls in a family-filled log cabin. Everyone welcomed him, saying, "Rooney! We all thought you were dead." Clare himself looked at his father, overcome with affection and shyness. Gradually he always understood that, in fact, the man was dead. He had no will, no love, and no way to express his embarrassment for the overexcited living. He was an apparition the family's hopes could not sustain; his form faded as their faith failed, and where he had stood was only the sooty log wall. Now, as winter left the coast that year and spring wore on, Clare dreamed this dream again, and others like it.

Everywhere he went he saw Obenchain. Friday it was Obenchain brooding at the new post office, his lower lip hanging. Last week he became aware of Obenchain at the grocer's when, from the corner of his eye, he saw one pale forehead as high as his own above the other heads, as if the two men were lighthouses. From a high school window he saw Obenchain pacing the center of the street below, agitated, wearing his hat over one ear. Twice from parlor windows he saw him looming tense in the vacant lot below the house, cast in silhouette against the bay.

One January Saturday he and June were replenishing the woodpile, and Clare had glanced up to see Obenchain just disappearing down the back alley. The alley ran through a tangle of blackberry bushes. Clare had leaned on his maul and peered hard through the thorns to learn if the ungainly, wrinkled form that was Obenchain had kept moving or stopped. He could not tell; he could not decide if he had seen a dark piece of a man moving, or if he was now seeing a man holding still, or a patch of gloom and no man at all. He had stood and studied and pondered, until he began to see not Obenchain, but his own self, as a man with a revolver behind blackberry thorns might see him: a target as isolated and still as some poor stiff before a firing squad. Would he then fall handily in his own yard on Lambert Street, with his wife at his side?

June was carrying two alder rounds to the chopping block; she had not noticed anything. Small beads of drizzle like bird shot made a halo around her hair. Clare felt immense in his own yard and stripped, like a barked tree. Could it be that he, who had been a fearless boy, was a cowardly man? His mouth had gone dry. He quit the yard then, tucked tail like a dog, ducked back into the house without a word, and sat idle, clapping his hands repeatedly over his bony knees, away from the windows.

Since that day, over two months ago, he had not felt fear. He could not bear to, so he had looked steadily past it until it left. In the post office on Friday, Clare fronted Obenchain, looked at him, and Obenchain had turned away.

He had told June, on New Year's Day. They were alone downstairs, late. He had fallen asleep over tea in the parlor and wakened to see June clearing his place, with her head cocked like a robin's, looking at him.

He told her right then—she started, for he spoke as soon as his eyes opened—that he had not long to live, that he would die one of these days or nights soon, that he knew because Beal Obenchain had told him on Christmas Eve that he was going to kill him, and she was not to worry because nothing could be done.

As it happened, June never worried because she never believed that "nothing could be done." Something could always be done; that is what people were for.

She sat down and it sunk in. Her black-sleeved arms rested on the chair's brocade arms and her head alternately bent and raised as she thought of things. She was thirty-four to Clare's forty-two, fair-skinned and brown-haired, restless. High and curving brows made her look alert. Now her tender expression firmed. "What does Beal Obenchain have against you?" "Nothing. It was just some notion he seized." It sunk in some more.

She could, June had said in her soft, Maryland voice, shoot Beal Obenchain. It would be easy. He lived alone in the woods by the tracks, where any vagrant, any swindler or gambler or ruined miner or drunken logger, could shoot him for any reason. No one would find him for days—maybe even "till Almighty crack"—and no one would ever suspect Clare Fishburn, never mind June Fishburn. Why would these ordinary, quiet townspeople want to murder someone?

"Why indeed?" Clare said. Obenchain was not all-the-way normal. What if he was just blowing off steam? Why should anyone go murder a poor lonely bugger who raved? Clare knew that Obenchain was not just bloviating, that Obenchain was, as he put it to himself, a bad hat in earnest, and would do him in. Clare did not, however, intend to murder, and said so. Capital threats are not capital crimes; you do not shoot a man unless he is actually in the process of harming you or your family. You do not cold-bloodedly kill a man under any circumstances, and you by golly do not let your wife do it.

He had thought of everything, and here was June thinking of it all again. "Where's your shotgun?" He had oiled it, and taken it to his shop in the high school. He had bought the Colt Lightning. His thinking was running, however, to knives. With a Bowie knife, a fighter could rip open a man up close before either could draw a revolver. He could throw a knife faster than Obenchain could raise and aim a gun—if he were a knife fighter. He had passed a few fine years as a boy throwing a Bowie knife at tree trunks and hay bales, and he knew enough about it to know it would take another few years to get the skill back. Of course he had thought of corralling his friends George Bacon and Jim O'Shippy to stand guard or fight.

Don't go near the water; don't go out alone. "—And we must move." June's round head turned toward him, and away, and back. "We can move to Portland, and tell no one where we are going. We can sell this house for cash—it must be worth thousands now. You take the train tomorrow, and your mother and I will follow with Mabel when we have everything packed."

Clare saw that June was pink and heated. Her skin was always a thin membrane; she changed colors faster than a cloud. Her face seemed everywhere as liquid and live as her eyes. She subsided, looking down at her lap, but her cheeks still glowed.

"And when do we come back?"

June thought it through and fired up, "Anytime we're ready for you to die, we just hop a train."

He reminded her that his livelihood was here. He directed the course in physical sciences and in manual training. He would probably be vice-principal before long. His voice was steady. He wanted to set a brave example for his young, small wife, who had been reared delicately among women. He kept forgetting that she noticed when he tried to set an example, and flared up.

"You can't be vice-principal if you're dead." June sounded to Clare awfully contemptuous, as though he thought he could. He poured himself cold tea. The parlor's high windows were glossy and black, and the lamp's light streaked them.

He brought out, "I have no preferment in Portland, and no position, and know of no proposition." Clare talked this way when the thought of her powerful family in Baltimore shamed him. In fact, the galling thing, if he lived in any strange town, would be not knowing what was happening every day.

"We have no need of further prospects." She lowered her voice to a resonant bass, to startle and reconcile him, a trick he knew, which usually worked anyway. "My legacy has advanced— tripled or quadrupled, at least—these past few years. We can live in Portland without your making a stir in anything."

"I fancy making a stir in something," Clare said. Having never lived in any big city, Clare had a horror of them all, and supposed their citizens must live perpetually as lost, footsore, cleaned out, and lonesome as he was when he visited. He repeated, "When do we come back?"

"We don't come back. We don't come back!"

Clare tended to stare at the grapes when he was in the parlor. June had draped a fringed scarf over a picture frame's corner, and heaped blue glass grapes there, as if women commonly stored grapes on picture frames.

He broke out in a fresh start, "Then do we live in Portland as nobodies, hoping every minute Obenchain never finds us, or wondering every minute if he actually meant to kill me at all? That's sorry living. Or do we hope he decides to murder someone else? Who?" Clare regretted this latter tack, for arguments from universal morality tended to pass June right by when she was roused.

He was waiting for her to coil down. He could not see her expression when she bent her head; he saw the untidy curved parting of her dark hair. It would take her several days, he thought, to study their possibilities as he had studied them, and get to the bottom facts—several days to conclude that nothing could, reasonably and honorably, be done.

As the weeks and months had passed, however, Clare learned he been wrong. June did not "coil down." She wanted to move. As she began to adjust to a new life based on Obenchain's threat—as the days passed and Clare still lived—she wanted to move. She was willing to give up her familiar friends to struggle somewhere as a stranger. She had, Clare reflected, some sand in her.

Their brightest hope next to moving, June held, was beating Obenchain to it. Clare should send Obenchain to his reward, without witnesses. The two sifted it all through again. People in town would make a complete row if Obenchain killed Clare, and hardly any row if Clare killed Obenchain. If Obenchain killed first, he would leave town or hang for it, but Clare "would be dead," June said. If Clare, who possessed respectability, got the jump on Obenchain, he might go to prison, but he would get out alive, in time, and they could go on. She preferred "any degree of disgrace"—she once said ardently, her voice rising and hoarse—to losing him. Clare was surprised by her vehemence. "You truly want to save my bacon," he said, and smiled at her; she had glared at him. He was touched. This was a wealthy woman. She set him to thinking as much as Obenchain had.

*   *   *

Clare considered these things throughout the early spring. In the light and changing rain he rode his bicycle to school one morning along Lambert Street and down the hill. June had always seen things in him no one else ever saw. Of course she was fond of him. Why was he surprised?

He saw she acted from an unmentioned source of feeling, a source that, he discovered, he tapped as well. It had been there all along. He asked himself if she was conscious of it and understood at once that she was, that she probably had been since Mabel's birth, when their courting talk had hushed and let go, loosing them to drift into the great silence. She had been waiting for him to notice it, and she understood his doltishness in advance. Wherever he found himself, in whatever deep caves and vaulted mazes of understanding, he discovered her already there before him, her arched eyes glinting with amused sensibility, her untidy, small form seeming to beckon him onward. She mocked him, guided him, forgave him, and tantalized him, at every level of depth he reached. What else did she know that he did not?

He steered his bicycle through the morning crowds on Commercial Street. At real estate offices, men stood smoking under dripping awnings. Women held their dark skirts out of the mud. There was Obenchain, ducking into the pharmacy. Let him. Two teams of black mules hauled a covered wagon from the docks. The mule shoes and the wagon wheels knocked planks. Clare and June quarreled about moving. Whatcom is better than Portland, he said; he chose to live and die there. He knew that June saw only a new fatalism in his decision, and he wondered if she missed his old carelessness. He did not.

Clare imagined June's tilted round head, her unfathomable silences. How had they found the courage to marry, when they had known nothing? Clare felt a bottomlessness in himself. He felt a bottomlessness in his attachment to June that made him teeter, and he felt a parcel of infinity between them, over which their days floated like chips.

*   *   *

All that April it rained. The Nooksack River flooded its banks and spread over the farmers' fields on the plain.

South of Whatcom, the new cemetery became a low lake where green-winged teal dabbled and dove among headstones and logs. In town Clare took Mabel to the bridge over Whatcom Creek. They saw a henhouse tumble by. Clare rode his bicycle to school one day and told Jim O'Shippy that the roads were "slick as calf slobbers."

When the water went down it was May. Cold sun lighted the snow in the mountains. Townsmen forgot the flooding; they began to mend nets and scrape hulls, to make railroad excursions and dig clams. In the Lummi reservation orchards, the pruning was over and the bees were out.

People became fitful, bold, or melancholy. Spring pried open their jaws and poured sunlight down their throats. The light picked them up and floated them as spring tides lifted logs on the beach: lightly, taking their heaviness from them, and setting them free. They moved pianos, adopted puppies, drove buggies out to look at land in the county, staked sweet peas. The schoolchildren grew careless and distraught; when school let out in June they hit the streets. There were boy gangs and girl gangs all over town—on the wharf and along the beaches and at the sawmills' edges—gangs composed of children few adults recognized. The light never quit. The old people knew the season by heart, and their hearts turned over anyway, as lakes turn over by the season.

By the third week in May it was light in earnest. Sunlight spread like a crescendo; June was a blare. The sockeye came leaping and leaping northward offshore. The winds left and the clouds dried up and the sun rolled almost all the way around the sky. Time expanded. The day widened, pulled from both ends by the shrinking dark, as if darkness itself were a pair of hands and daylight a skein between them, now flung wide. The fishermen fished day and night while the salmon ran, and the cannery worked around the clock. Loggers logged the forests, and their teams of oxen dragged the logs away. It was summer and no one seemed to sleep. The sky had fallen open like a clamshell. The days were round and lighted one after the other without end.

Four weeks later, the town of Whatcom was on its beam ends. Financial panic was sudden and dire. In June, every bank in Whatcom County had failed and closed. Across the nation, fifteen thousand banks failed, most in the south and west. In Whatcom, people were soon to be poor as snakes, and they knew it. Already a few steamships had dropped Whatcom from their schedule. Already wholesalers were closing. Farm prices fell so badly that potatoes sold for fourteen dollars a ton. A man could insulate his house with potatoes.

Clare Fishburn straddled a cedar shake bolt in his backyard and split shakes. He tapped the froe, and the shakes popped off the bolt.

Of the seventeen thousand dollars in holdings he possessed that spring, nothing remained but one thousand dollars of Whatcom Gas Company shares he had purchased for five thousand dollars. The bank certificates were worthless; the Northern Pacific Railroad had suspended dividends and fallen into the hands of receivers. The lost money was mostly June's—her wedding present and legacy.

June had never said so, but her father's circumstance made it plain, that she could have found a suitor to match her fortune, not lose it. Clare's simple pride before men, that a rich and beautiful young woman should have lighted on him, had long since changed to shame before men, that his wife was rich. Now he and June would be, as he said, scuffling for themselves like everybody else. He still had his job, but the principal cut his pay. The principal even intimated, when they talked yesterday, that the school system might have to pay in scrip instead of cash. If Obenchain killed him now, June would have nothing to shift with.

Facing him a few feet away, June was kneeling to weave the shakes he had shaved yesterday. She had her sleeves rolled up. Until recently he had doubted she chose this life freely; perhaps, he thought now, he doubted because he himself would have chosen luxury, in a trice.

Clare set on edge one of the last shake bolts, and split it in two with an old crab-apple wedge that was his father's. Then he set the heavy froe blade in position along one billet's grain, and tapped it with a mallet. A shake split off as if goosed. He adjusted the blade a notch and tapped again. The red shakes crackled at his feet. He worked through both bolts, whistling. He turned to the bolt he had sat on, reduced it to a clatter of shakes. He moved to the shaving horse and, with a two-handled knife, shaved those shakes into shingles. He was kneeling at the horse, for he was too tall to work the knife bent over. It was not yet nine o'clock in the morning.

He stood and flexed his back. He surveyed the littered yard; would the grass reseed this fall? Old Ada opened the back door and Mabel came out, holding on to the dog. Clare had taken to looking at things as if for the last time. This practice caused him to see them as if for the first time: yesterday the principal's dark and freckled forehead, now the froe leaning on the back step, sunlit, and the crab-apple wedge beside it. The crab-apple wedge top was furred from blows. It looked to be outlined in the blue shadow that streamed behind most everything; it held its shape for now, vivid and stubborn against the current, as he did.

When the bank failed, Clare dreaded June's contempt. Ordinarily he would have quailed at the worse possibility that she might hide her contempt, thereby demonstrating that she felt her very life to be a calamity entire—he would have quailed, that is, except that he could barely fix his mind on any aspect of the loss. He chided himself: What was a man's duty but to provide for his family? What species of scoundrel would lose all his wife's money? He felt himself, however, more substantial than before. The Panic was showing all Whatcom what people could live without. No one would knock on the Fishburn door at midnight and threaten to take away anything they needed. Clare had never clapped eyes on piles of gold; he had only signed papers, and brought papers for June to sign. He had done nothing more with the money than buy June an organ with it, and imagine buying a boat or two, and a horse, and a carriage. He had prized the money as evidence of his rise. Now he found he rather liked falling; there was some solidity to it. A man knew where he was bound.

These days June was eager to pitch in. Kneeling in her skirt, she wove shingles by alternating thick sides and thin sides so the bundles came out square. The skin on her face was puffed and red. She gave out rather more of her usual ironic brand of affection lately, and never blamed him. "She really is a daisy," he thought—for those were all the words he found for his increasing sensation of participation, of glory, even, in a world of flux.

Together they would weave up these last shingles and load them in the wagon. Then there was nothing more Clare could do but wait until tomorrow, when he could take them down to the railyard. Now fair-weather clouds were forming overhead. It seemed to Clare that a man in his situation, on such a day, in such a possible world, just ought to go fishing.

Beal Obenchain sat outside his stump house, on a stool. His long feet were bare and white save for streaks of orange callus where his trouser cuffs scraped them; his high-crowned derby eclipsed half his brow. He pulled from his mouth an orange crab leg, which he bit delicately up its length, then upended and sucked. High overhead, fir and cedar needles shredded the sunlight till it was gone.

Earlier that afternoon, Obenchain had rowed out and found a big male Dungeness crab and most of a smaller male in his crab pot. He reset the pot with dogfish skin and carried the crabs by their hind legs up the embankment and into the woods. Now he was eating them. The boiling vat lay on the needled ground beside him. From time to time he shook the broken shells from the tops of his feet.

It had not worked with Clare Fishburn, whose life he now knew. "You are going to die," he had said, and this simple townsman believed him. He seemed, however, singularly unaffected by it. In the first months, Obenchain knew, Fishburn avoided the south side of town and the deep timber. He stayed out of the saloon and the hotel bar all winter and spring, and hauled his bed away from the upstairs window. Beal had scared him out of his own garden once. He wore a sidearm outside. Obenchain even knew that the man's wife was badgering him to move.

He knew also that, despite these alarms, the man was not yet ontologically dead. He persisted in thinking his own thoughts, and Obenchain was uncertain what those thoughts might be. A boyish, unchastened stupidity had left Fishburn's face—that was good. The face, however, had not merely flinched or emptied. When he walked or bicycled in town, he no longer searched the streets and glanced behind him, as he had during the winter. His gait wakened, and he looked sharp, but not strictly in fear. It was no longer a pleasure for Obenchain to surprise Fishburn in the street; the subject failed to react. Now Obenchain hated him, when he recalled him.

He rose and bent to a pan of dough on the ground. He punched the dough down, slid the pan over the gray ground to a patch of sunlight that had moved, and sat back.

He had meant to observe and preside over the corruption of a man's spirit. He had meant to dramatize to an ordinary man, by the threat of death, the spectacle of his own cowardice. He had meant to reveal to the man his own lifelong ignorance and self-satisfaction, and to display both his helplessness and his insignificance. He had meant to murder Fishburn without leaving a corpse—to own him by possessing his thoughts, to kill him legally, by the power of suggestion. The suggestion had failed. Fishburn was not tormenting himself with uncertainty. Who could live with the certain knowledge that he would die? Only, apparently, the truly stupid. Fishburn's self-satisfaction had, if anything, apparently increased.

Obenchain had seen Fishburn with his family at a boat launching the evening before. Fishburn was among the men who had hoisted the new hull in the builder's shed, hauled it down to the beach, and heaved it into the water. Obenchain watched from a log. Fishburn carried himself, following his sharp nose, as if he owned the earth. He looked to Obenchain as though he fancied he had personally built the boat and the beach and the water, all in his little shop. After the launching the town made a picnic on the beach. The man and his wife looked at the water, at the men taking turns rowing the new dory up and down the mild shore; they kindled a fire. Limber but not slack, Fishburn looked as though he owned all the time in the world. He had learned absolutely nothing. His self-deception overpowered any truth. He paid Obenchain no mind. Once he nodded at him and, in what was possibly open mockery, passed the jug to someone else.

Obenchain cracked crab legs in his teeth. There were many things on his mind this June. There was an artist, a painter of shipwrecks, new in town this summer. He was an insignificant personage—what could more properly be termed a "booger"—whom everyone worshiped as a species of god, and who was seeking to destroy Obenchain's reputation as an intellectual. There was a rich book collector, too, in LaConner, a book collector of delicate sensibility and strikingly youthful appearance, whose fortune insulted Obenchain and whose image appeared in his mind. Finally there was Fishburn, a shrivel of a man, who would not give up the ghost.

He had admired the idea of kicking the struts away from a man one by one, so the false front fell. The spectacle of Fishburn's decline was meant to be, among other things, a moral display for the town. That the town would likely not notice it dramatized it further. None of this was coming to pass, however. Obenchain had endured a bellyful of Fishburn. Now a new idea was provoking his mind.

What Obenchain considered, crumbling crabs, was this. Although Fishburn was afraid, he was not destroyed, not owned. Likely, fear alone could not deliver a man into his hands, not if it presented a clear challenge. Perhaps uncertainty alone could destroy. Perhaps the Chinaman tied to the wharf had not suffered at all as he waited for the tide to rise and drown him—because he was certain the tide would rise. Perhaps, then, his own weapons were, hitherto, crude. If uncertainty was the last hope of destroying Fishburn, then he would furnish him with more of it.

He would take it all back. He would tell him he was by no means going to kill him. Tell him it was a joke, or an experiment, something finished. Then . . . what would Fishburn do?

Would he be acute enough to reckon the experiment just begun?

Obenchain could say, "What I told you in December was a lie, and now . . . this is the truth: I am not going to kill you." Since Fishburn was alive so long after he told him he was going to die, Fishburn had reason to doubt Obenchain, and disbelieve him. He might think Obenchain was an inveterate liar, like one of the Cretans in the epistle to Titus—"always liars, evil beasts, slow bellies." A liar who told you he would not kill you actually meant to kill you in earnest. Fishburn might think Obenchain sometimes lied and sometimes spoke the truth. In these uncertainties, Fishburn could stew. Obenchain was losing interest in him, but he would allow him this last chance to furnish him with diversion.

Obenchain determined, then, to find Clare Fishburn tomorrow, and tell him this new thing. He stood up, and fine sand and triangles of orange shell fell from his pants. He moved the dough pan again. He poured the crab water over the bracken ferns by the door.

Before noon the next day, Mabel Fishburn, her puttylike face sunburned below her eyes, returned from her cousin's house and was sitting on the front porch, waiting for her mother to prepare lunch. A man came along the front alley and stopped at the foot of the porch steps. He was as big as her father, and fatter. He wore no shirt or coat. He smiled at her and said, "Where is your father?" Mabel tried to remember.

"Gone fishing," she said, looking away. People were always trying to get her to look in their faces.

"Where has he gone . . . fishing?"

Mabel rose and went inside. She returned in a minute, with her stockings pulled up; she sat again on the edge of the porch and said, "On the river."

"Which river?"

Mabel rolled her eyes at the botheration to which life ceaselessly subjected her. She went inside and returned to stand in the doorway—she had no intention of sitting any longer on the porch—and said, "The Nooksack."

* * *

Clare Fishburn came walking over the Nooksack plain. He was heading home after an afternoon alone on the river. He carried a pole and a knotted sack containing one cleaned two-pound trout. He followed the lazy dirt track that traced the Nooksack down and swept east toward the bay. The river lay low and sleeping. The poured plain lay slow and flat as the river, and the sky lay monumental over the world.

Miles away at the eastern rim of the plain, the snowed mountains lighted their portion of sky. Mount Baker and the other peaks appeared to rise behind the very bank of the river, the plain was so flat. In every other direction the fields gave way directly to light; the farmers' yellow flax and green pea fields and hayfields curved beyond sight. Clare walked toward the train tracks to town. It was afternoon; overhead the sun was ample. Above the earth rode fifteen or twenty tall clouds. Clare watched the clouds—clouds like rocks you could chip, edged with light, caked in grit. They bulged and piled.

Beside him a dense hedge of berries darkened the lip where the fields met a delta meander. Goldfinches were feeding in the hedges—wild canaries, his mother called them. As Clare moved across the plain, the goldfinches swept before him, burst by burst, then flew behind him after he passed. He flushed flock after flock; they looped down the riverside before him. He was walking home.

He was walking home and remembering a Sunday last spring. In the drizzle after church, children were playing in Clare's front yard.

Mabel and her cousin Nesta, and two other children, were tying each other to the cottonwood tree. They had found a length of line. Clare watched from the parlor. He had forgotten this piece of information: children tie one another to trees. Children find wild eggs, treasure, and corpses; they make trails, huts, and fires; they hit one another, hold hands, and tie one another to trees. They tied a small boy to the tree, and he cried. They tied Mabel to the tree; her Easter hat fell, and she could not break away.

That day Clare had looked out past the porch and the lilacs.

Here is a solid planet, he thought, stocked with mountains and cliffs, where stone banks jut and deeply rooted trees hang on. Among these fixed and enduring features wander the flimsy people. The earth rolls down and the people die; their survivors derive solace from clinging, not to the rocks, not to the cliffs, not to the trees, but to each other. It was striking. Loose people clung in families, holding on for dear life. Grasping at straws! One would think people would beg to be tied to trees.

Mabel stood, dubious in her white ruffled dress, lashed in manila rope to the wet cottonwood trunk. She looked up and saw him in the window. June, old Ada, and the other women were in the kitchen, preparing a big dinner. If the children tied him to the tree, Obenchain could shoot him. How soft-shelled Mabel was, with her bones inside her! She could break, burn, suffocate, puncture, or freeze, this Mabel, for whom everything had been made so smooth. Clare's mother came bending around the house to the back door in her church finery; the children were calling her. "No," she said from the doorway, "I am too old."

Now Clare had walked all day. He saw a marsh hawk riding the air slopes low over the plain. The big clouds brightened; the sunlight shone yellow on their bossy sides. What could be unthinkable? When the river curved north, Clare left its banks and cut westward past pea fields north of town. He flushed the goldfinches, and the goldfinches flew; the sky colored up, and a killdeer ran calling. After two or three miles he saw patches of forest ahead—the uncut railroad right-of-way on the bluff past the trestle—forest, and a forest-broken lighted band of water. After another mile his path joined the railroad track. It entered a strip of timber and burst out on the grade up to the shore.

Clare lowered his hat, looking out at water. White gulls dropped cockles on the roadbed and lumbered down to feed on broken bits. The sun was low. The tide was in; water covered the beach below past the cobbles, where the mud began. Clare shifted his sack and pole, changing arms, and started up the tracks toward the trestle. Looking ahead, he saw Obenchain almost at once.

It looked like Obenchain. The man lounged inert on the point of the bluff where the trestle's log foundation met its ties. His body pointed out toward the water, and his head lay sideways, resting on naked shoulder and arm, facing down the track toward Clare. It was certainly Obenchain, from his size and his hat. His chest and arms were bare. Clare could not see if he had a gun. Clare had his Lightning; he had also a fish knife. Unless Clare could shoot him first, and if Obenchain had no gun, he would simply throw Clare from the trestle. His back would break, or his legs, and he would drown. He sifted his options without emotion. He would not shoot Obenchain in cold blood, as if for lounging on the trestle. If the two tangled, could he use his knife? Should he open it now? He decided he should not open his knife, or uncover his revolver. There was no use asking for trouble. It always came down to a man's size. Obenchain could point any weapon Clare held in any direction Obenchain preferred. He would, slightly, rather drown in cold water than get stuck by his own knife or shot.

There was no one else near; no farm boys bringing in the cows, no crewmen inspecting track, no men in boats on the water. Obenchain alone was in sight, and Clare was in sight of Obenchain and the yellow clouds. Obenchain looked for all the world as if he was expecting Clare and waiting for him.

So Clare carried on up the tracks toward Obenchain. Obenchain raised his head from his arm; he made no move to stand. Clare came pacing the roadbed cinders toward Obenchain because Obenchain sat in his path.

He walked from the long habit of walking, as if he were opening the air as a canoe bow opens the river. He saw himself being opened as if Obenchain were a table saw. He was a clod of dirt that the light splits.

Obenchain stood and stopped him, his face thickened under his hat.

"I am not . . . going to kill you," Obenchain said. "You are not . . . going to die." Clare looked out over the trestle toward town.

Obenchain offered a view he had to reject. Of course he was going to die. He walked around the man. He saw Obenchain's head turn as he passed; he made no move to follow. The tide on the bay was slack at the flood. There was a plank walkway on the trestle by the rails. Clare moved onto the walkway, nodding. The trestle quit the shore, and Clare stepped out over the bay and the strait in a socket of light. Sky pooled under his shoulders and arched beneath his feet. Time rolled back and bore him; he was porous as bones.

"No," he said to Obenchain—but Obenchain was already far behind him on the bluff, his head swaying up like a blind man's. No, indeed. He was not willing to lose this life. He would return home and fry the trout. He had shingles to split, too, here on top. He saw the sun drenching the blue westward islands and battering a path down the water. He saw the town before him to the south, where the trestle lighted down. Then, far on the Nooksack plain to the east, he saw a man walking. The distant figure was turning pea rows under in perfect silence. He held and guided the plow a horse drew. His feet trod his figure's long blue shadow, and the plow cut its long blue shadow in the ground. The man turned back as if to look along the furrow, to check its straightness. Clare saw again on the plain farther north another man, walking behind a horse and turning the green ground under. Then before him on the trestle over the water he saw the earth itself walking, the earth walking darkly as it always walks in every season: it was plowing the men under, and the horses, and the plows.

The earth was plowing the men under, and the horses under, and the plows. No generation sees it happen, and the broken new fields grow up forgetting. Clare was burrowing in light upstream. All the living were breasting into the crest of the present together. All men and women and children ran spread in a long line, holding aloft a ribbon or banner; they ran up a field as wide as earth, opening time like a path in the grass, and he was borne along with them. No, he said, peeling the light back, walking in the sky toward home; no.

The trestle lit down in town above the wharves. Clare paused to look back down the beach. The water's face showed a flaw of wind rake over it like fingers; the water's surface pulled the near blue islands down in reflections that boats cut in streaks. His eye followed the long curve of stones and logs on the bay. He heard a glad shout.

There were some Lummi Indian men on the beach below. He watched one man heave a plank of driftwood high over the water, crying a cry. The other three, whose laughing he could faintly hear, shied cobbles at the plank as it fell. Everything splashed into the water. Clare stepped onto the beach and picked up a few stones, thinking to join the men, but he remembered the trout, so he turned and headed up the five steep blocks to Lambert Street.

1978/1994

THE DEER AT PROVIDENCIA

THERE WERE FOUR OF US North Americans in the jungle, in the Ecuadorian jungle on the banks of the Napo River in the Amazon watershed. The other three North Americans were metropolitan men. We stayed in tents in one riverside village, and visited others. At the village called Providencia we saw a sight which moved us, and which shocked the men.

The first thing we saw when we climbed the riverbank to the village of Providencia was the deer. It was roped to a tree on the grass clearing near the thatch shelter where we would eat lunch.

The deer was small, about the size of a whitetail fawn, but apparently full-grown. It had a rope around its neck and three feet caught in the rope. Someone said that the dogs had caught it that morning and the villagers were going to cook and eat it that night.

This clearing lay at the edge of the little thatched-hut village. We could see the villagers going about their business, scattering feed corn for hens about their houses, and wandering down paths to the river to bathe. The village headman was our host; he stood beside us as we watched the deer struggle. Several village boys were interested in the deer; they formed part of the circle we made around it in the clearing. So also did four businessmen from Quito, who were attempting to guide us around the jungle. Few of the very different people standing in this circle had a common language. We watched the deer, and no one said much.

The deer lay on its side at the rope's very end, so the rope lacked slack to let it rest its head in the dust. It was "pretty," delicate of bone, like all deer, and thin-skinned for the tropics. Its skin looked virtually hairless, in fact, and almost translucent, like a membrane. Its neck was no thicker than my wrist; it was rubbed open on the rope, and gashed. Trying to paw itself free of the rope, the deer had scratched its own neck with its hooves. The raw underside of its neck showed red stripes and some bruises bleeding inside the muscles. Now three of its feet were hooked in the rope under its jaw. It could not stand, of course, on one leg, so it could not move to slacken the rope and ease the pull on its throat and enable it to rest its head.

Repeatedly the deer paused, motionless, its eyes veiled, with only its rib cage in motion, and its breaths the only sound. Then, after I would think, "It has given up; now it will die," it would heave. The rope twanged; the tree leaves clattered; the deer's free foot beat the ground. We stepped back and held our breaths. It thrashed, kicking, but only one leg moved; the other three legs tightened inside the rope's loop. Its hip jerked; its spine shook. Its eyes rolled; its tongue, thick with spittle, pushed in and out. Then it rested again. We watched this for fifteen minutes.

Once three young native boys charged in, released its trapped legs, and jumped back to the circle of people. But instantly the deer scratched up its neck with its hooves and snared its forelegs in the rope again. It was easy to imagine a third and then a fourth leg soon stuck, like Brer Rabbit and the Tar Baby.

We watched the deer from the circle, and then we drifted on to lunch. Our palm-roofed shelter stood on a grassy promontory, from which we could see the deer tied to the tree, pigs and hens walking under village houses, and black-and-white cattle standing in the river. There was even a breeze.

Lunch, which was the second and better lunch we had that day, was hot and fried. There was a big fish called *doncella*, a kind of catfish, dipped whole in corn flour and beaten egg, then deep fried. With our fingers we pulled soft fragments of it from its sides to our plates, and ate; it was delicate fish flesh, fresh and mild. Someone found the roe, and I ate of that, too—it was fat and stronger, like egg yolk, naturally enough, and warm.

There was also a stew of meat in shreds, with rice and pale-brown gravy. I had asked what kind of deer it was tied to the tree; Pepe had answered in Spanish, *"Gama."* Now they told us this was *gama*, too, stewed. I suspect the word means merely game or venison. At any rate, I heard that the village dogs had cornered another deer just yesterday, and it was this deer that we were now eating in full sight of the whole article. It was good. I was surprised at its tenderness. But it is a fact that high levels of lactic acid, which builds up in muscle tissues during exertion, tenderize.

After the fish and meat we ate bananas fried in chunks and served on a tray; they were sweet and full of flavor. I felt terrific. My shirt was wet and cool from swimming; I had had a night's sleep, two decent walks, three meals, and a swim—everything tasted good. From time to time each one of us, separately, would look beyond our shaded roof to the sunny spot where the deer was still convulsing in the dust. Our meal completed, we walked around the deer and back to the boats.

That night I learned that while we were watching the deer, the others were watching me.

We four North Americans grew close in the jungle in a way that was not the usual artificial intimacy of travelers. We liked each other. We stayed up all that night talking, murmuring, as though we rocked on hammocks slung above time. The others were from big cities: New York, Washington, Boston. They all said that I had no expression on my face when I was watching the deer—or at any rate, not the expression they expected.

They had looked to see how I, the only woman, and the youngest, was taking the sight of the deer's struggles. I looked detached, apparently, or hard, or calm, or focused, still. I don't know. I was thinking. I remember feeling very old and energetic. I could say like Thoreau that I have traveled widely in Roanoke, Virginia. I have thought a great deal about carnivorousness; I eat meat. These things are not issues; they are mysteries.

*   *   *

Gentlemen of the city, what surprises you? That there is suffering here, or that I know it?

We lay in the tent and talked. "If it had been my wife," one man said with special vigor, amazed, "she wouldn't have cared *what* was going on; she would have dropped *everything* right at that moment and gone in the village from here to there to there, she would not have *stopped* until that animal was out of its suffering one way or another. She couldn't *bear* to see a creature in agony like that."

I nodded.

Now I am home. When I wake I comb my hair before the mirror above my dresser. Every morning for the past two years I have seen in that mirror, beside my sleep-softened face, the blackened face of a burned man. It is a wire-service photograph, clipped from a newspaper and taped to my mirror. The caption reads: "Alan McDonald in Miami hospital bed." All you can see in the photograph is a smudged triangle of face from his eyelids to his lower lip; the rest is bandages. You cannot see the expression in his eyes; the bandages shade them.

The story, headed MAN BURNED FOR SECOND TIME, begins:

> "Why does God hate me?" Alan McDonald asked from his hospital bed.
>
> "When the gunpowder went off, I couldn't believe it," he said. "I just couldn't believe it. I said, 'No, God couldn't do this to me again.'"

He was in a burn ward in Miami, in serious condition. I do not even know if he lived. I wrote him a letter at the time, cringing.

He had been burned before, thirteen years previously, by flaming gasoline. For years he had been having his body restored and his face remade in dozens of operations. He had been a boy, and then a burned boy. He had already been stunned by what could happen, by how life could veer.

Once I read that people who survive bad burns tend to go crazy; they have a very high suicide rate. Medicine cannot ease their pain; drugs just drip away, soaking the sheets, because there is no skin to hold them in. The people just lie there and weep. Later they kill themselves. They had not known, before they were burned, that the world included such suffering, that life could permit them personally such pain.

This time a bowl of gunpowder had exploded on McDonald.

"I didn't realize what had happened at first," he recounted. "And then I heard that sound from 13 years ago. I was burning. I rolled to put the fire out and I thought, 'Oh God, not again.'

"If my friend hadn't been there, I would have jumped into a canal with a rock around my neck."

His wife concludes the piece, "Man, it just isn't fair."

I read the whole clipping again every morning. This is the Big Time here, every minute of it. Will someone please explain to Alan McDonald in his dignity, to the deer at Providencia in his dignity, what is going on? And mail me the carbon.

When we walked by the deer at Providencia for the last time, I said to Pepe, with a pitying glance at the deer, *"Pobrecito"*—"poor little thing." But I was trying out Spanish. I knew at the time it was a ridiculous thing to say.

1975

LIVING LIKE
WEASELS

A WEASEL IS WILD. Who knows what he thinks? He sleeps in his underground den, his tail draped over his nose. Sometimes he lives in his den for two days without leaving. Outside, he stalks rabbits, mice, muskrats, and birds, killing more bodies than he can eat warm, and often dragging the carcasses home. Obedient to instinct, he bites his prey at the neck, either splitting the jugular vein at the throat or crunching the brain at the base of the skull, and he does not let go. One naturalist refused to kill a weasel who was socketed into his hand deeply as a rattlesnake. The man could in no way pry the tiny weasel off, and he had to walk half a mile to water, the weasel dangling from his palm, and soak him off like a stubborn label.

I have been thinking about weasels because I saw one last week. I startled a weasel who startled me, and we exchanged a long glance.

Near my house in Virginia is a pond—Hollins Pond. It covers two acres of bottomland near Tinker Creek with six inches of water and six thousand lily pads. There is a fifty-five mph highway at one end of the pond, and a nesting pair of wood ducks at the other. Under every bush is a muskrat hole or a beer can. The far end is an alternating series of fields and woods, fields and woods, threaded everywhere with motorcycle tracks— in whose bare clay wild turtles lay eggs.

One evening last week at sunset, I walked to the pond and sat on a downed log near the shore. I was watching the lily pads at my feet tremble and part over the thrusting path of a carp. A yellow warbler appeared to my right and flew behind me. It caught my eye; I swiveled around—and the next instant, inexplicably, I was looking down at a weasel, who was looking up at me.

*   *   *

Weasel! I had never seen one wild before. He was ten inches long, thin as a curve, a muscled ribbon, brown as fruitwood, soft-furred, alert. His face was fierce, small and pointed as a lizard's; he would have made a good arrowhead. There was just a dot of chin, maybe two brown hairs' worth, and then the pure white fur began that spread down his underside. He had two black eyes I did not see, any more than you see a window.

The weasel was stunned into stillness as he was emerging from beneath an enormous shaggy wild-rose bush four feet away. I was stunned into stillness, twisted backward on the tree trunk. Our eyes locked, and someone threw away the key.

Our look was as if two lovers, or deadly enemies, met unexpectedly on an overgrown path when each had been thinking of something else: a clearing blow to the gut. It was also a bright blow to the brain, or a sudden beating of brains, with all the charge and intimate grate of rubbed balloons. It emptied our lungs. It felled the forest, moved the fields, and drained the pond; the world dismantled and tumbled into that black hole of eyes. If you and I looked at each other that way, our skulls would split and drop to our shoulders. But we don't. We keep our skulls.

He disappeared. This was only last week, and already I don't remember what shattered the enchantment. I think I blinked, I think I retrieved my brain from the weasel's brain, and tried to memorize what I was seeing, and the weasel felt the yank of separation, the careening splashdown into real life and the urgent current of instinct. He vanished under the wild rose. I waited motionless, my mind suddenly full of data and my spirit with pleadings, but he didn't return.

Please do not tell me about "approach-avoidance conflicts." I tell you I've been in that weasel's brain for sixty seconds, and he was in mine. Brains are private places, muttering through unique and secret tapes—but the weasel and I both plugged into another tape simultaneously, for a sweet and shocking time. Can I help it if it was a blank?

What goes on in his brain the rest of the time? What does a weasel think about? He won't say. His journal is tracks in clay, a

spray of feathers, mouse blood and bone: uncollected, uncon-
nected, loose-leaf, and blown.

I would like to learn, or remember, how to live. I come to
Hollins Pond not so much to learn how to live as, frankly, to forget about it. That is, I don't think I can learn from a wild animal
how to live in particular—shall I suck warm blood, hold my tail
high, walk with my footprints precisely over the prints of my
hands?—but I might learn something of mindlessness, something of the purity of living in the physical senses and the dignity of living without bias or motive. The weasel lives in necessity and we live in choice, hating necessity and dying at the last
ignobly in its talons. I would like to live as I should, as the
weasel lives as he should. And I suspect that for me the way is
like the weasel's: open to time and death painlessly, noticing
everything, remembering nothing, choosing the given with a
fierce and pointed will.

I missed my chance. I should have gone for the throat. I
should have lunged for that streak of white under the weasel's
chin and held on, held on through mud and into the wild rose,
held on for a dearer life. We could live under the wild rose wild
as weasels, mute and uncomprehending. I could very calmly go
wild. I could live two days in the den, curled, leaning on mouse
fur, sniffing bird bones, blinking, licking, breathing musk, my
hair tangled in the roots of grasses. Down is a good place to go,
where the mind is single. Down is out, out of your ever-loving
mind and back to your careless senses. I remember muteness as
a prolonged and giddy fast, where every moment is a feast of
utterance received. Time and events are merely poured, unre-
marked, and ingested directly, like blood pulsed into my gut
through a jugular vein. Could two live that way? Could two live
under the wild rose, and explore by the pond, so that the
smooth mind of each is as everywhere present to the other, and
as received and as unchallenged, as falling snow?
We could, you know. We can live any way we want. People
take vows of poverty, chastity, and obedience—even of
silence—by choice. The thing is to stalk your calling in a certain

skilled and supple way, to locate the most tender and live spot and plug into that pulse. This is yielding, not fighting. A weasel doesn't "attack" anything; a weasel lives as he's meant to, yielding at every moment to the perfect freedom of single necessity.

I think it would be well, and proper, and obedient, and pure, to grasp your one necessity and not let it go, to dangle from it limp wherever it takes you. Then even death, where you're going no matter how you live, cannot you part. Seize it and let it seize you up aloft even, till your eyes burn out and drop; let your musky flesh fall off in shreds, and let your very bones unhinge and scatter, loosened over fields, over fields and woods, lightly, thoughtless, from any height at all, from as high as eagles.

1974

From

AN AMERICAN
CHILDHOOD

WHEN EVERYTHING ELSE HAS GONE from my brain—the President's name, the state capitals, the neighborhoods where I lived, and then my own name and what it was on earth I sought, and then at length the faces of my friends, and finally the faces of my family—when all this has dissolved, what will be left, I believe, is topology: the dreaming memory of land as it lay this way and that.

I will see the city poured rolling down the mountain valleys like slag, and see the city lights sprinkled and curved around the hills' curves, rows of bonfires winding. At sunset a red light like housefires shines from the narrow hillside windows; the houses' bricks burn like glowing coals.

The three wide rivers divide and cool the mountains. Calm old bridges span the banks and link the hills. The Allegheny River flows in brawling from the north, from near the shore of Lake Erie, and from Lake Chautauqua in New York and eastward. The Monongahela River flows in shallow and slow from the south, from West Virginia. The Allegheny and the Monongahela meet and form the westward-wending Ohio.

Where the two rivers join lies an acute point of flat land from which rises the city. The tall buildings rise lighted to their tips. Their lights illumine other buildings' clean sides, and illumine the narrow city canyons below, where people move, and shine reflected red and white at night from the black waters.

When the shining city, too, fades, I will see only those forested mountains and hills, and the way the rivers lie flat and moving among them, and the way the low land lies wooded among them, and the blunt mountains rise in darkness from the rivers' banks, steep from the rugged south and rolling from the north, and from farther, from the inclined eastward plateau where the high ridges begin to run so long north and south unbroken that to get around them you practically have to navigate Cape Horn.

In those first days, people said, a squirrel could run the long length of Pennsylvania without ever touching the ground. In those first days, the woods were white oak and chestnut, hickory, maple, sycamore, walnut, wild ash, wild plum, and white pine. The pine grew on the ridgetops where the mountains' lumpy spines stuck up and their skin was thinnest.

The wilderness was uncanny, unknown. Benjamin Franklin had already invented his stove in Philadelphia by 1753, and Thomas Jefferson was a schoolboy in Virginia; French soldiers had been living in forts along Lake Erie for two generations. But west of the Alleghenies in western Pennsylvania, there was not even a settlement, not even a cabin. No Indians lived there, or even near there.

Wild grapevines tangled the treetops and shut out the sun. Few songbirds lived in the deep woods. Bright Carolina parakeets—red, green, and yellow—nested in the dark forest. There were ravens then, too. Woodpeckers rattled the big trees' trunks, ruffed grouse whirred their tail feathers in the fall, and every long once in a while a nervous gang of empty-headed turkeys came hustling and kicking through the leaves—but no one heard any of this, no one at all.

In 1753, young George Washington surveyed for the English this point of land where rivers met. To see the forest-blurred lay of the land, he rode his horse to a ridgetop and climbed a tree. He judged it would make a good spot for a fort. An English fort it became, and a depot for Indian traders to the Ohio country, and later a French fort and way station to New Orleans.

But it would be another ten years before any settlers lived there on that land where the rivers met, lived to draw in the flowery scent of June rhododendrons with every breath. It would be another ten years before, for the first time on earth, tall men and women lay exhausted in their cabins, sleeping in the sweetness, worn out from planting corn.

IN 1955, WHEN I WAS TEN, my father's reading went to his head.

My father's reading during that time, and for many years before and after, consisted for the most part of *Life on the Mississippi*. He was a young executive in the old family firm, American Standard; sometimes he traveled alone on business. Traveling, he checked into a hotel, found a bookstore, and chose for the night's reading, after what I fancy to have been long deliberation, yet another copy of *Life on the Mississippi*. He brought all these books home. There were dozens of copies of *Life on the Mississippi* on the living-room shelves. From time to time, I read one.

Down the Mississippi hazarded the cub riverboat pilot, down the Mississippi from Saint Louis to New Orleans. His chief, the pilot Mr. Bixby, taught him how to lay the boat in her marks and dart between points; he learned to pick a way fastidiously inside a certain snag and outside a shifting shoal in the black dark; he learned to clamber down a memorized channel in his head. On tricky crossings the leadsmen sang out the soundings, so familiar I seemed to have heard them the length of my life: "Mark four! . . . Quarter-less-four! . . . Half three! . . . Mark three! . . . Quarter-less . . . " It was an old story.

When all this reading went to my father's head, he took action. From Pittsburgh he went down the river. Although no one else that our family knew kept a boat on the Allegheny River, our father did, and now he was going all the way with it. He quit the firm his great-grandfather had founded a hundred years earlier down the river at his family's seat in Louisville, Kentucky; he sold his own holdings in the firm. He was taking off for New Orleans.

*   *   *

New Orleans was the source of the music he loved: Dixieland jazz, O Dixieland. In New Orleans men would blow it in the air and beat it underfoot, the music that hustled and snapped, the music whose zip matched his when he was a man-about-town at home in Pittsburgh, working for the family firm; the music he tapped his foot to when he was a man-about-town in New York for a few years after college, working for the family firm by day and by night hanging out at Jimmy Ryan's on Fifty-second Street with Zutty Singleton, the black drummer, who befriended him, and the rest of the house band. A certain kind of Dixieland suited him best. They played it at Jimmy Ryan's, and Pee Wee Russell and Eddie Condon played it too—New Orleans Dixieland chilled a bit by its journey up the river, and smoothed by its sojourns in Chicago and New York.

Back in New Orleans where he was headed they would play the old stuff, the hot, rough stuff—bastardized for tourists, but still the big and muddy source of it all. Back in New Orleans where he was headed the music would smell like the river itself, maybe, like a thicker, older version of the Allegheny River at Pittsburgh, where he heard the music beat in the roar of his boat's inboard motor; like a thicker, older version of the wide Ohio River at Louisville, Kentucky, where at his family's summer house he'd spent his boyhood summers mucking about in boats.

Getting ready for the trip one Saturday, he roamed around our big brick house, snapping his fingers. He had put a record on: Sharkey Bonano, "Li'l Liza Jane." I was reading Robert Louis Stevenson on the sunporch: *Kidnapped*. I looked up from my book and saw him outside; he had wandered out to the lawn and was standing in the wind between the buckeye trees and looking up at what must have been a small patch of wild sky. Old Low-Pockets. He was six feet four, all lanky and leggy; he had thick brown hair and shaggy brows, and a mild and dreamy expression in his blue eyes.

When our mother met Frank Doak, he was twenty-seven: witty, boyish, bookish, unsnobbish, a good dancer. He had grown up an only child in Pittsburgh, attended Shady Side Academy, and Washington and Jefferson College in Pennsylvania, where he studied history. He was a lapsed Presbyterian and a believing Republican. "Books make the man," read the blue bookplate in all his books. "Frank Doak." The bookplate's woodcut showed a square-rigged ship under way in a steep following sea. Father had hung around jazz in New York, and half-heartedly played the drums; he had smoked marijuana, written poems, begun a novel, painted in oils, imagined a career as a riverboat pilot, and acted for more than ten seasons in amateur and small-time professional theater. At American Standard, Amstan Division, he was the personnel manager.

But not for long, and never again; Mother told us he was quitting to go down the river. I was sorry he'd be leaving the Manufacturers' Building downtown. From his office on the fourteenth floor, he often saw suicides, which he reported at dinner. The suicides grieved him, but they thrilled us kids. My sister Amy was seven.

People jumped from the Sixth Street bridge into the Allegheny River. Because the bridge was low, they shinnied all the way up the steel suspension cables to the bridge towers before they jumped. Father saw them from his desk in silhouette, far away. A man vigorously climbed a slanting cable. He slowed near the top, where the cables hung almost vertical; he paused on the stone tower, seeming to sway against the sky, high over the bridge and the river below. Priests, firemen, and others—presumably family members or passersby—gathered on the bridge. In about half the cases, Father said, these people talked the suicide down. The ones who jumped kicked off from the tower so they'd miss the bridge, and fell tumbling a long way down.

Pittsburgh was a cheerful town, and had far fewer suicides than most other cities its size. Yet people jumped so often that Father and his colleagues on the fourteenth floor had a betting pool going. They guessed the date and time of day the next jumper would appear. If a man got talked down before he jumped, he still counted for the betting pool, thank God; no manager of American Standard ever wanted to hope, even in the smallest part of himself, that the fellow would go ahead and jump. Father said he and the other men used to gather at the biggest window and holler, "No! Don't do it, buddy, don't!" Now he was leaving American Standard to go down the river, and he was a couple of bucks in the hole.

While I was reading *Kidnapped* on this Saturday morning, I heard him come inside and roam from the kitchen to the pantry to the bar, to the dining room, the living room, and the sunporch, snapping his fingers. He was snapping the fingers of both hands, and shaking his head, to the record—"Li'l Liza Jane"— the sound that was beating, big and jivey, all over the house. He walked lightly, long-legged, like a soft-shoe hoofer barely in touch with the floor. When he played the drums, he played lightly, coming down soft with the steel brushes that sounded like a Slinky falling, not making the beat but just sizzling along with it. He wandered into the sunporch, unseeing; he was snapping his fingers lightly, too, as if he were feeling between them a fine layer of Mississippi silt. The big buckeyes outside the glass sunporch walls were waving.

A week later, he bade a cheerful farewell to us—to Mother, who had encouraged him, to us oblivious daughters, ten and seven, and to the new baby girl, six months old. He loaded his twenty-four-foot cabin cruiser with canned food, pushed off from the dock of the wretched boat club that Mother hated, and pointed his bow downstream, down the Allegheny River. From there it was only a few miles to the Ohio River at Pittsburgh's point, where the Monongahela came in. He wore on westward down the Ohio; he watched West Virginia float past his port bow and Ohio past his starboard. It was 138 river miles to New Martinsville, West Virginia, where he lingered for some races. Back on the move, he tied up nights at club docks he'd seen on the charts; he poured himself water for drinks from dockside hoses. By day he rode through locks, twenty of them in all. He conversed with the lockmasters, those lone men who paced silhouetted in overalls on the concrete lock-chamber walls and threw the big switches that flooded or drained the locks: "Hello, up there!" "So long, down there!"

He continued down the river along the Kentucky border

with Ohio, bumping down the locks. He passed through Cincinnati. He moved along down the Kentucky border with Indiana. After 640 miles of river travel, he reached Louisville, Kentucky. There he visited relatives at their summer house on the river.

It was a long way to New Orleans, at this rate another couple of months. He was finding the river lonesome. It got dark too early. It was September; people had abandoned their pleasure boats for the season; their children were back in school. There were no old salts on the docks talking river talk. People weren't so friendly as they were in Pittsburgh. There was no music except the dreary yacht-club jukeboxes playing "How Much Is That Doggie in the Window?" Jazz had come up the river once and for all; it wasn't still coming, he couldn't hear it across the water at night, rambling and blowing and banging along high and tuneful, sneaking upstream to Chicago to get educated. He wasn't free so much as loose. He was living alone on beans in a boat and having witless conversations with lockmasters. He mailed out sad postcards.

From phone booths all down the Ohio River he talked to Mother. She told him that she was lonesome, too, and that three children—maid and nanny or no—were a handful. She said, further, that people were starting to talk. She knew Father couldn't bear people's talking. For all his dreaminess, he prized respectability above all; it was our young mother, whose circumstances bespoke such dignity, who loved to shock the world. After only six weeks, then—on the Ohio River at Louisville—he sold the boat and flew home.

I was just waking up then, just barely. Other things were changing. The highly entertaining new baby, Molly, had taken up residence in a former guest room. The great outer world hove into view and began to fill with things that had apparently been there all along: mineralogy, detective work, lepidopterology, ponds and streams, flying, society. My younger sister Amy and I were to start at private school that year: the Ellis School, on Fifth Avenue. I would start dancing school.

*   *   *

Children ten years old wake up and find themselves here, discover themselves to have been here all along; is this sad? They wake like sleepwalkers, in full stride; they wake like people brought back from cardiac arrest or from drowning: *in medias res,* surrounded by familiar people and objects, equipped with a hundred skills. They know the neighborhood, they can read and write English, they are old hands at the commonplace mysteries, and yet they feel themselves to have just stepped off the boat, just converged with their bodies, just flown down from a trance, to lodge in an eerily familiar life already well under way.

I woke in bits, like all children, piecemeal over the years. I discovered myself and the world, and forgot them, and discovered them again. I woke at intervals until, by that September when Father went down the river, the intervals of waking tipped the scales, and I was more often awake than not. I noticed this process of waking, and predicted with terrifying logic that one of these years not far away I would be awake continuously and never slip back, and never be free of myself again.

Consciousness converges with the child as a landing tern touches the outspread feet of its shadow on the sand: precisely, toe hits toe. The tern folds its wings to sit; its shadow dips and spreads over the sand to meet and cup its breast.

Like any child, I slid into myself perfectly fitted, as a diver meets her reflection in a pool. Her fingertips enter the fingertips on the water, her wrists slide up her arms. The diver wraps herself in her reflection wholly, sealing it at the toes, and wears it as she climbs rising from the pool, and ever after.

I never woke, at first, without recalling, chilled, all those other waking times, those similar stark views from similarly lighted precipices: dizzying precipices from which the distant, glittering world revealed itself as a brooding and separated scene—and so let slip a queer implication, that I myself was both observer and observable, and so a possible object of my own humming awareness. Whenever I stepped into the porcelain bathtub, the bath's hot water sent a shock traveling up my bones. The skin on my arms pricked up, and the hair rose on the back of my skull. I saw my own firm foot press the tub, and the pale shadows waver over it, as if I were looking down from the sky and remembering this scene forever. The skin on my face tightened, as it had always done whenever I stepped into the tub, and remembering it all drew a swinging line, loops connecting the dots, all the way back. You again.

THE STORY STARTS BACK IN 1950, when I was five.

Oh, the great humming silence of the empty neighborhoods in those days, the neighborhoods abandoned everywhere across continental America—the city residential areas, the new "suburbs," the towns, and villages on the peopled highways, the cities, towns, and villages on the rivers, the shores, in the Rocky and Appalachian mountains, the piedmont, the dells, the bayous, the hills, the Great Basin, the Great Valley, the Great Plains—oh, the silence!

For every morning the neighborhoods emptied, and all vital activity, it seemed, set forth for parts unknown.

The men left in a rush: they flung on coats, they slid kisses at everybody's cheeks, they slammed house doors, they slammed car doors; they ground their cars' starters till the motors caught with a jump.

And the Catholic schoolchildren left in a rush; I saw them from our dining-room windows. They burst into the street buttoning their jackets; they threw dry catalpa pods at the stop sign and at each other. They hugged their brown-and-tan workbooks to them, clumped and parted, and proceeded toward Saint Bede's church school almost by accident.

The men in their oval, empty cars drove slowly among the schoolchildren. The boys banged the cars' fenders with their hands, with their jackets' elbows, or their books. The men in cars inched among the children; they edged around corners and vanished from sight. The waving knots of children zigzagged and hollered up the street and vanished from sight. And inside all the forgotten houses in all the abandoned neighborhoods, the day of silence and waiting had begun.

*　　*　　*

The war was over. People wanted to settle down, apparently, and calmly blow their way out of years of rationing. They wanted to bake sugary cakes, burn gas, go to church together, get rich, and make babies.

I had been born at the end of April 1945, on the day Hitler died; Roosevelt had died eighteen days before. My father had been 4-F in the war, because of a collapsing lung—despite his repeated and chagrined efforts to enlist. Now—five years after V-J Day—he still went out one night a week as a volunteer to the Civil Air Patrol; he searched the Pittsburgh skies for new enemy bombers. By day he worked downtown for American Standard.

Every woman stayed alone in her house in those days, like a coin in a safe. Amy and I lived alone with our mother most of the day. Amy was three years younger than I. Mother and Amy and I went our separate ways in peace.

The men had driven away and the schoolchildren had paraded out of sight. Now a self-conscious and stricken silence overtook the neighborhood, overtook our white corner house and myself inside. "Am I living?" In the kitchen I watched the unselfconscious trees through the screen door, until the trees' autumn branches like fins waved away the silence. I forgot myself, and sank into dim and watery oblivion.

A car passed. Its rush and whine jolted me from my blankness. The sound faded again and I faded again down into my hushed brain until the icebox motor kicked on and prodded me awake. "You are living," the icebox motor said. "It is morning, morning, here in the kitchen, and you are in it," the icebox motor said, or the dripping faucet said, or any of the hundred other noisy things that only children can't stop hearing. Cars started, leaves rubbed, trucks' brakes whistled, sparrows peeped. Whenever it rained, the rain spattered, dripped, and ran, for the entire length of the shower, for the entire length of days-long rains, until we children were almost insane from hearing it rain because we couldn't stop hearing it rain. "Rinso white!" cried the man on the radio. "Rinso blue." The silence, like all silences, was made poignant and distinct by its sounds.

What a marvel it was that the day so often introduced itself with a firm footfall nearby. What a marvel it was that so many times a day the world, like a church bell, reminded me to recall and contemplate the durable fact that I was here, and had awakened once more to find myself set down in a going world.

In the living room the mail slot clicked open and envelopes clattered down. In the back room, where our maid, Margaret Butler, was ironing, the steam iron thumped the muffled ironing board and hissed. The walls squeaked, the pipes knocked, the screen door trembled, the furnace banged, and the radiators clanged. This was the fall the loud trucks went by. I sat mindless and eternal on the kitchen floor, stony of head and solemn, playing with my fingers. Time streamed in full flood beside me on the kitchen floor; time roared raging beside me down its swollen banks; and when I woke I was so startled I fell in.

Who could ever tire of this heart-stopping transition, of this breakthrough shift between seeing and knowing you see, between being and knowing you be? It drives you to a life of concentration, it does, a life in which effort draws you down so very deep that when you surface you twist up exhilarated with a yelp and a gasp.

Who could ever tire of this radiant transition, this surfacing to awareness and this deliberate plunging to oblivion—the theater curtain rising and falling? Who could tire of it when the sum of those moments at the edge—the conscious life we so dread losing—is all we have, the gift at the moment of opening it?

Six xylophone notes chimed evenly from the radio in the back room where Margaret was ironing, and then seven xylophone notes chimed. With carefully controlled emotion, a radio woman sang:

> What will the weather be?
> Tell us, Mister Weather Man.

Mother picked up Amy, who was afraid of the trucks. She called the painters on the phone; it was time to paint the outside trim again. She ordered groceries on the phone. Larry, from

Lloyd's Market, delivered. He joked with us in the kitchen while Mother unpacked the groceries' cardboard box.

I wandered outside. It was afternoon. No cars passed on the empty streets; no people passed on the empty sidewalks. The brick houses, the frame and stucco houses, white and red behind their high hedges, were still. A small woman appeared at the far, high end of the street, in silhouette against the sky; she pushed a black baby carriage, tall and chromed as a hearse. The leaves in the Lombardy poplars were turning brown.

"Lie on your back," my mother said. She was kind, imaginative. She had joined me in one of the side yards. "Look at the clouds and figure out what they look like. A hat? I see a camel."

Must I? Could this be anybody's idea of something worth doing?

I was hoping the war would break out again, here. I was hoping the streets would fill and I could shoot my cap gun at people instead of at mere sparrows. My project was to ride my swing all around, over the top. I bounced a ball against the house; I fired gravel bits from an illegal slingshot Mother gave me. Sometimes I looked at the back of my hand and tried to memorize it. Sometimes I dreamed of a coal furnace, a blue lake, a redheaded woodpecker who turned into a screeching hag. Sometimes I sang uselessly in the yard, "Blithar, blithar, blithar, blithar."

It rained and it cleared and I sent Popsicle sticks and twigs down the gritty rivulet below the curb. Soon the separated neighborhood trees lost their leaves, one by one. On Saturday afternoons I watched the men rake leaves into low heaps at the curb. They tried to ignite the heaps with matches. At length my father went into the house and returned with a yellow can of lighter fluid. The daylight ended early, before all the men had burned all their leaves.

It snowed and it cleared and I kicked and pounded the snow. I roamed the darkening snowy neighborhood, oblivious. I bit and crumbled on my tongue the sweet, metallic worms of ice that had formed in rows on my mittens. I took a mitten off to fetch some wool strands from my mouth. Deeper the blue shadows grew on the sidewalk snow, and longer; the blue shadows joined and spread upward from the streets like rising water. I walked wordless and unseeing, dumb and sunk in my skull, until—what was that?

The streetlights had come on—yellow, bing—and the new light woke me like noise. I surfaced once again and saw: it was winter now, winter again. The air had grown blue dark; the skies were shrinking; the streetlights had come on; and I was here outside in the dimming day's snow, alive.

THE INTERIOR LIFE IS OFTEN stupid. Its egoism blinds it and deafens it; its imagination spins out ignorant tales, fascinated. It fancies that the western wind blows on the Self, and leaves fall at the feet of the Self for a reason, and people are watching. A mind risks real ignorance for the sometimes paltry prize of an imagination enriched. The trick of reason is to get the imagination to seize the actual world—if only from time to time.

When I was five, growing up in Pittsburgh in 1950, I would not go to bed willingly because something came into my room. This was a private matter between me and it. If I spoke of it, it would kill me.

Who could breathe as this thing searched for me over the very corners of the room? Who could ever breathe freely again? I lay in the dark.

My sister Amy, two years old, was asleep in the other bed. What did she know? She was innocent of evil. Even at two she composed herself attractively for sleep. She folded the top sheet tidily under her prettily outstretched arm; she laid her perfect head lightly on an unwrinkled pillow, where her thick curls spread evenly in rays like petals. All night long she slept smoothly in a series of pleasant and serene, if artificial-looking, positions, a faint smile on her closed lips, as if she were posing for an ad for sheets. There was no messiness in her, no roughness for things to cling to, only a charming and charmed innocence that seemed then to protect her, an innocence I needed but couldn't muster. Since Amy was asleep, furthermore, and since when I needed someone most I was afraid to stir enough to wake her, she was useless.

I lay alone and was almost asleep when the damned thing

entered the room by flattening itself against the open door and sliding in. It was a transparent, luminous oblong. I could see the door whiten at its touch; I could see the blue wall turn pale where it raced over it, and see the maple headboard of Amy's bed glow. It was a swift spirit; it was an awareness. It made noise. It had two joined parts, a head and a tail, like a Chinese dragon. It found the door, wall, and headboard; and it swiped them, charging them with its luminous glance. After its fleet, searching passage, things looked the same, but weren't.

I dared not blink or breathe; I tried to hush my whooping blood. If it found another awareness, it would destroy it.

Every night before it got to me it gave up. It hit my wall's corner and couldn't get past. It shrank completely into itself and vanished like a cobra down a hole. I heard the rising roar it made when it died or left. I still couldn't breathe. I knew—it was the worst fact I knew, a very hard fact—that it could return again alive that same night.

Sometimes it came back, sometimes it didn't. Most often, restless, it came back. The light stripe slipped in the door, ran searching over Amy's wall, stopped, stretched lunatic at the first corner, raced wailing toward my wall, and vanished into the second corner with a cry. So I wouldn't go to bed.

It was a passing car, whose windshield reflected the corner streetlight outside. I figured it out one night.

Figuring it out was as memorable as the oblong itself. Figuring it out was a long and forced ascent to the very rim of being, to the membrane of skin that both separates and connects the inner life and the outer world. I climbed deliberately from the depths like a diver who releases the monster in his arms and hauls himself hand over hand up an anchor chain till he meets the ocean's sparkling membrane and bursts through it; he sights the sunlit, becalmed hull of his boat, which had bulked so ominously from below.

I recognized the noise it made when it left. That is, the noise it made called to mind, at last, my daytime sensations when a car passed—the sight and noise together. A car came roaring down hushed Edgerton Avenue in front of our house, stopped at the corner stop sign, and passed on shrieking as its engine shifted up the gears. What, precisely, came into the bedroom? A reflection from the car's oblong windshield. Why did it travel in two parts? The window sash split the light and cast a shadow.

Night after night I labored up the same long chain of reasoning, as night after night the thing burst into the room where I lay awake and Amy slept prettily and my loud heart thrashed and I froze.

There was a world outside my window and contiguous to it. If I was so all-fired bright, as my parents, who had patently no basis for comparison, seemed to think, why did I have to keep learning this same thing over and over? For I had learned it a summer ago, when men with jackhammers broke up Edgerton Avenue. I had watched them from the yard; the street came up in jagged slabs like floes. When I lay to nap, I listened. One restless afternoon I connected the new noise in my bedroom with the jackhammer men I had been seeing outside. I understood abruptly that these worlds met, the outside and the inside. I traveled the route in my mind: You walked downstairs from here, and outside from downstairs. "Outside," then, was conceivably just beyond my windows. It was the same world I reached by going out the front or the back door. I forced my imagination yet again over this route.

The world did not have me in mind; it had no mind. It was a coincidental collection of things and people, of items, and I myself was one such item—a child walking up the sidewalk, whom anyone could see or ignore. The things in the world did not necessarily cause my overwhelming feelings; the feelings were inside me, beneath my skin, behind my ribs, within my skull. They were even, to some extent, under my control.

I could be connected to the outer world by reason, if I chose, or I could yield to what amounted to a narrative fiction, to a tale of terror whispered to me by the blood in my ears, a show in light projected on the room's blue walls. As time passed, I learned to amuse myself in bed in the darkened room by entering the fiction deliberately and replacing it by reason deliberately.

When the low roar drew nigh and the oblong slid in the door, I threw my own switches for pleasure. It's coming after me; it's a car outside. It's after me. It's a car. It raced over the wall, lighting it blue wherever it ran; it bumped over Amy's maple headboard in a rush, paused, slithered elongate over the corner, shrank, flew my way, and vanished into itself with a wail. It was a car.

OUR PARENTS AND GRANDPARENTS, AND all their friends, seemed insensible to their own prominent defect, their limp, coarse skin.

We children had, for instance, proper hands; our fluid, pliant fingers joined their skin. Adults had misshapen, knuckly hands loose in their skin like bones in bags; it was a wonder they could open jars. They were loose in their skins all over, except at the wrists and ankles, like rabbits.

We were whole, we were pleasing to ourselves. Our crystalline eyes shone from firm, smooth sockets; we spoke in pure, piping voices through dark, tidy lips. Adults were coming apart, but they neither noticed nor minded. My revulsion was rude, so I hid it. Besides, we could never rise to the absolute figural splendor they alone could on occasion achieve. Our beauty was a mere absence of decrepitude; their beauty, when they had it, was not passive but earned; it was grandeur; it was a party to power, and to artifice, even, and to knowledge. Our beauty was, in the long run, merely elfin. We could not, finally, discount the fact that in some sense they owned us, and they owned the world.

Mother let me play with one of her hands. She laid it flat on a living-room end table beside her chair. I picked up a transverse pinch of skin over the knuckle of her index finger and let it drop. The pinch didn't snap back; it lay dead across her knuckle in a yellowish ridge. I poked it; it slid over intact. I left it there as an experiment and shifted to another finger. Mother was reading *Time* magazine.

Carefully, lifting it by the tip, I raised her middle finger an inch and released it. It snapped back to the tabletop. Her insides, at least, were alive. I tried all the fingers. They all worked. Some I could lift higher than others.

"That's getting boring."

"Sorry, Mama."

I refashioned the ridge on her index-finger knuckle; I made the ridge as long as I could, using both my hands. Moving quickly, I made parallel ridges on her other fingers—a real mountain chain, the Alleghenies; Indians crept along just below the ridgetops, eyeing the frozen lakes below them through the trees.

Skin was earth; it was soil. I could see, even on my own skin, the joined trapezoids of dust specks God had wetted and stuck with his spit the morning he made Adam from dirt. Now, all these generations later, we people could still see on our skin the inherited prints of the dust specks of Eden.

I loved this thought, and repeated it for myself often. I don't know where I got it; my parents cited Adam and Eve only in jokes. Someday I would count the trapezoids, with the aid of a mirror, and learn precisely how many dust specks Adam comprised—one single handful God wetted, shaped, blew into, and set firmly into motion and left to wander about in the fabulous garden, bewildered.

The skin on my mother's face was smooth, fair, and tender; it took impressions readily. She napped on her side on the couch. Her face skin pooled on the low side; it piled up in the low corners of her deep-set eyes and drew down her lips and cheeks. How flexible was it? I pushed at a puddle of it by her nose.

She stirred and opened her eyes. I jumped back.

She reminded me not to touch her face while she was sleeping. Anybody's face.

When she sat up, her cheek and brow bone bore a deep red gash, the mark of a cushion's welting. It was textured inside precisely with the upholstery's weave and brocade.

Another day, after a similar nap, I spoke up about this gash. I told her she had a mark on her face where she'd been sleeping.

"Do I?" she said; she ran her fingers through her hair. Her hair was short, blond, and wavy. She wore it swept back from her high, curved forehead. The skin on her forehead was both tight and soft. It would only barely shift when I tried to move it. She went to the kitchen. She was not interested in the hideous mark on her face. "It'll go away," I said. "What?" she called.

I noticed the hair on my father's arms and legs; each hair sprang from a dark dot on his skin. I lifted a hair and studied the puckered tepee of skin it pulled with it. Those hairs were in there tight. The greater the strain I put on the hair, the more puckered the tepee became, and shrunken within, concave. I could point it every which way.

"Ouch! Enough of that."

"Sorry, Daddy."

At the beach I felt my parents' shinbones. The bones were flat and curved, like the slats in a venetian blind. The long edges were sharp as swords. But they had unexplained and, I thought, possibly diseased irregularities: nicks, bumps, small hard balls, shallow ridges, and soft spots. I was lying between my parents on an enormous towel through which I could feel the hot sand.

Loose under their shinbones, as in a hammock, hung the relaxed flesh of their calves. You could push and swing this like a baby in a sling. Their heels were dry and hard, sharp at the curved edge. The bottoms of their toes had flattened, holding the imprint of life's smooth floors even when they were lying down. I would not let this happen to me. Under certain conditions, the long bones of their feet showed under their skin. The bones rose up long and miserably thin in skeletal rays on the slopes of their feet. This terrible sight they ignored also.

In fact, they were young. Mother was twenty-two when I was born, and Father twenty-nine; both appeared to other adults much younger than they were. They were a handsome couple. I felt it overwhelmingly when they dressed for occasions. I never lost a wondering awe at the transformation of an

everyday, tender, nap-creased mother into an exalted and dazzling beauty who chatted with me as she dressed.

Her blue eyes shone and caught the light, and so did the
platinum waves in her hair and the pearls at her ears and throat.
She was wearing a black dress. The smooth skin on her breast-
bone rent my heart, it was so familiar and beloved; the black silk
bodice and the simple necklace set off its human fineness.
Mother was perhaps a bit vain of her long and perfect legs, but
not too vain for me; despite her excited pleasure, she did not
share my view of her beauty.

"Look at your father," she said. We were all in the dressing
room. I found him in one of the long mirrors, where he waggled
his outthrust chin over the last push of his tie knot. For me he
made his big ears jiggle on his skull. It was a wonder he could
ever hear anything; his head was loose inside him.

Father's enormousness was an everyday, stunning fact; he
was taller than everyone else. He was neither thin nor stout; his
torso was supple, his long legs nimble. Before the dressing-room
mirror he produced an anticipatory soft-shoe, and checked to
see that his cuffs stayed down.

Now they were off. I hoped they knocked them dead; I
hoped their friends knew how witty they were, and how splendid. Their parties at home did not seem very entertaining,
although they laughed loudly and often fetched the one-man
percussion band from the basement, or an old trumpet, or a
snare drum. We children could have shown them how to have a
better time. Kick the Can, for instance, never palled. A private
game called Spider Cow, played by the Spencer children, also
had possibilities: The spider cow hid and flung a wet washcloth
at whoever found it, and erupted from hiding and chased him
running all over the house.

But implicitly and emphatically, my parents and their
friends were not interested. They never ran. They did not
choose to run. It went with being old, apparently, and having
their skin half off.

THERE WAS A BIG SNOW that same year, 1950. Traffic vanished; in the first week, nothing could move. The mailman couldn't get to us; the milkman couldn't come. Our long-legged father walked four miles with my sled to the dairy across Fifth Avenue and carried back milk for the neighborhood.

We had a puppy, who was shorter than the big snow. Our parents tossed it for fun in the yard and it disappeared, only to pop up somewhere else at random like a loon in a lake. After a few days of this game, the happy puppy went crazy and died. It had distemper. While it was crazy it ran around the house crying, upstairs and down.

One night during the second week of the big snow I saw Jo Ann Sheehy skating on the street. I remembered this sight for its beauty and strangeness.

I was aware of the Sheehy family; they were Irish Catholics from a steep part of the neighborhood. One summer when I was walking around the block, I had to walk past skinny Tommy Sheehy and his fat father, who were hunched on their porch doing nothing. Tommy's eleven-year-old sister, Jo Ann, brought them iced tea.

"Go tell your maid she's a nigger," Tommy Sheehy said to me.

What?

He repeated it, and I did it, later, when I got home. That night, Mother came into our room after Amy was asleep. She explained, and made sure I understood. She was steely. Where had my regular mother gone? Did she hate me? She told me a passel of other words that some people use for other people. I was never to use such words, and never to associate with people who did, so long as I lived; I was to apologize to Margaret Butler first thing in the morning; and I was to have no further dealings with the Sheehys.

The night Jo Ann Sheehy skated on the street, it was dark inside our house. We were having dinner in the dining room— my mother, my father, my younger sister Amy, and I. There were lighted ivory candles on the table. The only other light inside was the blue fluorescent lamp over the fish tank, on a sideboard. Inside the tank, neon tetras, black mollies, and angelfish circled, illumined, through the light-shot water. When I turned the fluorescent lamp off, I had learned, the fish still circled their tank in the dark. The still water in the tank's center barely stirred.

Now we sat in the dark dining room, hushed. The big snow outside, the big snow on the roof, silenced our words and the scrape of our forks and our chairs. The dog was gone, the world outside was dangerously cold, and the big snow held the houses down and the people in.

Behind me, tall chilled windows gave out onto the narrow front yard and the street. A motion must have caught my mother's eye; she rose and moved to the windows, and Father and I followed. There we saw the young girl, the transfigured Jo Ann Sheehy, skating alone under the streetlight.

She was turning on ice skates inside the streetlight's yellow cone of light—illumined and silent. She tilted and spun. She wore a short skirt, as if Edgerton Avenue's asphalt had been the ice of an Olympic arena. She wore mittens and a red knitted cap below which her black hair lifted when she turned. Under her skates the street's packed snow shone; it illumined her from below, the cold light striking her under her chin.

I stood at the tall window, barely reaching the sill; the glass fogged before my face, so I had to keep moving or hold my breath. What was she doing out there? Was everything beautiful so bold? I expected a car to run over her at any moment: the open street was a fatal place, where I was forbidden to set foot.

Once, the skater left the light. She winged into the blackness beyond the streetlight and sped down the street; only her white skates showed, and the white snow. She emerged again under another streetlight, in the continuing silence, just at our corner stop sign where the trucks' brakes hissed. Inside that second cone of light she circled backward and leaning. Then she reversed herself in an abrupt half-turn—as if she had skated backward into herself, absorbed her own motion's impetus, and rebounded from it; she shot forward into the dark street and appeared again becalmed in the first streetlight's cone. I exhaled; I looked up. Distant over the street, the night sky was moonless and foreign, a frail, bottomless black, and the cold stars speckled it without moving.

This was for many years the center of the maze, this still, frozen evening inside, the family's watching through glass the Irish girl skate outside on the street. Here were beauty and mystery outside the house, and peace and safety within. I watched passive and uncomprehending, as in summer I watched Lombardy poplar leaves turn their green sides out, and then their silver sides out—watched as if the world were a screen on which played interesting scenes for my pleasure. But there was danger in this radiant sight, in the long glimpse of the lone girl skating, for it was night, and killingly cold. The open street was fatal and forbidden. And the apparently invulnerable girl was Jo Ann Sheehy, Tommy Sheehy's sister, part of the Sheehy family, whose dark ways were a danger and a crime.

"Tell your maid she's a nigger," he had said, and when I said to Margaret, "You're a nigger," I had put myself in danger—I felt at the time, for Mother was so enraged—of being put out, tossed out in the cold, where I would go crazy, and die, like the dog.

That night Jo Ann alone outside in the cold had performed recklessly. My parents did not disapprove; they loved the beauty of it, and the queerness of skating on a street. The next morning I saw from the dining-room windows the street shrunken again and ordinary, tracked by tires, and the streetlights inconspicuous, and Jo Ann Sheehy walking to school in a blue plaid skirt.

WHEN SHE WAS IN HER twenties, my mother's taste ran to modernism. In our living room on Edgerton Avenue we had a free-form blond coffee table, Jean Arp style, shaped something like a kidney and also something like a boomerang. Over a heat register Mother hung a black iron Calder-like mobile. The mobile's disks spun and orbited slowly before a window all winter when the heat was on, and replaced for me the ensorcellizing waving of tree leaves. On the wall above the couch she hung a large print of Gauguin's *Fatata te miti;* those enormous rounded women, with their muscular curving backs, sat before a blue river in a flat and speckled jungle. On an end table she placed the first piece of art she ever bought: a Yoruba wood sculpture, a long-headed abstract woman with pointy breasts and a cold coil of wire around her neck.

Mother must have cut a paradoxical figure in her modernist living room, with her platinum-blond hair, her brisk motions, her slender, urbane frame, her ironic wit (one might even say "lip")—and her wee Scotticisms. "Sit you doon," Mother said cordially to guests. If the room was too bright, she asked one of us to douse the glim. When we were babies, she bade each of us in turn, "Put your wee headie down." If no one could locate Amy when she was avoiding her nap, it was because she'd found herself a hidey-hole. Sometimes after school we discovered in our rooms a wee giftie. If Mother wanted a favor, she asked, heartrendingly, "Would you grant me a boon?"

This was all the more remarkable because Mother was no more Scotch, or Scotch-Irish, than the Pope. She was, if anyone cared to inquire, Pennsylvania Dutch and French. But the Pittsburgh in which we lived—and that Pittsburgh only—was so strongly Scotch-Irish it might have been seventeenth-century Donegal; almost all old Pittsburgh families were Scotch-Irish. Scotticisms fairly flew in the air. And Mother picked up every sort of quaint expression.

She delighted in using queer nouns from the mountains, too. Her family hailed from Somerset, the mountain-county seat near Pittsburgh: Whiskey Rebellion country. They were pretty well educated, but they heard plenty of mountain terms.

"Where's the woolly brush?" "I need a gummy"—that is, a gum band, or rubber band. She keenly enjoyed these archaisms, and whenever she used one, she stopped enthusiastically in midsentence to list the others: "And do you know what a poke is?" We did indeed.

Her speech was an endlessly interesting, swerving path of old punch lines, heartfelt cris de coeur, puns new and old, dramatic true confessions, challenges, witty one-liners, wee Scotticisms, tag lines from Frank Sinatra songs, obsolete mountain nouns, and moral exhortations.

"I'll show him," she'd say. "I'll show him which way the bear went through the buckwheat. It'll be Katy-bar-the-door around here." "He'll be gone," Father would add wistfully, "where the woodbine twineth."

Mother woke Amy and me in the mornings by dashing into our room, wrenching aside the window curtains, cranking open our old leaded windows, shouting mysteriously, "It smells like a French whorehouse in here," and dashing out. When we got downstairs we might find her—that same morning—sitting half asleep, crumpled-of-skin in her soft bathrobe, staring at her foot in its slipper, or even with her eyes closed. If we began to whisper, we soon heard her murmur affectionately if unconvincingly into her bathrobe collar, "I'm awake."

She moved vigorously, laughed easily, spoke rapidly and boldly, and analyzed with restless force. Her moods shifted; her utterances changed key and pitch. She was fond of ending any long explanation with the sudden, puzzling kicker, "And that's why I can't imitate four Hawaiians." She stroked our heads tenderly, called us each a dozen endearing names; she thrilled, apparently, to tales of our adventures, and admired inordinately our drawings and forts. She taught us to curtsy; she taught us to play poker.

Mother's Somerset family were respectable Millers and good-looking, prominent, wild Lamberts. The Lambert women were beautiful; they married rich men. The Lambert men were charmers; they drank hard and came to early ends. They flourished during Prohibition, and set a dashing, doomed tone for the town.

Mother's handsome father was the mayor. He was so well liked that no one in town voted for his opponent. He won a contest by writing the slogan, "When better automobiles are built, Buick will build them." He and a friend journeyed to Detroit to pick up the contest prize. The trip was a famous spree; it lasted a month. He died not long after, at forty-one, when Mother was seven, and left her forever full of longing.

Late at night on Christmas Eve, she carried us each to our high bedroom, and darkened the room, and opened the window, and held us awed in the freezing stillness, saying—and we could hear the edge of tears in her voice—"Do you hear them? Do you hear the bells, the little bells, on Santa's sleigh?" We marveled and drowsed, smelling the piercingly cold night and the sweetness of Mother's warm neck, hearing in her voice so much pent emotion, feeling the familiar strength in the crook of her arms, and looking out over the silent streetlights and the chilled stars above the rooftops of the town. "Very faint, and far away—can you hear them coming?" And we could hear them coming, very faint and far away, the bells on the flying sleigh.

SOME BOYS TAUGHT ME TO play football. This was fine sport. You thought up a new strategy for every play and whispered it to the others. You went out for a pass, fooling everyone. Best, you got to throw yourself mightily at someone's running legs. Either you brought him down or you hit the ground flat out on your chin, with your arms empty before you. It was all or nothing. If you hesitated in fear, you would miss and get hurt: you would take a hard fall while the kid got away, or you would get kicked in the face while the kid got away. But if you flung yourself wholeheartedly at the back of his knees—if you gathered and joined body and soul and pointed them diving fearlessly— then you likely wouldn't get hurt, and you'd stop the ball. Your fate, and your team's score, depended on your concentration and courage. Nothing girls did could compare with it.

Boys welcomed me at baseball, too, for I had, through enthusiastic practice, what was weirdly known as a boy's arm. In winter, in the snow, there was neither baseball nor football, so the boys and I threw snowballs at passing cars. I got in trouble throwing snowballs, and have seldom been happier since.

On one weekday morning after Christmas, six inches of new snow had just fallen. We were standing up to our boot tops in snow on a front yard on trafficked Reynolds Street, waiting for cars. The cars traveled Reynolds Street slowly and evenly; they were targets all but wrapped in red ribbons, cream puffs. We couldn't miss.

I was seven; the boys were eight, nine, and ten. The oldest two Fahey boys were there—Mikey and Peter—polite blond boys who lived near me on Lloyd Street, and who already had four brothers and sisters. My parents approved Mikey and Peter

Fahey. Chickie McBride was there, a tough kid, and Billy Paul and Mackie Kean, too, from across Reynolds, where the boys grew up dark and furious, grew up skinny, knowing, and skilled. We had all drifted from our houses that morning looking for action, and had found it here on Reynolds Street.

It was cloudy but cold. The cars' tires laid behind them on the snowy street a complex trail of beige chunks like crenellated castle walls. I had stepped on some earlier; they squeaked. We could have wished for more traffic. When a car came, we all popped it one. In the intervals between cars we reverted to the natural solitude of children.

I started making an iceball—a perfect iceball, from perfectly white snow, perfectly spherical, and squeezed perfectly translucent so no snow remained all the way through. (The Fahey boys and I considered it unfair actually to throw an iceball at somebody, but it had been known to happen.)

I had just embarked on the iceball project when we heard tire chains come clanking from afar. A black Buick was moving toward us down the street. We all spread out, banged together some regular snowballs, took aim, and, when the Buick drew nigh, fired.

A soft snowball hit the driver's windshield right before the driver's face. It made a smashed star with a hump in the middle.

Often, of course, we hit our target, but this time, the only time in all of life, the car pulled over and stopped. Its wide black door opened; a man got out of it, running. He didn't even close the car door.

He ran after us, and we ran away from him, up the snowy Reynolds sidewalk. At the corner, I looked back; incredibly, he was still after us. He was in city clothes: a suit and tie, street shoes. Any normal adult would have quit, having sprung us into flight and made his point. This man was gaining on us. He was a thin man, all action. All of a sudden, we were running for our lives.

Wordless, we split up. We were on our turf; we could lose ourselves in the neighborhood backyards, everyone for himself. I paused and considered. Everyone had vanished except Mikey Fahey, who was just rounding the corner of a yellow brick house. Poor Mikey—I trailed him. The driver of the Buick sensibly picked the two of us to follow. The man apparently had all day.

He chased Mikey and me around the yellow house and up a backyard path we knew by heart: under a low tree, up a bank, through a hedge, down some snowy steps, and across the grocery store's delivery driveway. We smashed through a gap in another hedge, entered a scruffy backyard, and ran around its back porch and tight between houses to Edgerton Avenue; we ran across Edgerton to an alley and up our own sliding woodpile to the Halls' front yard; he kept coming. We ran up Lloyd Street and wound through mazy backyards toward the steep hilltop at Willard and Lang.

He chased us silently, block after block. He chased us silently over picket fences, through thorny hedges, between houses, around garbage cans, and across streets. Every time I glanced back, choking for breath, I expected he would have quit. He must have been as breathless as we were. His jacket strained over his body. It was an immense discovery, pounding into my hot head with every sliding, joyous step, that this ordinary adult evidently knew what I thought only children who trained at football knew: that you have to fling yourself at what you're doing, you have to point yourself, forget yourself, aim, dive.

Mikey and I had nowhere to go, in our own neighborhood or out of it, but away from this man who was chasing us. He impelled us forward; we compelled him to follow our route. The air was cold; every breath tore my throat. We kept running, block after block; we kept improvising, backyard after backyard, running a frantic course and choosing it simultaneously, failing always to find small places or hard places to slow him down, and discovering always, exhilarated, dismayed, that only bare speed could save us—for he would never give up, this man—and we were losing speed.

He chased us through the backyard labyrinths of ten blocks before he caught us by our jackets. He caught us and we all stopped.

We three stood staggering, half blinded, coughing, in an obscure hilltop backyard: a man in his twenties, a boy, a girl. He had released our jackets, our pursuer, our captor, our hero: he knew we weren't going anywhere. We all played by the rules. Mikey and I unzipped our jackets. I pulled off my sopping mittens. Our tracks multiplied in the backyard's new snow. We had been breaking new snow all morning. We didn't look at each other. I was cherishing my excitement. The man's lower pant legs were wet; his cuffs were full of snow, and there was a prow of snow beneath them on his shoes and socks. Some trees bordered the little flat backyard, some messy winter trees. There was no one around: a clearing in a grove, and we the only players.

It was a long time before he could speak. I had some difficulty at first recalling why we were there. My lips felt swollen; I couldn't see out of the sides of my eyes; I kept coughing.

"You stupid kids," he began perfunctorily.

We listened perfunctorily indeed, if we listened at all, for the chewing out was redundant, a mere formality, and beside the point. The point was that he had chased us passionately without giving up, and so he had caught us. Now he came down to earth. I wanted the glory to last forever.

But how could the glory have lasted forever? We could have run through every backyard in North America until we got to Panama. But when he trapped us at the lip of the Panama Canal, what precisely could he have done to prolong the drama of the chase and cap its glory? I brooded about this for the next few years. He could only have fried Mikey Fahey and me in boiling oil, say, or dismembered us piecemeal, or staked us to anthills. None of which I really wanted, and none of which any adult was likely to do, even in the spirit of fun. He could only chew us out there in the Panamanian jungle, after months or years of exalting pursuit. He could only begin, "You stupid kids," and continue in his ordinary Pittsburgh accent with his normal righteous anger and the usual common sense.

If in that snowy backyard the driver of the black Buick had cut off our heads, Mikey's and mine, I would have died happy, for nothing has required so much of me since as being chased all over Pittsburgh in the middle of winter—running terrified, exhausted—by this sainted, skinny, furious redheaded man who wished to have a word with us. I don't know how he found his way back to his car.

OUR PARENTS WOULD SOONER HAVE left us out of Christmas than leave us out of a joke. They explained a joke to us while they were still laughing at it; they tore a still-kicking joke apart, so we could see how it worked. When we got the first Tom Lehrer album in 1954, Mother went through the album with me, cut by cut, explaining. B.V.D.s are men's underwear. Radiation makes you sterile, and lead protects from radiation, so the joke is . . .

Our father kept in his breast pocket a little black notebook. There he noted jokes he wanted to remember. Remembering jokes was a moral obligation. People who said, "I can never remember jokes," were like people who said, obliviously, "I can never remember names," or "I don't bathe."

"No one tells jokes like your father," Mother said. Telling a good joke well—successfully, perfectly—was the highest art. It was an art because it was up to you: if you did not get the laugh, you had told it wrong. Work on it, and do better next time. It would have been reprehensible to blame the joke, or, worse, the audience.

As we children got older, our parents discussed with us every technical, theoretical, and moral aspect of the art. We tinkered with a joke's narrative structure: "Maybe you should begin with the Indians." We polished the wording. There is a Julia Randall story, set in Baltimore, which we smoothed together for years. How does the lady word the question? Does she say, "How are you called?" No, that is needlessly awkward. She just says, "What's your name?" And he says, "Folks generally call me Bominitious." No, he can just say, "They call me Bominitious."

We analyzed many kinds of pacing. We admired with Father the leisurely meanders of the shaggy-dog story. "A young couple

161

moved to the Swiss Alps," one story of his began, "with their grand piano"; it ended, to a blizzard of thrown napkins, ". . . Oppernockity tunes but once." "Frog goes into a bank," another story began, to my enduring pleasure. The joke was not great, but with what a sweet light splash you could launch it! "Frog goes into a bank," you said, and your canoe had slipped delicately and surely into the water, into Lake Champlain with painted Indians behind every tree, and there was no turning back.

Father was also very fond of stories set in bars that starred zoo animals or insects. These creatures apparently came into bars all over America, either accompanied or alone, and sat down to face incredulous, sarcastic bartenders. (It was a wonder the bartenders were always so surprised to see talking dogs or drinking monkeys or performing ants, so surprised year after year, when clearly this sort of thing was the very essence of bar life.) In the years he had been loose, swinging aloft in the airy interval between college and marriage, Father had frequented bars in New York, listening to jazz. Bars had no place whatever in the small Pittsburgh world he had grown up in, and lived in now. Bars were so far from our experience that I had assumed, in my detective work, that their customers were ipso facto crooks. Father's bar jokes—"and there were the regulars, all sitting around"—gave him the raffish air of a man who was at home anywhere. (How poignant were his "you know"s directed at me: you know how bartenders are; you know how the regulars would all be sitting around. For either I, a nine-year-old girl, knew what he was talking about, then or ever, or nobody did. Only because I read a lot, I often knew.)

Our mother favored a staccato, stand-up style; if our father could perorate, she could condense. Fellow goes to a psychiatrist. "You're crazy." "I want a second opinion!" "You're ugly." "How do you get an elephant out of the theater? You can't; it's in his blood."

What else in life so required, and so rewarded, such care?

"Tell the girls the one about the four-by-twos, Frank."

"Let's see. Let's see."

"Fellow goes into a lumberyard . . . "

"Yes, but it's tricky. It's a matter of point of view." And Father would leave the dining room, rubbing his face in concentration, or as if he were smearing on greasepaint, and return when he was ready.

"Ready with the four-by-twos?" Mother said.

Our father hung his hands in his pockets and regarded the far ceiling with fond reminiscence.

"Fellow comes into a lumberyard," he began.

"Says to the guy, 'I need some four-by-twos.' 'You mean two-by-fours?' 'Just a minute. I'll find out.' He walks out to the parking lot, where his buddies are waiting in the car. They roll down the car window. He confers with them awhile and comes back across the parking lot and says to the lumberyard guy, 'Yes. I mean two-by-fours.'

"Lumberyard guy says, 'How long do you want them?' 'Just a minute,' fellow says, 'I'll find out.' He goes out across the parking lot and confers with the people in the car and comes back across the parking lot to the lumberyard and says to the guy, 'A long time. We're building a house.'"

After any performance Father rubbed the top of his face with both hands, as if it had all been a dream. He sat back down at the dining-room table, laughing and shaking his head. "And when you tell a joke," Mother said to Amy and me, "laugh. It's mean not to."

We were brought up on the classics. Our parents told us all the great old American jokes, practically by number. They collaborated on, and for our benefit specialized in, the painstaking paleontological reconstruction of vanished jokes from extant tag lines. They could vivify old *New Yorker* cartoons, source of many tag lines. The lines themselves—"Back to the old drawing board," and "I say it's spinach and I say the hell with it," and "A simple yes or no will suffice"—were no longer funny; they were instead something better, they were fixtures in the language. The tag lines of old jokes were the most powerful expressions we learned at our parents' knees. A few words suggested a complete story and a wealth of feelings. Learning our culture backward, Amy and Molly and I heard only later about *The Divine*

Comedy and the Sistine Chapel ceiling, and still later about the Greek and Roman myths, which held no residue of feeling for us at all—certainly not the vibrant suggestiveness of old American jokes and cartoons.

Our parents reserved a few select jokes, such as "Archibald à Soulbroke," like vintage wines for extraordinary occasions. We heard about or witnessed those rare moments—maybe three or four in a lifetime—when circumstances combined to float our father to the top of the world, from which precarious eminence he would consent to fling himself into "Archibald à Soulbroke."

Telling "Archibald à Soulbroke" was for Father an exhilarating ordeal, like walking a tightrope over Niagara Falls. It was a long, absurdly funny, excruciatingly tricky tour de force he had to tell fast, and it required beat-perfect concentration. He had to go off alone and rouse himself to an exalted, superhuman pitch in order to pace the hot coals of its dazzling verbal surface. Often enough he returned from his prayers to a crowd whose moment had passed. We knew that when we were grown, the heavy, honorable mantle of this heart-pounding joke would fall on us.

There was another very complicated joke, also in a select category, which required a long weekend with tolerant friends.

You had to tell a joke that was not funny. It was a long, pointless story about a construction job that ended with someone's throwing away a brick. There was nothing funny about it at all, and when your friends did not laugh, you had to pretend you'd muffed it. (Your husband in the crowd could shill for you: "'Tain't funny, Pam. You told it all wrong.")

A few days later, if you could contrive another occasion for joke telling, and if your friends still permitted you to speak, you set forth on another joke, this one an old nineteenth-century chestnut about angry passengers on a train. The lady plucks the lighted, smelly cigar from the man's mouth and flings it from the moving train's window. The man seizes the little black poodle from her lap and hurls the poor dog from the same window. When at last the passengers draw unspeaking into the station, what do they see coming down the platform but the black poodle, and guess what it has in its mouth? "The cigar," say your friends, bored sick and vowing never to spend another weekend with you. "No," you say, triumphant, "the brick." This was Mother's kind of joke. Its very riskiness excited her. It wasn't funny, but it was interesting to set up, and it elicited from her friends a grudging admiration.

How long, I wondered, could you stretch this out? How boldly could you push an audience—not, in Mother's terms, to "slay them" but to please them in some grand way? How could you convince the listeners that you knew what you were doing, that the payoff would come? Or conversely, how long could you lead them to think you were stupid, a dumb blonde, to enhance their surprise at the punch line and heighten their pleasure in the good story you had controlled all along? Alone, energetic and trying to fall asleep, or walking the residential streets long distances every day, I pondered these things.

Our parents were both sympathetic to what professional comedians call flop sweat. Boldness was all at our house, and of course you would lose some. Anyone could be misled by poor judgment into telling a "woulda hadda been there." Telling a funny story was harder than telling a joke; it was trying out, as a tidy unit, some raveling shred of the day's fabric. You learned to gauge what sorts of thing would "tell." You learned that some people, notably your parents, could rescue some things by careful narration from the category "woulda hadda been there" to the category "it tells."

At the heart of originating a funny story was recognizing it as it floated by. You scooped the potentially solid tale from the flux of history. Once I overheard my parents arguing over a thirty-year-old story's credit line. "It was my mother who said that," Mother said. "Yes, but"—Father was downright smug—"I was the one who noticed she said that."

The sight gag was a noble form, and the running gag was a noble form. In combination they produced the top of the line, the running sight gag, like the sincere and deadpan Nairobi Trio interludes on Ernie Kovacs. How splendid it was when my parents could get a running sight gag going. We heard about these legendary occasions with a thrill of family pride, as other children hear about their progenitors' war exploits.

The sight gag could blur with the practical joke—not a noble form but a friendly one, which helps the years pass. My parents favored practical jokes of the sort you set up and then retire from, much as one writes books, possibly because imagining people's reactions beats witnessing them. They procured a living hen and "hypnotized" it by setting it on the sink before the bathroom mirror in a friend's cottage by the New Jersey shore. They spent weeks constructing a ten-foot sea monster—from truck inner tubes, cement blocks, broomsticks, lumber, pillows—and set it afloat in a friend's pond. On Sanibel Island, Florida, they baffled the shell collectors each Saint Patrick's Day by boiling a bucketful of fine shells in green dye and strewing the green shells up and down the beach before dawn. I woke one Christmas morning to find in my stocking, hung from the mantel with care, a leg. Mother had charmed a department store display manager into lending her one.

When I visited my friends, I was well advised to rise when their parents entered the room. When my friends visited me, they were well advised to duck.

Central in the orders of merit, and the very bread and butter of everyday life, was the crack. Our mother excelled at the crack. We learned early to feed her lines just to watch her speed to the draw. If someone else fired a crack simultaneously, we compared their concision and pointedness and declared a winner.

Feeding our mother lines, we were training as straight men. The straight man's was an honorable calling, a bit like that of the rodeo clown: despised by the ignorant masses, perhaps, but revered among experts who understood the skills required and the risks run. We children mastered the deliberate misunderstanding, the planted pun, the Gracie Allen know-nothing remark, which can make of any interlocutor an instant hero.

How very gracious is the straight man!—or, in this case, the straight girl. She spreads before her friend a gift-wrapped, beribboned gag line he can claim for his own, if only he will pick it up instead of pausing to contemplate what a nitwit he's talking to.

WE HAD MOVED WHEN I was eight. We moved from Edgerton Avenue to Richland Lane, a hushed dead-end street on the far side of Frick Park. We expanded into a brick house on two lots. There was a bright sunporch under buckeye trees; there was a golden sandstone wall with fireplace and bench that Mother designed, which ran the length of the living room.

It was into this comfortable house that the last of us sisters, Molly, was born, two years later. It was from this house that Father would leave to go down the river to New Orleans, and to this house that he would return early, from the river at Louisville. Here Mother told the contractor where she wanted kitchen walls knocked out. Here on the sunporch Amy tended her many potentially well-dressed dolls, all of whom were, unfortunately, always sick in bed. Here I began a life of reading books, and drawing, and playing at the sciences. Here also I began to wake in earnest, and shed superstition, and plan my days.

Every August when Amy and I returned from our summer at Lake Erie with our grandmother, we saw that workmen had altered the house in our absence—the dining room seemed bigger, the kitchen was lighter—but we couldn't recall how it had been. I thought Mother was a genius for thinking up these improvements, for the house always seemed fine to me, yet it got better and better.

This August, the summer I was ten, we returned from the Lake and found our shared room uncannily tidy and stilled, dark, while summer, the summer in which we had been immersed, played outside the closed windows like a movie. So it always was, those first few minutes in an emptied room. They made you self-conscious; you felt yourself living your life. As soon as you unzipped your suitcase and opened the window, you broke the spell; you plunged again into the rush and weather.

While we were gone, Molly had learned to crawl. She pulled herself up and stood singing in her playpen on the flat part of the front lawn; the buckeye boughs stirred far overhead, and waved over her round arms their speckled lights.

Usually when it was hot the family swam at the distant country-club pool. Now that we were back from the Lake, all that resumed—a nasty comedown after the Lake, to whose neighborhood beach I had gone alone, and where we were all kids among kids who owned the beach and our days. There, at the Lake, if you wanted to leave, you simply kicked the bike's kickstand and sprang into the seat and away, in one skilled gesture like cowboys' mounting horses, rode away on the innocent Ohio roads under old, still trees. At the country club, you often wanted to leave as soon as you had come, but there was no leaving to be had. The country-club pool drew a society as complex and constraining, if not so entertaining, as any European capital's drawing room did. You forgot an old woman's name at some peril to your entire family. What if you actually, physically, ran into her? Knocked her off her pins? It was no place for children.

One country-club morning this August, I saw a red blotch moving in a dense hedge by the club's baby pool. I crept up on the red blotch in my cold bathing suit and discovered that it was a rose-breasted grosbeak. I had never seen one. This living, wild bird, which could fetch up anyplace it pleased, had inexplicably touched down at our country club. It scratched around in a hedge between the baby pool and the sixth hole. The dumb cluck, why a country club?

Mother said Father was going down the river in his boat pretty soon. It sounded like a swell idea.

One windy Saturday morning, after the Lake and before the new private school started, I hung around the house. It was too early for action in the neighborhood. To wake up, I read on the sunporch.

The sunporch would wake anybody up; Father had now put

on the record: Sharkey Bonano, "Li'l Liza Jane." He was bop-ping around, snapping his fingers; now he had wandered outside and stood under the big buckeye trees. I could see him through the sunporch's glass walls. He peered up at a patch of sky as if it could tell him, old salt that he was, right there on Richland Lane, how the weather would be next week on the Ohio River.

I was starting *Kidnapped*. It began in Scotland; David Balfour's father asked that a letter be delivered "when the house is redd up." Some people in Pittsburgh redd up houses, too. The hard-working parents of my earliest neighborhood friends said it: You kids redd up this room. It meant clean up, or ready up. I never expected to find "redd up" in so grand a thing as a book. Appar-ently it was Scots. I hadn't heard the phrase since we moved.

I rode back to Edgerton Avenue from time to time after we moved—to look around, and to fix in my mind the route back: past the lawn bowlers in Frick Park, past the football field, and beyond the old elementary school yard, where a big older boy had said to me, "Why, you're a regular Ralph Kiner." Touring that old neighborhood, I saw the Saint Bede's nuns. I sped past them, careless, on my bike.

"Redd up," David Balfour's father said in *Kidnapped*. I was reading on the sunporch, on the bright couch. "Oh, Li'l Liza!" said the music on the record. "Li'l Liza Jane." Next week Father was going down the river to New Orleans. Maybe they'd let him sit in a set on the drums; maybe Zutty Singleton would be there and holler out to him—"Hey, Frank!"

The wind rattled the windowed sunporch walls beside me. I could see, without getting up, some green leaves blowing down from the buckeye branches overhead. Everything in the room was bright, even the bookshelves, even Amy's melancholy dolls. The blue shadows of fast clouds ran over the far walls and floor. Father snapped his fingers and wandered, tall and loose-limbed, over the house.

I was ten years old now, up into the double numbers, where I would likely remain till I died. I am awake now forever, I thought suddenly; I have converged with myself in the present. My hands were icy from holding *Kidnapped* up; I always read lying down. I felt time in full stream, and I felt consciousness in full stream joining it, like the rivers.

WHILE FATHER WAS MOTORING DOWN the river, my reading was giving me a turn.

At a neighbor boy's house, I ran into Kimon Nicolaides' *The Natural Way to Draw.* This was a manual for students who couldn't get to Nicolaides' own classes at New York's Art Students League. I was amazed that there were books about things one actually did. I had been drawing in earnest, but at random, for two years. Like all children, when I drew I tried to reproduce schema. The idea of drawing from life had astounded me two years previously, but I had gradually let it slip, and my drawing, such as it was, had sunk back into facile sloth. Now this book would ignite my fervor for conscious drawing, and bind my attention to both the vigor and the detail of the actual world.

For the rest of August, and all fall, this urgent, hortatory book ran my life. I tried to follow its schedules: every day, sixty-five gesture drawings, fifteen memory drawings, an hour-long contour drawing, and "The Sustained Study in Crayon, Clothed" or "The Sustained Study in Crayon, Nude."

While Father was gone, I outfitted an attic bedroom as a studio, and moved in. Every summer or weekend morning at eight o'clock I taped that day's drawing schedule to a wall. Since there was no model, nude or clothed, I drew my baseball mitt.

I drew my baseball mitt's gesture—its tense repose, its expectancy, which ran up its hollows like a hand. I drew its contours—its flat fingertips strung on square rawhide thongs. I drew its billion grades of light and dark in detail, so the glove weighed vivid and complex on the page, and the trapezoids small as dust motes in the leather fingers cast shadows, and the pale palm leather was smooth as a belly and thick. "Draw anything," said the book. "Learning to draw is really a matter of learning to see," said the book. "Imagine that your pencil point is touching the model instead of the paper." "All the student need concern himself with is reality."

With my pencil point I crawled over the mitt's topology. I slithered over each dip and rise; I checked my bearings, admired the enormous view, and recorded it like Meriwether Lewis mapping the Rockies.

One thing struck me as odd and interesting. A gesture drawing took forty-five seconds; a Sustained Study took all morning. From any still-life arrangement or model's pose, the artist could produce either a short study or a long one. Evidently, a given object took no particular amount of time to draw; instead the artist took the time, or didn't take it, at pleasure. Similarly, things themselves possessed no fixed and intrinsic amount of interest; instead things were interesting as long as you had attention to give them. How long does it take to draw a baseball mitt? As much time as you care to give it. Not an infinite amount of time, but more time than you first imagined. For many days, so long as you want to keep drawing that mitt, and studying that mitt, there will always be a new and finer layer of distinctions to draw out and lay in. Your attention discovers— seems thereby to produce—an array of interesting features in any object, like a lamp.

By noon, all this drawing would have gone to my head. I slipped into the mitt, quit the attic, quit the house, and headed up the street, looking for a ball game.

My friend had sought permission from his father for me to borrow *The Natural Way to Draw;* it was his book. Grown men and growing children rarely mingled then. I had lived two doors away from this family for several years, and had never clapped eyes on my good friend's father; still, I now regarded him as a man after my own heart. Had he another book about drawing? He had; he owned a book about pencil drawing. This book began well enough, with the drawing of trees. Then it devoted a chapter to the schematic representation of shrubbery. At last it dwindled into its true subject, the drawing of buildings.

My friend's father was an architect. All his other books were about buildings. He had been a boy who liked to draw, according to my friend, so he became an architect. Children who drew, I learned, became architects; I had thought they became painters. My friend explained that it was not proper to become a painter; it couldn't be done. I resigned myself to architecture school and a long life of drawing buildings. It was a pity, for I disliked buildings, considering them only a stiffer and more ample form of clothing, and no more important.

I began reading books, reading books to delirium. I began by vanishing from the known world into the passive abyss of reading, but soon found myself engaged with surprising vigor because the things in the books, or even the things surrounding the books, roused me from my stupor. From the nearest library I learned every sort of surprising thing—some of it, though not much of it, from the books themselves.

The Homewood branch of Pittsburgh's Carnegie Library system was in a Negro section of town—Homewood. This branch was our nearest library; Mother drove me to it every two weeks for many years, until I could drive myself. I only very rarely saw other white people there.

I understood that our maid, Margaret Butler, had friends in Homewood. I never saw her there, but I did see Henry Watson, who drove for my grandmother.

I was getting out of Mother's car in front of the library, when Henry appeared on the sidewalk; he was walking with some other old men. I had never before seen him at large; it must have been his day off. He had gold-rimmed glasses, a gold front tooth, and a frank, open expression. It would embarrass him, I thought, if I said hello to him in front of his friends. I was wrong. He spied me, picked me up—books and all—swung me as he always did, and introduced Mother and me to his friends. Later, as we were climbing the long stone steps to the library's door, Mother said, "That's what I mean by good manners."

The Homewood Library had graven across its enormous stone facade: FREE TO THE PEOPLE. In the evenings, neighborhood people—the men and women of Homewood—browsed in the library, and brought their children. By day, the two vaulted rooms, the adults' and children's sections, were almost empty. The kind Homewood librarians, after a trial period, had given me a card to the adult section. This was an enormous silent room with marble floors. Nonfiction was on the left.

Beside the farthest wall, and under leaded windows set ten feet from the floor, so that no human being could ever see anything from them—next to the wall, and at the farthest remove from the idle librarians at their curved wooden counter, and from the oak bench where my mother waited in her camel's-hair coat, chatting with the librarians or reading—stood the last and darkest and most obscure of the tall nonfiction stacks: NEGRO HISTORY and NATURAL HISTORY. It was in Natural History, in the cool darkness of a bottom shelf, that I found *The Field Book of Ponds and Streams.*

The Field Book of Ponds and Streams was a small, blue-bound book printed in fine type on thin paper, like *The Book of Common Prayer.* Its third chapter explained how to make sweep nets, plankton nets, glass-bottomed buckets, and killing jars. It specified how to mount slides, how to label insects on their pins, and how to set up a freshwater aquarium.

One was to go into "the field" wearing hip boots and perhaps a head net for mosquitoes. One carried in a "rucksack" half a dozen corked test tubes, a smattering of screw-top baby-food jars, a white enamel tray, assorted pipettes and eyedroppers, an artillery of cheesecloth nets, a notebook, a hand lens, perhaps a map, and *The Field Book of Ponds and Streams.* This field—unlike the fields I had seen, such as the field where Walter Milligan played football—was evidently very well watered, for there one could find, and distinguish among, daphniae, planaria, water pennies, stonefly larvae, dragonfly nymphs, salamander larvae, tadpoles, snakes, and turtles, all of which one could carry home.

That anyone had lived the fine life described in Chapter 3 astonished me. Although the title page indicated quite plainly that one Ann Haven Morgan had written *The Field Book of Ponds and Streams,* I nevertheless imagined, perhaps from the authority and freedom of it, that its author was a man. It would be good to write him and assure him that someone had found his book, in the dark near the marble floor at the Homewood Library. I would, in the same letter or in a subsequent one, ask him a question outside the scope of his book, which was where I personally might find a pond, or a stream. But I did not know how to address such a letter, of course, or how to learn if he was still alive.

I was afraid, too, that my letter would disappoint him by betraying my ignorance, which was just beginning to attract my own notice. What, for example, was this noisome-sounding substance called cheesecloth, and what do scientists do with it? What, when you really got down to it, was enamel? If candy could, notoriously, "eat through enamel," why would anyone make trays out of it? Where—short of robbing a museum— might a fifth-grade student at the Ellis School on Fifth Avenue obtain such a legendary item as a wooden bucket?

The Field Book of Ponds and Streams was a shocker from beginning to end. The greatest shock came at the end.

When you checked out a book from the Homewood Library, the librarian wrote your number on the book's card and stamped the due date on a sheet glued to the book's last page. When I checked out *The Field Book of Ponds and Streams* for the second time, I noticed the book's card. It was almost full. There were numbers on both sides. My hearty author and I were not alone in the world, after all. With us, and sharing our enthusiasm for dragonfly larvae and single-celled plants, were, apparently, many Negro adults.

Who were these people? Had they, in Pittsburgh's Homewood section, found ponds? Had they found streams? At home, I read the book again; I studied the drawings; I reread Chapter 3; then I settled in to study the due-date slip. People read this book in every season. Seven or eight people were reading this book every year, even during the war.

Every year, I read again *The Field Book of Ponds and Streams*. Often, when I was in the library, I simply visited it. I sat on the marble floor and studied the book's card. There we all were. There was my number. There was the number of someone else who had checked it out more than once. Might I contact this person and cheer him up? For I assumed that, like me, he had found pickings pretty slim in Pittsburgh.

The people of Homewood, some of whom lived in visible poverty, on crowded streets among burned-out houses—they dreamed of ponds and streams. They were saving to buy microscopes. In their bedrooms they fashioned plankton nets. But their hopes were even more vain than mine, for I was a child, and anything might happen; they were adults, living in Homewood. There was neither pond nor stream on the streetcar routes. The Homewood residents whom I knew had little money and little free time. The marble floor was beginning to chill me. It was not fair.

I had been driven into nonfiction against my wishes. I wanted to read fiction, but I had learned to be cautious about it.

"When you open a book," the sentimental library posters said, "anything can happen." This was so. A book of fiction was a bomb. It was a land mine you wanted to go off. You wanted it to blow your whole day. Unfortunately, hundreds of thousands of books were duds. They had been rusting out of everyone's way for so long that they no longer worked. There was no way to distinguish the duds from the live mines except to throw yourself at them headlong, one by one.

The suggestions of adults were uncertain and incoherent. They gave you Nancy Drew with one hand and *Little Women* with the other. They mixed good and bad books together because they could not distinguish between them. Any book that contained children, or short adults, or animals, was felt to be a children's book. So also was any book about the sea—as though danger or even fresh air were a child's prerogative—or any book by Charles Dickens or Mark Twain. Virtually all British books, actually, were children's books; no one understood children like the British. Suited to female children were love stories set in any century but this one. Consequently one had read, exasperated often to fury, *Pickwick Papers*, *Désirée*, *Wuthering Heights*, *Lad, a Dog*, *Gulliver's Travels*, *Gone with the Wind*, *Robinson Crusoe*, Nordhoff and Hall's *Bounty* trilogy, *Moby-*

Dick, The Five Little Peppers, Innocents Abroad, Lord Jim, Old Yeller.
The fiction stacks at the Homewood Library, their volumes alphabetized by author, baffled me. How could I learn to choose a novel? That I could not easily reach the top two shelves helped limit choices a little. Still, on the lower shelves I saw too many books: Mary Johnson, *Sweet Rocket;* Samuel Johnson, *Rasselas;* James Jones, *From Here to Eternity.* I checked out the last because I had heard of it; it was good. I decided to check out books I had heard of. I had heard of *The Mill on the Floss.* I read it, and it was good. On its binding was printed a figure, a man dancing or running; I had noticed this figure before. Like so many children before and after me, I learned to seek out this logo, the Modern Library colophon.

The going was always rocky. I couldn't count on Modern Library the way I could count on, say, *Mad* magazine, which never failed to slay me. *Native Son* was good, *Walden* was pretty good, *The Interpretation of Dreams* was okay, and *The Education of Henry Adams* was awful. *Ulysses,* a very famous book, was also awful. *Confessions* by Augustine, whose title promised so much, was a bust. *Confessions* by Jean-Jacques Rousseau was much better, though it fell apart halfway through.

In fact, it was a plain truth that most books fell apart halfway through. They fell apart as their protagonists quit, without any apparent reluctance, like idiots diving voluntarily into buckets, the most interesting part of their lives, and entered upon decades of unrelieved tedium. I was forewarned, and would not so bobble my adult life; when things got dull, I would go to sea.

Jude the Obscure was the type case. It started out so well. Halfway through, its author forgot how to write. After Jude got married, his life was over, but the book went on for hundreds of pages while he stewed in his own juices. The same thing happened in *The Little Shepherd of Kingdom Come,* which Mother brought me from a fair. It was simply a hazard of reading. Only a heartsick loyalty to the protagonists of the early chapters, to the eager children they had been, kept me reading chronological narratives to their bitter ends. Perhaps later, when I had become an architect, I would enjoy the latter halves of books more.

*   *   *

This was the most private and obscure part of life, this Homewood Library: a vaulted marble edifice in a decent Negro neighborhood, the silent stacks of which I plundered in deep concentration for many years. There seemed then, happily, to be an infinitude of books.

I no more expected anyone else on earth to have read a book I had read than I expected someone else to have twirled the same blade of grass. I would never meet those Homewood people who were borrowing *The Field Book of Ponds and Streams;* the people who read my favorite books were invisible or in hiding, underground. Father occasionally raised his big eyebrows at the title of some volume I was hurrying off with, quite as if he knew what it contained—but I thought he must know of it by hearsay, for none of it seemed to make much difference to him. Books swept me away, one after the other, this way and that; I made endless vows according to their lights, for I believed them.

THE PIRATES WERE IN THE cellar again. They lived in the cellar, like trolls. They hadn't won a pennant since 1927. Nobody could even remember when they won ball games, the bums. They had some hitters, but no pitchers.

On the yellow back wall of our Richland Lane garage, I drew a target in red crayon. The target was a batter's strike zone. The old garage was dark inside; I turned on the bare bulb. Then I walked that famously lonely walk out to the mound, our graveled driveway, and pitched.

I squinted at the strike zone, ignoring the jeers of the batter—oddly, Ralph Kiner. I received no impressions save those inside the long aerial corridor that led to the target. I threw a red-and-blue rubber ball, one of those with a central yellow band. I wound up; I drew back. The target held my eyes. The target set me spinning as the sun from a distance winds the helpless spheres. Entranced and drawn, I swung through the moves and woke up with the ball gone. It felt as if I'd gathered my own body, pointed it carefully, and thrown it down a tunnel bored by my eyes.

I pitched in a blind fever of concentration. I pitched, as I did most things, in order to concentrate. Why do elephants drink? To forget. I loved living at my own edge, as an explorer on a ship presses to the ocean's rim; mind and skin were one joined force curved out and alert, prow and telescope. I pitched, as I did most things, in a rapture.

Now here's the pitch. I followed the ball as if it had been my own head, and watched it hit the painted plastered wall. High and outside; ball one. While I stood still stupefied by the effort of the pitch, while I stood agog, unbreathing, mystical, and unaware, here came the daggone rubber ball again, bouncing out of the garage. And I had to hustle up some snappy fielding, or lose the ball in a downhill thicket next door.

The red, blue, and yellow ball came spinning out to the driveway, and sprang awry on the gravel; if I nabbed it, it was apt to bounce out of my mitt. Sometimes I threw the fielded grounder to first—sidearm—back to the crayon target, which had become the first baseman. Fine, but the moronic first baseman spat it back out again at once, out of the dark garage and bouncing crazed on the gravel; I bolted after it, panting. The pace of this game was always out of control.

So I held the ball now, and waited, and breathed, and fixed on the target till it mesmerized me into motion. In there, strike one. Low, ball two.

Four balls, and they had a man on. Three strikeouts, and you had retired the side. Happily, the opposing batters, apparently paralyzed by admiration, never swung at a good pitch. Unfortunately, though, you had to keep facing them; the retired side resurrected immediately from its ashes, fresh and vigorous, while you grew delirious—nutsy, that is, from fielding a bouncing ball every other second and then stilling your heart and blinking the blood from your eyes so you could concentrate on the pitch.

Amy's friend Tibby had an older brother, named Ricky; he was younger than I was, but available. We had no laughing friendship, such as I enjoyed with Pin Ford, but instead a working relationship: we played a two-handed baseball game. Tibby and Ricky's family lived secluded at the high dead end of Richland Lane. Their backyard comprised several kempt and gardened acres. It was here in the sweet mown grass, here between the fruit trees and the rhubarb patch, that we passed long, hot afternoons pitching a baseball. Ricky was a sober, good-looking boy, very dark; his father was a surgeon.

We each pitched nine innings. The other caught, hunkered down, and called each pitch a ball or a strike. That was the essence of it: Catcher called it. Four walks scored a side. Three outs retired a side, and the catcher's side came on to pitch.

This was practically the majors. You had a team to root for, a team that both received pitches and dished them out. You kept score. The pitched ball came back right to you—after a proper, rhythmical interval. You had a real squatting catcher. Best, you had a baseball.

The game required the accuracy I was always working on. It also required honor. If when you were catching you made some iffy calls, you would be sorry when it was your turn to pitch. Ricky and I were, in this primitive sense, honorable. The tag ends of summer—before or after camp, before or after Lake Erie—had thrown us together for this one activity, this chance to do some pitching. We shared a catcher's mitt every inning; we pitched at the catcher's mitt. I threw as always by imagining my whole body hurled into the target; the rest followed naturally. I had one pitch, a fast ball. I couldn't control the curve. When the game was over, we often played another. Then we thanked each other formally, drank some hot water from a garden hose, and parted—like, perhaps, boys.

On Tuesday summer evenings I rode my bike a mile down Braddock Avenue to a park where I watched Little League teams play ball. Little League teams did not accept girls, a ruling I looked into for several years in succession. I parked my bike and hung outside the chain-link fence and watched and rooted and got mad and hollered, "Idiot, catch the ball!" "Play's at first!" Maybe some coach would say, "Okay, sweetheart, if you know it all, you go in there." I thought of disguising myself. None of this was funny. I simply wanted to play the game earnestly, on a diamond, until it was over, with eighteen players who knew what they were doing, and an umpire. My parents were sympathetic, if amused, and not eager to make an issue of it.

At school we played softball. No bunting, no stealing. I had settled on second base, a spot Bill Mazeroski would later sanctify: lots of action, lots of talk, and especially a chance to turn the double play. Dumb softball: so much better than no ball at all, that I reluctantly grew to love it. As I got older, and the prospect of having anything to do with young Ricky up the street became out of the question, I had to remind myself, with all loyalty and nostalgia, how a baseball, a real baseball, felt.

A baseball weighted your hand just so, and fit it. Its red stitches, its good leather and hardness like skin over bone, seemed to call forth a skill both easy and precise. On the catch—the grounder, the fly, the line drive—you could snag a baseball in your mitt, where it stayed, snap, like a mouse locked in its trap, not like some pumpkin of a softball you merely halted, with a terrible sound like a splat. You could curl your fingers around a baseball, and throw it in a straight line. When you hit it with a bat it cracked—and your heart cracked, too, at the sound. It took a grass stain nicely, stayed round, smelled good, and lived lashed in your mitt all winter, hibernating.

There was no call for overhand pitches in softball; all my training was useless. I was playing with twenty-five girls, some of whom did not, on the face of it, care overly about the game at hand. I waited out by second and hoped for a play to the plate.

A TORNADO HIT OUR NEIGHBORHOOD one morning. Our neighborhood was not only leafy Richland Lane and its hushed side streets, but also Penn Avenue, from which Richland Lane loftily arose. Old Penn Avenue was a messy, major thoroughfare, still cobblestoned in the middle lanes, and full of stoplights and jammed traffic. There were drugstores there, old apartment buildings, and some old mansions. Penn Avenue was the city—tangled and muscular, a broad and snarled fist. The tornado broke all the windows in the envelope factory on Penn Avenue and ripped down mature oaks and maples on Richland Lane and its side streets—trees about which everyone would make, in my view, an unconscionable fuss, not least perhaps because they would lie across the streets for a week.

After the tornado passed I roamed around and found a broken power line. It banged violently by the Penn Avenue curb; it was shooting sparks into the street. I couldn't bring myself to leave the spot.

The power line was loosing a fireball of sparks that melted the asphalt. It was a thick twisted steel cable usually strung overhead along Penn Avenue; it carried power—4,500 kilovolts of it—from Wilkinsburg ("City of Churches") to major sections of Pittsburgh, to Homewood and Brushton, Shadyside, and Squirrel Hill.

It was melting a pit for itself in the street. The live wire's hundred twisted ends spat a thick sheaf of useless yellow sparks that hissed. The sparks were cooking the asphalt gummy; they were burning a hole. I watched the cable relax and sink into its own pit; I watched the yellow sparks pool and crackle around the cable's torn end and splash out of the pit and over the asphalt in a stream toward the curb and my shoes. My bare shins could feel the heat. I smelled tarry melted asphalt and steel so hot it smoked.

"If you touch that," my father said, needlessly, "you're a goner."

I had gone back to the house to get him so he could see this violent sight, this cable all but thrashing like a cobra and shooting a torrent of sparks.

The torn cable lay near the curb, away from traffic. Its loose power dissipated in the air, a random destructiveness. If you touched it, you would turn into Reddy Kilowatt. Your skin would wiggle up in waves like an electrified cat's in a cartoon; your hair would rise stiff from your head; anyone who touched you by mistake would stick to you wavy-skinned and paralyzed. You would be dead but still standing, the power surging through your body in electrical imitation of life. Passersby would have to knock you away from the current with planks.

Father placed a ring of empty Coke bottles around the hissing power line and went back home to call Duquesne Light. I stayed transfixed. Other neighborhood children showed up, looked at the cable shooting sparks, and wandered away to see the great killed trees. I stood and watched the thick billion bolts swarm in the street. The cable was as full as a waterfall, never depleted; it dug itself a pit in which the yellow sparks spilled like water. I stayed at the busy Penn Avenue curb all day, staring, until, late in the afternoon, someone somewhere turned off the juice.

What can we make of the inexpressible joy of children? It is a kind of gratitude, I think—the gratitude of the ten-year-old who wakes to her own energy and the brisk challenge of the world. You thought you knew the place and all its routines, but you see you hadn't known. Whole stacks at the library held books devoted to things you knew nothing about. The boundary of knowledge receded, as you poked about in books, like Lake Erie's rim as you climbed its cliffs. And each area of knowledge disclosed another, and another. Knowledge wasn't a body, or a tree, but instead air, or space, or being—whatever pervaded, whatever never ended and fitted into the smallest cracks and the widest space between stars.

Any way you cut it, colors and shadows flickered from multiple surfaces. Just enough work had already been done on everything—moths, say, or meteorites—to get you started and interested, but not so much there was nothing left to do. Often I wondered: Was it being born just now, in this century, in this country? And I thought: No, any time could have been like this, if you had the time and weren't sick; you could, especially if you were a boy, learn and do. There was joy in concentration, and the world afforded an inexhaustible wealth of projects to concentrate on. There was joy in effort, and the world resisted effort to just the right degree, and yielded to it at last. People cut Mount Rushmore into faces; they chipped here and there for years. People slowed the spread of yellow fever; they sprayed the Isthmus of Panama puddle by puddle. Effort alone I loved. Some days I would have been happy to push a pole around a threshing floor like an ox, for the pleasure of moving the heavy stone and watching my knees rise in turn.

I was running down the Penn Avenue sidewalk, revving up for an act of faith. I was conscious and self-conscious. I knew well that people could not fly—as well as anyone knows it—but I also knew the kicker: that, as the books put it, with faith all things are possible.

Just once I wanted a task that required all the joy I had. Day after day I had noticed that if I waited long enough, my strong unexpressed joy would dwindle and dissipate inside me, over many hours, like a fire subsiding, and I would at last calm down. Just this once I wanted to let it rip. Flying rather famously required the extra energy of belief, and this, too, I had in superabundance.

There were boxy yellow thirties apartment buildings on those Penn Avenue blocks, and the Evergreen Café, and Miss Frick's house set back behind a wrought-iron fence. There were some side yards of big houses, some side yards of little houses, some streetcar stops, and a drugstore from which I had once tried to heist a five-pound box of chocolates, a Whitman's Sampler, confusing "sampler" with "free sample." It was past all this that I ran that late fall afternoon, up old Penn Avenue on the cracking cement sidewalks—past the drugstore and bar, past the old and new apartment buildings and the long dry lawn behind Miss Frick's fence.

I ran the sidewalk full tilt. I waved my arms ever higher and faster; blood balled in my fingertips. I knew I was foolish. I knew I was too old really to believe in this as a child would, out of ignorance; instead I was experimenting as a scientist would, testing both the thing itself and the limits of my own courage in trying it miserably self-conscious in full view of the whole world. You can't test courage cautiously, so I ran hard and waved my arms hard, happy.

Up ahead I saw a business-suited pedestrian. He was coming stiffly toward me down the walk. Who could ever forget this first test, this stranger, this thin young man appalled? I banished the temptation to straighten up and walk right. He flattened himself against a brick wall as I passed flailing—although I had left him plenty of room. He had refused to meet my exultant eye. He looked away, evidently embarrassed. How surprisingly easy it was to ignore him! What I was letting rip, in fact, was my willingness to look foolish, in his eyes and in my own. Having chosen this foolishness, I was a free being. How could the world ever stop me, how could I betray myself, if I was not afraid?

I was flying. My shoulders loosened, my stride opened, my heart banged the base of my throat. I crossed Carnegie and ran up the block waving my arms. I crossed Lexington and ran up the block waving my arms.

A linen-suited woman in her fifties did meet my exultant eye. She looked exultant herself, seeing me from far up the block. Her face was thin and tanned. We converged. Her warm, intelligent glance said she knew what I was doing—not because she herself had been a child but because she herself took a few loose aerial turns around her apartment every night for the hell of it, and by day played along with the rest of the world and took the streetcar. So Teresa of Ávila checked her unseemly joy and hung on to the altar rail to hold herself down. The woman's smiling, deep glance seemed to read my own awareness from my face, so we passed on the sidewalk—a beautifully upright woman walking in her tan linen suit, a kid running and flapping her arms—we passed on the sidewalk with a look of accomplices who share a humor just beyond irony. What's a heart for?

I crossed Homewood and ran up the block. The joy multiplied as I ran—I ran never actually quite leaving the ground—and multiplied still as I felt my stride begin to fumble and my knees begin to quiver and stall. The joy multiplied even as I slowed bumping to a walk. I was all but splitting, all but shooting sparks. Blood coursed free inside my lungs and bones, a light-shot stream like air. I couldn't feel the pavement at all.

I was too aware to do this, and had done it anyway. What could touch me now? For what were the people on Penn Avenue to me, or what was I to myself, really, but a witness to any boldness I could muster, or any cowardice if it came to that, any giving up on heaven for the sake of dignity on earth? I had not seen a great deal accomplished in the name of dignity, ever.

ONE SUNDAY AFTERNOON MOTHER WANDERED through our kitchen, where Father was making a sandwich and listening to the ball game. The Pirates were playing the New York Giants at Forbes Field. In those days, the Giants had a utility infielder named Wayne Terwilliger. Just as Mother passed through, the radio announcer cried—with undue drama—"Terwilliger bunts one!"

"Terwilliger bunts one?" Mother cried back, stopped short. She turned. "Is that English?"

"The player's name is Terwilliger," Father said. "He bunted."

"That's marvelous," Mother said. "'Terwilliger bunts one.' No wonder you listen to baseball. 'Terwilliger bunts one.'"

For the next seven or eight years, Mother made this surprising string of syllables her own. Testing a microphone, she repeated, "Terwilliger bunts one"; testing a pen or a typewriter, she wrote it. If, as happened surprisingly often in the course of various improvised gags, she pretended to whisper something else in my ear, she actually whispered, "Terwilliger bunts one." Whenever someone used a French phrase, or a Latin one, she answered solemnly, "Terwilliger bunts one." If Mother had had, like Andrew Carnegie, the opportunity to cook up a motto for a coat of arms, hers would have read simply and tellingly, "Terwilliger bunts one." (Carnegie's was "Death to Privilege.")

She served us with other words and phrases. On a Florida trip, she repeated tremulously, "That . . . is a royal poinciana." I don't remember the tree; I remember the thrill in her voice. She pronounced it carefully, and spelled it. She also liked to say "portulaca."

The drama of the words "Tamiami Trail" stirred her, we

learned on the same Florida trip. People built Tampa on one coast, and they built Miami on another. Then—the height of visionary ambition and folly—they piled a slow, tremendous road through the terrible Everglades to connect them. To build the road, men stood sunk in muck to their armpits. They fought off cottonmouth moccasins and six-foot alligators. They slept in boats, wet. They blasted muck with dynamite, cut jungle with machetes; they laid logs, dragged drilling machines, hauled dredges, heaped limestone. The road took fourteen years to build up by the shovelful, a Panama Canal in reverse, and cost hundreds of lives from tropical, mosquito-carried diseases. Then, capping it all, some genius thought of the word Tamiami: they called the road from Tampa to Miami, this very road under our spinning wheels, the Tamiami Trail. Anyone could drive over this road without a thought.

Back home, Mother cut clips from reels of talk, as it were, and played them back at leisure. She noticed that many Pittsburghers confuse "leave" and "let." One kind relative brightened our morning by mentioning why she'd brought her son to visit: "He wanted to come with me, so I left him." Mother filled in Amy and me on locutions we missed. "I can't do it on Friday," her pretty sister told a crowded dinner party, "because Friday's the day I lay in the stores."

(All unconsciously, though, we ourselves used some pure Pittsburghisms. We said "tele pole," pronounced "telly pole," for that splintery sidewalk post I loved to climb. We said "slippy"—the sidewalks are "slippy." We said, "That's all the farther I could go." And we said, as Pittsburghers do say, "This glass needs washed," or "The dog needs walked"—a usage our father eschewed; he knew it was not standard English, nor even comprehensible English, but he never let on.)

"Spell 'poinsettia,'" Mother would throw out at me, smiling with pleasure. "Spell 'sherbet.'" The idea was not to make us whizzes, but, quite the contrary, to remind us—and I, especially, needed reminding—that we didn't know it all just yet.

"There's a deer standing in the front hall," she told me one quiet evening in the country.

"Really?"

"No. I just wanted to tell you something once without your saying, 'I know.'"

Supermarkets in the middle 1950s began luring, or bothering, customers by giving out Top Value Stamps or Green Stamps. When, shopping with Mother, we got to the head of the checkout line, the checker, always a young man, asked, "Save stamps?"

"No," Mother replied genially, week after week, "I build model airplanes." I believe she originated this line. It took me years to determine where the joke lay.

Anyone who met her verbal challenges she adored. She had surgery on one of her eyes. On the operating table, just before she conked out, she appealed feelingly to the surgeon, saying, as she had been planning to say for weeks, "Will I be able to play the piano?" "Not on me," the surgeon said. "You won't pull that old one on me."

It was, indeed, an old one. The surgeon was supposed to answer, "Yes, my dear, brave woman, you will be able to play the piano after this operation," to which Mother intended to reply, "Oh, good, I've always wanted to play the piano." This pat scenario bored her; she loved having it interrupted. It must have galled her that usually her acquaintances were so predictably unalert; it must have galled her that, for the length of her life, she could surprise everyone so continually, so easily, when she had been the same all along. At any rate, she loved anyone who, as she put it, saw it coming and called her on it.

She regarded the instructions on bureaucratic forms as straight lines. "Do you advocate the overthrow of the United States government by force or violence?" After some thought she wrote, "Force." She regarded children, even babies, as straight men. When Molly learned to crawl, Mother delighted in buying her gowns with drawstrings at the bottom, like Swee'pea's, because, as she explained energetically, you could easily step on the drawstring without the baby's noticing, so that she crawled and crawled and crawled and never got anywhere except into a small ball at the gown's top.

*   *   *

When we children were young, she mothered us tenderly and dependably; as we got older, she resumed her career of anarchism. She collared us into her gags. If she answered the phone on a wrong number, she told the caller, "Just a minute," and dragged the receiver to Amy or me, saying, "Here, take this, your name is Cecile," or, worse, just, "It's for you." You had to think on your feet. But did you want to perform well as Cecile, or did you want to take pity on the wretched caller?

During a family trip to the Highland Park Zoo, Mother and I were alone for a minute. She approached a young couple holding hands on a bench by the seals, and addressed the young man in dripping tones: "Where have you been? Still got those baby-blue eyes; always did slay me. And this"—a swift nod at the dumbstruck young woman, who had removed her hand from the man's—"must be the one you were telling me about. She's not so bad, really, as you used to make out. But listen, you know how I miss you, you know where to reach me, same old place. And there's Ann over there—see how she's grown? See the blue eyes?"

And off she sashayed, taking me firmly by the hand, and leading us around briskly past the monkey house and away. She cocked an ear back, and both of us heard the desperate man begin, in a high-pitched wail, "I swear, I never saw her before in my life. . . ."

On a long, sloping beach by the ocean, she lay stretched out sunning with Father and friends, until the conversation gradually grew tedious, when without forethought she gave a little push with her heel and rolled away. People were stunned. She rolled deadpan and apparently effortlessly, arms and legs extended and tidy, down the beach to the distant water's edge, where she lay at ease just as she had been, but half in the surf, and well out of earshot.

She dearly loved to fluster people by throwing out a game's rules at whim—when she was getting bored, losing in a dull sort of way, and when everybody else was taking it too seriously. If you turned your back, she moved the checkers around on the board. When you got them all straightened out, she denied she'd touched them; the next time you turned your back, she lined them up on the rug or hid them under your chair. In a betting rummy game called Michigan, she routinely played out of turn, or called out a card she didn't hold, or counted backward, simply to amuse herself by causing an uproar and watching the rest of us do double takes and have fits. (Much later, when serious suitors came to call, Mother subjected them to this fast card game as a trial by ordeal; she used it as an intelligence test and a measure of spirit. If the poor man could stay a round without breaking down or running out, he got to marry one of us, if he still wanted to.)

She excelled at bridge, playing fast and boldly, but when the stakes were low and the hands dull, she bid slams for the devilment of it, or raised her opponents' suit to bug them, or showed her hand, or tossed her cards in a handful behind her back in a characteristic swift motion accompanied by a vibrantly innocent look. It drove our stolid father crazy. The hand was over before it began, and the guests were appalled. How do you score it, who deals now, what do you do with a crazy person who is having so much fun? Or they were down seven, and the guests were appalled. "Pam!" "Dammit, Pam!" He groaned. What ails such people? What on earth possesses them? He rubbed his face.

She was an unstoppable force; she never let go. When we moved across town, she persuaded the U.S. Post Office to let her keep her old address—forever—because she'd had stationery printed. I don't know how she did it. Every new post office worker, over decades, needed to learn that although the Doaks' mail is addressed to here, it is delivered to there.

Mother's energy and intelligence suited her for a greater role in a larger arena—mayor of New York, say—than the one she had. She followed American politics closely; she had been known to vote for Democrats. She saw how things should be run, but she had nothing to run but our household. Even there, small minds bugged her; she was smarter than the people who designed the things she had to use all day for the length of her life.

"Look," she said. "Whoever designed this corkscrew never used one. Why would anyone sell it without trying it out?" So she invented a better one. She showed me a drawing of it. The spirit of American enterprise never faded in Mother. If capitalizing and tooling up had been as interesting as theorizing and thinking up, she would have fired up a new factory every week, and chaired several hundred corporations.

"It grieves me," she would say, "it grieves my heart," that the company that made one superior product packaged it poorly, or took the wrong tack in its advertising. She knew, as she held the thing mournfully in her two hands, that she'd never find another. She was right. We children wholly sympathized, and so did Father; what could she do, what could anyone do, about it? She was Samson in chains. She paced.

She didn't like the taste of stamps, so she didn't lick stamps; she licked the corner of the envelope instead. She glued sandpaper to the sides of kitchen drawers, and under kitchen cabinets, so she always had a handy place to strike a match. She designed, and hounded workmen to build against all norms, doubly wide kitchen counters and elevated bathroom sinks. To splint a finger, she stuck it in a lightweight cigar tube. Conversely, to protect a pack of cigarettes, she carried it in a Band-Aid box. She drew plans for an over-the-finger toothbrush for babies, an oven rack that slid up and down, and—the family favorite—Lendalarm. Lendalarm was a beeper you attached to books (or tools) you loaned friends. After ten days, the beeper sounded. Only the rightful owner could silence it.

She repeatedly reminded us of P. T. Barnum's dictum: You could sell anything to anybody if you marketed it right. The adman who thought of making Americans believe they needed underarm deodorant was a visionary. So, too, was the hero who made a success of a new product, Ivory soap. The executives were horrified, Mother told me, that a cake of this stuff floated. Soap wasn't supposed to float. Anyone would be able to tell it was mostly whipped-up air. Then some inspired adman made a leap: Advertise that it floats. Flaunt it. The rest is history.

She respected the rare few who broke through to new ways. "Look," she'd say, "here's an intelligent apron." She called upon us to admire intelligent control knobs and intelligent pan handles, intelligent andirons and picture frames and knife sharpeners. She questioned everything, every pair of scissors, every knitting needle, gardening glove, tape dispenser. Hers was a restless mental vigor that just about ignited the dumb household objects with its force.

Torpid conformity was a kind of sin; it was stupidity itself, the mighty stream against which Mother would never cease to struggle. If you held no minority opinions, or if you failed to risk total ostracism for them daily, the world would be a better place without you.

Always I heard Mother's emotional voice asking Amy and me the same few questions: Is that your own idea? Or somebody else's? "*Giant* is a good movie," I pronounced to the family at dinner. "Oh, really?" Mother warmed to these occasions. She all but rolled up her sleeves. She knew I hadn't seen it. "Is that your considered opinion?"

She herself held many unpopular, even fantastic, positions. She was scathingly sarcastic about the McCarthy hearings while they took place, right on our living-room television; she frantically opposed Father's wait-and-see calm. "We don't know enough about it," he said. "I do," she said. "I know all I need to know."

She asserted, against all opposition, that people who lived in trailer parks were not bad but simply poor, and had as much right to settle on beautiful land, such as rural Ligonier, Pennsylvania, as did the oldest of families in the finest of hidden houses. Therefore, the people who owned trailer parks, and sought zoning changes to permit trailer parks, needed our help. Her profound belief that the country-club pool sweeper was a person, and that the department-store saleslady, the bus driver, telephone operator, and housepainter were people, and even, in groups, the steelworkers who carried pickets and the Christmas shoppers who clogged intersections were people—this was a conviction common enough in democratic Pittsburgh, but not altogether common among our friends' parents, or even, perhaps, among our parents' friends.

Opposition emboldened Mother, and she would take on anybody on any issue—the chairman of the board, at a cocktail party, on the current strike; she would fly at him in a flurry of passion, as a songbird selflessly attacks a big hawk.

"Eisenhower's going to win," I announced after school. She lowered her magazine and looked me in the eyes: "How do you know?" I was doomed. It was fatal to say, "Everyone says so." We all knew well what happened. "Do you consult this Everyone before you make your decisions? What if Everyone decided to round up all the Jews?" Mother knew there was no danger of cowing me. She simply tried to keep us all awake. And in fact it was always clear to Amy and me, and to Molly when she grew old enough to listen, that if our classmates came to cruelty, just as much as if the neighborhood or the nation came to madness, we were expected to take, and would be each separately capable of taking, a stand.

AFTER I READ *The Field Book of Ponds and Streams* several times, I longed for a microscope. Everybody needed a microscope. Detectives used microscopes, both for the FBI and at Scotland Yard. Although usually I had to save my tiny allowance for things I wanted, that year for Christmas my parents gave me a microscope kit.

In a dark basement corner, on a white enamel table, I set up the microscope kit. I supplied a chair, a lamp, a batch of jars, a candle, and a pile of library books. The microscope kit supplied a blunt black three-speed microscope, a booklet, a scalpel, a dropper, an ingenious device for cutting thin segments of fragile tissue, a pile of clean slides and cover slips, and a dandy array of corked test tubes.

One of the test tubes contained "hay infusion." Hay infusion was a wee brown chip of grass blade. You added water to it, and after a week it became a jungle in a drop, full of one-celled animals. This did not work for me. All I saw in the microscope after a week was a wet chip of dried grass, much enlarged.

Another test tube contained "diatomaceous earth." This was, I believed, an actual pinch of the white cliffs of Dover. On my palm it was an airy, friable chalk. The booklet said it was composed of the silicaceous bodies of diatoms—one-celled creatures that lived in, as it were, small glass jewelry boxes with fitted lids. Diatoms, I read, come in a variety of transparent geometrical shapes. Broken and dead and dug out of geological deposits, they made chalk, and a fine abrasive used in silver polish and toothpaste. What I saw in the microscope must have been the fine abrasive—grit enlarged. It was years before I saw a recognizable, whole diatom. The kit's diatomaceous earth was a bust.

All that winter I played with the microscope. I prepared slides from things at hand, as the books suggested. I looked at the transparent membrane inside an onion's skin and saw the cells. I looked at a section of cork and saw the cells, and at scrapings from the inside of my cheek, ditto. I looked at my blood and saw not much; I looked at my urine and saw long iridescent crystals, for the drop had dried.

All this was very well, but I wanted to see the wildlife I had read about. I wanted especially to see the famous amoeba, who had eluded me. He was supposed to live in the hay infusion, but I hadn't found him there. He lived outside in warm ponds and streams, too, but I lived in Pittsburgh, and it had been a cold winter.

Finally late that spring I saw an amoeba. The week before, I had gathered puddle water from Frick Park; it had been festering in a jar in the basement. This June night after dinner I figured I had waited long enough. In the basement at my microscope table I spread a scummy drop of Frick Park puddle water on a slide, peeked in, and lo, there was the famous amoeba. He was as blobby and grainy as his picture; I would have known him anywhere.

Before I had watched him at all, I ran upstairs. My parents were still at table, drinking coffee. They, too, could see the famous amoeba. I told them, bursting, that he was all set up, that they should hurry before his water dried. It was the chance of a lifetime.

Father had stretched out his long legs and was tilting back in his chair. Mother sat with her knees crossed, in blue slacks, smoking a Chesterfield. The dessert dishes were still on the table. My sisters were nowhere in evidence. It was a warm evening; the big dining-room windows gave onto blooming rhododendrons.

Mother regarded me warmly. She gave me to understand that she was glad I had found what I had been looking for, but that she and Father were happy to sit with their coffee, and would not be coming down.

She did not say, but I understood at once, that they had their pursuits (coffee?) and I had mine. She did not say, but I began to understand then, that you do what you do out of your private passion for the thing itself.

I had essentially been handed my own life. In subsequent years my parents would praise my drawings and poems, and supply me with books, art supplies, and sports equipment, and listen to my troubles and enthusiasms, and supervise my hours, and discuss and inform, but they would not get involved with my detective work, nor hear about my reading, nor inquire about my homework or term papers or exams, nor visit the salamanders I caught, not listen to me play the piano, nor attend my field hockey games, nor fuss over my insect collection with me, or my poetry collection or stamp collection or serious rock and mineral collection. My days and nights were my own to plan and fill.

When I left the dining room that evening and started down the dark basement stairs, I had a life. I sat to my wonderful amoeba, and there he was, rolling his grains more slowly now, extending an arc of his edge for a foot and drawing himself along by that foot, and absorbing it again and rolling on. I gave him some more pond water.

I had hit pay dirt. For all I knew, there were paramecia, too, in that pond water, or daphniae, or stentors, or any of the many other creatures I had read about and never seen: volvox, the spherical algal colony; euglena with its one red eye; the elusive, glassy diatom; hydra, rotifers, water bears, worms. Anything was possible. The sky was the limit.

WHAT DOES IT FEEL LIKE to be alive?

Living, you stand under a waterfall. You leave the sleeping shore deliberately; you shed your dusty clothes, pick your barefoot way over the high, slippery rocks, hold your breath, choose your footing, and step into the waterfall. The hard water pelts your skull, bangs in bits on your shoulders and arms. The strong water dashes down beside you and you feel it along your calves and thighs rising roughly back up, up to the roiling surface, full of bubbles that slide up your skin or break on you at full speed. Can you breathe here? Here where the force is greatest and only the strength of your neck holds the river out of your face? Yes, you can breathe even here. You could learn to live like this. And you can, if you concentrate, even look out at the peaceful far bank where maples grow straight and their leaves lean down. For a joke you try to raise your arms. What a racket in your ears, what a scattershot pummeling!

It is time pounding at you, time. Knowing you are alive is watching on every side your generation's short time falling away as fast as rivers drop through air, and feeling it hit.

Who turned on the lights? You did, by waking up: you flipped the light switch, started up the wind machine, kicked on the flywheel that spins the years. Can you catch hold of a treetop, or will you fly off the diving planet as she rolls? Can you ride out the big blow on a coconut palm's trunk until you fall asleep again, and the winds let up? You fall asleep again, and you slide in a dream to the palm tree's base; the winds die off, the lights dim, the years slip away as you idle there till you die in your sleep, till death sets you cruising down the Tamiami Trail.

Knowing you are alive is feeling the planet buck under you,

rear, kick, and try to throw you; you hang on to the ring. It is riding the planet like a log downstream, whooping. Or, conversely, you step aside from the dreaming fast loud routine and feel time as a stillness about you, and hear the silent air asking in so thin a voice, Have you noticed yet that you will die? Do you remember, remember, remember? Then you feel your life as a weekend, a weekend you cannot extend, a weekend in the country.

O Augenblick verweile.

My friend Judy Schoyer was a thin, messy, shy girl whose thick blond curls lapped over her glasses. Her cheeks, chin, nose, and blue eyes were round; the lenses and frames of her glasses were round, and so were her heavy curls. Her long spine was supple; her legs were long and thin, so her knee socks fell down. She did not care if her knee socks fell down. When I first knew her, as my classmate at the Ellis School, she sometimes forgot to comb her hair. She was so shy she tended not to move her head, but only let her eyes rove about. If my mother addressed her, or a teacher, she held her long-legged posture lightly, alert, like a fawn ready to bolt but hoping its camouflage will work a little longer.

Judy's family were members of the oldest, most liberal, and best-educated ranks of Pittsburgh society. They were Unitarians. I visited her Unitarian Sunday school once. There we folded paper to make little geese; it shocked me to the core. One of her linear ancestors, Edward Holyoke, had been president of Harvard University in the eighteenth century, which fact paled locally before the greater one, that her great-grandfather's brother had been one of the founding members of Pittsburgh's Duquesne Club. She was related also to Pittsburgh's own Stephen Foster.

Judy and her family passed some long weekends at a family farmhouse in the country on a little river, the nearest town to which was Paw Paw, West Virginia. When they were going to the farm, they said they were going to Paw Paw. The trip was a four-hour drive from Pittsburgh. Often they invited me along.

There in Paw Paw for the weekend I imagined myself in the distant future remembering myself now, twelve years old with

Judy. We stood on the high swinging plank bridge over the river, in early spring, watching the first hatch of small flies hover below us.

The river was a tributary of the distant Potomac—a tributary so stony, level, and shallow that Judy's grandmother regularly drove her old Model A Ford right through it, while we hung out over the running boards to try and get wet. From above the river, from the hanging center of the swinging bridge, we could see the forested hill where the big house stood. There at the big house we would have dinner, and later look at the Gibson girls in the wide, smelly old books in the cavernous living room, only recently and erratically electrified.

And from the high swinging bridge we could see in the other direction the log cabin, many fields away from the big house, where we children stayed alone: Judy and I, and sometimes our friend Margaret, who had a dramatic, somewhat morbid flair and who wrote poetry, and Judy's good-natured younger brother. We cooked pancakes in the cabin's fireplace; we drew water in a bucket from the well outside the door.

By Friday night when we'd carried our duffel and groceries from the black Model A at the foot of the hill, or over the undulating bridge if the river was high, when we children had banged open the heavy log-cabin door, smelled the old logs and wood dust, found matches and lighted the kerosene lanterns, and in the dark outside had drawn ourselves a bucket of sweet water (feeling the rope go slack and hearing the bucket hit, then feeling the rope pull as the bucket tipped and filled), and hunted up wood for a fire, smelled the loamy nighttime forest again, and heard the whippoorwill—by that time on Friday night I was already grieving and mourning, only just unpacking my nightgown, because here it was practically Sunday afternoon and time to go.

"What you kids need," Mrs. Schoyer used to say, "is more exercise."

How exhilarating, how frightening, to ride the tippy Model A over the shallow river to the farm at Paw Paw, to greet again in a new season the swaying bridge, the bare hills, the woods behind the log cabin, the hayloft in the barn—and know I had just so many hours. From the minute I set foot on that land across the river, I started ticking like a timer, fizzing like a fuse.

On Friday night in the log cabin at Paw Paw I watched the wild firelight on Judy's face as she laughed at something her cheerful brother said, laughed shyly even here. When she laughed, her cheeks rose and formed spheres. I loved her spherical cheeks and knocked myself out to make her laugh. I could hardly see her laughing eyes behind her glasses under hanging clumps of dark-blond curls. She was nimble, swaybacked, long-limbed, and languid as a heron, and as abrupt. In Pittsburgh she couldn't catch a ball—nearsighted; she perished of bashfulness at school sports. Here she could climb a tree after a kitten as smoothly as a squirrel could, and run down her nasty kicking pony with authority, and actually hit it, and scoop up running hens with both swift arms. She spoke softly and not often.

Judy treated me with amused tolerance. At school I was, if not a central personage, at least a conspicuous one, and I had boyfriends all along and got invited to the boys' school dances. Nevertheless, Judy put up with me, not I with Judy. She possessed a few qualities that, although they counted for nothing at school, counted, I had to admit, with me. Her goodness was both intrinsic and a held principle. This thin, almost speechless child had moral courage. She intended her own life—starting when she was about ten—to be not only harmless but good. I considered Judy's goodness, like Judy's farm, a nice place to visit. She put up with my fast-talking avoidance of anything that smacked of manual labor. That she was indulging me altogether became gradually clear to both of us—though I pretended I didn't know it, and Judy played along.

On Saturday mornings in Paw Paw we set out through the dewy fields. I could barely lay one foot before the other along the cowpath through the pasture, I was so nostalgic for this scene already, this day just begun, when Judy and I were twelve. With Margaret we boiled and ate blue river mussels; we wrote and staged a spidery melodrama. We tried to ride the wretched untrained pony, which scraped us off under trees. We chopped down a sassafras tree and made a dirty tea, and we started to clean a run-over snake, in order to make an Indian necklace from its delicate spine, but it smelled so bad we quit.

After Saturday-night dinner in the big-house dining room—its windows gave out on the cliffside treetops—Mr. Schoyer told us, in his calm, ironic voice, Victor Hugo's story of a French sailor who was commended for having heroically captured a cannon loose on the warship's deck, and then hanged for having loosed the cannon in the first place. There were usually a dozen or more of us around the table, rapt. When the household needed our help, Mrs. Schoyer made mild, wry suggestions, almost diffidently.

I would have liked going to prison with the Schoyers. My own family I loved with all my heart; the Schoyers fascinated me. They were not sharply witty but steadily wry. In Pittsburgh they invited foreigners to dinner. They went to art galleries, they heard the Pittsburgh Symphony. They weren't tan. Mr. Schoyer, who was a corporation lawyer, had majored in classical history and literature at Harvard. Like my father, he had studied something that had no direct bearing on the clatter of coin. He was always the bemused scholar, mild and democratic, posing us children friendly questions as if Pittsburgh or Paw Paw were Athens and he fully expected to drag from our infant brains the Pythagorean theorem. What do you make of our new President? Your position on capital punishment? Or, conversationally, after I had been branded as a lover of literature, "You recall that speech of Pericles, don't you?" or "Won't you join me in reading 'A Shropshire Lad' or 'The Ballad of East and West'?" At Paw Paw the Schoyers did every wholesome thing but sing. None of them could carry a tune.

If there was no moon that night, we children took a flashlight down the steep dirt driveway from the big house and across the silvery pastures to the edge of the woods where the log cabin stood. The log cabin stayed empty, behind an old vine-hung gate, except when we came. In front of the cabin we drew water from the round stone well; under the cabin we put milk and butter in the cold cellar, which was only a space dug in the damp black dirt—dirt against which the butter's wrap looked too thin.

That was the farm at Paw Paw, West Virginia. The farm lay far from the nearest highway, off three miles of dirt road. When at the end of the long darkening journey from Pittsburgh we turned down the dirt road at last, the Schoyers' golden retriever not unreasonably began to cry, and so, unreasonably, invisibly, did I. Some years when the Schoyers asked me to join them I declined miserably, refused in a swivet, because I couldn't tolerate it, I loved the place so.

I knew what I was doing at Paw Paw: I was beginning the lifelong task of tuning my own gauges. I was there to brace myself for leaving. I was having my childhood. But I was haunting it, as well, practically reading it, and preventing it. How much noticing could I permit myself without driving myself round the bend? Too much noticing and I was too self-conscious to live; I trapped and paralyzed myself, and dragged my friends down with me, so we couldn't meet each other's eyes, my own loud awareness damning us both. Too little noticing, though—I would risk much to avoid this—and I would miss the whole show. I would wake on my deathbed and say, What was that?

I INTENDED TO LIVE THE way the microbe hunters lived. I wanted to work. Hard work on an enormous scale was the microbe hunters' stock-in-trade. They took a few clear, time-consuming steps and solved everything. In those early days of germ theory, large disease-causing organisms, whose cycles traced straightforward patterns, yielded and fell to simple procedures. I would know just what to do. I would seize on the most casual remarks of untutored milkmaids. When an untutored milkmaid remarked to me casually, "Oh, everyone knows you won't get the smallpox if you've had the cowpox," I would perk right up.

Microbe Hunters sent me to a biography of Louis Pasteur. Pasteur's was the most enviable life I had yet encountered. It was his privilege to do things until they were done. He established the germ theory of disease; he demonstrated convincingly that yeasts ferment beer; he discovered how to preserve wine; he isolated the bacillus in a disease of silkworms; he demonstrated the etiology of anthrax and produced a vaccine for it; he halted an epidemic of cholera in fowls and inoculated a boy for hydrophobia. Toward the end of his life, in a rare idle moment, he chanced to read some of his early published papers and exclaimed (someone overheard), "How beautiful! And to think that I did it all!" The tone of this exclamation was, it seemed to me, astonished and modest, for he had genuinely forgotten, moving on.

Pasteur had not used up all the good work. Mother told me again and again about one of her heroes, a doctor working for a federal agency who solved a problem that arose in the late forties. Premature babies, and only premature babies, were turning up blind, in enormous numbers. Why? What do premature babies have in common?

"Look in the incubators!" Mother would holler, and knock the side of her head with the heel of her hand, holler outraged, glaring far behind my head as she was telling me this story, holler, "Look in the incubators!" as if at her wit's end facing a roomful of doctors who wrung their useless hands and accepted this blindness as one of life's tough facts. Mother's hero, like all of Mother's heroes, accepted nothing. She rolled up her sleeves, looked in the incubators, and decided to see what happened if she reduced the oxygen in the incubator air. That worked. Too much oxygen had been blinding them. Now the babies throve; they got enough oxygen, and they weren't blinded. Hospitals all over the world changed the air mixture for incubators, and prematurity no longer carried a special risk of blindness.

Mother liked this story, and told it to us fairly often. Once she posed it as a challenge to Amy. We were all in the living room, waiting for dinner. "What would you do if you noticed that all over the United States, premature babies were blind?" Without even looking up from her homework, Amy said, "Look in the incubators. Maybe there's something wrong in the incubators." Mother started to whoop for joy before she realized she'd been had.

Problems still yielded to effort. Only a few years ago, to the wide-eyed attention of the world, we had seen the epidemic of poliomyelitis crushed in a twinkling, right here in Pittsburgh.

We had all been caught up in the polio epidemic: the early neighbor boy who wore one tall shoe, to which his despairing father added another two soles every year; the girl in the iron lung reading her schoolbook in an elaborate series of mirrors while a volunteer waited to turn the page; my friend who limped, my friend who rolled everywhere in a wheelchair, my friend whose arm hung down, Mother's friend who walked with crutches. My beloved dressed-up aunt, Mother's sister, had come to visit one day and, while she was saying hello, flung herself on the couch in tears; her son had it. Just a touch, they said, but who could believe it?

When Amy and I had asked, Why do we have to go to bed so early? Why do we have to wash our hands again? we knew

Mother would kneel to look us in the eyes and answer in a low, urgent voice, So you do not get polio. We heard polio discussed once or twice a day for several years.

And we had all been caught up in its prevention, in the wild ferment of the early days of the Salk vaccine, the vaccine about which Pittsburgh talked so much, and so joyously, you could probably have heard the crowd noise on the moon.

In 1953, Jonas Salk's Virus Research Laboratory at the University of Pittsburgh had produced a controversial vaccine for polio. The small stories in the Pittsburgh *Press* and the *Post-Gazette* were coming out in *Life* and *Time*. It was too quick, said medical colleagues nationwide: Salk had gone public without first publishing everything in the journals. He rushed out a killed-virus serum without waiting for a safe live-virus one, which would probably be better. Doctors walked out of professional meetings; some quit the foundation that funded the testing. Salk was after personal glory, they said. Salk was after money, they said. Salk was after big prizes.

Salk tested the serum on five thousand Pittsburgh schoolchildren, of whom I was three, because I kept changing elementary schools. Our parents, like 95 percent of all Pittsburgh parents, signed the consent forms. Did the other mothers then bend over the desk in relief and sob? I don't know. But I don't suppose any of them gave much of a damn what Salk had been after.

When Pasteur died, near a place wonderfully called Saint-Cloud, he murmured to the devoted assistants who surrounded his bed, "*Il faut travailler.*"

Il faut indeed *travailler*—no one who grew up in Pittsburgh could doubt it. And no one who grew up in Pittsburgh could doubt that the great work was ongoing. We breathed in optimism—not coal dust—with every breath. What couldn't be done with good hard *travail?*

The air in Pittsburgh had been dirty; now we could see it was clean. An enormous, pioneering urban renewal was under way; the newspapers pictured fantastic plans, airy artists' watercolors, which we soon saw laid out and built up in steel and glass downtown. The Republican Richard King Mellon had approached Pittsburgh's Democratic, Catholic mayor, David L. Lawrence, and together with a dozen business leaders they were razing the old grim city and building a sparkling new one; they were washing the very air. The Russians had shot Sputnik into outer space. In Shippingport, just a few miles down the Ohio River, people were building a generating plant that used atomic energy—an idea that seemed completely dreamy, but there it was. A physicist from Bell Laboratories spoke to us at school about lasers; he was about as wrought up a man as I had ever seen. You could not reasonably believe a word he said, but you could see that he believed it.

We knew that "Doctor Salk" had spent many years and many dollars to produce the vaccine. He commonly worked sixteen-hour days, six days a week. Of course. In other laboratories around the world, other researchers were working just as hard, as hard as Salk and Pasteur. Hard work bore fruit. This is what we learned growing up in Pittsburgh, growing up in the United States.

Salk had isolated seventy-four strains of polio virus. It took him three years to verify the proposition that a workable vaccine would need samples of only three of these strains. He grew the virus in tissues cultured from monkey kidneys. The best broth for growing the monkey tissue proved to be Medium Number 199; it contained sixty-two ingredients in careful proportion.

This was life itself: the big task. Nothing exhilarated me more than the idea of a life dedicated to a monumental worthwhile task. Doctor Salk never watched it rain and wished he had never been born. How many shovelfuls of dirt did men move to dig the Panama Canal? Two hundred and forty million cubic yards. It took ten years and twenty-one thousand lives and $336,650,000, but it was possible.

I thought a great deal about the Panama Canal, and always contemplated the same notion: You could take more time, and do it with teaspoons. I saw myself and a few Indian and Caribbean co-workers wielding teaspoons from our kitchen: Towle, Rambling Rose. And our grandchildren, and their grandchildren. Digging the canal across the isthmus at Panama would tear through a good many silver spoons. But it could be done, in theory and therefore in fact. It was like Mount Rushmore, or Grand Coulee Dam. You hacked away at the landscape and made something, or you did not do anything and just died.

How many filaments had Thomas Edison tried, over how many years, before he found one workable for incandescence? How many days and nights over how many years had Marie Curie labored in a freezing shed to isolate radium? I read a biography of George Washington Carver: so many years on the soybean, the peanut, the sweet potato, the waste from ginning cotton. I read biographies of Abraham Lincoln, Thomas Edison, Daniel Boone.

It was all the same story. You have a great idea and spend grinding years at dull tasks, still charged by your vision. All the people about whom biographies were not written were people who failed to find something that took years to do. People could count the grains of sand. In my own life, as a sideline, and for starters, I would learn all the world's languages.

What if people said it could not be done? So much the better. We grew up with the myth of the French Impressionist painters, and its queer implication that rejection and ridicule guaranteed, or at any rate signaled, a project's worth. When little George Westinghouse at last figured out how to make air brakes, Cornelius Vanderbilt of the New York Central Railroad said to him, "Do you mean to tell me with a straight face that a moving train can be stopped with wind?" "They laughed at Orville," Mother used to say when someone tried to talk her out of a wild scheme, "and they laughed at Wilbur."

I had small experience of the evil hopelessness, pain, starvation, and terror that the world spread about; I had barely seen people's malice and greed. I believed that in civilized countries, torture had ended with the Enlightenment. Of nations' cruel options I knew nothing. My optimism was endless; it grew sky-high within the narrow bounds of my isolationism. Because I was all untried courage, I could not allow that the loss of courage was a real factor to be reckoned in. I put my faith in willpower, that weak notion by which children seek to replace the loving devotion that comes from intimate and dedicated knowledge. I believed that I could resist aging by willpower.

I believed then, too, that I would never harm anyone. I usually believed I would never meet a problem I could not solve. I would overcome any weakness, any despair, any fear. Hadn't I overcome my fear of the ghosty oblong that coursed round my room, simply by thinking it through? Everything was simple. You found good work, learned all about it, and did it.

Questions of how to act were also transparent to reason. Right and wrong were easy to discern: I was right, and Amy was wrong. Many of my classmates stole things, but I did not. Sometimes, in a very tight spot, when at last I noticed I had a moral question on my hands, I asked myself: What would Christ have done? I had picked up this method (very much on the sly—we were not supposed really to believe these things) from Presbyterian Sunday school, from summer camp, or from any of the innumerable righteous orange-bound biographies I read. I had not known it to fail in the two times I had applied it.

As for loss, as for parting, as for bidding farewell, so long, thanks, to love or a land or a time—what did I know of parting, of grieving, mourning, loss? Well, I knew one thing; I had known it all along. I knew it was the kicker. I knew life pulled you in two; you never healed. Mother's emotions ran high, and she suffered sometimes from a web of terrors, because, she said, her father died when she was seven; she still missed him.

My parents played the Cole Porter song "It's All Right with Me." When Ella Fitzgerald sang, "There's someone I'm trying so hard to forget—don't you want to forget someone too?," these facile, breathy lyrics struck me as an unexpectedly true expression of how it felt to be alive. This was experience at its most private and inarticulate: longing and loss. "It's the wrong time, it's the wrong place, though your face is charming, it's the wrong face." I was a thirteen-year-old child; I had no one to miss, had lost no one. Yet I suspect most children feel this way, probably all children feel this way, as adults do; they mourn this absence or loss of someone, and sense that unnamable loss as a hole or hollow moving beside them in the air.

Loss came around with the seasons, blew into the house

when you opened the windows, piled up in the bottom desk and dresser drawers, accumulated in the back of closets, heaped in the basement starting by the furnace, and came creeping up the basement stairs. Loss grew as you did, without your consent; your losses mounted beside you like earthworm castings. No willpower could prevent someone's dying. And no willpower could restore someone dead, breathe life into that frame and set it going again in the room with you to meet your eyes. That was the fact of it. The strongest men and women who had ever lived had presumably tried to resist their own deaths, and now they were dead. It was on this fact that all the stirring biographies coincided, concurred, and culminated.

Time itself bent you and cracked you on its wheel. We were getting ready to move again. I knew I could not forever keep riding my bike backward into ever-older neighborhoods to look the ever-older houses in the face. I tried to memorize the layout of this Richland Lane house, but I couldn't force it into my mind while it was still in my bones.

I saw already that I could not in good faith renew the increasingly desperate series of vows by which I had always tried to direct my life. I had vowed to love an older boy forever; now I could recall neither his face nor my feeling, but only this quondam urgent vow. I had vowed to keep exploring Pittsburgh by bicycle no matter how old I got, and planned an especially sweeping tour for my hundredth birthday in 2045. I had vowed to keep hating Amy in order to defy Mother, who kept prophesying I would someday not hate Amy. In short, I always vowed, one way or another, not to change. Not me. I needed the fierceness of vowing because I could scarcely help but notice, visiting the hatchling robins at school every day, that it was mighty unlikely.

As a life's work, I would remember everything—everything, against loss. I would go through life like a plankton net. I would trap and keep every teacher's funny remark, every face on the street, every microscopic alga's sway, every conversation, configuration of leaves, every dream, and every scrap of overhead cloud. Who would remember Molly's infancy if not me?

(Unaccountably, I thought that only I had noticed—not Molly, but time itself. No one else, at least, seemed bugged by it. Children may believe that they alone have interior lives.)

Some days I felt an urgent responsibility to each change of light outside the sunporch windows. Who would remember any of it, any of this our time, and the wind thrashing the buckeye limbs outside? Somebody had to do it, somebody had to hang on to the days with teeth and fists, or the whole show had been in vain. That it was impossible never entered my reckoning. For work, for a task, I had never heard the word.

SINCE WE HAD MOVED, MY reading had taken a new turn.

Books wandered in and out of my hands, as they had always done, but now most of them had a common theme. This new theme was the source of imagination at its most private—never mentioned, rarely even brought to consciousness. It was, essentially, a time, and a series of places, to which I returned nightly. So also must thousands, or millions, of us who grew up in the 1950s, reading what came to hand. What came to hand in those years were books about the past war: the war in England, France, Belgium, Norway, Italy, Greece; the war in Africa; the war in the Pacific, in Guam, New Guinea, the Philippines; the war, Adolf Hitler, and the camps.

We read Leon Uris's popular novels *Exodus* and, better, *Mila 18*, about the Warsaw ghetto. We read Hersey's *The Wall*—again, the Warsaw ghetto. We read *Time* magazine, and *Life*, and *Look*. It was in the air, that there had been these things. We read, above all, and over and over, for we were young, Anne Frank's *The Diary of a Young Girl*. This was where we belonged; here we were at home.

I say "we," but in fact I did not know anyone else who read these things. Perhaps my parents did, for they brought the books home. What were my friends reading? We did not then talk about books; our reading was private, and constant, like the interior life itself. Still, I say, there must have been millions of us. The theaters of war—the lands, the multiple seas, the very corridors of air—and the death camps in Europe, with their lines of starved bald people . . . these, combined, were the settings in which our imaginations were first deeply stirred.

Earlier generations of children, European children, I inferred, had had on their minds heraldry and costumed adventure. They read *The Count of Monte Cristo* and *The Three Musketeers.* They read about King Arthur and Lancelot and Galahad; they read about Robin Hood. I had read some of these things and considered them behind me. It would have been pleasant, I suppose, to close your eyes and imagine yourself in a suit of armor, astride an armored horse, fighting a battle for honor with broadswords on a pennanted plain, or in a copse of trees.

But of what value was honor when, in book after book, the highest prize was a piece of bread? Of what use was a broadsword, or even a longbow, against Hitler's armies that occupied Europe, against Hitler's Luftwaffe, Hitler's Panzers, Hitler's U-boats, or against Hitler's S.S., who banged on the door and led Anne Frank and her family away? We closed our eyes and imagined how we would survive the death camps— maybe with honor and maybe not. We imagined how we would escape the death camps, imagined how we would liberate the death camps. How? We fancied and schemed, but we had read too much, and knew there was no possible way. This was a novel concept: Can't do. We were in for the duration. We closed our eyes and waited for the Allies, but the Allies were detained.

Now and over the next few years, the books appeared and we read them. We read *The Bridge Over the River Kwai, The Young Lions.* In the background sang a chorus of smarmy librarians:

> The world of books is a child's
> Land of enchantment.
> When you open a book and start reading
> You enter another world—the world
> Of make-believe—where anything can happen.

We read *Thirty Seconds Over Tokyo,* and *To Hell and Back.* We read *The Naked and the Dead; Run Silent, Run Deep;* and *Tales of the South Pacific,* in which American sailors saw native victims of elephantiasis pushing their own enlarged testicles before them in wheelbarrows. We read *The Caine Mutiny, Some Came Running.*

I was a skilled bombardier. I could run a submarine with one hand, and evade torpedoes, depth charges, and mines. I could disembowel a soldier with a bayonet, survive under a tarp in a lifeboat, and parachute behind enemy lines. I could contact the Resistance with my high-school French and eavesdrop on the Germans with my high-school German:

"Du! Kleines Mädchen! Bist du französisches Mädchen oder bist du Amerikanischer spy?"

"Je suis une jeune fille de la belle France, Herr S.S. Officer."

"Prove it!"

"Je suis, tu es, il est, nous sommes, vous êtes, ils sont."

"Very gut. Run along and play."

What were librarians reading these days? One librarian pressed on me a copy of *Look Homeward, Angel.* "How I envy you," she said, "having a chance to read this for the very first time." But it was too late, several years too late.

At last Hitler fell, and scientists working during the war came up with the atomic bomb. We read *On the Beach, A Canticle for Leibowitz;* we read *Hiroshima.* Reading about the bomb was a part of reading about the war: these were actual things and events, large in their effects on millions of people, vivid in their nearness to each man's or woman's death. It was a relief to turn from life to something important.

At school we had air-raid drills. We took the drills seriously; surely Pittsburgh, which had the nation's steel, coke, and aluminum, would be the enemy's first target.

I knew that during the war, our father had "watched the skies." We all knew that people still watched the skies. But when the keen-eyed watcher spotted the enemy bomber over Pittsburgh, what, precisely, would be his moves? Surely he could only calculate, just as we in school did, what good it would do him to get under something.

When the air-raid siren sounded, our teachers stopped talking and led us to the school basement. There the gym teachers lined us up against the cement walls and steel lockers, and showed us how to lean in and fold our arms over our heads. Our small school ran from kindergarten through twelfth grade. We had air-raid drills in small batches, four or five grades together, because there was no room for us all against the walls. The teachers had to stand in the middle of the basement rooms: those bright Pittsburgh women who taught Latin, science, and art, and those educated, beautifully mannered European women who taught French, history, and German, who had landed in Pittsburgh at the end of their respective flights from Hitler, and who had baffled us by their common insistence on tidiness, above all, in our written work.

The teachers stood in the middle of the room, not talking to each other. We tucked against the walls and lockers: dozens of clean girls wearing green jumpers, green knee socks, and pink-soled white bucks. We folded our skinny arms over our heads, and raised to the enemy a clatter of gold scarab bracelets and gold bangle bracelets.

If the bomb actually came, should we not let the little kids—the kindergartners like Molly, and the first and second graders—go against the wall? We older ones would stand in the middle with the teachers. The European teachers were almost used to this sort of thing. We would help them keep spirits up; we would sing "Frère Jacques," or play Buzz.

Our house was stone. In the basement was a room furnished with a long wooden bar, tables and chairs, a leather couch, a refrigerator, a sink, an ice maker, a fireplace, a piano, a record player, and a set of drums. After the bomb, we would live, in the manner of Anne Frank and her family, in this basement. It had also a larger set of underground rooms, which held a washer and a dryer, a workbench, and, especially, food: shelves of canned fruits and vegetables, and a chest freezer. Our family could live in the basement for many years, until the radiation outside blew away. Amy and Molly would grow up there. I would teach them all I knew, and entertain them on the piano. Father would build a radiation barrier for the basement's sunken windows. He would teach me to play the drums. Mother would feed us and tend to us. We would grow close.

I had spent the equivalent of years of my life, I fancied, in concentration camps, in ghettos, in prison camps, and in lifeboats. I knew how to ration food and water. We would each have four ounces of food a day and eight ounces of water, or maybe only four ounces of water. I knew how to stretch my rations by hoarding food in my shirt, by chewing slowly, by sloshing water around in my mouth and wetting my tongue well before I swallowed. If the water gave out in the taps, we could drink club soda or tonic. We could live on the juice in canned food. I figured the five of us could live many years on the food in the basement—but I was not sure.

One day I asked Mother: How long could we last on the food in the basement? She did not know what I had been reading. How could she have known?

"The food in the basement? In the freezer and on the shelves? Oh, about a week and a half. Two weeks."

She knew, as I knew, that there were legs of lamb in the freezer, turkeys, chickens, pork roasts, shrimp, and steaks. There were pounds of frozen vegetables, quarts of ice cream, dozens of Popsicles. By her reckoning, that wasn't many family dinners: a leg of lamb one night, rice, and vegetables; steak the next night, potatoes, and vegetables.

"Two weeks! We could live much longer than two weeks!"

"There's really not very much food down there. About two weeks' worth."

I let it go. What did I know about feeding a family? On the other hand, I considered that if it came down to it, I would have to take charge.

It was clear that adults, including our parents, approved of children who read books, but it was not at all clear why this was so. Our reading was subversive, and we knew it. Did they think we read to improve our vocabularies? Did they want us to read and not pay the least bit of heed to what we read, as they wanted us to go to Sunday school and ignore what we heard?

I was now believing books more than I believed what I saw and heard. I was reading books about the actual, historical, moral world—in which somehow I felt I was not living.

The French and Indian War had been, for me, a purely literary event. Skilled men in books could survive it. Those who died, an arrow through the heart, thrilled me by their last words. This recent war's survivors, some still shaking, some still in mourning, taught in our classrooms. *"Wir waren ausgebombt,"* one dear old white-haired Polish lady related in German class, her family was "bombed out," and we laughed, we smart girls, because this was our slang for "drunk." Those who died in this war's books died whether they were skilled or not. Bombs fell on their cities or ships, or they starved in the camps or were gassed or shot, or they stepped on land mines and died surprised, trying to push their intestines back in their abdomens with their fingers and thumbs.

What I sought in books was imagination. It was depth, depth of thought and feeling; some sort of extreme of subject matter; some nearness to death; some call to courage. I myself was getting wild; I wanted wildness, originality, genius, rapture, hope. I wanted strength, not tea parties. What I sought in books was a world whose surfaces, whose people and events and days lived, actually matched the exaltation of the interior life. There you could live.

Those of us who read carried around with us like martyrs a secret knowledge, a secret joy, and a secret hope: There is a life worth living where history is still taking place; there are ideas worth dying for, and circumstances where courage is still prized. This life could be found and joined, like the Resistance. I kept this exhilarating faith alive in myself, concealed under my uniform shirt like an oblate's ribbon; I would not be parted from it.

We who had grown up in the Warsaw ghetto, who had seen all our families gassed in the death chambers, who had shipped before the mast, and hunted sperm whale in Antarctic seas; we who had marched from Moscow to Poland and lost our legs to the cold; we who knew by heart every snag and sandbar on the Mississippi River south of Cairo, and knew by heart Morse code, forty parables and psalms, and lots of Shakespeare; we who had battled Hitler and Hirohito in the North Atlantic, in North Africa, in New Guinea and Burma and Guam, in the air over London, in the Greek and Italian hills; we who had learned to man minesweepers before we learned to walk in high heels— were we going to marry Holden Caulfield's roommate, and buy a house in Point Breeze, and send our children to dancing school?

THE BOYS WERE CHANGING. Those froggy little beasts had elongated and transformed into princes and gods. When it happened, I must have been out of the room. Suddenly here they all were, Richie and Rickie and Dan and all, diverse in their varied splendors, each powerful and mysterious, immense, and possessed of an inexplicable knowledge of arcana.

The boys wandered the neighborhoods now, and showed up at girls' houses, as if by accident. They would let us listen to them talk, and we heard them mention the state legislature, say, or some opinion of Cicero's, or the Battle of the Marne—and those things abruptly became possible topics in society because those magnificent boys had pronounced their names.

Where had they learned all this, or more pertinently, why had they remembered it? We girls knew precisely the limits of the possible and the thinkable, we thought, and were permanently astonished to learn that we were wrong. Whose idea of sophistication was it, after all, to pay attention in Latin class? It was the boys' idea. Everything was. Everything they thought of was bold and original like that.

Each year as we rose through the grades, dancing school met an hour later, until one year it vanished into the darkness, and was replaced by, or transmogrified into, another institution altogether, that of country-club subscription dances.

The engraved invitation came in the mail: The Sewickley Country Club was hosting a subscription dinner dance several weeks thence.

We showed up at our own country club in pale spaghetti-strap dresses and silk shoes, to board a yellow bus in the snow. There we all were: the same boys, the same girls. How did they know? I wondered which of those remote country-club powers, those white-haired sincere men, those golden-haired, long-toothed, ironic women, had met on what firm cloud over western Pennsylvania to apportion and schedule these events among the scattered country clubs, and had pored over what unthinkable list of schoolchildren to discuss which schoolchildren should be asked to these dances they held for what reason. If you were part Jewish, would they find you out, like Hitler? How small a part could they detect?

We dined that night in faraway Sewickley, at long linen-covered tables marked by place cards. During dessert the band straggled in and set up by the freezing French doors to the terrace. The band struck up, not surprisingly, "Mountain Greenery." This frenzied sequence of notes had been our cue, conditioned since we were ten. We danced.

Here was a light-shouldered boy who could jitterbug, old style, and would; he was more precious than gold, yea, than much fine gold. We jitterbugged. It was an exultant and concentrated collaboration, such as aerialists enjoy—and I hope they enjoy it—when they catch each other twirling in midair. Only the strength in our fingertips kept us alive. If they weakened or slipped, his fingertips or mine, we'd fall spinning backward across the length of the room and out through the glass French doors to the snowy terrace, and if we were any good we'd make sure we fell on the downbeat, snow or no snow. For this was rock and roll. We danced in front of the band; I wished the music were louder.

The last dance was slow; the lights dimmed. The light-shouldered blond boy moved me over and across the golden dark floor and in and out of his arms. He released me and caught me, slowly, and turned me and spun me, and paused on the odd long note so I had to raise a leg from the hip to keep us afloat, and I held him loosely but surely for the count of four, amazed.

He was bare-handed, as were all the boys at these dances. We retained our white cotton gloves. It was easy to imagine his warmth, the heel of his naked left hand on my glove. But it still required imagination. The thick cotton stretched flat across the dip of my palm like a trampoline; it repelled the bulge of his hand and held away his heat.

"Keep your back straight," my mother had told me years before. "Don't let your arm weigh and drag on a boy's shoulder, no matter how tired you are. Dance on the balls of your feet, no matter how tall you are. Chin up."

The drummer stretched in the dark and rubbed the back of his neck. He began packing up, retaining, however, his brushes for "Good Night, Ladies," at whose opening bars we all groaned.

We groaned because we had to part and lacked the words to manage it smoothly. We groaned because we had to ride back through the snow for an hour and a half with our boys on a bus, and we never figured out how to conduct ourselves on this bus. Were we to kiss, or sing camp songs?

"How was it?" my mother asked the next morning. She lowered the Sunday paper she'd been paging through. How was what? I could barely remember. Someone's father had picked us up at our club and driven us another hour home. I didn't get in till after two. Now it was Sunday morning. I was dressed up again and looking for a pair of clean white cotton gloves for church. So was Amy. If there was such a pair, I wanted to find it first.

"How was it?" she asked, and then I remembered and began to understand how it was. It was wonderful, that's how it was. It was absolutely wonderful.

THAT MORNING IN CHURCH AFTER our first subscription dance, we reconvened on the balcony of the Shadyside Presbyterian Church. I sat in the first balcony row, and resisted the impulse to stretch my Charleston-stiff legs on the balcony's carved walnut rail. The blond boy I'd met at the dance was on my mind, and I intended to spend the church hour recalling his every word and gesture, but I couldn't concentrate. Beside me sat my friend Linda. Last night at the dance she had been a laughing, dimpled girl with an advanced sense of the absurd. Now in church she was grave, and didn't acknowledge my remarks.

Near us in the balcony's first row, and behind us, were the boys—the same boys with whom we had traveled on a bus to and from the Sewickley Country Club dance. Below us spread the main pews, filling with adults. Almost everyone in the church was long familiar to me. But this particular Sunday in church bore home to me with force a new notion: that I did not really know any of these people at all. I thought I did—but, being now a teenager, I thought I knew almost everything. Only the strongest evidence could penetrate this illusion, which distorted everything I saw. I knew I approved almost nothing. That is, I liked, I adored, I longed for, everyone on earth, especially India and Africa, and particularly everyone on the streets of Pittsburgh—all those friendly, democratic, openhearted, sensible people—and at Forbes Field, and in all the office buildings, parks, streetcars, churches, and stores, excepting only the people I knew, none of whom was up to snuff.

The church building, where the old Scotch-Irish families assembled weekly, was a Romanesque chunk of rough, carved stone and panes of dark slate. Covered in creeper, long since encrusted into its quietly splendid site, it looked like a Scottish rock in the rain.

Everywhere outside and inside the church and parish hall, sharp carved things rose from the many dim tons of stone. There were grainy crossed keys, pelicans, anchors, a phoenix, ivy vines, sheaves of wheat, queer and leering mammal heads like gargoyles, thistles for Scotland, lizards, scrolls, lions, and shells. It looked as if someone had once in Pittsburgh enjoyed a flight or two of fancy. If your bare hand or arm brushed against one of the stone walls carelessly, the stone would draw blood.

My wool coat sat empty behind me; its satin lining felt cool on the backs of my arms. I hated being here. It looked as if the boys did, too. Their mouths were all open, and their eyelids half down. We were all trapped. At home before church, I had been too rushed to fight about it.

I imagined the holy war each boy had fought with his family this morning, and lost, resulting in his sullen and suited presence in church. I thought of Dan there, ruddy-cheeked, and of wild, sweet Jamie beside him, each flinging his silk tie at his hypocrite father after breakfast, and making a desperate stand in some dark dining room lighted upward by snowlight from the lawns outside—struggling foredoomed to raise the stone-and-walnut weight of this dead society's dead institutions, battling for liberty, freedom of conscience, and so forth.

The boys, at any rate, slumped. Possibly they were hung over.

While the nave filled we examined, or glared at, the one thing before our eyes: the apse's enormous gold mosaic of Christ. It loomed over the chancel; every pew in the nave and on the balcony looked up at it. It was hard to imagine what long-ago board of trustees had voted for this Romish-looking mosaic, so glittering, with which we had been familiarizing ourselves in a lonely way since infancy, when our eyes could first focus on distance.

Christ stood barefoot, alone and helpless-looking, his palms outcurved at his sides. He was wearing his robes. He wasn't standing on anything, but instead floated loose and upright inside a curved, tiled dome. The balcony's perspective fore-

shortened the dome's curve, so Christ appeared to drift flattened and clumsy, shriveled but glorious. Barefoot as he was,
and with the suggestion of sandstone scarps behind him, he
looked rural. Below me along the carpeted marble aisles crept
the church's families; the women wore mink and sable stoles.
Hushed, they sat and tilted their hatted heads and looked at the
rural man. His skies of shattered gold widened over the sanctu-
ary and almost met the square lantern tower, gold-decorated,
over the nave.

The mosaic caught the few church lights—lights like tapers
in a castle—and spread them dimly, a dusting of gold like
pollen, throughout the vast and solemn space. There was nothing you could see well in this rich, Rembrandt darkness—nothing save the minister's shining face and Christ's gold vault—and
yet there was no corner, no scratchy lily work, you couldn't see
at all.

It was a velvet cord, maroon, with brass fittings, that reserved
our ninth-grade balcony section for us. We sat on velvet cush-
ions. Below us, filling the yellow pews with dark furs, were the
rest of the families of the church, who seemed to have been
planted here in dignity—by a God who could see how hard they
worked and how few pleasures they took for themselves—just
after the Flood went down. There were Linda's parents and
grandparents and one of her great-grandparents. Always, the
same old Pittsburgh families ran this church. The men, for
whose forefathers streets all over town were named, served as
deacons, trustees, and elders. The women served in many ways,
and ran the Christmas bazaar.

I knew these men; they were friends and neighbors. I knew
what they lived for, I thought. The men wanted to do the right
thing, at work and in the community. They wore narrow, tight
neckties. Close-mouthed, they met, in volunteer boardrooms
and in club locker rooms, the same few comfortable others they
had known since kindergarten. Their wives and children, in
those days, lived around them on their visits home. Some men
found their families bewildering, probably; a man might wonder, wakened by reports of the outstanding misdeeds of this son
or that son, how everyone had so failed to understand what he

expected. Some of these men held their shoulders and knuckles tight; their laughter was high and embarrassed; they seemed to be looking around for the entrance to some other life. Only some of the doctors, it seemed to me, were conspicuously interested and glad. During conversations, they looked at people calmly, even at their friends' little daughters; their laughter was deep, long, and joyful; they asked questions; and they knew lots of words.

I knew the women better. The women were wise and strong. Even among themselves, they prized gaiety and irony, gaiety and irony come what may. They coped. They sighed, they permitted themselves a remark or two, they lived essentially alone. They reared their children with their own two hands, and did all their own cooking and driving. They had no taste for waste or idleness. They volunteered their considerable energies, wisdom, and ideas at the church or the hospital or the service organization or charity.

Life among these families partook of all the genuine seriousness of life in time. A child's birth was his sole entrée, just as it is to life itself. His birthright was a regiment of families and a phalanx of institutions that would accompany him, solidly but at a distance, through this vale of tears.

Families whose members have been acquainted with each other for as long as anyone remembers grow not close, but respectful. They accumulate dignity by being seen at church every Sunday for the duration of life, despite their troubles and sorrows. They accumulate dignity at club luncheons, dinners, and dances, by gracefully and persistently, with tidy hair and fitted clothes, occupying their slots.

In this world, some grown women went carefully wild from time to time. They appeared at parties in outlandish clothes, hair sticking out, faces painted in freckles. They shrieked, sang, danced, and parodied anything—that is, anything at all outside the tribe—so that nothing, almost, was sacred. These clowns were the best-loved women, and rightly so, for their own sufferings had taught them what dignity was worth, and every few years they reminded the others, and made them laugh till they cried.

My parents didn't go to church. I practically admired them for it. Father would drive by at noon and scoop up Amy and me, saying, "Hop in quick!" so no one would see his weekend khaki pants and loafers.

Now, in unison with the adults in the dimness below, we read responsively, answering the minister. Our voices blended low, so their joined sound rose muffled and roaring, rhythmic, like distant seas, and soaked into the rough stone vaults and plush fittings, and vanished, and rose again:

> The heavens declare the glory of God;
> AND THE FIRMAMENT SHOWETH HIS
>   HANDIWORK.
> Day unto day uttereth speech,
> AND NIGHT UNTO NIGHT SHOWETH
>   KNOWLEDGE.
> There is no speech nor language, where their voice is not heard.

The minister was a florid, dramatic man who commanded a batch of British vowels, for which I blamed him absolutely, not knowing he came from a Canadian farm. His famous radio ministry attracted letters and even contributions from Alaskan lumberjacks and fishermen. The poor saps. What if one of them, a lumberjack, showed up in Pittsburgh wearing a lumberjack shirt and actually tried to enter the church building? Maybe the ushers were really bouncers.

I had got religion at summer camp, and had prayed nightly there, and in my bed at home, to God, asking for a grateful heart, and receiving one insofar as I requested it. Inasmuch as I despised everything and everyone about me, of course, it was taken away, and I was left with the blackened heart I had chosen instead. As the years wore on, the intervals between Julys at camp stretched, and filled with country-club evenings, filled with the slang of us girls, our gossip, and our intricately shifting friendships, filled with the sight of the boys whose names themselves were a litany, and with the absorbing study of their nonchalance and gruff ease. All of which I professed, from time to time, when things went poorly, to disdain.

Nothing so inevitably blackened my heart as an obligatory Sunday at the Shadyside Presbyterian Church: the sight of camp orphan-girl Liz's "Jesus" tricked out in gilt; the minister's Britishy accent; the putative hypocrisy of my parents, who forced me to go, though they did not; the putative hypocrisy of the expensive men and women who did go. I knew enough of the Bible to damn these people to hell, citing chapter and verse. My house shall be called the house of prayer; but ye have made it a den of thieves. Every week I had been getting madder; now I was going to plain quit. One of these days, when I figured out how.

After the responsive reading there was a pause, an expectant hush. It was the first Sunday of the month, I remembered, shocked. Today was Communion. I would have to sit through Communion, with its two species, embarrassment and tedium—and I would be late getting out and Father would have to drive around the block a hundred times. I had successfully avoided Communion for years.

From their pews below rose the ushers and elders—everybody's father and grandfather, from Mellon Bank & Trust et cetera—in tailcoats. They worked the crowd smoothly, as always. When they collected money, I noted, they were especially serene. Collecting money was, after all, what they did during the week; they were used to it. Down each pew an usher thrust a long-handled velvet butterfly net, into the invisible interior of which we each inserted a bare hand to release a crushed, warm dollar bill we'd stored in a white glove's palm.

Now with dignity the ushers and elders hoisted the round sterling silver trays that bore Communion. A loaded juice tray must have weighed ten pounds. From a cunning array of holes in its top layer hung wee, tapered, lead-crystal glasses. Each held one-half ounce of Welch's grape juice.

The seated people passed the grape-juice trays down the pews. After the grape juice came bread: flat silver salvers bore heaps of soft bread cubes, as if for stuffing a turkey. The elders and ushers spread swiftly and silently over the marble aisles in discreet pairs, some for bread cubes, some for grape juice, communicating by eyebrow only. An unseen organist, behind stone screens, played a muted series of single notes, a restless, breathy strain in a minor key, to kill time.

Soon the ushers reached the balcony where we sat. There our prayers had reached their intensest pitch, so fervent were we in our hopes not to drop the grape-juice tray.

I passed up the Welch's Grape Juice, I passed up the cubed bread, and sat back against my coat. Was all this not absurd? I glanced at Linda beside me. Apparently it was not. Her hands lay folded in her lap. Both her father and her uncle were elders.

It was not surprising, really, that I alone in this church knew what the barefoot Christ, if there had been such a person, would think about things—grape juice, tailcoats, British vowels, sable stoles. It was not surprising because it was becoming quite usual. After all, I was the intelligentsia around these parts, single-handedly. The intelligentsium. I knew why these people were in church: to display to each other their clothes. These were sophisticated men and women, such as we children were becoming. In church they made business connections; they saw and were seen. The boys, who, like me, were starting to come out for freedom and truth, must be having fits, now that the charade of Communion was in full swing.

I stole a glance at the boys, then looked at them outright, for I had been wrong. The boys, if mine eyes did not deceive me, were praying. Why? The intelligentsia, of course, described itself these days as "agnostic"—a most useful word. Around me, in seeming earnest, the boys prayed their unthinkable private prayers. To whom? It was wrong to watch, but I watched.

On the balcony's first row, to my right, big Dan had pressed his ruddy cheeks into his palms. Beside him, Jamie bent over his knees. Over one eye he had jammed a fist; his other eye was crinkled shut. Another boy, blond Robert, lay stretched over his arms, which clasped the balcony rail. His shoulders were tight; the back of his jacket rose and fell heavily with his breathing. It had been a long time since I'd been to Communion. When had this praying developed?

Dan lowered his hands and leaned back slowly. He opened

his eyes, unfocused to the high, empty air before him. Wild Jamie moved his arm; he picked up a fistful of hair from his forehead and held it. His eyes fretted tightly shut; his jaws worked. Robert's head still lay low on his outstretched sleeves; it moved once from side to side and back again. So they struggled on. I finally looked away.

Below the balcony, in the crowded nave, men and women were also concentrating, it seemed. Were they perhaps pretending to pray? All heads were bent; no one moved. I began to doubt my own omniscience. If I bowed my head, too, and shut my eyes, would this be apostasy? No, I'd keep watching the people, in case I'd missed some clue that they were actually doing something else—bidding bridge hands.

For I knew these people, didn't I? I knew their world, which was, in some sense, my world, too, since I could not, outside of books, name another. I knew what they loved: their families, their houses, their country clubs, hard work, the people they knew best, and summer parties with old friends full of laughter. I knew what they hated: labor unions, laziness, spending, wildness, loudness. They didn't buy God. They didn't buy anything if they could help it. And they didn't work on spec.

Nevertheless, a young father below me propped his bowed head on two fists stacked on a raised knee. The ushers and their trays had vanished. The people had taken Communion. No one moved. The organist hushed. All the men's heads were bent—black, white, red, yellow, and brown. The men sat absolutely still. Almost all the women's heads were bent down, too, and some few tilted back. Some hats wagged faintly from side to side. All the people seemed scarcely to breathe.

I was alert enough now to feel, despite myself, some faint, thin stream of spirit braiding forward from the pews. Its flawed and fragile rivulets pooled far beyond me at the altar. I felt, or saw, its frail strands rise to the wide tower ceiling, and mass in the gold mosaic's dome.

The gold tesserae scattered some spirit like light back over the cavernous room, and held some of it, like light, in its deep curve. Christ drifted among floating sandstone ledges and deep, absorbent skies. There was no speech nor language. The people had been praying, praying to God, just as they seemed to be praying. That was the fact. I didn't know what to make of it.

I left Pittsburgh before I had a grain of sense. Who IS my neighbor? I never learned what the strangers around me had known and felt in their lives—those lithe, sarcastic boys in the balcony, those expensive men and women in the pews below— but it was more than I knew, after all.

FATHER PICKED UP AMY AND me after church. When we got out of the car in the garage, we could hear Dixieland, all rambling brasses and drums, coming from the house. We hightailed it inside through the snow on the back walk and kicked off our icy dress shoes. I was in stockings. I could eat something, and go to my room. I had my own room now, and when I was home I stayed there and read or sulked.

While we were making sandwiches, though, Father started explaining the world to us once again. I stuck around. There in the kitchen, Father embarked upon an explanation of American economics. I don't know what prompted it. His voice took on urgency; he paced. Money worked like water, he said.

We were all listening, even little Molly. Molly, at four, had an open expression, smooth and quick, and fine blond hair; she was eating on the hoof, like the rest of us, and looking up, a pale face at thigh level, following the conversation. Mother futzed around the kitchen in camel-colored wool slacks; she rarely ate.

Did we know how water got up to our attic bathroom? Money worked the same way, he said, worked the way locks on the river worked, worked the way water flowed down from high water towers into our attic bathroom, the way the Allegheny and the Monongahela flowed into the Ohio, and the Ohio flowed into the Mississippi and out into the Gulf of Mexico at New Orleans. The money, once you got enough of it high enough, would flow by gravitation, all over everybody.

"It doesn't work that way," our mother said. She offered Molly tidbits: a drumstick, a beet slice, cheese. "Remember those shacks we saw in Georgia? Those barefoot little children who have to quit school to work in the fields, their poor mothers not able to feed them enough"—we could all hear in her voice that she was beginning to cry—"not even able to keep them dressed?" Molly was looking at her, wide-eyed; she was bent over, looking at Molly, wide-eyed.

"They shouldn't have so many kids," Father said. "They must be crazy."

The trouble was, I no longer believed him. It was beginning to strike me that Father, who knew the real world so well, got some of it wrong. Not much; just some.

WHEN I WAS FIFTEEN, I felt it coming; now I was sixteen, and it hit.

My feet had imperceptibly been set on a new path, a fast path into a long tunnel like those many turnpike tunnels near Pittsburgh, turnpike tunnels whose entrances bear on brass plaques a roll call of those men who died blasting them. I wandered witlessly forward and found myself going down, and saw the light dimming; I adjusted to the slant and dimness, traveled further down, adjusted to greater dimness, and so on. There wasn't a whole lot I could do about it, or about anything. I was going to hell on a handcart, that was all, and I knew it and everyone around me knew it, and there it was.

I was growing and thinning, as if pulled. I was getting angry, as if pushed. I morally disapproved most things in North America, and blamed my innocent parents for them. My feelings deepened and lingered. The swift moods of early childhood—each formed by and suited to its occasion—vanished. Now feelings lasted so long they left stains. They arose from nowhere, like winds or waves, and battered at me or engulfed me.

When I was angry, I felt myself coiled and longing to kill someone or bomb something big. Trying to appease myself, during one winter I whipped my bed every afternoon with my uniform belt. I despised the spectacle I made in my own eyes— whipping the bed with a belt, like a creature demented!—and I often began halfheartedly, but I did it daily after school as a desperate discipline, trying to rid myself and the innocent world of my wildness. It was like trying to beat back the ocean.

Sometimes in class I couldn't stop laughing; things were too funny to be borne. It began then, my surprise that no one else saw what was so funny.

I read some few books with such reverence I didn't close them at the finish, but only moved the pile of pages back to the start, without breathing, and began again. I read one such book, an enormous novel, six times that way—closing the binding between sessions, but not between readings.

On the piano in the basement I played the maniacal "Poet and Peasant Overture" so loudly, for so many hours, night after night, I damaged the piano's keys and strings. When I wasn't playing this crashing overture, I played boogie-woogie, or something else, anything else, in octaves—otherwise, it wasn't loud enough. My fingers were so strong I could do push-ups with them. I played one piece with my fists. I banged on a steel-stringed guitar till I bled, and once on a particularly piercing rock-and-roll downbeat I broke straight through one of Father's snare drums.

I loved my boyfriend so tenderly, I thought I must transmogrify into vapor. It would take spectroscopic analysis to locate my molecules in thin air. No possible way of holding him was close enough. Nothing could cure this bad case of gentleness except, perhaps, violence: maybe if he swung me by the legs and split my skull on a tree? Would that ease this insane wish to kiss too much his eyelids' outer corners and his temples, as if I could love up his brain?

I envied people in books who swooned. For two years I felt myself continuously swooning and continuously unable to swoon; the blood drained from my face and eyes and flooded my heart; my hands emptied, my knees unstrung, I bit at the air for something worth breathing—but I failed to fall, and I couldn't find the way to black out. I had to live on the lip of a waterfall, exhausted.

When I was bored I was first hungry, then nauseated, then furious and weak. "Calm yourself," people had been saying to me all my life. Since early childhood I had tried one thing and then another to calm myself, on those few occasions when I truly wanted to. Eating helped; singing helped. Now sometimes I truly wanted to calm myself. I couldn't lower my shoulders; they seemed to wrap around my ears. I couldn't lower my voice although I could see the people around me flinch. I waved my arm in class till the very teachers wanted to kill me.

I was what they called a live wire. I was shooting out sparks that were digging a pit around me, and I was sinking into that pit. Laughing with Ellin at school recess, or driving around after school with Judy in her jeep, exultant, or dancing with my boyfriend to Louis Armstrong across a polished dining-room floor, I got so excited I looked around wildly for aid; I didn't know where I should go or what I should do with myself. People in books split wood.

When rage or boredom reappeared, each seemed never to have left. Each so filled me with so many years' intolerable accumulation it jammed the space behind my eyes, so I couldn't see. There was no room left even on my surface to live. My rib cage was so taut I couldn't breathe. Every cubic centimeter of atmosphere above my shoulders and head was heaped with last straws. Black hatred clogged my very blood. I couldn't peep, I couldn't wiggle or blink; my blood was too mad to flow.

For as long as I could remember, I had been transparent to myself, unselfconscious, learning, doing, most of every day. Now I was in my own way; I myself was a dark object I could not ignore. I couldn't remember how to forget myself. I didn't want to think about myself, to reckon myself in, to deal with myself every livelong minute on top of everything else—but swerve as I might, I couldn't avoid it. I was a boulder blocking my own path. I was a dog barking between my own ears, a barking dog who wouldn't hush.

So this was adolescence. Is this how the people around me had died on their feet—inevitably, helplessly? Perhaps their own selves eclipsed the sun for so many years the world shriveled around them, and when at last their inescapable orbits had passed through these dark egoistic years it was too late, they had adjusted.

Must I then lose the world forever, that I had so loved? Was it all, the whole bright and various planet, where I had been so ardent about finding myself alive, only a passion peculiar to children, that I would outgrow even against my will?

NOW IT WAS MAY. DAYLIGHT saving time had begun; the colored light of the long evenings fairly split me with joy. White trillium had bloomed and gone on the forested slopes in Fox Chapel. The cliffside and riverside patches of woods all over town showed translucent ovals of yellow or ashy greens; the neighborhood trees on Glen Arden Drive had blossomed in white and red.

Baseball season had begun, a season that recalled but could never match last year's National League pennant and seventh-game World Series victory over the Yankees, when we at school had been so frenzied for so many weeks they finally and wisely opened the doors and let us go. I had walked home from school one day during that series and seen Pittsburgh's Fifth Avenue emptied of cars, as if the world were over.

A year of wild feelings had passed, and more were coming. Without my noticing, the drummer had upped the tempo. Someone must have slipped him a signal when I wasn't looking; he'd speeded things up. The key was higher, too. I had a driver's license. When I drove around in Mother's old Dodge convertible, the whole town smelled good. And I did drive around the whole town. I cruised along the blue rivers and across them on steel bridges, and steered up and down the scented hills. I drove winding into and out of the steep neighborhoods across the Allegheny River, neighborhoods where I tried in vain to determine in what languages the signs on storefronts were written. I drove onto boulevards, highways, beltways, freeways, and the turnpike. I could drive to Guatemala, drive to Alaska. Why, I asked myself, did I drive to—of all spots on earth—our garage? Why home, why school?

*　　*　　*

Throughout the long, deadly school afternoons, we junior and senior girls took our places in study hall. We sat at desks in a roomful of desks, whether or not we had something to do, until four o'clock.

Now this May afternoon a teacher propped open the study hall's back door. The door gave onto our hockey field and, behind it, Pittsburgh's Nabisco plant, whence, O Lordy, issued the smell of shortbread today; they were baking Lorna Doones. Around me sat forty or fifty girls in green cotton jumpers and spring-uniform white bucks. They rested their chins on the heels of both hands and leaned their cheeks on curled fingers; their propped heads faced the opened pages of *L'Étranger*, *Hamlet*, *Vanity Fair*. Some girls leaned back and filed their nails. Some twisted stiff pieces of their hair, to stay not so much awake as alive. Sometimes in health class, when we were younger, we had all been so bored we hooked our armpits over our chairs' backs so we cut off all circulation to one arm, in an effort to kill that arm for something to do, or cause a heart attack, whichever came first. We were, in fact, getting a dandy education. But sometimes we were restless. Weren't there some wars being fought somewhere that I, for one, could join?

I wrote a name on a notebook. I looked at the study-hall ceiling and tried to see that boy's familiar face—light and dark, bold-eyed, full of feeling—on the inside of my eyelids. Failing that, I searched for his image down the long speckled tunnel or corridor I saw with my eyes closed. As if visual memory were a Marx Brothers comedy, I glimpsed swift fragments—a wry corner of his lip, a pointy knuckle, a cupped temple—which crossed the corridor so fast I recognized them only as soon as they vanished. I opened my eyes and wrote his name. His depth and complexity were apparently infinite. From the tip of his lively line of patter to the bottom of his heartbroken, hopeful soul was the longest route I knew, and the best.

The heavy, edible scent of shortbread maddened me in my seat, made me so helpless with longing my wrists gave out; I couldn't hold a pen. I looked around constantly to catch someone's eye, anyone's eye.

It was a provocative fact, which I seemed to have discovered, that we students outnumbered our teachers. Must we then huddle here like sheep? By what right, exactly, did these few women keep us sitting here in this clean, bare room to no purpose? Lately I had been trying to inflame my friends with the implications of our greater numbers. We could pull off a riot. We could bang on the desks and shout till they let us out. Then we could go home and wait for dinner. Or we could bear our teachers off on our shoulders, and—what? Throw them into the Lorna Doone batter? I got no takers.

I had finished my work long ago. "Works only on what interests her," the accusation ran—as if, I reflected, obedience outranked passion, as if sensible people didn't care what they stuck in their minds. Today as usual no one around me was ready for action. I took a fresh sheet of paper and copied on it random lines in French:

Ô saisons, ô châteaux!
Is it through these endless nights that you sleep in exile
Ô million golden birds, ô future vigor?

Oh, that my keel would split! Oh, that I would
go down in the sea!

I had struck upon the French Symbolists, like a canyon of sharp crystals underground, like a long and winding corridor lined with treasure. These poets popped into my ken in an odd way: I found them in a book I had rented from a drugstore. Carnegie and school libraries filled me in. I read Enid Starkie's Rimbaud biography. I saved my allowance for months and bought two paperbound poetry books, the Penguin *Rimbaud*, and a Symbolist anthology in which Paul Valéry declaimed, "*Azure! c'est moi* ... " I admired Gérard de Nerval. This mad writer kept a lobster as a pet. He walked it on a leash along the sidewalks of Paris, saying, "It doesn't bark, and knows the secrets of the deep."

I loved Rimbaud, who ran away, loved his skinny, furious face with the wild hair and snaky, unseeing eyes pointing in two directions, and his poems' confusion and vagueness, their overwritten longing, their hatred, their sky-shot lyricism, and their oracular fragmentation, which I enhanced for myself by reading and retaining his stuff in crazed bits, mostly from *Le Bateau Ivre,* The Drunken Boat.

Now in study hall I saw that I had drawn all over this page; I got out another piece of paper. Rimbaud was damned. He said so himself. Where could I meet someone like that? I wrote down another part:

> There is a cathedral that goes down and a lake that
> goes up.
> There is a troupe of strolling players in costume, glimpsed
> on the road through the edge of the trees.

I looked up from the new page I had already started to draw all over. Except for my boyfriend, the boys I knew best were out of town. They were older, prep school and college boys whose boldness, wit, breadth of knowledge, and absence of scruples fascinated me. They cruised the deb party circuit all over Pennsylvania, holding ever younger girls up to the light like chocolates, to determine how rich their centers might be. I smiled to recall one of these boys: he was so accustomed to the glitter of society, and so sardonic and graceful, that he carried with him at all times, in his jacket pocket, a canister of dance wax. Ordinary boys carried pocket knives for those occasions which occur unexpectedly, and this big, dark-haired boy carried dance wax for the same reason. When the impulse rose, he could simply sprinkle dance wax on any hall or dining-room floor, take a girl in his arms and whirl her away. I had known these witty, handsome boys for years, and only recently understood that when they were alone, they read books. In public, they were lounge lizards; they drank; they played word games, filling in the blanks desultorily; they cracked wise. These boys would be back in town soon, and my boyfriend and I would join them.

Whose eye could I catch? Everyone in the room was bent over her desk. Ellin Hahn was usually ready to laugh, but now she was working on something. She would call me as soon as we got home. Every day on the phone, I unwittingly asked Ellin some blunt question about the social world around us, and at every question she sighed and said to me, "You still don't get it"—or often, as if addressing a jury of our incredulous peers, "She still doesn't get it!"

Looking at the study-hall ceiling, I dosed myself almost fatally with the oxygen-eating lines of Verlaine's "The long sobs / of the violins / of autumn / wound my heart / with a languor / monotone."

This unsatisfying bit of verse I repeated to myself for ten or fifteen minutes, by the big clock, over and over, clobbering myself with it, the way Molly, when she had been a baby, banged the top of her head on her crib.

Ô world, ô college, ô dinner . . .
Ô unthinkable task . . .

Funny how badly I'd turned out. Now I was always in trouble. It felt as if I was doing just as I'd always done—I explored the neighborhood, turning over rocks. The latest rocks were difficult. I'd been in a drag race, of all things, the previous September, and in the subsequent collision, and in the hospital; my parents saw my name in the newspapers, and their own names in the newspapers. Some boys I barely knew had cruised by that hot night and said to a clump of us girls on the sidewalk, "Anybody want to come along for a drag race?" I did, absolutely. I loved fast driving.

It was then, in the days after the drag race, that I noticed the ground spinning beneath me, all bearings lost, and recognized as well that I had been loose like this—detached from all I saw and knowing nothing else—for months, maybe years. I whirled through the air like a bull-roarer spun by a lunatic who'd found his rhythm. The pressure almost split my skin. What else can you risk with all your might but your life? Only a moment ago I was climbing my swing set, holding one cold metal leg between my two legs tight, and feeling a piercing oddness run the length of my gut—the same sensation that plucked me when my

tongue touched tarnish on a silver spoon. Only a moment ago I
was gluing squares of paper to rocks; I leaned over the bedroom
desk. I was drawing my baseball mitt in the attic, under the
plaster-stain ship; a pencil study took all Saturday morning. I
was capturing the flag, turning the double play, chasing butterflies by the country-club pool. Throughout these many years of
childhood, a transparent sphere of timelessness contained all my
running and spinning as a glass paperweight holds flying snow.
The sphere of this idyll broke; time unrolled before me in a
line. I woke up and found myself in juvenile court. I was hanging from crutches; for a few weeks after the drag race, neither
knee worked. (No one else got hurt.) In juvenile court, a police-
man wet all ten of my fingertips on an ink pad and pressed
them, one by one, using his own fingertips, on a form for the
files.

Turning to the French is a form of suicide for the American
who loves literature—or, as the joke might go, it is at least a cry
for help. Now, when I was sixteen, I had turned to the French. I
flung myself into poetry as into Niagara Falls. Beauty took away
my breath. I twined away; I flew off with my eyes rolled up; I
dove down and succumbed. I bought myself a plot in Valéry's
marine cemetery, and moved in: cool dirt on my eyes, my brain
smooth as a cannonball. It grieves me to report that I tried to see
myself as a sobbing fountain, apparently serene, tall and thin
among the chill marble monuments of the dead. Rimbaud wrote
a lyric that gently described a man sleeping out in the grass; the
sleeper made a peaceful picture, until, in the poem's last line,
we discover in his right side two red holes. This, and many
another literary false note, appealed to me.

I'd been suspended from school for smoking cigarettes.
That was a month earlier, in early spring. Both my parents wept.
Amy saw them weeping; horrified, she began to cry herself.
Molly cried. She was six, missing her front teeth. Like Mother
and me, she had pale skin that turned turgid and red when she
cried; she looked as if she were dying of wounds. I didn't cry,
because, actually, I was an intercontinental ballistic missile, with
an atomic warhead; they don't cry.

Why didn't I settle down, straighten out, shape up? I wondered, too. I thought that joy was a childish condition that had forever departed; I had no glimpse then of its return the minute I got to college. I couldn't foresee the pleasure—or the possibility—of shedding sophistication, walking away from rage, and renouncing French poets.

Late one night, my parents and I sat at the kitchen table; there was a truce. We were all helpless, and tired of fighting. Amy and Molly were asleep.

"What are we going to do with you?"

Mother raised the question. Her voice trembled and rose with emotion. She couldn't sit still; she kept getting up and roaming around the kitchen. Father stuck out his chin and rubbed it with his big hands. I covered my eyes. Mother squeezed white lotion into her hands, over and over. We all smoked; the ashtray was full. Mother walked over to the sink, poured herself some ginger ale, ran both hands through her short blond hair to keep it back, and shook her head.

She sighed and said again, looking up and out of the night-black window, "Dear God, what are we going to do with you?" My heart went out to them. We all seemed to have exhausted our options. They asked me for fresh ideas, but I had none. I racked my brain, but couldn't come up with anything. The U.S. Marines didn't take sixteen-year-old girls.

I GREW UP IN PITTSBURGH in the 1950s, in a house full of comedians, reading books. Possibly because Father had loaded his boat one day and gone down the Ohio River, I confused leaving with living, and vowed that when I got my freedom, I would be the one to do both.

Sometimes after dinner, when my sisters and I were young, Mother could persuade Father to perform Goofus—to "do" Goofus. Goofus, he explained, was an old road-show routine, older than vaudeville, that traveling actors brought to the cities of the young republic, and out into the frontier towns. It was a pantomime, a character, and a song.

Doing Goofus, Father shambled, holding his tall frame unstrung like one of those toy figures whose string collapses when you press the bottoms of their stands. He walked onstage a hayseed, a farm boy, a rube, sticking his neck forward. He sang the syncopated song, dipping his knees mock-idiotically on the beats:

> I was born on a farm down in Ioway,
> Flaming youth who was bound that he'd fly away . . .

Between verses of the song the rube stepped forward and concentrated on some absurdity, like balancing on his finger an imaginary hair plucked from his head. He stiffened the hair with his fingers and, wincing horribly, inserted it into one of his ears. He pushed it through to the other ear till he could grasp it; then he drew it sawing back and forth through his skull with both hands, in one ear and out the other, grinning stupidly in the character of the rube. That was the flaming youth.

"Do you know what you call that?" he asked as he sat back down. The intelligence had come back to his eyes. What? "That," he said. "What you do up there. That is called a 'business.'"

Our father taught us the culture into which we were born. American culture was Dixieland above all, Dixieland pure and simple, and next to Dixieland, jazz. It was the pioneers who went West singing "Bang away my Lulu." When someone died on the Oregon Trail, as someone was always doing, the family scratched a shallow grave right by the trail, because the wagon train couldn't wait. Everyone paced on behind the oxen across the empty desert, and some families sang "Bang away my Lulu" that night, and some didn't.

Our culture was the stock-market crash—the biggest and best crash a country ever had. Father explained the mechanics of the crash to young Amy and me, around the dining-room table. He tried to explain why men on Wall Street had jumped from skyscrapers when the stock market crashed: "They lost everything!"—but of course I thought they lost everything only when they jumped. It was the breadlines of the Depression, and the Okies fleeing the Dust Bowl, and the proud men begging on city streets, and families on the move seeking work—dusty women, men in black hats pulled over their eyes, haunted, hungry children: what a mystifying spectacle, this almost universal misery, city families living in cars, farm families eating insects, because—why? Because all the businessmen realized at once, on the same morning, that paper money was only paper. What terrible fools. What did they think it was?

American culture was the World's Fair in Chicago, baseball, the Erie Canal, fancy nightclubs in Harlem, silent movies, summer-stock theater, the California forty-niners, the Alaska gold rush, Henry Ford and his bright idea of paying workers enough to buy cars, P.T. Barnum and his traveling circus, Buffalo Bill Cody and his Wild West Show. It was the Chrysler Building in New York and the Golden Gate Bridge in San Francisco; the *Concord* and the *Merrimack*, the Alamo, the Little Bighorn, Gettysburg, Shiloh, Bull Run, and "Strike the tent."

It was Pittsburgh's legendary Joe Magarac, the mighty Hungarian steelworker, who took off his shirt to reveal his body made of high-grade steel, and who squeezed out steel rail between his knuckles by the ton. It was the brawling rivermen on the Ohio River, the sandhogs who dug Hudson River tunnels, silver miners in Idaho, cowboys in Texas, and the innocent American Indian Jim Thorpe, who had to give all his Olympic gold medals back. It was the men of every race who built the railroads, and the boys of every race who went to war.

Above all, it was the man who wandered unencumbered by family ties: Johnny Appleseed in our own home woods, Daniel Boone in Kentucky, Jim Bridger crossing the Rockies. Father described for us the Yankee peddler, the free trapper, the roaming cowhand, the whalerman, roustabout, gandy dancer, tramp. His heroes, and my heroes, were Raymond Chandler's city detective Marlowe going, as a man must, down these mean streets; Huck Finn lighting out for the territories; and Jack Kerouac on the road.

Every time we danced, Father brought up Jack Kerouac, *On the Road*.

We did a lot of dancing at our house, fast dancing; everyone in the family was a dancing fool. I always came down from my room to dance. When the music was going, who could resist? I bounced down the stairs to the rhythm and began to whistle a bit, helpless as a marionette whose strings jerk her head and feet.

We danced by the record player in the dining room. For fast dancing, Mother only rarely joined in; perhaps Amy, Molly, and I had made her self-conscious. We waved our arms a lot. I bumped into people, because I liked to close my eyes.

"Turn that record player down!" Mother suggested from the living room. She was embroidering a pillow. Father opened the cabinet and turned the volume down a bit. I opened my eyes.

"Remember that line in *On the Road?*" He addressed me, because between us we had read *On the Road* approximately a million times. Like *Life on the Mississippi*, it was the sort of thing we read. I thought of his blue bookplate: "Books make the man." The bookplate's ship struggled in steep seas, and crowded on too much sail.

I nodded; I knew what he was going to say, because he said it every time we played music; it was always a pleasure. We both reined in our dancing a bit, so we could converse. Sure I remembered that line in *On the Road*.

"Kerouac's in a little bar in Mexico. He says that was the only time he ever got to hear music played loud enough—in that little bar in Mexico. It was in *On the Road*. The only time he ever got to hear the music loud enough. I always remember that."

He laughed, shaking his head; he turned the record player down another notch. If it had ever been at all, it had been a long time since Father had heard the music played loud enough. Maybe he was still imagining it, fondly, some little bar back away somewhere, so small he and the other regulars sat in the middle of the blaring band, or stood snapping their fingers, drinking bourbon, telling jokes between sets. He knew a lot of jokes. Did he think of himself as I thought of him, as the man who had cut out of town and headed, wearing tennis shoes and a blue cap, down the river toward New Orleans?

I was gaining momentum. It was only a matter of months. Downstairs in the basement, I played "Shake, Rattle, and Roll" on the piano. Why not take up the trumpet, why not marry this wonderful boy, write an epic, become a medical missionary to the Amazon as I always intended? What happened to painting, what happened to science? My boyfriend never seemed to sleep. "I can sleep when I'm dead," he said. Was this not grand?

I was approaching escape velocity. What would you do if you had fifteen minutes to live before the bomb went off? Quick: What would you read? I drove up and down the boulevards, up and down the highways, around Frick Park fast, over the flung bridges and up into the springtime hills. My boyfriend and I played lightning chess, ten games an hour. We drove up the Allegheny River into New York and back, and up the Monongahela River into West Virginia and back. In my room I shuffled cards. I wrote poems about the sea. I wrote poems imitating the psalms. I held my pen on the red paper label of the modern jazz record on the turntable, played that side past midnight over and over, and let the pen draw a circle hours thick. In New Orleans—if you could get to New Orleans—would the music be loud enough?

1987

POEMS

BIVOUAC

I

The she-wolf whelps in thunder.
The newborn prophet licks his palms
to clean his face like a cat.
You wake on the shore, weeping,
biting your own salt knee.

> You remember, don't you?
> You remember the sea,
> the deep sea, the pressure,
> and the pebbled shallows
> where the nurse sharks wait
> to heave you toward the light. . . .

You wake on the shore,
sand and gravel under your back,
wrack and sand in your hair.
Blink, and the light gives way
to the fixed and waterless stars.

You wake. The ocean
is furling its green tons down.
Volcano weather.
The sharp shinned hawk
cleaves with intricate strain
to the skin of air rivers rising,
spreading, peeling half over
and off to the side like a leaf.

This is the mainland,
this heaping of stones and the pines.
And the barnacles—
remember?—
when the water came over,
you waved your feathery arms.

The sky never ceases to widen,
hollow, over your head.
You can fashion
a fish-life here on the coast,
willow-strip, driftwood
and dugout, or go in
to a land already planted.

    You remember, don't you?
    You remember the forest,
    the deep jungle, the tree ferns,
    the club mosses, the green air;
    turning a golden eye to watch
    the lizards still on the stones. . . .

There's forest inside, straight wood,
a mud clearing, and a man
on his knees shaking feathers,
owl feathers, owl tongues, twisted
in sinew and thong.

And there's desert inside,
caves, and a woman
splitting her lips with a thorn.
This is your son, and your daughter.

    You remember, don't you?
    You remember the plains,
    the wind, the hot grass,
    hefting a gritty rock
    to split thick bones and suck
    the bloody grease. . . .

Follow the rivers, look for a pass,
or follow the ridges, rise.
There are no eyes on you.
You were kindled from a clot
and washed on the beach like a conch
from one more witless wave.

II

You have never been so tired.

The wooded ridges roll under the sun
like water, and none of the mountains home,
and all of the mountains bivouac,
campaigner; lean-to, hoe-down, shack-up: run.

III

A baby is a pucker
of the earth's thin skin;
he swells, circles, and lays him down.

The lakes fill, the ice rolls back
(the ice rolls up!), the ice rolls back,
the skin wrinkles and splits—
fishes, grass—the skin
bunches and smooths.

You die, you die.
First you go wet
and then you go dry.

This is the end,
the dry channel,
the splintered sluice,
where you slake your thirst on chert.
There's a spread to the light
and a rising, a way
that even the air is a cobra;
and at night
the rock moon and the desert rock
bat the dead light back
and forth till it snaps.

You sleep
under a ledge away from the riverbed;

you wake
to the sun looming low like the mouth
of a tunnel to hell.
A scale-legged bird is eating a snake.
Dig for mice. Smell
your shoulder. There's been
flash-flood, dust-storm,
rivers run in and move out
like haunts, and still those two round lights,
the fire-light and the ash;
and still you wake, you wake a million days,
and walk.

Oh yes,
it's a hard slide,
it's a rough winter,
what with the sharp gravel
and acid salts in the sand.
You're softshell and peeled,
with nothing to keep out the wind—
the williwaw, cheechako—
that splits the cell and drains it dry as ash.

IV

You have walked beyond
the highest tide and seen
how, where birds have landed,
walked, and flown,
their tracks begin in sand,
and go, and suddenly end.
Our tracks do that, but we go down.

Where have we been,
and why do we go down?
At night your best-loved dead appear
back, and start their stare.
You wake; you greet them;

you wake again; the dead still steer
their sleeping course,
their sleeping heels in the air.

Hold fast.
Duck.
There's a flat-out, flinging way
the clouds begin their dive,
there's a scurf of earth and air
so thin
you'd step clear through
or blow clean off.

You remember it all:
how you lungless lay in slime,
how you shied across the plain
on your sharp split hoof,
the mist, the sip of ozone on the tongue. . . .

You wake. This is the mainland.
Here you must look
at each thing with the elephant eye:
greeting it now for the first time,
and bidding, forever, good-bye.

Ease her when she pitches.
Keep your tinder dry.

1972

THE MAN WHO WISHES TO FEED
ON MAHOGANY

*Chesterton tells us that if someone wished to feed exclusively on
mahogany, poetry would not be able to express this. Instead, if a
man happens to love and not be loved in return, or if he mourns
the absence or loss of someone, then poetry is able to express these
feelings precisely because they are commonplace.*

—BORGES, INTERVIEW IN *ENCOUNTER*, APRIL 1969

Not the man who wishes to feed on mahogany
and who happens to love and not be loved in return;
not mourning in autumn the absence or loss of someone,
remembering how, in a yellow dress, she leaned
light-shouldered, lanky, over a platter of pears—
no; no tricks. Just the man and his wish, alone.

That there should be mahogany, real, in the world,
instead of no mahogany, rings in his mind
like a gong—that in humid Haitian forests are trees,
hard trees, not holes in air, not nothing, no Haiti,
no zone for trees nor time for wood to grow:
reality rounds his mind like rings in a tree.

Love is the factor, love is the type, and the poem.
Is love a trick, to make him commonplace?
He wishes, cool in his windy rooms. He thinks:
of all earth's shapes, her coils, rays, and nets,
mahogany I love, this sunburnt red,
this close-grained, scented slab, my fellow creature.

He knows he can't feed on the wood he loves, and he won't.
But desire walks on lean legs down halls of his sleep,
desire to drink and sup at mahogany's mass.
His wishes weight his belly. Love holds him here,
love nails him to the world, this windy wood,
as to a cross. Oh, this lanky, sunburnt cross!

Is he sympathetic? Do you care?
And you, sir: perhaps you wish to feed
on your bright-eyed daughter, on your baseball glove,
on your outboard motor's pattern in the water.
Some love weights your walking in the world;
Some love molds you heavier than air.

Look at the world, where vegetation spreads
and peoples air with weights of green desire.
Crosses grow as trees and grasses everywhere,
writing in wood and leaf and flower and spore,
marking the map, "Some man loved here;
and one loved something here; and here; and here."

1971

FOUR FOUND POEMS

Poems seldom require explanation, but these do. I did not write a word of them. Other hands composed the poems' lines—the poems' sentences. These are found poems. They differ, however, from what we usually think of as found poems. Instead of presenting whole texts as "found," these poems derive from sentences of broken text. The poems are original as poems; their themes and their orderings are invented. Their sentences are not. Their sentences come from the books named; I lifted them. Sometimes I dropped extra words; I never added a word. (There is a forthcoming book of such, *Mornings Like This*.)

Dash It
  —MIKHAIL PRISHVIN, *NATURE'S DIARY*, 1925, TRANS. L. NAVROZOV

How wonderfully it was all arranged that each
Of us had not too long to live. This is one
Of the main snags—the shortness of the day.
The whole wood was whispering, "Dash it, dash it . . . "

What joy—to walk along that path! The snow
Was so fragrant in the sun! What a fish!
Whenever I think of death, the same stupid
Question arises: "What's to be done?"

As for myself, I can only speak of what
Made me marvel when I saw it for the first time.
I remember my own youth when I was in love.
I remember a puddle rippling, the insects aroused.

I remember our own springtime when my lady told me:
You have taken my best. And then I remember
How many evenings I have waited, how much
I have been through for this one evening on earth.

1993

I Am Trying to Get at Something Utterly Heart-Broken.
> —V. VAN GOGH, LETTERS, 1873–1890, ED. I. STONE,
> TRANS. JOHANNA VAN GOGH

I
At the end of the road is a small cottage,
And over it all the blue sky.
I am trying to get at something utterly heart-broken.

The flying birds, the smoking chimneys,
And that figure loitering below in the yard—
**If we do not learn from this, then from what shall we
    learn?**

The miners go home in the white snow at twilight.
These people are quite black. Their houses are small.
The time for making dark studies is short.

A patch of brown heath through which a white
Path leads, and sky just delicately tinged,
Yet somewhat passionately brushed.
We who try our best to live, why do we not live more?

II
The branches of poplars and willows rigid like wire.
It may be true that there is no God here,
But there must be one not far off.

A studio with a cradle, a baby's high chair.
Those colors which have no name
Are the real foundation of everything.

What I want is more beautiful huts far away on the heath.
If we are tired, isn't it then because
We have already walked a long way?

The cart with the white horse brings
a wounded man home from the mines.

Bistre and bitumen, well applied,
Make the colouring ripe and mellow and generous.

III
A ploughed field with clods of violet earth;
Over all a yellow sky with a yellow sun.
So there is every moment something that moves one
   intensely.

A bluish-grey line of trees with a few roofs.
I simply could not restrain myself or keep
My hands off it or allow myself to rest.

A mother with her child, in the shadow
Of a large tree against the dune.
To say how many green-greys there are is impossible.

I love so much, so very much, the effect
Of yellow leaves against green trunks.
This is not a thing that I have sought,
But it has come across my path and I have seized it.

1993

An Acquaintance in the Heavens
—MARTHA EVANS MARTIN, WHO SEEMED LONELY IN *THE FRIENDLY STARS*, 1907, REV. DONALD HOWARD MENZEL, 1964

A window in my bedroom opens towards
The northeast. Many times I have suddenly
Opened my eyes in the night. Betelgeuse
Pushes its red face up over the horizon.

One begins in February to watch the handle
Of the Dipper, so clearly pointing to something
Important just below the horizon.

It has pulled into the view the steady
Shining face of Arcturus. The hawks
And crows are among the high trees.

There comes a soft June evening. The blue
Jays have become stealthy. One walks
To the end of the porch and looks for Altair.

Orion: We watch for it in October.
One jewel after another emerges
From the storehouse below the horizon until

The whole splendid figure is before us.
We remember then that the juncos
Came that day and we heard them.

The birds have ceased to sing and are seeking
Shadows. Fomalhaut the lonely:
When the days are growing shorter, some evening,

Just after dark, one sees it, trailing
Over the small arc of its circle
With no companion near it, and no need.

1993

The Sign of Your Father

—E. HENNECKE, *NEW TESTAMENT APOCRYPHA*, VOL. I, ED. WILHELM
SCHNEEMELCHER, ENGLISH TRANS. ED. BY R. McL. WILSON, 1963

I
(The grain of wheat) . . .
Place shut in . . .
It was laid beneath and invisible . . .
Its wealth imponderable?

And as they were in perplexity
At his strange question, Jesus
On his way came (to the) bank
Of the (riv)er Jordan,
Stretched out (hi)s right
Hand, (fill)ed it with . . .
And sowed . . . on the . . .
And then . . . water . . . And . . .
Before (their eyes),
Brought fruit . . . much
To the jo(y?) . . .

Jesus said: "Become
Passers-by."

He said: "Lord, there are many
Around the cistern, but
Nobody in the cistern."

And we said to him, "O Lord,
Are you speaking again
In parables to us?" And he said
To us, "Do not be grieved . . . "

II
(His) disciples ask him (and s)ay:
How should we fas(t and how

Should we pr)ay and how (. . .
. . .) and what should we observe
(Of the traditions?) Jesus says (. . . . .
. . . . .) do not (. . . . .
. . . . .) truth (. . . . .
. . . . .) hidden (. . . . .

"This saying has been handed down
In a particularly sorry condition."

They all wondered and were afraid.
The Redeemer (σωτήρ) smiled
And spake to them: Of what
Are you thinking, or (ἤ) about what
Are you at a loss (ἀπορεῖν), or
(ἤ) what are you seeking?

If they ask you: "What
Is the sign of your Father in you?"
You say to them: "It is a movement
And a rest (ἀνάπαυσις)."

1976

THE BOOK OF
LUKE

IT IS A FAULT OF infinity to be too small to find. It is a fault of eternity to be crowded out by time. Before our eyes we see an unbroken sheath of colors. We live over a bulk of things. We walk amid a congeries of colored things that part before our steps to reveal more colored things. Above us hurtle more things, which fill the universe. There is no crack. Unbreakable seas lie flush on their beds. Under the Greenland icecap lies not so much as a bubble. Mountains and hills, lakes, deserts, forests, and plains fully occupy their continents. Where, then, is the gap through which eternity streams? In holes at the roots of forest cedars I find spiders and chips. I have rolled plenty of stones away, to no avail. Under the lily pads on the lake are flatworms and lake water. Materials wrap us seamlessly; time propels us ceaselessly. Muffled and bound we pitch forward from one filled hour to the next, from one filled landscape or house to the next. No rift between one note of the chorus and the next opens on infinity. No spear of eternity interposes itself between work and lunch.

And this is what we love: this human-scented skull, the sheen on the skin of a face, this exhilarating game, this crowded feast, these shifting mountains, the dense water and its piercing lights. It is our lives we love, our times, our generation, our pursuits. And are we called to forsake these vivid and palpable goods for an idea of which we experience not one trace? Am I to believe eternity outranks my child's finger?

The idea of infinity is that it is bigger, infinitely bigger, than our universe, which floats, held, upon it, as a leaf might float on a shoreless sea. The idea of eternity is that it bears time in its side like a hole. You believe it. Surely it is an idea suited for minds deranged by solitude, people who run gibbering from caves, who rave on mountaintops, who forgot to sleep and starved.

Let us rest the material view and consider, just consider, that the weft of materials admits of a very few, faint, unlikely gaps. People are, after all, still disappearing, still roping robes on themselves, still braving the work of prayer, insisting they hear something, even fighting and still dying for it. The impulse to a spiritual view persists, and the evidence of that view's power among historical forces and among contemporary ideas persists, and the claim of reasoning men and women that they know God from experience persists.

"A young atheist cannot be too careful of his reading," C. S. Lewis observed with amusement. Any book on any subject—a book by a writer the young atheist least suspects of apostasy— may abruptly and unabashedly reveal its author's theist conviction. It may quote the Bible—that fetish of Grandma's—as if it possessed real authority. The young atheist reels—is he crazy, or is everyone else?

This Bible, this ubiquitous, persistent black chunk of a bestseller, is a chink—often the only chink—through which winds howl. It is a singularity, a black hole into which our rich and multiple world strays and vanishes. We crack open its pages at our peril. Many educated, urbane, and flourishing experts in every aspect of business, culture, and science have felt pulled by this anachronistic, semibarbaric mass of antique laws and fabulous tales from far away; they entered its queer, strait gates and were lost. Eyes open, heads high, in full possession of their critical minds, they obeyed the high, inaudible whistle, and let the gates close behind them.

Respectable parents who love their children leave this absolutely respectable book lying about, as a possible safeguard against, say, drugs; alas, it is the book that kidnaps the children, and hooks them.

> But he . . . said unto Jesus, And who is my neighbor?
> And Jesus answering said, A certain man went down
> from Jerusalem to Jericho, and fell among thieves. . . .

And he said unto him, Who is my neighbor?

But a certain Samaritan . . . came where he was. . . .

And went to him, and bound up his wounds . . . and brought him to an inn, and took care of him.

And he said unto him, Which now, thinkest thou, was neighbor unto him that fell among the thieves?

And he said unto him, Who IS my neighbor?

And Jesus answering said, A certain man went down from Jerusalem to Jericho, and fell among thieves.

Who IS my neighbor?

Then said Jesus unto him, Go, and do thou likewise.

This and similar fragments of biblical language played in my mind like a record on which the needle has stuck, moved at the root of my tongue, and sounded deep in my ears without surcease. Who IS my neighbor?

Every July for four years, my sister and I trotted off to Presbyterian church camp. It was cheap, wholesome, and nearby. There we were happy, loose with other children under pines. If our parents had known how pious and low-church this camp was, they would have yanked us. We memorized Bible chapters, sang rollicking hymns around the clock, held nightly devotions with extemporaneous prayers, and filed out of the woods to chapel twice on Sunday dressed in white shorts. The faith-filled theology there was only half a step out of a tent; you could still smell the sawdust.

I had a head for religious ideas. They were the first ideas I ever encountered. They made other ideas seem mean.

For what shall it profit a man, if he shall gain the whole world and lose his own soul? And lose his own soul? Know ye that the Lord he is God: it is he that hath made us, and not we ourselves; we are his people, and the sheep of his pasture. Arise, take up thy bed, and walk.

Who shall ascend into the hill of the Lord? or who shall stand in his holy place? He that hath clean hands, and a pure heart; who hath not lifted up his soul unto vanity, nor sworn deceitfully.

The earth is the Lord's, and the fulness thereof; the world, and they that dwell therein. The heavens declare the glory of

God; and the firmament sheweth his handiwork. Verily I say unto you, that one of you shall betray me.

Every summer we memorized these things at camp. Every Sunday, at home in Pittsburgh, we heard these things in Sunday school. Every Thursday we studied these things, and memorized them, too (strictly as literature, they said), at our private school. I had miles of Bible in memory: some perforce, but most by hap, like the words to songs. There was no corner of my brain where you could not find, among the files of clothing labels and heaps of rocks and minerals, among the swarms of protozoans and shelves of novels, whole tapes and snarls and reels of Bible. I wrote poems in deliberate imitation of its sounds, those repeated feminine endings followed by thumps, or those long hard beats followed by softness. Selah.

The Bible's was an unlikely, movie-set world alongside our world. Light-shot and translucent in the pallid Sunday-school watercolors on the walls, stormy and opaque in the dense and staggering texts they read us placidly, sweet-mouthed and earnest, week after week, this world interleaved our waking world like dream.

I saw Jesus in watercolor, framed, on the walls. We Sunday-school children sat in a circle and said dimly with Samuel, "Here am I." Jesus was thin as a veil of tinted water; he was awash. Bearded men lay indolent about him in pastel robes, and shepherd boys, and hooded women with clear, round faces. The River Jordan, the Sea of Galilee—it was all watercolor; I could see the paper through it. The southern sun, the Asian sun, bleached the color from thick village walls, from people's limbs and eyes. These pastel illustrations were as exotic, and as peculiar to children's sentimental educations, as watercolor depictions of lions and giraffes.

We studied the Gospel of Luke. In that world, people had time on their hands. Simon Peter, James, and John dropped their nets and quit their two boats full of fresh fish: "And when they had brought their ships to land, they forsook all, and followed him." They had time to gather at the side of the lake and hear harsh words. They had time to stand for the Sermon on the Mount and the sermon on the plain. A multitude followed Jesus and the twelve into a desert place belonging to the city of Bethsaida. The day wore away while Jesus spoke to them of the Kingdom of God; then he had his disciples feed them—"about five thousand men"—on five loaves of bread and two fishes, which Jesus blessed and broke, looking up to heaven.

Luke's is the most reasoned, calm, plausible, and orderly Gospel. It does not claim divinity for Christ, but a glorious messiahship; Jesus is the holy teacher who shows the way; he leads Israel and all the world back to a prayerful acknowledgment of the fatherhood of the one God. The coming of Jesus, attended by signs from heaven, does not interrupt the sacred history of Israel; it fulfills it. But Luke's Gospel is calm and plausible only compared to the swirling bewilderments of Mark and the intergalactic leapings of John. All of the Gospels are unprecedented, unequaled, singular texts. Coming at Luke from our world, we stagger and balk. Luke is a piece torn from wildness. It is a blur of power, violent in its theological and narrative heat, abrupt and inexplicable. It shatters and jolts. Its grand-scale, vivid, and shifting tableaux call all in doubt.

In a hurried passage, Jesus walks by Levi the tax collector and says, "Follow me." That is all there is to that. He calms the storm on the lake from his skiff. He heals the centurion's servant at a distance from his house; he raises a widow's young son from his funeral bier. He drives demons into the Gadarene swine and over the cliff. He performs all with his marble calm, by his fiery power which seems to derive from his very otherness, his emptiness as a channel to God. He moves among men who, being fishermen, could not have been panicky, but who nevertheless seem so in contrast to him: "Master, master, we perish!" Jesus is tranquil in his dealings with maniacs, rich young men, synagogue leaders, Roman soldiers, weeping women, Pilate, Herod, and Satan himself in the desert. Resurrected (apparently as a matter of course), he is distant, enlarged, and calm, even subdued; he explicates Scripture, walks from town to town, and puts up with the marveling disciples. These things are in Luke, which of all the Gospels most stresses and vivifies Christ's common humanity.

Long before any rumor of resurrection, the narrative is wild. Jesus dines with a Pharisee. A woman—a sinner—from the town walks in; she has heard that Jesus is in that house for dinner. In she walks with no comment at all, just as later a man with dropsy appears before Jesus at another house where he is eating. The woman stands behind him in tears; the men apparently ignore her. Her tears, which must have been copious, wet Jesus's feet. She bends over and wipes the wetness away with her hair. She kisses his feet and anoints them with perfume from an alabaster flask.

After some time and conversation with the Pharisee, Jesus says, "Seest thou this woman? . . . Thou gavest me no kiss: but this woman since the time I came in hath not ceased to kiss my feet. . . . Her sins, which are many, are forgiven; for she loved much." To the woman he says, "Thy faith hath saved thee; go in peace." (This is in Luke alone.)

The light is raking; the action is relentless. Once in a crushing crowd, Jesus is trying to make his way to Jairus's twelve-year-old daughter, who is dying. In the crowd, a woman with an unstoppable issue of blood touches the border of his robe. Jesus says, "Who touched me?" Peter and the other disciples point out, with exasperated sarcasm, that "the multitude throng thee and press thee, and sayest thou, Who touched me?" Jesus persists, "Somebody hath touched me: for I perceive that virtue is gone out of me." The woman confesses, and declares she was healed immediately; Jesus blesses her; a message comes from Jairus's house that the daughter has already died—"Trouble not the Master."

"Fear not," says Jesus; he enters the child's chamber with her parents and Peter, James, and John; says, "Maid, arise." She arises straightway, and he commands her parents to give her meat. Then he calls the twelve together, gives them authority over devils and power to heal, and sends them out to teach and heal. When they come back he preaches to multitudes whom he feeds. He prays, teaches the disciples, heals, preaches to throngs, and holds forth in synagogues. And so on without surcease, event crowded on event. Even as he progresses to his own crucifixion, his saving work continues: in the garden where soldiers seize him, he heals with a touch the high priest's servant's ear, which a disciple impetuously lopped off; hanging on his cross, he blesses the penitent thief, promising him a place in paradise "this very day."

Historians of every school agree—with varying enthusiasm—that this certain Jewish man lived, wandered in Galilee and Judaea, and preached a radically spiritual doctrine of prayer, poverty, forgiveness, and mercy for all under the fathership of God; he attracted a following and was crucified by soldiers of the occupying Roman army. There is no reason to hate him, unless the idea of a God who knows, hears, and acts—which idea he proclaimed—is itself offensive.

In Luke, Jesus makes no claims to be the only Son of God. Luke is a monotheist: Jesus is the Son of Man, and the Messiah, but Jesus is not God's only-begotten Son, of one substance with the Father, who came down from heaven. Luke never suggests that Christ was begotten before all worlds, that he was very God of very God, that eternity interrupted time with his coming, or that faith in his divinity is the sole path to salvation. The substance of his teaching is his way; he taught God, not Christ. The people in Luke are a rogues' gallery of tax collectors, innkeepers, fallen women, shrewd bourgeois owners, thieves, Pharisees, and assorted unclean Gentiles. He saves them willy-nilly; they need not, and do not, utter creeds first.

Salvation in Luke, for the followers of Christ, consists in a life of prayer, repentance, and mercy; it is a life in the world with God. Faith in Christ's divinity has nothing to do with it. The cross as God's own sacrifice has nothing to do with it; the cross is Jesus' own sacrifice, freely and reluctantly chosen, and of supreme moment on that head. That Jesus was resurrected in flesh and blood means in Luke, I think, that he was indeed the Messiah whom God had promised to lead the people—now all people—by his teaching and example, back to prayerful and spiritual obedience to God their father and creator.

*   *   *

Still, his teachings are as surprising as his life. Their require-
ments are harsh. Do not ask your goods back from anyone who
has taken them from you. Sell all that thou hast, and give it to
the poor. Do not stop to perform a son's great duty, to bury a
father. Divorce and remarriage is adultery. Forgive an enemy
seven times in one day, without limit. Faith is not a gift but a
plain duty. Take no thought for your life. Pray without ceasing.
Unto everyone which hath shall be given; and from him that
hath not, even that he hath shall be taken away.

The teachings that are not harsh are even more radical, and
harder to swallow.

Consider the lilies how they grow: they toil not, they spin
not; and yet I say unto you, that Solomon in all his glory was not
arrayed like one of these.

If then God so clothe the grass, which is to day in the field,
and to morrow is cast into the oven; how much more will he
clothe you, O ye of little faith?. . .

Your Father knoweth that you have need of these things.

But rather seek ye the kingdom of God; and all these things
shall be added unto you.

Fear not, little flock. . . .

Ask, and it shall be given you; seek, and ye shall find;
knock, and it shall be opened unto you.

For every one that asketh receiveth; and he that seeketh
findeth; and to him that knocketh it shall be opened.

"Fear not, little flock": this seems apt for those pious watercolor people so long ago, those blameless and endearing shepherds and fishermen, in colorful native garb, whose lives seem
pure, because they are not our lives. They were rustics, silent
and sunlit, outdoors, whom we sentimentalize and ignore. They
are not in our world. They had some nascent sort of money, but
not the kind to take seriously. They got their miracles, perhaps,
but they died anyway, long ago, and so did their children.
Salvation is obviously for them, and so is God, for they are, like
the very young and the very old in our world, peripheral.
Religion is for outcasts and victims; Jesus made that clear.

Religion suits primitives. They have time to work up their touching faith in unverifiable promises, and they might as well, having bugger-all else.

Our lives are complex. There are many things we must consider before we go considering any lilies. There are many things we must fear. We are in charge; we are running things in a world we made; we are nobody's little flock.

In Luke, Christ's ministry enlarges in awfulness—from the sunny Galilean days of eating and drinking, preaching on lakesides, saying lovely things, choosing disciples, healing the sick, making the blind see, casting out demons, and raising the dead—enlarges in awfulness from this exuberant world, where all is possible and God displays his power and love, to the dark messianic journey which begins when Peter acknowledges him ("Who do you think I am?") as the Christ, and culminates in the eerie night-long waiting at the lip of the vortex as Pilate and Herod pass Jesus back and forth and he defends himself not.

Jesus creates his role and succumbs to it. He understands his destiny only gradually, through much prayer; he decides on it, foretells it, and sets his face to meet it. On the long journey to Jerusalem, which occupies many chapters of Luke, he understands more and more. The narrative builds a long sober sense of crushing demand on Jesus the man, and the long sober sense of his gradually strengthening himself to see it, to cause it, and to endure it. (The account of his ministry's closure parallels the account of its beginning three years previously; Jesus very gradually, and through prayer, chooses, creates, and assumes his tremendous and transcendent role. He chooses his life, and he chooses his death.)

In that final long journey to Jerusalem, the austerity of Jesus deepens; his mystery and separateness magnify. The party is over. Pressure rises from crowds, pressure rises from the Jewish authorities.

His utterances become vatic and Greekish. Behold, we go up to Jerusalem, he tells his disciples. If anyone wishes to follow me, let him deny himself, take up his cross day after day, and so follow me. For the Son of Man is coming into his glory. What awaits him is uncertain, unspecified, even unto the cross and upon it; but in the speeches of his last days, in this village and that, his awareness becomes stonily clearer. Privately, often, and urgently, he addresses his disciples in dire terms: When they call you before the magistrates, do not trouble yourself about what you are to say. I have a baptism to undergo. The days will come when ye shall desire to see one of the days of the Son of Man, and ye shall not see it. "And they understood none of these things."

On the way to Jerusalem he addresses the Pharisees, who bring him a message from Herod ("that fox"): "I must walk to day, and to morrow, and the day following: for it cannot be that a prophet perish out of Jerusalem." He adds an apostrophe: "O Jerusalem, Jerusalem, which killest the prophets, and stonest them that are sent unto thee; how often would I have gathered they children together, as a hen doth gather her brood under her wings, and ye would not!"

And he does walk, that day, and the next day, and the day following, soberly, wittingly, and freely, going up to Jerusalem for the Passover in which he will not be passed over. There is little mingling with crowds, and only four healings, two of them provokingly on the Sabbath. His words are often harsh and angry. "Thou fool," he has God saying to a rich man. "Ye hypocrites," he calls his disciples. In one of his stories an outraged master says, "Depart from me, all ye workers of iniquity." I am come to send fire on the earth. But those mine enemies . . . bring hither, and slay them before me.

He enters the city on a "colt" and is at once discovered driving the money changers out of the Temple. "Whosoever shall fall upon that stone shall be broken; but on whomsoever it shall fall, it will grind him to powder." As for the temple in which they stand, "there shall not be left one stone upon another. . . . These be the days of vengeance."

The crowds around Jesus are so great in Jerusalem that the Roman authorities must take him at night, as he quits the garden. There he has prayed in an agony, "Father, if thou be willing, remove this cup from me: nevertheless not my will, but thine, be done." Then he has prayed *more* earnestly, and his sweat fell down to the ground. Betrayed to the soldiers, he shuttles back and forth between Pilate and Herod all night; the cock crows; Peter denies him; and in the morning Pilate takes him— him supremely silent, magnificent, and vulnerable—before the chief priests and Jewish rulers, and before an unspecified crowd. They cry, "Release unto us Barabbas." And their voices and those of the chief priests prevail. As Roman soldiers lead Jesus away, "there followed him a great company of people." Where were they a minute ago, that they could not outshout the claque for Barabbas?

In Luke alone, after Jesus on the cross commends his spirit to the hands of God and dies, a Roman soldier is moved to say, "Certainly this was a righteous man." Luke alone recounts the incident on the road to Emmaus. Two disciples walking to Emmaus are talking about Jesus' crucifixion, which has occurred three days previously, when a stranger joins them and asks what they are talking about; the disciples, surprised, explain. The stranger interprets messianic prophecies in Scripture for them, beginning with Moses, which seems to surprise them not at all. In the village, they invite the stranger in. When at table he takes the loaf, gives thanks, and breaks it, then their eyes are opened, they recognize him, and he vanishes.

Amazed, they walk that night all the way back to Jerusalem—another seven miles—and tell the others. And while they are speaking, Jesus appears yet again. They are "terrified," but Jesus says, "Why are ye troubled? and why do thoughts arise in your hearts?" He shows them his wounded hands and feet, and they are full of joy and wondering, and very far from recognizing that, among other things, ordinary hospitality is called for—so Jesus has to ask, "Have ye here any meat?" (They give him broiled fish and a piece of honeycomb.) Then the resurrected Jesus explains scriptural prophecies concerning the Messiah's death and his resurrection on the third day; charges them to preach to all nations; leads them out as far as Bethany (two miles east); blesses them; and is carried up to heaven.

*   *   *

When I was a child, the adult members of Pittsburgh society adverted to the Bible unreasonably often. What arcana! Why did they spread this scandalous document before our eyes? If they had read it, I thought, they would have hid it. They did not recognize the lively danger that we would, through repeated exposure, catch a dose of its virulent opposition to their world. Instead they bade us study great chunks of it, and think about those chunks, and commit them to memory, and ignore them. By dipping us children in the Bible so often, they hoped, I think, to give our lives a serious tint, and to provide us with quaintly magnificent snatches of prayer to produce as charms while, say, being mugged for our cash or jewels.

In Sunday school at the Shadyside Presbyterian Church, the handsome father of rascal Jack from dancing school, himself a vice-president of Jones & Laughlin Steel, whose wife was famous at the country club for her tan, held a birch pointer in his long fingers and shyly tapped the hanging paper map—shyly because he could see we were not listening. Who would listen to this? Why on earth were we here? There in blue and yellow and green were Galilee, Samaria itself, and Judaea, he said (and I pretended to pay attention as a courtesy), the Sea of Galilee, the River Jordan, and the Dead Sea. I saw on the hanging map the coasts of Judaea by the far side of Jordan, on whose unimaginable shores the pastel Christ had maybe uttered such cruel, stiff, thrilling words: "Sell all that thou hast. . . ."

The Gospel of Luke ends immediately and abruptly after the Ascension outside Bethany, on that Easter Sunday when the disciples had walked so much and kept receiving visitations from the risen Christ. The skies have scarcely closed around Christ's heels when the story concludes on the disciples: "And [they] were continually in the temple, praising and blessing God. Amen."

What a pity, that so hard on the heels of Christ come the Christians. There is no breather. The disciples turn into the early Christians between one rushed verse and another. What a dismaying pity, that here come the Christians already, flawed to the core, full of wild ideas and hurried self-importance. They are already blocking, with linked arms, the howling gap in the weft of things that their man's coming and going tore.

For who can believe in the Christians? They are, we know by hindsight, suddenly not at all peripheral. They set out immediately to take over the world, and they pretty much did it. They converted emperors, raised armies, lined their pockets with real money, and did evil things large and small, in century after century, including this one. They are smug and busy, just like us, and who could believe in them? They are not innocent, they are not shepherds and fishermen in rustic period costume, they are men and women just like us, in polyester. Who could believe salvation is for these rogues? That God is for these rogues? For they are just like us, and salvation's time is past.

Unless, of course—

Unless Christ's washing the disciples' feet, their dirty toes, means what it could, possibly, mean: that it is all right to be human. That God knows we are human, and full of evil, all of us, and we are his people anyway, and the sheep of his pasture.

Unless those colorful scamps and scalawags who populate Jesus' parables were just as evil as we are, and evil in the same lazy, cowardly, and scheming ways. Unless those pure disciples themselves and those watercolor women—who so disconcertingly turned into The Christians overnight—were complex and selfish humans also, who lived in the material world, and whose errors and evils were not pretty but ugly, and had real consequences. If they were just like us, then Christ's words to them are addressed to us, in full and merciful knowledge—and we are lost. There is no place to hide.

1989

From

PILGRIM AT
TINKER CREEK

*It ever was, and is, and shall
be, ever-living Fire, in measures being kindled and in
measures going out.*

—HERACLITUS

I USED TO HAVE A cat, an old fighting tom, who would jump through the open window by my bed in the middle of the night and land on my chest. I'd half awaken. He'd stick his skull under my nose and purr, stinking of urine and blood. Some nights he kneaded my bare chest with his front paws, powerfully, arching his back, as if sharpening his claws, or pummeling a mother for milk. And some mornings I'd wake in daylight to find my body covered with paw prints in blood; I looked as though I'd been painted with roses.

It was hot, so hot the mirror felt warm. I washed before the mirror in a daze; my twisted summer sleep still hung about me like sea kelp. What blood was this, and what roses? It could have been the rose of union, the blood of murder, or the rose of beauty bare and the blood of some unspeakable sacrifice or birth. The sign on my body could have been an emblem or a stain, the keys to the kingdom or the mark of Cain. I never knew. I never knew as I washed, and the blood streaked, faded, and finally disappeared, whether I'd purified myself or ruined the blood sign of the passover. We wake, if we ever wake at all, to mystery, rumors of death, beauty, violence. . . . "Seem like we're just set down here," a woman said to me recently, "and don't nobody know why."

These are morning matters, pictures you dream as the final wave heaves you up on the sand to the bright light and drying air. You remember pressure, and a curved sleep you rested against, soft, like a scallop in its shell. But the air hardens your skin; you stand; you leave the lighted shore to explore some dim headland, and soon you're lost in the leafy interior, intent, remembering nothing.

*   *   *

I still think of that old tomcat, mornings, when I wake. Things are tamer now; I sleep with the window shut. The cat and our rites are gone and my life is changed, but the memory remains of something powerful playing over me. I wake expectant, hoping to see a new thing. If I'm lucky I might be jogged awake by a strange birdcall. I dress in a hurry, imagining the yard flapping with auks, or flamingos. This morning it was a wood duck, down at the creek. It flew away.

I live by a creek, Tinker Creek, in a valley in Virginia's Blue Ridge. An anchorite's hermitage is called an anchorhold; some anchorholds were simple sheds clamped to the side of a church like a barnacle to a rock. I think of this house clamped to the side of Tinker Creek as an anchorhold. It holds me at anchor to the rock bottom of the creek itself and it keeps me steadied in the current, as a sea anchor does, facing the stream of light pouring down. It's a good place to live; there's a lot to think about. The creeks—Tinker and Carvin's—are an active mystery, fresh every minute. Theirs is the mystery of the continuous creation and all that providence implies: the uncertainty of vision, the horror of the fixed, the dissolution of the present, the intricacy of beauty, the pressure of fecundity, the elusiveness of the free, and the flawed nature of perfection. The mountains—Tinker and Brushy, McAfee's Knob and Dead Man—are a passive mystery, the oldest of all. Theirs is the one simple mystery of creation from nothing, of matter itself, anything at all, the given. Mountains are giant, restful, absorbent. You can heave your spirit into a mountain and the mountain will keep it, folded, and not throw it back as some creeks will. The creeks are the world with all its stimulus and beauty; I live there. But the mountains are home.

The wood duck flew away. I caught only a glimpse of something like a bright torpedo that blasted the leaves where it flew. Back at the house I ate a bowl of oatmeal; much later in the day came the long slant of light that means good walking.

If the day is fine, any walk will do; it all looks good. Water in particular looks its best, reflecting blue sky in the flat, and chopping it into graveled shallows and white chute and foam in the riffles. On a dark day, or a hazy one, everything's washed out and lackluster but the water. It carries its own lights. I set out for the railroad tracks, for the hill the flocks fly over, for the woods where the white mare lives. But I go to the water.

Today is one of those excellent January partly cloudies in which light chooses an unexpected part of the landscape to trick out in gilt, and then shadow sweeps it away. You know you're alive. You take huge steps, trying to feel the planet's roundness arc between your feet. Kazantzakis says that when he was young he had a canary and a globe. When he freed the canary, it would perch on the globe and sing. All his life, wandering the earth, he felt as though he had a canary on top of his mind, singing.

West of the house, Tinker Creek makes a sharp loop, so that the creek is both in back of the house, south of me, and on the other side of the road, north of me. I like to go north. There the afternoon sun hits the creek just right, deepening the reflected blue and lighting the sides of trees on the banks. Steers from the pasture across the creek come down to drink; I always flush a rabbit or two there; I sit on a fallen trunk in the shade and watch the squirrels in the sun. There are two separated wooden fences suspended from cables that cross the creek just upstream from my tree-trunk bench. They keep the steers from escaping up or down the creek when they come to drink. Squirrels, the neighborhood children, and I use the downstream fence as a swaying bridge across the creek. But the steers are there today.

I sit on the downed tree and watch the black steers slip on the creek bottom. They are all bred beef: beef heart, beef hide, beef hocks. They're a human product like rayon. They're like a field of shoes. They have cast-iron shanks and tongues like foam insoles. You can't see through to their brains as you can with other animals; they have beef fat behind their eyes, beef stew.

I cross the fence six feet above the water, walking my hands down the rusty cable and tightroping my feet along the narrow edge of the planks. When I hit the other bank and terra firma, some steers are bunched in a knot between me and the barbed-wire fence I want to cross. So I suddenly rush at them in an enthusiastic sprint, flailing my arms and hollering, "Lightning! Copperhead! Swedish meatballs!" They flee, still in a knot, stumbling across the flat pasture. I stand with the wind on my face.

When I slide under a barbed-wire fence, cross a field, and run over a sycamore trunk felled across the water, I'm on a little island shaped like a tear in the middle of Tinker Creek. On one side of the creek is a steep forested bank; the water is swift and deep on that side of the island. On the other side is the level field I walked through next to the steers' pasture; the water between the field and the island is shallow and sluggish. In summer's low water, flags and bulrushes grow along a series of shallow pools cooled by the lazy current. Water striders patrol the surface film, crayfish hump along the silt bottom eating filth, frogs shout and glare, and shiners and small bream hide among roots from the sulky green heron's eye. I come to this island every month of the year. I walk around it, stopping and staring, or I straddle the sycamore log over the creek, curling my legs out of the water in winter, trying to read. Today I sit on dry grass at the end of the island by the slower side of the creek. I'm drawn to this spot. I come to it as to an oracle; I return to it as a man years later will seek out the battlefield where he lost a leg or an arm.

A couple of summers ago I was walking along the edge of the island to see what I could see in the water, and mainly to scare frogs. Frogs have an inelegant way of taking off from invisible positions on the bank just ahead of your feet, in dire panic, emitting a froggy "Yike!" and splashing into the water. Incredibly, this amused me, and, incredibly, it amuses me still. As I walked along the grassy edge of the island, I got better and better at seeing frogs both in and out of the water. I learned to recognize, slowing down, the difference in texture of the light reflected from mudbank, water, grass, or frog. Frogs were flying all around me. At the end of the island I noticed a small green frog. He was exactly half in and half out of the water, looking like a schematic diagram of an amphibian, and he didn't jump.

He didn't jump; I crept closer. At last I knelt on the island's winter-killed grass, lost, dumbstruck, staring at the frog in the creek just four feet away. He was a very small frog, with wide, dull eyes. And just as I looked at him, he slowly crumpled and began to sag. The spirit vanished from his eyes as if snuffed. His skin emptied and drooped; his very skull seemed to collapse and settle like a kicked tent. He was shrinking before my eyes like a deflating football. I watched the taut, glistening skin on his shoulders ruck, and rumple, and fall. Soon, part of his skin, formless as a pricked balloon, lay in floating folds like bright scum on top of the water: it was a monstrous and terrifying thing. I gaped, bewildered, appalled. An oval shadow hung in the water behind the drained frog; then the shadow glided away. The frogskin bag started to sink.

I had read about the giant water bug, but never seen one. "Giant water bug," is really the name of the creature, which is an enormous, heavy-bodied brown true bug. It eats insects, tadpoles, fish, and frogs. Its grasping forelegs are mighty and hooked inward. It seizes a victim with these legs, hugs it tight, and paralyzes it with enzymes injected during a vicious bite. That one bite is the only bite it ever takes. Through the puncture shoot the poisons that dissolve the victim's muscles and bones and organs—all but the skin—and through it the giant water bug sucks out the victim's body, reduced to a juice. This event is quite common in warm fresh water. The frog I saw was being sucked by a giant water bug. I had been kneeling on the island grass; when the unrecognizable flap of frogskin settled on the creek bottom, swaying, I stood up and brushed the knees of my pants. I couldn't catch my breath.

Of course, many carnivorous animals devour their prey alive. The usual method seems to be to subdue the victim by drowning or grasping it so it can't flee, then eating it whole or in a series of bloody bites. Frogs eat everything whole, stuffing prey into their mouths with their thumbs. People have seen frogs with their wide jaws so full of live dragonflies they couldn't close them. Ants don't even have to catch their prey: in the spring they swarm over newly hatched, featherless birds in the nest and eat them tiny bite by bite.

That it's rough out there and chancy is no surprise. Every live thing is a survivor on a kind of extended emergency bivouac. But at the same time we are also created. In the Koran,

Allah asks, "The heaven and the earth and all in between, thinkest thou I made them *in jest?*" It's a good question. What do we think of the created universe, spanning an unthinkable void with an unthinkable profusion of forms? Or what do we think of nothingness, those sickening reaches of time in either direction? If the giant water bug was not made in jest, was it then made in earnest? Pascal uses a nice term to describe the notion of the creator's, once having called for the universe, turning his back to it: *Deus Absconditus.* Is this what we think happened? Was the sense of it there, and God absconded with it, ate it, like a wolf who disappears round the edge of the house with the Thanksgiving turkey? "God is subtle," Einstein said, "but not malicious." Again, Einstein said that "nature conceals her mystery by means of her essential grandeur, not by her cunning." It could be that God has not absconded but spread, as our vision and understanding of the universe have spread, to a fabric of spirit and sense so grand and subtle, so powerful in a new way, that we can only feel blindly of its hem. In making the thick darkness a swaddling band for the sea, God "set bars and doors" and said, "Hitherto shalt thou come, but no further." But have we come even that far? Have we rowed out to the thick darkness, or are we all playing pinochle in the bottom of the boat?

Cruelty is a mystery, and the waste of pain. But if we describe a world to compass these things, a world that is a long, brute game, then we bump against another mystery: the inrush of power and light, the canary that sings on the skull. Unless all ages and races of men have been deluded by the same mass hypnotist (who?), there seems to be such a thing as beauty, a grace wholly gratuitous. About five years ago I saw a mockingbird make a straight vertical descent from the roof gutter of a four-story building. It was an act as careless and spontaneous as the curl of a stem or the kindling of a star.

The mockingbird took a single step into the air and dropped. His wings were still folded against his sides as though he were singing from a limb and not falling, accelerating thirty-two feet per second per second, through empty air. Just a breath before he would have been dashed to the ground, he unfurled his wings with exact, deliberate care, revealing the broad bars of white, spread his elegant, white-banded tail, and so floated onto the grass. I had just rounded a corner when his insouciant step caught my eye; there was no one else in sight. The fact of his free fall was like the old philosophical conundrum about the tree that falls in the forest. The answer must be, I think, that beauty and grace are performed whether or not we will or sense them. The least we can do is try to be there.

Another time I saw another wonder: sharks off the Atlantic coast of Florida. There is a way a wave rises above the ocean horizon, a triangular wedge against the sky. If you stand where the ocean breaks on a shallow beach, you see the raised water in a wave is translucent, shot with lights. One late afternoon at low tide a hundred big sharks passed the beach near the mouth of a tidal river in a feeding frenzy. As each green wave rose from the churning water, it illuminated within itself the six- or eight-foot-long bodies of twisting sharks. The sharks disappeared as each wave rolled toward me; then a new wave would swell above the horizon, containing in it, like scorpions in amber, sharks that roiled and heaved. The sight held awesome wonders: power and beauty, grace tangled in a rapture with violence.

We don't know what's going on here. If these tremendous events are random combinations of matter run amok, the yield of millions of monkeys at millions of typewriters, then what is it in us, hammered out of those same typewriters, that they ignite? We don't know. Our life is a faint tracing on the surface of mystery, like the idle, curved tunnels of leaf miners on the face of a leaf. We must somehow take a wider view, look at the whole landscape, really see it, and describe what's going on here. Then we can at least wail the right question into the swaddling band of darkness, or, if it comes to that, choir the proper praise.

At the time of Lewis and Clark, setting the prairies on fire was a well-known signal that meant, "Come down to the water." It was an extravagant gesture, but we can't do less. If the landscape reveals one certainty, it is that the extravagant gesture is the very stuff of creation. After the one extravagant gesture of creation in the first place, the universe has continued to deal exclusively in extravagances, flinging intricacies and colossi down aeons of emptiness, heaping profusions on profligacies with ever fresh vigor. The whole show has been on fire from the word go. I come down to the water to cool my eyes. But everywhere I look I see fire; that which isn't flint is tinder, and the whole world sparks and flames.

I have come to the grassy island late in the day. The creek is up; icy water sweeps under the sycamore-log bridge. The frogskin, of course, is utterly gone. I have stared at that one spot on the creek bottom for so long, focusing past the rush of water, that when I stand, the opposite bank seems to stretch before my eyes and flow grassily upstream. When the bank settles down I cross the sycamore log and enter again the big plowed field next to the steers' pasture.

The wind is terrific out of the west; the sun comes and goes. I can see the shadow on the field before me deepen uniformly and spread like a plague. Everything seems so dull I am amazed I can even distinguish objects. And suddenly the light runs across the land like a comber, and up the trees, and goes again in a wink: I think I've gone blind or died. When it comes again, the light, you hold your breath, and if it stays you forget about it until it goes again.

It's the most beautiful day of the year. At four o'clock the eastern sky is a dead stratus black flecked with low white clouds. The sun in the west illuminates the ground, the mountains, and especially the bare branches of trees, so that everywhere silver trees cut into the black sky like a photographer's negative of a landscape. The air and the ground are dry; the mountains are going on and off like neon signs. Clouds slide east as if pulled from the horizon, like a tablecloth whipped off a table. The hemlocks by the barbed-wire fence are flinging themselves east as though their backs would break. Purple shadows are racing east; the wind makes me face east, and again I feel the dizzying, drawn sensation I felt when the creek bank reeled.

At four-thirty the sky in the east is clear; how could that big blackness be blown? Fifteen minutes later another darkness is coming overhead from the northwest; and it's here. Everything is drained of its light as if sucked. Only at the horizon do inky mountains give way to distant, lighted mountains—lighted not by direct illumination but rather paled by glowing sheets of mist hung before them. Now the blackness is in the east; everything is half in shadow, half in sun, every clod, tree, mountain, and hedge. I can't see Tinker Mountain through the line of hemlock, till it comes on like a streetlight, ping, *ex nihilo*. Its sandstone cliffs pink and swell. Suddenly the light goes; the cliffs recede as if pushed. The sun hits a clump of sycamores between me and the mountains; the sycamore arms light up, and *I can't see the cliffs*. They're gone. The pale network of sycamore arms, which a second ago was transparent as a screen, is suddenly opaque, glowing with light. Now the sycamore arms snuff out, the mountains come on, and there are the cliffs again.

I walk home. By five-thirty the show has pulled out. Nothing is left but an unreal blue and a few banked clouds low in the north. Some sort of carnival magician has been here, some fast-talking worker of wonders who has the act backward. "Something in this hand," he says, "something in this hand, something up my sleeve, something behind my back . . . ," and abracadabra, he snaps his fingers, and it's all gone. Only the bland, blank-faced magician remains, in his unruffled coat, barehanded, acknowledging a smattering of baffled applause. When you look again the whole show has pulled up stakes and moved on down the road. It never stops. New shows roll in from over the mountains, and the magician reappears unannounced from a fold in the curtain you never dreamed was an opening. Scarves of clouds, rabbits in plain view, disappear into the black hat forever. Presto chango. The audience, if there is an audience at all, is dizzy from head-turning, dazed.

Like the bear who went over the mountain, I went out to see what I could see. And I might as well warn you that, like the bear, all I could see was the other side of the mountain: more of same. On a good day I might catch a glimpse of another wooded ridge rolling under the sun like water, another bivouac. I propose to keep here what Thoreau called "a meteorological journal of the mind," telling some tales and describing some of the sights of this rather tamed valley, and exploring, in fear and trembling, some of the unmapped dim reaches and unholy fastnesses to which those tales and sights so dizzyingly lead.

I am no scientist. I explore the neighborhood. An infant who has just learned to hold his head up has a frank and forthright way of gazing about him in bewilderment. He hasn't the faintest clue where he is, and he aims to learn. In a couple of years, what he will have learned instead is how to fake it: he'll have the cocksure air of a squatter who has come to feel he owns the place. Some unwonted, taught pride diverts us from our original intent, which is to explore the neighborhood, view the landscape, to discover at least *where* it is that we have been so startlingly set down, if we can't learn why.

So I think about the valley. It is my leisure as well as my work, a game. It is a fierce game I have joined because it is being played anyway, a game of both skill and chance, played against an unseen adversary—the conditions of time—in which the payoffs, which may suddenly arrive in a blast of light at any moment, might as well come to me as anyone else. I stake the time I'm grateful to have, the energies I'm glad to direct. I risk getting stuck on the board, so to speak, unable to move in any direction, which happens enough, God knows; and I risk the searing, exhausting nightmares that plunder rest and force me facedown all night long in some muddy ditch seething with hatching insects and crustaceans.

But if I can bear the nights, the days are a pleasure. I walk out; I see something, some event that would otherwise have been utterly missed and lost; or something sees me, some enormous power brushes me with its clean wing, and I resound like a beaten bell.

I am an explorer, then, and I am also a stalker, or the instrument of the hunt itself. Certain Indians used to carve long grooves along the wooden shafts of their arrows. They called the grooves "lightning marks," because they resembled the curved fissure lightning slices down the trunks of trees. The function of lightning marks is this: if the arrow fails to kill the game, blood from a deep wound will channel along the lightning mark, streak down the arrow shaft, and spatter to the ground, laying a trail dripped on broad-leaves, on stones, that the barefoot and trembling archer can follow into whatever deep or rare wilderness it leads. I am the arrow shaft, carved along my length by unexpected lights and gashes from the very sky, and this book is the straying trail of blood.

Something pummels us, something barely sheathed. Power broods and lights. We're played on like a pipe; our breath is not our own. James Houston describes two young Eskimo girls sitting cross-legged on the ground, mouth on mouth, blowing by turns each other's throat cords, making a low, unearthly music. When I cross again the bridge that is really the steers' fence, the wind has thinned to the delicate air of twilight; it crumples the water's skin. I watch the running sheets of light raised on the creek's surface. The sight has the appeal of the purely passive, like the racing of light under clouds on a field, the beautiful dream at the moment of being dreamed. The breeze is the merest puff, but you yourself sail headlong and breathless under the gale force of the spirit.

WHEN I WAS SIX OR seven years old, growing up in Pittsburgh, I used to take a precious penny of my own and hide it for someone else to find. It was a curious compulsion; sadly, I've never been seized by it since. For some reason I always "hid" the penny along the same stretch of sidewalk up the street. I would cradle it at the roots of a sycamore, say, or in a hole left by a chipped-off piece of sidewalk. Then I would take a piece of chalk and, starting at either end of the block, draw huge arrows leading up to the penny from both directions. After I learned to write I labeled the arrows: SURPRISE AHEAD or MONEY THIS WAY. I was greatly excited, during all this arrow drawing, at the thought of the first lucky passerby who would receive in this way, regardless of merit, a free gift from the universe. But I never lurked about. I would go straight home and not give the matter another thought until, some months later, I would be gripped by the impulse to hide another penny.

It is still the first week in January, and I've got great plans. I've been thinking about seeing. There are lots of things to see, unwrapped gifts and free surprises. The world is fairly studded and strewn with pennies cast broadside from a generous hand. But—and this is the point—who gets excited by a mere penny? If you follow one arrow, if you crouch motionless on a bank to watch a tremulous ripple thrill on the water and are rewarded by the sight of a muskrat kit paddling from its den, will you count that sight a chip of copper only, and go your rueful way? It is dire poverty indeed when a man is so malnourished and fatigued that he won't stoop to pick up a penny. But if you cultivate a healthy poverty and simplicity, so that finding a penny will literally make your day, then, since the world is in fact planted in pennies, you have with your poverty bought a life-time of days. It is that simple. What you see is what you get.

I used to be able to see flying insects in the air. I'd look ahead and see, not the row of hemlocks across the road, but the air in front of it. My eyes would focus along that column of air, picking out flying insects. But I lost interest, I guess, for I dropped the habit. Now I can see birds. Probably some people can look at the grass at their feet and discover all the crawling creatures. I would like to know grasses and sedges—and care. Then my least journey into the world would be a field trip, a series of happy recognitions. Thoreau, in an expansive mood, exulted, "What a rich book might be made about buds, includ-ing, perhaps, sprouts!" It would be nice to think so. I cherish mental images of three perfectly happy people. One collects stones. Another—an Englishman, say—watches clouds. The third lives on a coast and collects drops of seawater, which he examines microscopically and mounts. But I don't see what the specialist sees, and so I cut myself off, not only from the total picture, but from the various forms of happiness.

Unfortunately, nature is very much a now-you-see-it, now-you-don't affair. A fish flashes, then dissolves in the water before my eyes like so much salt. Deer apparently ascend bod-ily into heaven; the brightest oriole fades into leaves. These dis-appearances stun me into stillness and concentration; they say of nature that it conceals with a grand nonchalance, and they say of vision that it is a deliberate gift, the revelation of a dancer who for my eyes only flings away her seven veils. For nature does reveal as well as conceal: now you don't see it, now you do. For a week last September, migrating red-winged blackbirds were feeding heavily down by the creek at the back of the house. One day I went out to investigate the racket; I walked up to a tree, an Osage orange, and a hundred birds flew away. They simply materialized out of the tree. I saw a tree, then a whisk of color, then a tree again. I walked closer, and another hundred blackbirds took flight. Not a branch, not a twig budged: the birds were apparently weightless as well as invisi-ble. Or it was as if the leaves of the Osage orange had been freed from a spell in the form of red-winged blackbirds; they flew from the tree, caught my eye in the sky, and vanished. When I looked again at the tree, the leaves had reassembled as if nothing had happened. Finally I walked directly to the trunk of the tree, and a final hundred, the real diehards, appeared, spread, and vanished. How could so many hide in the tree without my seeing them? The Osage orange, unruffled, looked just as it had looked from the house, when three hundred red-winged blackbirds cried from its crown. I looked downstream where they flew, and they were gone. Searching, I couldn't spot one. I wandered downstream to force them to play their hand, but they'd crossed the creek and scattered. One show to a customer. These appearances catch at my throat; they are the free gifts, the bright coppers at the roots of trees.

It's all a matter of keeping my eyes open. Nature is like one of those line drawings of a tree that are puzzles for children: Can you find hidden in the leaves a duck, a house, a boy, a bucket, a zebra, and a boot? Specialists can find the most incredibly well-hidden things. A book I read when I was young recommended an easy way to find caterpillars to rear: you simply find some fresh caterpillar droppings, look up, and there's your caterpillar. More recently an author advised me to set my mind at ease about those piles of cut stems on the ground in grassy fields. Field mice make them; they cut the grass down by degrees to reach the seeds at the head. It seems that when the grass is tightly packed, as in a field of ripe grain, the blade won't topple at a single cut through the stem; instead the cut stem simply drops vertically, held in the crush of grain. The mouse severs the bottom again and again, the stem keeps dropping an inch at a time, and finally the head is low enough for the mouse to reach the seeds. Meanwhile, the mouse is positively littering the field with its little piles of cut stems, into which, presumably, the author of the book is constantly stumbling.

If I can't see these minutiae, I still try to keep my eyes open. I'm always on the lookout for ant lion traps in sandy soil, monarch pupae near milkweed, skipper larvae in locust leaves. These things are utterly common, and I've not seen one. I bang on hollow trees near water, but so far no flying squirrels have appeared. In flat country I watch every sunset in hopes of seeing the green ray. The green ray is a seldom-seen streak of light that rises from the sun like a spurting fountain at the moment of sunset; it throbs into the sky for two seconds and disappears. One more reason to keep my eyes open. A photography professor at the University of Florida just happened to see a bird die in midflight; it jerked, died, dropped, and smashed on the ground. I squint at the wind because I read Stewart Edward White: "I have always maintained that if you looked closely enough you could *see* the wind—the dim, hardly-made-out, fine débris fleeing high in the air." White was an excellent observer, and devoted an entire chapter of *The Mountains* to the subject of seeing deer: "As soon as you can forget the naturally obvious and construct an artificial obvious, then you too will see deer."

But the artificial obvious is hard to see. My eyes account for less than one percent of the weight of my head; I'm bony and dense; I see what I expect. I once spent a full three minutes looking at a bullfrog that was so unexpectedly large I couldn't see it even though a dozen enthusiastic campers were shouting directions. Finally I asked, "What color am I looking for?" and a fellow said, "Green." When at last I picked out the frog, I saw what painters are up against: the thing wasn't green at all, but the color of wet hickory bark.

The lover can see, and the knowledgeable. I visited an aunt and uncle at a quarter-horse ranch in Cody, Wyoming. I couldn't do much of anything useful, but I could, I thought, draw. So as we all sat around the kitchen table after supper, I produced a sheet of paper and drew a horse. "That's one lame horse," my aunt volunteered. The rest of the family joined in: "Only place to saddle that one is his neck"; "Looks like we better shoot the poor thing, on account of those terrible growths." Meekly, I slid the pencil and paper down the table. Everyone in that family, including my three young cousins, could draw a horse. Beautifully. When the paper came back, it looked as though five shining, real quarter horses had been corraled by mistake with a papier-mâché moose; the real horses seemed to gaze at the monster with a steady, puzzled air. I stay away from horses now, but I can do a creditable goldfish. The point is that I just don't know what the lover knows; I just can't see the artificial obvious that those in the know construct. The herpetologist asks the native, "Are there snakes in that ravine?" "Nosir." And the herpetologist comes home with, yessir, three bags full. Are there butterflies on that mountain? Are the bluets in bloom, are there arrowheads here, or fossil shells in the shale?

Peeping through my keyhole, I see within the range of only about 30 percent of the light that comes from the sun; the rest is infrared and some little ultraviolet, perfectly apparent to many animals, but invisible to me. A nightmare network of ganglia, charged and firing without my knowledge, cuts and splices what I do see, editing it for my brain. Donald E. Carr points out that the sense impressions of one-celled animals are *not* edited for the brain: "This is philosophically interesting in a rather mournful way, since it means that only the simplest animals perceive the universe as it is."

A fog that won't burn away drifts and flows across my field of vision. When you see fog move against a backdrop of deep pines, you see not the fog itself but streaks of clearness floating across the air in dark shreds. So I see only tatters of clearness through a pervading obscurity. I can't distinguish the fog from the overcast sky; I can't be sure if the light is direct or reflected. Everywhere darkness and the presence of the unseen appalls. We estimate now that only one atom dances alone in every cubic meter of intergalactic space. I blink and squint. What planet or power yanks Halley's Comet out of orbit? We haven't seen that force yet; it's a question of distance, density, and the pallor of reflected light. We rock, cradled in the swaddling band of darkness. Even the simple darkness of night whispers suggestions to the mind. Last summer, in August, I stayed at the creek too late.

Where Tinker Creek flows under the sycamore-log bridge to the tear-shaped island, it is slow and shallow, fringed thinly in cattail marsh. At this spot an astonishing bloom of life supports vast breeding populations of insects, fish, reptiles, birds, and mammals. On windless summer evenings I stalk along the creekbank or straddle the sycamore log in absolute stillness, watching for muskrats. The night I stayed too late, I was hunched on the log, staring spellbound at spreading, reflected stains of lilac on the water. A cloud in the sky suddenly lighted as if turned on by a switch; its reflection just as suddenly materialized on the water upstream, flat and floating, so that I couldn't see the creek bottom, or life in the water under the cloud. Downstream, away from the cloud on the water, water turtles smooth as beans were gliding down with the current in a series of easy, weightless push-offs, as men bound on the moon. I didn't know whether to trace the progress of one turtle I was sure of, risking sticking my face in one of the bridge's spiderwebs made invisible by the gathering dark, or take a chance on seeing the carp, or scan the mud bank in hope of seeing a muskrat, or follow the last of the swallows who caught at my heart and trailed it after them like streamers as they appeared from directly below, under the log, flying upstream with their tails forked, so fast.

But shadows spread, and deepened, and stayed. After thousands of years we're still strangers to darkness, fearful aliens in an enemy camp with our arms crossed over our chests. I stirred. A land turtle on the bank, startled, hissed the air from its lungs and withdrew into its shell. An uneasy pink here, an unfathomable blue there, gave great suggestion of lurking beings. Things were going on. I couldn't see whether that sere rustle I heard was a distant rattlesnake, slit-eyed, or a nearby sparrow kicking in the dry flood debris slung at the foot of a willow. Tremendous action roiled the water everywhere I looked, big action, inexplicable. A tremor welled up beside a gaping muskrat burrow in the bank, and I caught my breath, but no muskrat appeared. The ripples continued to fan upstream with a steady, powerful thrust. Night was knitting over my face an eyeless mask, and I still sat transfixed. A distant airplane, a delta wing out of nightmare, made a gliding shadow on the creek's bottom that looked like a stingray cruising upstream. At once a black fin slit the pink cloud on the water, shearing it in two. The two halves merged together and seemed to dissolve before my eyes. Darkness pooled in the cleft of the creek and rose, as water collects in a well. Untamed, dreaming lights flickered over the sky. I saw hints of hulking underwater shadows, two pale splashes out of the water, and round ripples rolling close together from a blackened center.

At last I stared upstream, where only the deepest violet remained of the cloud, a cloud so high its underbelly still glowed feeble color reflected from a hidden sky lighted in turn by a sun halfway to China. And out of that violet, a sudden enormous black body arced over the water. I saw only a cylindrical sleekness. Head and tail, if there was a head and tail, were both submerged in cloud. I saw only one ebony fling, a headlong dive to darkness; then the waters closed, and the lights went out.

I walked home in a shivering daze, up hill and down. Later I lay openmouthed in bed, my arms flung wide at my sides to steady the whirling darkness. At this latitude I'm spinning 836 miles an hour round the earth's axis; I often fancy I feel my sweeping fall as a breakneck arc like the dive of dolphins, and the hollow rushing of wind raises hair on my neck and the side of my face. In orbit around the sun I'm moving 64,800 miles an hour. The solar system as a whole, like a merry-go-round unhinged, spins, bobs, and blinks at the speed of 43,200 miles an hour along a course set east of Hercules. Someone has piped, and we are dancing a tarantella until the sweat pours. I open my eyes and I see dark, muscled forms curl out of water, with flapping gills and flattened eyes. I close my eyes and I see stars, deep stars giving way to deeper stars, deeper stars bowing to deepest stars at the crown of an infinite cone.

"Still," wrote van Gogh in a letter, "a great deal of light falls on everything." If we are blinded by darkness, we are also blinded by light. When too much light falls on everything, a special terror results. Peter Freuchen describes the notorious kayak sickness to which Greenland Eskimos are prone. "The Greenland fjords are peculiar for the spells of completely quiet weather, when there is not enough wind to blow out a match and the water is like a sheet of glass. The kayak hunter must sit in his boat without stirring a finger so as not to scare the shy seals away.... The sun, low in the sky, sends a glare into his eyes, and the landscape around moves into the realm of the unreal. The reflex from the mirror-like water hypnotizes him, he seems to be unable to move, and all of a sudden it is as if he were floating in a bottomless void, sinking, sinking, and sinking.... Horror-stricken, he tries to stir, to cry out, but he cannot, he is completely paralyzed, he just falls and falls." Some hunters are especially cursed with this panic, and bring ruin and sometimes starvation to their families.

Sometimes here in Virginia at sunset, a low cloud on the southern or northern horizon is completely invisible in the lighted sky. I only know one is there because I can see its reflection in still water. The first time I discovered this mystery, I looked from cloud to no-cloud in bewilderment, checking my bearings over and over, thinking maybe the ark of the covenant was just passing by south of Dead Man Mountain. Only much later did I read the explanation: polarized light from the sky is very much weakened by reflection, but the light in clouds isn't polarized. So invisible clouds pass among visible clouds, till all slide over the mountains; so a greater light extinguishes a lesser as though it didn't exist.

In the great meteor shower of August, the Perseid, I wail all day for the shooting stars I miss. They're out there showering down, committing hara-kiri in a flame of fatal attraction, and hissing perhaps at last into the ocean. But at dawn what looks like a blue dome clamps down over me like a lid on a pot. The stars and planets could smash, and I'd never know. Only a piece of ashen moon occasionally climbs up or down the inside of the dome, and our local star without surcease explodes on our heads. We have really only that one light, one source for all power, and yet we must turn away from it by universal decree. Nobody here on the planet seems aware of this strange, powerful taboo, that we all walk about carefully averting our faces, this way and that, lest our eyes be blasted forever.

Darkness appalls and light dazzles; the scrap of visible light that doesn't hurt my eyes hurts my brain. What I see sets me swaying. Size and distance and the sudden swelling of meanings confuse me, bowl me over. I straddle the sycamore-log bridge over Tinker Creek in the summer. I look at the lighted creek bottom: snail tracks tunnel the mud in quavering curves. A crayfish jerks, but by the time I absorb what has happened, he's gone in a billowing smoke screen of silt. I look at the water: minnows and shiners. If I'm thinking minnows, a carp will fill my brain till I scream. I look at the water's surface: skaters, bubbles, and leaves sliding down. Suddenly my own face, reflected, startles me witless. Those snails have been tracking my face! Finally, with a shuddering wrench of the will, I see clouds, cirrus clouds. I'm dizzy, I fall in. This looking business is risky.

Once I stood on a humped rock on nearby Purgatory Mountain, watching through binoculars the great autumn hawk migration below, until I discovered that I was in danger of joining the hawks on a vertical migration of my own. I was used to binoculars, but not, apparently, to balancing on humped rocks while looking through them. I staggered. Everything advanced and receded by turns; the world was full of unexplained foreshortenings and depths. A distant huge tan object, a hawk the size of an elephant, turned out to be the browned bough of a nearby loblolly pine. I followed a sharp-shinned hawk against a featureless sky, rotating my head unawares as it flew, and when I lowered the glass a glimpse of my own looming shoulder sent me staggering. What prevents the men on Palomar from falling, voiceless and blinded, from their tiny, vaulted chairs?

I reel in confusion; I don't understand what I see. With the naked eye I can see two million light-years to the Andromeda galaxy. Often I slop some creek water in a jar, and when I get home I dump it in a white china bowl. After the silt settles I return and see tracings of minute snails on the bottom, a planarian or two winding round the rim of water, roundworms shimmying frantically, and finally, when my eyes have adjusted to these dimensions, amoebae. At first the amoebae look like muscae volitantes, those curled moving spots you seem to see in your eyes when you stare at a distant wall. Then I see the amoebae as drops of water congealed, bluish, translucent, like chips of sky in the bowl. At length I choose one individual and give myself over to its idea of an evening. I see it dribble a grainy foot before it on its wet, unfathomable way. Do its unedited sense impressions include the fierce focus of my eyes? Shall I take it outside and show it Andromeda, and blow its little endoplasm? I stir the water with a finger, in case it's running out of oxygen. Maybe I should get a tropical aquarium with motorized bubblers and lights, and keep this one for a pet. Yes, it would tell its fissioned descendants, the universe is two feet by five, and if you listen closely you can hear the buzzing music of the spheres.

Oh, it's mysterious lamplit evenings, here in the galaxy, one after the other. It's one of those nights when I wander from window to window, looking for a sign. But I can't see. Terror and a beauty insoluble are a ribband of blue woven into the fringes of garments of things both great and small. No culture explains, no bivouac offers real haven or rest. But it could be that we are not seeing something. Galileo thought comets were an optical illusion. This is fertile ground: since we are certain that they're not, we can look with fresh hope at what our scientists have been saying. What if there are *really* gleaming, castellated cities hung upside down over the desert sand? What limpid lakes and cool date palms have our caravans always passed untried? Until, one by one, by the blindest of leaps, we light on the road to these places, we must stumble in darkness and hunger. I turn from the window. I'm blind as a bat, sensing only from every direction the echo of my own thin cries.

I chanced on a wonderful book by Marius von Senden, called *Space and Sight*. When Western surgeons discovered how to perform safe cataract operations, they ranged across Europe and America, operating on dozens of men and women of all ages who had been blinded by cataracts since birth. Von Senden collected accounts of such cases; the histories are fascinating. Many doctors had tested their patients' sense perceptions and ideas of space both before and after the operations. The vast majority of patients, of both sexes and all ages, had, in von Senden's opinion, no idea of space whatsoever. Form, distance, and size were so many meaningless syllables. A patient "had no idea of depth, confusing it with roundness." Before the operation a doctor would give a blind patient a cube and a sphere; the patient would tongue it or feel it with his hands, and name it correctly. After the operation the doctor would show the same objects to the patient without letting him touch them; now he had no clue whatsoever to what he was seeing. One patient called lemonade "square" because it pricked on his tongue as a square shape pricked on the touch of his hands. Of another postoperative patient, the doctor writes: "I have found in her no notion of size, for example, not even within the narrow limits which she might have encompassed with the aid of touch. Thus when I asked her to show me how big her mother was, she did not stretch out her hands, but set her two index-fingers a few inches apart." Other doctors reported their patients' own statements to similar effect. "The room he was in . . . he knew to be but part of the house, yet he could not conceive that the whole house could look bigger"; "Those who are blind from birth . . . have no real conception of height or distance. A house that is a mile away is thought of as nearby, but requiring the taking of a lot of steps. . . . The elevator that whizzes him up and down gives no more sense of vertical distance than does the train of horizontal."

For the newly sighted, vision is pure sensation unencumbered by meaning: "The girl went through the experience that we all go through and forget, the moment we are born. She saw, but it did not mean anything but a lot of different kinds of brightness." Again, "I asked the patient what he could see; he answered that he saw an extensive field of light, in which everything appeared dull, confused, and in motion. He could not distinguish objects." Another patient saw "nothing but a confusion of forms and colours." When a newly sighted girl saw photographs and paintings, she asked, "'Why do they put those dark marks all over them?' 'Those aren't dark marks,' her mother explained, 'those are shadows. That is one of the ways the eye knows that things have shape. If it were not for shadows many things would look flat.' 'Well, that's how things do look,' Joan answered. 'Everything looks flat with dark patches.'"

But it is the patients' concepts of space that are most revealing. One patient, according to his doctor, "practiced his vision in a strange fashion; thus he takes off one of his boots, throws it some way off in front of him, and then attempts to gauge the distance at which it lies; he takes a few steps towards the boot and tries to grasp it; on failing to reach it, he moves on a step or two and gropes for the boot until he finally gets hold of it. . . . But even at this stage, after three weeks' experience of seeing," von Senden goes on, "'space,' as he conceives it, ends with visual space, i.e. with colour-patches that happen to bound his view. He does not yet have the notion that a larger object (a chair) can mask a smaller one (a dog), or that the latter can still be present even though it is not directly seen."

In general the newly sighted see the world as a dazzle of color patches. They are pleased by the sensation of color, and learn quickly to name the colors, but the rest of seeing is tormentingly difficult. Soon after his operation, a patient "generally bumps into one of these colour-patches and observes them to be substantial, since they resist him as tactual objects do. In walking about it also strikes him—or can if he pays attention—that he is continually passing in between the colours he sees, that he can go past a visual object, that a part of it then steadily disappears from view; and that in spite of this, however he twists and turns—whether entering the room from the door, for example, or returning back to it—he always has a visual space in front of him. Thus he gradually comes to realize that there is also a space behind him, which he does not see."

The mental effort involved in these reasonings proves overwhelming for many patients. It oppresses them to realize, if they ever do at all, the tremendous size of the world, which they had previously conceived of as something touchingly manageable. It oppresses them to realize that they have been visible to people all along, perhaps unattractively so, without their knowledge or consent. A disheartening number of them refuse to use their new vision, continuing to go over objects with their tongues, and lapsing into apathy and despair. "The child can see, but will not make use of his sight. Only when pressed can he with difficulty be brought to look at objects in his neighbourhood; but more than a foot away it is impossible to bestir him to the necessary effort." Of a twenty-one-year-old girl, the doctor relates, "Her unfortunate father, who had hoped for so much from this operation, wrote that his daughter carefully shuts her eyes whenever she wishes to go about the house, especially when she comes to a staircase, and that she is never happier or more at ease than when, by closing her eyelids, she relapses into her former state of total blindness." A fifteen-year-old boy, who was in love with a girl at the asylum for the blind, finally blurted out, "No, really, I can't stand it any more; I want to be sent back to the asylum again. If things aren't altered, I'll tear my eyes out."

Some do learn to see, especially the young ones. But it changes their lives. One doctor comments on "the rapid and complete loss of that striking and wonderful serenity which is characteristic only of those who have never yet seen." A blind man who learns to see is ashamed of his old habits. He dresses up, grooms himself, and tries to make a good impression. While he was blind he was indifferent to objects unless they were edible; now, "a sifting of values sets in . . . his thoughts and wishes are mightily stirred and some few of the patients are thereby led into dissimulation, envy, theft and fraud."

On the other hand, many newly sighted people speak well of the world, and teach us how dull is our own vision. To one patient, a human hand, unrecognized, is "something bright and then holes." Shown a bunch of grapes, a boy calls out, "It is dark, blue and shiny. . . . It isn't smooth, it has bumps and hollows." A little girl visits a garden. "She is greatly astonished, and can scarcely be persuaded to answer, stands speechless in front of the tree, which she only names on taking hold of it, and then as 'the tree with the lights in it.'" Some delight in their sight and give themselves over to the visual world. Of a patient just after her bandages were removed, her doctor writes: "The first things to attract her attention were her own hands; she looked at them very closely, moved them repeatedly to and fro, bent and stretched the fingers, and seemed greatly astonished at the sight." One girl was eager to tell her blind friend that "men do not really look like trees at all" and astounded to discover that her every visitor had an utterly different face. Finally, a twenty-two-year-old girl was dazzled by the world's brightness and kept her eyes shut for two weeks. When at the end of that time she opened her eyes again, she did not recognize any objects, but, "the more she now directed her gaze upon everything about her, the more it could be seen how an expression of gratification and astonishment overspread her features; she repeatedly exclaimed: 'Oh God! How beautiful!'"

I saw color patches for weeks after I read this wonderful book. It was summer; the peaches were ripe in the valley orchards. When I woke in the morning, color patches wrapped round my eyes, intricately, leaving not one unfilled spot. All day long I walked among shifting color patches that parted before me like the Red Sea and closed again in silence, transfigured, wherever I looked back. Some patches swelled and loomed, while others vanished utterly, and dark marks flitted at random over the whole dazzling sweep. But I couldn't sustain the illusion of flatness. I've been around for too long. Form is condemned to an eternal danse macabre with meaning: I couldn't unpeach the peaches. Nor can I remember ever having seen without understanding; the color patches of infancy are lost. My brain then must have been smooth as any balloon. I'm told I reached for the moon; many babies do. But the color patches of infancy swelled as meaning filled them; they arrayed themselves in solemn ranks down distance that unrolled and stretched before me like a plain. The moon rocketed away. I live now in a world of shadows that shape and distance color, a world where space makes a kind of terrible sense. What gnosticism is this, and what physics? The fluttering patch I saw in my nursery window—silver and green and shape-shifting blue—is gone; a row of Lombardy poplars takes it place, mute, across the distant lawn. That humming oblong creature pale as light that stole along the walls of my room at night, stretching exhilaratingly around the corners, is gone too, gone the night I ate of the bittersweet fruit, put two and two together, and puckered forever my brain. Martin Buber tells this tale: "Rabbi Mendel once boasted to his teacher Rabbi Elimelekh that evenings he saw the angel who rolls away the light before the darkness, and mornings the angel who rolls away the darkness before the light. 'Yes,' said Rabbi Elimelekh, 'in my youth I saw that too. Later on you don't see these things any more.'"

Why didn't someone hand those newly sighted people paints and brushes from the start, when they still didn't know what anything was? Then maybe we all could see color patches too, the world unraveled from reason, Eden before Adam gave names. The scales would drop from my eyes; I'd see trees like men walking; I'd run down the road against all orders, hallooing and leaping.

* * *

Seeing is of course very much a matter of verbalization. Unless I call my attention to what passes before my eyes, I simply won't see it. It is, as Ruskin says, "not merely unnoticed, but in the full, clear sense of the word, unseen." My eyes alone can't solve analogy tests using figures, the ones that show, with increasing elaborations, a big square, then a small square in a big square, then a big triangle, and expect me to find a small triangle in a big triangle. I have to say the words, describe what I'm seeing. If Tinker Mountain erupted, I'd be likely to notice. But if I want to notice the lesser cataclysms of valley life, I have to maintain in my head a running description of the present. It's not that I'm observant; it's just that I talk too much. Otherwise, especially in a strange place, I'll never know what's happening. Like a blind man at the ball game, I need a radio.

When I see this way I analyze and pry. I hurl over logs and roll away stones; I study the bank a square foot at a time, probing and tilting my head. Some days, when a mist covers the mountains, when the muskrats won't show and the microscope's mirror shatters, I want to climb up the blank blue dome as a man would storm the inside of a circus tent, wildly, dangling, and with a steel knife claw a rent in the top, peep, and, if I must, fall.

But there is another kind of seeing, which involves a letting go. When I see this way I sway transfixed and emptied. The difference between the two days of seeing is the difference between walking with and without a camera. When I walk with a camera I walk from shot to shot, reading the light on a calibrated meter. When I walk without a camera, my own shutter opens, and the moment's light prints on my own silver gut. When I see this second way I am above all an unscrupulous observer.

It was sunny one evening last summer at Tinker Creek; the sun was low in the sky, upstream. I was sitting on the sycamore-log bridge with the sunset at my back, watching the shiners the size of minnows who were feeding over the muddy sand in skittery schools. Again and again, one fish, then another, turned for a split second across the current, and flash! the sun shot out from its silver side. I couldn't watch for it. It was always just happening somewhere else, and it drew my vision just as it disappeared: flash, like a sudden dazzle of the thinnest blade, a sparking over a dun-and-olive ground at chance intervals from every direction. Then I noticed white specks, some sort of pale petals, small, floating from under my feet on the creek's surface, very slow and steady. So I blurred my eyes and gazed toward the brim of my hat and saw a new world. I saw the pale-white circles roll up, roll up, like the world's turning, mute and perfect, and I saw the linear flashes, gleaming silver, like stars being born at random down a rolling scroll of time. Something broke and something opened. I filled up like a new wineskin. I breathed an air like light; I saw a light like water. I was the lip of a fountain the creek filled forever; I was ether, the leaf in the zephyr; I was flesh flake, feather, bone.

When I see this way I see truly. As Thoreau says, I return to my senses. I am the man who watches the baseball game in silence in an empty stadium. I see the game purely; I'm abstracted and dazed. When it's all over and the white-suited players lope off the green field to their shadowed dugouts, I leap to my feet; I cheer and cheer.

But I can't go out and try to see this way. I'll fail, I'll go mad. All I can do is try to gag the commentator, to hush the noise of useless interior babble that keeps me from seeing just as surely as a newspaper dangled before my eyes. The effort is really a discipline requiring a lifetime of dedicated struggle; it marks the literature of saints and monks of every order East and West, under every rule and no rule, discalced and shod. The world's spiritual geniuses seem to discover universally that the mind's muddy river, this ceaseless flow of trivia and trash, cannot be dammed, and that trying to dam it is a waste of effort that might lead to madness. Instead you must allow the muddy river to flow unheeded in the dim channels of consciousness; you raise your sights; you look along it, mildly, acknowledging its presence without interest and gazing beyond it into the realm of the real, where subjects and objects act and rest purely, without utterance. "Launch into the deep," says Jacques Ellul, "and you shall see."

The secret of seeing is, then, the pearl of great price. If I thought he could teach me to find it and keep it forever, I would stagger barefoot across a hundred deserts after any lunatic at all. But although the pearl may be found, it may not be sought. The literature of illumination reveals this above all: although it comes to those who wait for it, it is always, even to the most practiced and adept, a gift and a total surprise. I return from one walk knowing where the killdeer nests in the field by the creek and the hour the laurel blooms. I return from the same walk a day later scarcely knowing my own name. Litanies hum in my ears; my tongue flaps in my mouth Ailinon, alleluia! I cannot cause light; the most I can do is try to put myself in the path of its beam. It is possible, in deep space, to sail on solar wind. Light, be it particle or wave, has force: you rig a giant sail and go. The secret of seeing is to sail on solar wind. Hone and spread your spirit till you yourself are a sail, whetted, translucent, broadside to the merest puff.

When her doctor took her bandages off and led her into the garden, the girl who was no longer blind saw "the tree with the lights in it." It was for this tree I searched through the peach orchards of summer, in the forests of fall and down winter and spring for years. Then one day I was walking along Tinker Creek thinking of nothing at all, and I saw the tree with the lights in it. I saw the backyard cedar where the mourning doves roost charged and transfigured, each cell buzzing with flame. I stood on the grass with the lights in it, grass that was wholly fire, utterly focused and utterly dreamed. It was less like seeing than like being for the first time seen, knocked breathless by a powerful glance. The flood of fire abated, but I'm still spending the power. Gradually the lights went out in the cedar, the colors died, the cells unflamed and disappeared. I was still ringing. I had been my whole life a bell, and never knew it until at that moment I was lifted and struck. I have since only very rarely seen the tree with the lights in it. The vision comes and goes, mostly goes, but I live for it, for the moment when the mountains open and a new light roars in spate through the crack, and the mountains slam.

I HAVE JUST LEARNED TO see praying mantis egg cases. Suddenly I see them everywhere; a tan oval of light catches my eye, or I notice a blob of thickness in a patch of slender weeds. As I write I can see the one I tied to the mock orange hedge outside my study window. It is over an inch long and shaped like a bell, or like the northern hemisphere of an egg cut through its equator. The full length of one of its long sides is affixed to a twig; the side that catches the light is perfectly flat. It has a dead-straw, dead-weed color, and a curious brittle texture, hard as varnish, but pitted minutely, like frozen foam. I carried it home this afternoon, holding it carefully by the twig, along with several others—they were light as air. I dropped one without missing it until I got home and made a count.

Within the week I've seen thirty or so of these egg cases in a rose-grown field on Tinker Mountain, and another thirty in weeds along Carvin's Creek. One was on a twig of tiny dogwood on the mud lawn of a newly built house. I think the mail order houses sell them to gardeners at a dollar apiece. It beats spraying, because each case contains between one hundred twenty-five and three hundred fifty eggs. If the eggs survive ants, woodpeckers, and mice—and most do—then you get the fun of seeing the new mantises hatch, and the smug feeling of knowing, all summer long, that they're out there in your garden devouring gruesome numbers of fellow insects all nice and organically. When a mantis has crunched up the last shred of its victim, it cleans its smooth green face like a cat.

In late summer I often see a winged adult stalking the insects that swarm about my porch light. Its body is a clear, warm green; its naked, triangular head can revolve uncannily, so that I often see one twist its head to gaze at me as it were over its shoulder.

When it strikes, it jerks so suddenly and with such a fearful clatter of raised wings that even a hardened entomologist like J. Henri Fabre confessed to being startled witless every time.

Adult mantises eat more or less everything that breathes and is small enough to capture. They eat honeybees and butterflies, including monarch butterflies. People have actually seen them seize and devour garter snakes, mice, and even hummingbirds. Newly hatched mantises, on the other hand, eat small creatures like aphids and each other. When I was in elementary school, one of the teachers brought in a mantis egg case in a mason jar. I watched the newly hatched mantises emerge and shed their skins; they were spidery and translucent, all over joints. They trailed from the egg case to the base of the mason jar in a living bridge that looked like Arabic calligraphy, some baffling text from the Koran inscribed down the air by a fine hand. Over a period of several hours, during which time the teacher never summoned the nerve or the sense to release them, they ate each other until only two were left. Tiny legs were still kicking from the mouths of both. The two survivors grappled and sawed in the mason jar; finally both died of injuries. I felt as though I myself should swallow the corpses, shutting my eyes and washing them down like jagged pills, so all that life wouldn't be lost.

When mantises hatch in the wild, however, they straggle about prettily, dodging ants, till all vanish in the grass. So it was in hopes of seeing an eventual hatch that I pocketed my jackknife this afternoon before I set out to walk. Now that I can see the egg cases, I'm embarrassed to realize how many I must have missed all along. I walked east through the Adams' woods to the cornfield, cutting three undamaged egg cases I found at the edge of the field. It was a clear, picturesque day, a February day without clouds, without emotion or spirit, like a beautiful woman with an empty face. In my fingers I carried the thorny stems from which the egg cases hung like roses; I switched the bouquet from hand to hand, warming the free hand in a pocket. Passing the house again, deciding not to fetch gloves, I walked north to the hill by the place where the steers come to drink from Tinker Creek. There in the weeds on the hill I found another eight egg cases. I was stunned—I cross this hill several times a week, and I always look for egg cases here, because it was here that I had once seen a mantis laying her eggs.

It was several years ago that I witnessed this extraordinary procedure, but I remember, and confess, an inescapable feeling that I was watching something not real and present, but a horrible nature movie, a "secrets of nature" short, beautifully photographed in full color, that I had to sit through unable to look anywhere else but at the dimly lighted EXIT signs along the walls, and that behind the scenes some amateur moviemaker was congratulating himself on having stumbled across this little wonder, or even on having contrived so natural a setting, as though the whole scene had been shot very carefully in a terrarium in someone's greenhouse.

I was ambling across this hill that day when I noticed a speck of pure white. The hill is eroded; the slope is a rutted wreck of red clay broken by grassy hillocks and low wild roses whose roots clasp a pittance of topsoil. I leaned to examine the white thing and saw a mass of bubbles like spittle. Then I saw something dark like an engorged leech rummaging over the spittle, and then I saw the praying mantis.

She was upside down, clinging to a horizontal stem of wild rose by her feet, which pointed to heaven. Her head was deep in dried grass. Her abdomen was swollen like a smashed finger; it tapered to a fleshy tip out of which bubbled a wet, whipped froth. I couldn't believe my eyes. I lay on the hill this way and that, my knees in thorns and my cheeks in clay, trying to see as well as I could. I poked near the female's head with a grass; she was clearly undisturbed, so I settled my nose an inch from that pulsing abdomen. It puffed like a concertina, it throbbed like a bellows; it roved, pumping, over the glistening, clabbered surface of the egg case, testing and patting, thrusting and smoothing. It seemed to act so independently that I forgot the panting brown stick at the other end. The bubble creature seemed to have two eyes, a frantic little brain, and two busy, soft hands. It looked like a hideous, harried mother slicking up a fat daughter for a beauty pageant, touching her up, slobbering over her, patting and hemming and brushing and stroking.

The male was nowhere in sight. The female had probably eaten him. Fabre says that, at least in captivity, the female will mate with and devour up to seven males, whether she has laid her egg cases or not. The mating rites of mantises are well known: a chemical produced in the head of the male insect says, in effect, "No, don't go near her, you fool, she'll eat you alive." At the same time a chemical in his abdomen says, "Yes, by all means, now and forever yes."

While the male is making up what passes for his mind, the female tips the balance in her favor by eating his head. He mounts her. Fabre describes the mating, which sometimes lasts six hours, as follows: "The male, absorbed in the performance of his vital functions, holds the female in a tight embrace. But the wretch has no head; he has no neck; he has hardly a body. The other, with her muzzle turned over her shoulder, continues very placidly to gnaw what remains of the gentle swain. And, all the time, that masculine stump, holding on firmly, goes on with the business! . . . I have seen it done with my own eyes and have not yet recovered from my astonishment."

I watched the egg-laying for over an hour. When I returned the next day, the mantis was gone. The white foam had hardened and browned to a dirty suds; then, and on subsequent days, I had trouble pinpointing the case, which was only an inch or so off the ground. I checked on it every week all winter long. In the spring the ants discovered it; every week I saw dozens of ants scrambling over the sides, unable to chew a way in. Later in the spring I climbed the hill every day, hoping to catch the hatch. The leaves of the trees had long since unfolded, the butterflies were out, and the robins' first broods were fledged; still the egg case hung silent and full on the stem. I read that I should wait for June, but still I visited the case every day. One morning at the beginning of June everything was gone. I couldn't find the lower thorn in the clump of three to which the egg case was fixed. I couldn't find the clump of three. Tracks ridged the clay, and I saw the lopped stems: somehow my neighbor had contrived to run a tractor mower over that steep clay hill on which there grew nothing to mow but a few stubby thorns.

So. Today from this same hill I cut another three undamaged cases and carried them home with the others by their twigs. I also collected a suspiciously light cynthia moth cocoon. My fingers were stiff and red with cold, and my nose ran. I had forgotten the Law of the Wild, which is: "Carry Kleenex." At home I tied the twigs with their egg cases to various sunny bushes and trees in the yard. They're easy to find because I used white string; at any rate, I'm unlikely to mow my own trees. I hope the woodpeckers that come to the feeder don't find them, but I don't see how they'd get a purchase on them if they did.

Night is rising in the valley; the creek has been extinguished for an hour, and now only the naked tips of trees fire tapers into the sky like trails of sparks. The scene that was in the back of my brain all afternoon, obscurely, is beginning to rise from night's lagoon. It really has nothing to do with praying mantises. But this afternoon I threw tiny string lashings and hitches with frozen hands, gingerly, fearing to touch the egg cases even for a minute because I remembered the Polyphemus moth.

I have no intention of inflicting all my childhood memories on anyone. Far less do I want to excoriate my old teachers who, in their bungling, unforgettable way, exposed me to the natural world, a world covered in chitin, where implacable realities hold sway. The Polyphemus moth never made it to the past; it crawls in that crowded, pellucid pool at the lip of the great waterfall. It is as present as this blue desk and brazen lamp, as this blackened window before me in which I can no longer see even the white string that binds the egg case to the hedge, but only my own pale, astonished face.

Once, when I was ten or eleven years old, my friend Judy brought in a Polyphemus moth cocoon. It was January; there were doily snowflakes taped to the schoolroom panes. The teacher kept the cocoon in her desk all morning and brought it out when we were getting restless before recess. In a book, we found what the adult moth would look like; it would be beautiful. With a wingspread of up to six inches, the Polyphemus is one of the few huge American silk moths, much larger than, say, a giant or tiger swallowtail butterfly. The moth's enormous wings are velveted in a rich, warm brown and edged in bands of blue and pink delicate as a watercolor wash. A startling "eye-spot," immense and deep blue, melding to an almost translucent yellow, luxuriates in the center of each hind wing. The effect is one of a masculine splendor foreign to the butterflies, a fragility unfurled to strength. The Polyphemus moth in the picture looked like a mighty wraith, a beating essence of the hardwood forest, alien-skinned and brown, with spread, blind eyes. This was the giant moth packed in the faded cocoon. We closed the book and turned to the cocoon. It was an oak leaf sewn into a plump oval bundle; Judy had found it loose in a pile of frozen leaves.

We passed the cocoon around; it was heavy. As we held it in our hands, the creature within warmed and squirmed. We were delighted, and wrapped it tighter in our fists. The pupa began to jerk violently, in heart-stopping knocks. Who's there? I can still feel those thumps, urgent through a muffling of spun silk and leaf, urgent through the swaddling of many years, against the curve of my palm. We kept passing it around. When it came to me again it was hot as a bun; it jumped half out of my hand. The teacher intervened. She put it, still heaving and banging, in the inevitable mason jar.

It was coming. There was no stopping it now, January or not. One end of the cocoon dampened and gradually frayed in a furious battle. The whole cocoon twisted and slapped around in the bottom of the jar. The teacher fades, the classmates fade, I fade: I don't remember anything but that thing's struggle to be a moth or die trying. It emerged at last, a sodden crumple. It was a male; his long antennae were thickly plumed, as wide as his fat abdomen. His body was very thick, over an inch long, and deeply furred. A gray, furlike plush covered his head; a long, tan furlike hair hung from his wide thorax over his brown-furred, segmented abdomen. His multijointed legs, pale and powerful, were shaggy as a bear's. He stood still, but he breathed.

He couldn't spread his wings. There was no room. The chemical that coated his wings like varnish, stiffening them permanently, dried, and hardened his wings as they were. He was a monster in a mason jar. Those huge wings stuck on his back in a torture of random pleats and folds, wrinkled as a dirty tissue, rigid as leather. They made a single nightmare clump still racked with useless, frantic convulsions.

The next thing I remember, it was recess. The school was in Shadyside, a busy residential part of Pittsburgh. Everyone was playing dodgeball in the fenced playground or racing around the concrete schoolyard by the swings. Next to the playground a long delivery drive sloped downhill to the sidewalk and street. Someone—it must have been the teacher—had let the moth out. I was standing in the driveway, alone, stock-still but shivering. Someone had given the Polyphemus moth his freedom, and he was walking away.

He heaved himself down the asphalt driveway by infinite degrees, unwavering. His hideous crumpled wings lay glued and rucked on his back, perfectly still now, like a collapsed tent. The bell rang twice; I had to go. The moth was receding down the driveway, dragging on. I went; I ran inside. The Polyphemus moth is still crawling down the driveway, crawling down the driveway hunched, crawling down the driveway on six furred feet, forever.

Shading the glass with a hand, I can see how shadow has pooled in the valley. It washes up the sandstone cliffs on Tinker Mountain and obliterates them in a deluge; freshets of shadow leak into the sky. I am exhausted. In Pliny I read about the invention of clay modeling. A Sicyonian potter came to Corinth. There his daughter fell in love with a young man who had to make frequent long journeys away from the city. When he sat with her at home, she used to trace the outline of his shadow that a candle's light cast on the wall. Then, in his absence, she worked over the profile, deepening it, so that she might enjoy his face, and remember. One day the father slapped some potter's clay over the gouged plaster; when the clay hardened he removed it, baked it, and "showed it abroad." The story ends here. Did the boy come back? What did the girl think of her father's dragging her lover all over town by the hair? What I really want to know is this: Is the shadow still there? If I went

back and found the shadow of that face there on the wall by the
fireplace, I'd rip down the house with my hands for that hunk.

The shadow's the thing. Outside shadows are blue, I read,
because they are lighted by the blue sky and not the yellow sun.
Their blueness bespeaks infinitesimal particles scattered down
inestimable distance. Muslims, whose religion bans representational art as idolatrous, don't observe the rule strictly; but they
do forbid sculpture, because it casts a shadow. So shadows
define the real. If I no longer see shadows as "dark marks," as
do the newly sighted, then I see them as making some sort of
sense of the light. They give the light distance; they put it in its
place. They inform my eyes of my location here, here O Israel,
here in the world's flawed sculpture, here in the flickering
shade of the nothingness between me and the light.

Now that shadow has dissolved the heavens' blue dome, I
can see Andromeda again; I stand pressed to the window, rapt
and shrunk in the galaxy's chill glare. "Nostalgia of the
Infinite," di Chirico: cast shadows stream across the sunlit court-
yard, gouging canyons. There is a sense in which shadows are
actually cast, hurled with a power, cast as Ishmael was cast, *out*,
with a flinging force. This is the blue strip running through creation, the icy roadside stream on whose banks the mantis mates,
in whose unweighed waters the giant water bug sips frogs.
Shadow Creek is the blue subterranean stream that chills
Carvin's Creek and Tinker Creek; it cuts like ice under the ribs
of the mountains, Tinker and Dead Man. Shadow Creek storms
through limestone vaults under forests, or surfaces anywhere,
damp, on the underside of a leaf. I wring it from rocks; it seeps
into my cup. Chasms open at the glance of an eye; the ground
parts like a wind-rent cloud over stars. Shadow Creek: on my
least walk to the mailbox I may find myself knee-deep in its
sucking, frigid pools. I must either wear rubber boots, or dance
to keep warm.

Fish gotta swim and bird gotta fly; insects, it seems, gotta do
one horrible thing after another. I never ask why of a vulture or
shark, but I ask why of almost every insect I see. More than one
insect—the possibility of fertile reproduction—is an assault on

all human value, all hope of a reasonable god. Even that devout Frenchman J. Henri Fabre, who devoted his entire life to the study of insects, cannot restrain a feeling of unholy revulsion. He describes a bee-eating wasp, the Philanthus, who has killed a honeybee. If the bee is heavy with honey, the wasp squeezes its crop "so as to make her disgorge the delicious syrup, which she drinks by licking the tongue which her unfortunate victim, in her death-agony, sticks out of her mouth at full length. . . . At the moment of some such horrible banquet, I have seen the Wasp, with her prey, seized by the Mantis: the bandit was rifled by another bandit. And here is an awful detail: while the Mantis held her transfixed under the points of the double saw and was already munching her belly, the Wasp continued to lick the honey of her Bee, unable to relinquish the delicious food even amid the terrors of death. Let us hasten to cast a veil over these horrors."

The remarkable thing about the world of insects, however, is precisely that there is no veil cast over these horrors. These are mysteries performed in broad daylight before our very eyes; we can see every detail, and yet they are still mysteries. If, as Heraclitus suggests, God, like an oracle, neither "declares nor hides, but sets forth by signs," then clearly I had better be scrying the signs. The earth devotes an overwhelming proportion of its energy to these buzzings and leaps in the grass, to these brittle gnawings and crawlings about. Theirs is the biggest wedge of the pie: Why? I ought to keep a giant water bug in an aquarium on my dresser, so I can think about it. We have brass candlesticks in our houses now; we ought to display praying mantises in our churches. Why do we turn from the insects in loathing? Our competitors are not only cold-blooded, and green- and yellow-blooded, but also cased in a clacking horn. They lack the grace to go about as we do, soft-side out to the wind and thorns. They have rigid eyes and brains strung down their backs. But they make up the bulk of our comrades-at-life, so I look to them for a glimmer of companionship.

When a grasshopper landed on my study window last summer, I looked at it for a long time. Its hard wing covers were short; its body was a dead waxen yellow, with black-green, inde-

cipherable marks. Like all large insects, it gave me pause,
plenty pause, with its hideous horizontal, multijointed mouth-
parts and intricate, mechanical-looking feet, all cups and spikes.
I looked at its tapered, chitin-covered abdomen, plated and
barred as a tank tread, and was about to turn away when I saw it
breathe, puff puff, and I grew sympathetic. Yeah, I said, puff
puff, isn't it? It jerked away with a buzz like a rasping file, audi-
ble through the pane, and continued to puff in the grass. So puff
it is, and that's all there is; though I'm partial to honey myself.

Nature is, above all, profligate. Don't believe them when
they tell you how economical and thrifty nature is, whose leaves
return to the soil. Wouldn't it be cheaper to leave them on the
tree in the first place? This deciduous business alone is a radical
scheme, the brainchild of a deranged manic-depressive with
limitless capital. Extravagance! Nature will try anything once.
This is what the sign of the insects says. No form is too gruesome, no behavior too grotesque. If you're dealing with organic
compounds, then let them combine. If it works, if it quickens,
set it clacking in the grass; there's always room for one more;
you ain't so handsome yourself. This is a spendthrift economy;
though nothing is lost, all is spent.

That the insects have adapted is obvious. Their failures to
adapt, however, are dazzling. It is hard to believe that nature is
partial to such dim-wittedness. Howard Ensign Evans tells of
dragonflies trying to lay eggs on the shining hoods of cars. Other
dragonflies seem to test a surface, to learn if it's really water, by
dipping the tips of their abdomens in it. At the Los Angeles La
Brea tar pits, they dip their abdomens into the reeking tar and
get stuck. If by tremendous effort a dragonfly frees itself, Evans
reports, it is apt to repeat the maneuver. Sometimes the tar pits
glitter with the dry bodies of dead dragonflies.

J. Henri Fabre's pine processionaries speak to the same
point. Although the new studies show that some insects can on
occasion strike out into new territory, leaving instinct behind,
still a blindered and blinkered enslavement to instinct is the
rule, as the pine processionaries show. Pine processionaries are
moth caterpillars with shiny black heads, who travel about at

night in pine trees along a silken road of their own making. They straddle the road in a tight file, head to rear touching, and each caterpillar adds its thread to the original track first laid by the one who happens to lead the procession. Fabre interferes; he catches them on a daytime exploration approaching a circular track, the rim of a wide palm vase in his greenhouse. When the leader of the insect train completes a full circle, Fabre removes the caterpillars still climbing the vase and brushes away all extraneous silken tracks. Now he has a closed circuit of caterpillars, leaderless, trudging round his vase on a never-ending track. He wants to see how long it will take them to catch on. To his horror, they march not just an hour or so, but all day. When Fabre leaves the greenhouse at night, they are still tracing that wearying circle, although night is the time they usually feed.

In the chill of the next morning they are deadly still; when they rouse themselves, however, they resume what Fabre calls their "imbecility." They slog along all day, head to tail. The next night is bitterly cold; in the morning Fabre finds them slumped on the vase rim in two distinct clumps. When they line up again, they have two leaders, and the leaders in nature often explore to the sides of an already laid track. But the two ranks meet, and the entranced circle winds on. Fabre can't believe his eyes. The creatures have had neither water nor food nor rest; they are shelterless all day and all night long. Again the next night a hard frost numbs the caterpillars, who huddle in heaps. By chance the first one to wake is off the track; it strikes out in a new direction and encounters the soil in the pot. Six others follow his track. Now the ones on the vase have a leader, because there is a gap in the rim. But they drag on stubbornly around their circle of hell. Soon the seven rebels, unable to eat the palm in the vase, follow their trail back to the rim of the pot and join the doomed march. The circle often breaks as starved or exhausted caterpillars stagger to a halt; but they soon breach the gap they leave, and no leaders emerge.

The next day a heat spell hits. The caterpillars lean far over the rim of the vase, exploring. At last one veers from the track. Followed by four others, it explores down the long side of the vase; there, next to the vase, Fabre has placed some pine needles for them to feed on. They ramble within nine inches of the pine needles but, incredibly, wander upward to the rim and rejoin the dismal parade. For two more days the processionaries stagger on; at last they try the path laid down the vase by the last group. They venture out to new ground; they straggle at last to their nest. It has been seven days. Fabre himself, "already familiar with the abysmal stupidity of insects as a class whenever the least accident occurs," is nevertheless clearly oppressed by this new confirmation that the caterpillars lack "any gleam of intelligence in their benighted minds." "The caterpillars in distress," he concludes, "starved, shelterless, chilled with cold at night, cling obstinately to the silk ribbon covered hundreds of times, because they lack the rudimentary glimmers of reason which would advise them to abandon it."

I want out of this still air. What street-corner vendor wound the key on the backs of tin soldiers and abandoned them to the sidewalk, and crashings over the curb? Elijah mocked the prophets of Baal, who lay a bullock on a woodpile and begged Baal to consume it: "Cry aloud: for he is a god; either he is talking, or he is pursuing, or he is in a journey, or peradventure he sleepeth, and must be awaked." Cry aloud. It is the fixed that horrifies us, the fixed that assails us with the tremendous force of its mindlessness. The fixed is a mason jar, and we can't beat it open. The prophets of Baal gashed themselves with knives and lancets, and the wood stayed wood. The fixed is the world without fire—dead flint, dead tinder, and nowhere a spark. It is motion without direction, force without power, the aimless procession of caterpillars round the rim of a vase, and I hate it because at any moment I myself might step to that charmed and glistening thread. Last spring in the flood I saw a brown cattail bob in the high muddy water of Carvin's Creek, up and down, side to side, a jerk a second. I went back the next day and nothing had changed; that empty twitching beat on in an endless, sickening tattoo. What geomancy reads what the windblown sand writes on the desert rock? I read there that all things live by a generous power and dance to a mighty tune; or I read there that all things are scattered and hurled, that our every arabesque and grand jeté is a frantic variation on our one free fall.

Two weeks ago, in the dark of night, I bundled up and quit the house for Tinker Creek. Long before I could actually see the creek, I heard it shooting the sandstone riffles with a chilled rush and splash. It has always been a happy thought to me that the creek runs on all night, new every minute, whether I wish it or know it or care, as a closed book on a shelf continues to whisper to itself its own inexhaustible tale. So many things have been shown me on these banks, so much light has illumined me by reflection here where the water comes down, that I can hardly believe that this grace never flags, that the pouring from ever renewable sources is endless, impartial, and free. But that night Tinker Creek had vanished, usurped, and Shadow Creek blocked its banks. The night cold pulsed in my bones. I stood on the frozen grass under the Osage orange. The night was moonless; the mountains loomed over the stars. By half looking away I could barely make out the gray line of foam at the riffles; the skin tightened over the corners of my mouth, and I blinked in the cold. That night the fact of the creek's running on in the dark—from high on the unseen side of Tinker Mountain, miles away—smacked sinister. Where was the old exhilaration? This dumb dead drop over rocks was a hideous parody of real natural life, warm and willful. It was senseless and horrifying; I turned away. The damned thing was flowing because it was *pushed*.

That was two weeks ago; tonight I don't know. Tonight the moon is full, and I wonder. I'm pleased with my day's "work," with the cocoon and egg cases hung on the hedge. Van Gogh found nerve to call this world "a study that didn't come off," but I'm not so sure. Where do I get my standards that I fancy the fixed world of insects doesn't meet? I'm tired of reading; I pick up a book and learn that "pieces of the leech's body can also swim." Take a deep breath, Elijah: light your pile. Van Gogh is utterly dead; the world may be fixed, but it never was broken. And shadow itself may resolve into beauty.

*   *   *

Once, when Tinker Creek had frozen inches thick at a wide part near the bridge, I found a pileated woodpecker in the sky by its giant shadow flapping blue on the white ice below. It flew under the neighborhood children's skates; it soared whole and wholly wild though they sliced its wings. I'd like a chunk of that shadow, a pane of freshwater ice to lug with me everywhere, fluttering huge under my arm, to use as the Eskimos did for a window on the world. Shadow is the blue patch where the light doesn't hit. It is mystery itself, and mystery is the ancients' ultima Thule, the modern explorers' Point of Relative Inaccessibility, that boreal point most distant from all known lands. There the twin oceans of beauty and horror meet. The great glaciers are calving. Ice that sifted to earth as snow in the time of Christ shears from the pack with a roar and crumbles to water. It could be that our instruments have not looked deeply enough. The RNA deep in the mantis's jaw is a beautiful ribbon. Did the crawling Polyphemus have in its watery heart one cell, and in that cell one special molecule, and in that molecule one hydrogen atom, and round that atom's nucleus one wild, distant electron that, split, showed a forest, swaying?

In lieu of a pinochle game, I'll walk a step before bed. No hesitation about gloves now; I swath myself in wool and down from head to foot, and step into the night.

The air bites my nose like pepper. I walk down the road, leap a ditch, and mount the hill where today I clipped the egg cases, where years ago I watched the female mantis frothing out foam. The rutted clay is frozen tonight in shards; its scarps loom in the slanting light like pressure ridges in ice under aurora. The light from the moon is awesome, full and wan. It's not the luster of noonday it gives, but the luster of elf light, utterly lambent and utterly dreamed. I crash over clumps of brittle, hand-blown grass—and I stop still. The frozen twigs of the huge tulip poplar next to the hill clack in the cold like tin-snips.

I look to the sky. What do I know of deep space with its red giants and white dwarfs? I think of our own solar system, of the five mute moons of Uranus—Ariel, Umbriel, Titania, Oberon,

Miranda—spinning in their fixed sleep of thralldom. These our actors, as I foretold you, were all spirits. At last I look to the moon; it hangs fixed and full in the east, enormously scrubbed and simple. Our own hometown ultima moon. It must have been a wonderful sight from there, when the olive continents cracked and spread, and the white ice rolled down and up like a window blind. My eyes feel cold when I blink; this is enough of a walk tonight. I lack the apparatus to feel a warmth that few have felt—but it's there. According to Arthur Koestler, Kepler felt the focused warmth when he was experimenting on something entirely different, using concave mirrors. Kepler wrote, "I was engaged in other experiments with mirrors, without thinking of the warmth; I involuntarily turned around to see whether somebody was breathing on my hand." It was warmth from the moon.

CATCH IT IF YOU CAN.

It is early March. I am dazed from a long day of interstate driving homeward; I pull in at a gas station in Nowhere, Virginia, north of Lexington. The young boy in charge ("Chick 'at oll?") is offering a free cup of coffee with every gas purchase. We talk in the glass-walled office while my coffee cools enough to drink. He tells me, among other things, that the rival gas station down the road, whose FREE COFFEE sign is visible from the interstate, charges you fifteen cents if you want your coffee in a Styrofoam cup, as opposed, I guess, to your bare hands.

All the time we talk, the boy's new beagle puppy is skidding around the office, sniffing impartially at my shoes and at the wire rack of folded maps. The cheerful human conversation wakes me, recalls me, not to a normal consciousness, but to a kind of energetic readiness. I step outside, followed by the puppy.

I am absolutely alone. There are no other customers. The road is vacant, the interstate is out of sight and earshot. I have hazarded into a new corner of the world, an unknown spot, a Brigadoon. Before me extends a low hill trembling in yellow brome, and behind the hill, filling the sky, rises an enormous mountain ridge, forested, alive and awesome with brilliant blown lights. I have never seen anything so tremulous and live. Overhead, great strips and chunks of cloud dash to the northwest in a gold rush. At my back the sun is setting—how can I not have noticed before that the sun is setting? My mind has been a blank slab of black asphalt for hours, but that doesn't stop the sun's wild wheel. I set my coffee beside me on the curb; I smell loam on the wind; I pat the puppy; I watch the mountain.

My hand works automatically over the puppy's fur, following the line of hair under his ears, down his neck, inside his forelegs, along his hot-skinned belly.

Shadows lope along the mountain's rumpled flanks; they elongate like root tips, like lobes of spilling water, faster and faster. A warm purple pigment pools in each ruck and tuck of the rock; it deepens and spreads, boring crevasses, canyons. As the purple vaults and slides, it tricks out the unleafed forest and rumpled rock in gilt, in shape-shifting patches of glow. These gold lights veer and retract, shatter and glide in a series of dazzling splashes, shrinking, leaking, exploding. The ridge's bosses and hummocks sprout bulging from its side; the whole mountain looms miles closer; the light warms and reddens; the bare forest folds and pleats itself like living protoplasm before my eyes, like a running chart, a wildly scrawling oscillograph on the present moment. The air cools; the puppy's skin is hot. I am more alive than all the world.

This is it, I think, this is it, right now, the present, this empty gas station, here, this western wind, this tang of coffee on the tongue, and I am patting the puppy, I am watching the mountain. And the second I verbalize this awareness in my brain, I cease to see the mountain or feel the puppy. I am opaque, so much black asphalt. But at the same second, the second I know I've lost it, I also realize that the puppy is still squirming on his back under my hand. Nothing has changed for him. He draws his legs down to stretch the skin taut so he feels every fingertip's stroke along his furred and arching side, his flank, his flung-back throat.

I sip my coffee. I look at the mountain, which is still doing its tricks, as you look at a still-beautiful face belonging to a person who was once your lover in another country years ago: with fond nostalgia, and recognition, but no real feeling save a secret astonishment that you are now strangers. Thanks. For the memories. It is ironic that the one thing that all religions recognize as separating us from our creator—our very self-consciousness—is also the one thing that divides us from our fellow creatures. It was a bitter birthday present from evolution, cutting us off at both ends. I get in the car and drive home.

* * *

Catch it if you can. The present is an invisible electron; its lightning path traced faintly on a blackened screen is fleet, and fleeing, and gone.

That I ended this experience prematurely for myself—that I drew scales over my eyes between me and the mountain and gloved my hand between me and the puppy—is not the only point. After all, it would have ended anyway. I've never seen a sunset or felt a wind that didn't. The levitating saints came down at last, and their two feet bore real weight. No, the point is that not only does time fly and do we die, but that in these reckless conditions we live at all, and are vouchsafed, for the duration of certain inexplicable moments, to know it.

Stephen Graham startled me by describing this same gift in his antique and elegant book, *The Gentle Art of Tramping.* He wrote: "And as you sit on the hillside, or lie prone under the trees of the forest, or sprawl wet-legged on the shingly beach of a mountain stream, the great door, that does not look like a door, opens." That great door opens on the present, illuminates it as with a multitude of flashing torches.

I had thought, because I had seen the tree with the lights in it, that the great door, by definition, opens on eternity. Now that I have "patted the puppy"—now that I have experienced the present purely through my senses—I discover that, although the door to the tree with the lights in it was opened *from* eternity, as it were, and shone on that tree eternal lights, it nevertheless opened on the real and present cedar. It opened on time: Where else? That Christ's incarnation occurred improbably, ridiculously, at such and such a time, into such and such a place, is referred to—with great sincerity even among believers—as "the scandal of particularity." Well, the "scandal of particularity" is the only world that I, in particular, know. What use has eternity for light? We're all up to our necks in this particular scandal. Why, we might as well ask, not a plane tree, instead of a bo? I never saw a tree that was no tree in particular; I never met a man, not the greatest theologian, who filled infinity, or even whose hand, say, was undifferentiated, fingerless, like a griddlecake, and not lobed and split just so with the incursions of time.

I don't want to stress this too much. Seeing the tree with the lights in it was an experience vastly different in quality as well as in import from patting the puppy. On that cedar tree shone, however briefly, the steady, inward flames of eternity; across the mountain by the gas station raced the familiar flames of the falling sun. But on both occasions I thought, with rising exultation: This is it, this is it; praise the lord; praise the land. Experiencing the present purely is being emptied and hollow; you catch grace as a man fills his cup under a waterfall.

Consciousness itself does not hinder living in the present. In fact, it is only a heightened awareness that the great door to the present opens at all. Even a certain amount of interior verbalization is helpful to enforce the memory of whatever it is that is taking place. The gas station beagle puppy, after all, may have experienced those same moments more purely than I did, but he brought fewer instruments to bear on the same material, he had no data for comparison, and he profited only in the grossest of ways, by having an assortment of itches scratched.

Self-consciousness, however, does hinder the experience of the present. It is the one instrument that unplugs all the rest. So long as I lose myself in a tree, say, I can scent its leafy breath or estimate its board feet of lumber, I can draw its fruits or boil tea on its branches, and the tree stays tree. But the second I become aware of myself at any of these activities—looking over my own shoulder, as it were—the tree vanishes, uprooted from the spot and flung out of sight as if it had never grown. And time, which had flowed down into the tree bearing new revelations like floating leaves at every moment, ceases. It dams, stills, stagnates.

Self-consciousness is the curse of the city and all that sophistication implies. It is the glimpse of oneself in a storefront window, the unbidden awareness of reactions on the faces of other people—the novelist's world, not the poet's. I've lived there. I remember what the city has to offer: human companionship, major league baseball, and a clatter of quickening stimuli like a rush from strong drugs that leaves you drained. I remember how you bide your time in the city, and think, if you stop to think, "Next year . . . I'll start living; next year . . . I'll start my life." Innocence is a better world.

Innocence sees that this is it, and finds it world enough, and time. Innocence is not the prerogative of infants and puppies, and far less of mountains and fixed stars, which have no prerogatives at all. It is not lost to us; the world is a better place than that. Like any other of the spirit's good gifts, it is there if you want it, free for the asking, as has been stressed by stronger words than mine. It is possible to pursue innocence as hounds pursue hares: single-mindedly, driven by a kind of love, crashing over creeks, keening and lost in fields and forests, circling, vaulting over hedges and hills wide-eyed, giving loud tongue all unawares to the deepest, most incomprehensible longing, a root-flame in the heart, and that warbling chorus resounding back from the mountains, hurling itself from ridge to ridge over the valley, now faint, now clear, ringing the air through which the hounds tear, open-mouthed, the echoes of their own wails dimly knocking in their lungs.

What I call innocence is the spirit's unselfconscious state at any moment of pure devotion to any object. It is at once a receptiveness and a total concentration. One needn't be, shouldn't be, reduced to a puppy. If you wish to tell me that the city offers galleries, I'll pour you a drink and enjoy your company while it lasts; but I'll bear with me to my grave those pure moments at the Tate (was it the Tate?), where I stood planted, openmouthed, born, before that one particular canvas, that river, up to my neck, gasping, lost, receding into watercolor depth and depth to the vanishing point, buoyant, awed, and had to be literally hauled away. These are our few live seasons. Let us live them as purely as we can, in the present.

The color patches of vision part, shift, and re-form as I move through space in time. The present is the object of vision, and what I see before me at any given second is a full field of color patches scattered just so. The configuration will never be repeated. Living is moving; time is a live creek bearing changing lights. As I move, or as the world moves around me, the fullness of what I see shatters. This second of shattering is an *Augenblick*, a particular configuration, a slant of light shot in the open eye. Goethe's Faust risks all if he should cry to the moment, the *Augenblick*, *"Verweile doch!"* "Last forever!" Who hasn't prayed that prayer? But the *Augenblick* isn't going to *verweile*. You were lucky to get it in the first place. The present is a freely given canvas. That it is constantly being ripped apart and washed downstream goes without saying; it is a canvas, nevertheless.

I like the slants of light; I'm a collector. That's a good one, I say, that bit of bank there, the snakeskin and the aquarium, that patch of light from the creek on bark. Sometimes I spread my fingers into a viewfinder; more often I peek through a tiny square or rectangle—a frame of shadow—formed by the tips of index fingers and thumbs held directly before my eye. Speaking of the development of *papier collé* in late Cubism, Picasso said, "We tried to get rid of *trompe-l'oeil* to find a *trompe-l'esprit*." Trompe-l'esprit! I don't know why the world didn't latch onto the phrase. Our whole life is a stroll—or a forced march—through a gallery hung in trompes-l'esprit.

Once I visited a great university and wandered, a stranger, into the subterranean halls of its famous biology department. I saw a sign on a door: Ichthyology Department. The door was open a crack, and as I walked past I glanced in. I saw just a flash. There were two white-coated men seated opposite each other on high lab stools at a hard-surfaced table. They bent over identical white enamel trays. On one side, one man, with a lancet, was just cutting into an enormous preserved fish he'd taken from a jar. On the other side, the other man, with a silver spoon, was eating a grapefruit. I laughed all the way back to Virginia.

Michael Goldman wrote in a poem: "When the Muse comes She doesn't tell you to write; / She says get up for a minute, I've something to show you, stand here." What made me look up at that roadside tree?

The road to Grundy, Virginia, is, as you might expect, a narrow scrawl scribbled all over the most improbably peaked and hunched mountains you ever saw. The few people who live along the road also seem peaked and hunched. But what on earth—? It was hot, sunny summer. The road was just bending off sharply to the right. I hadn't seen a house in miles, and none was in sight. At the apogee of the road's curve grew an enormous oak, a massive bur oak two hundred years old, one hundred and fifty feet high, an oak whose lowest limb was beyond the span of the highest ladder. I looked up: there were clothes spread all over the tree. Red shirts, blue trousers, black pants, little baby smocks—they weren't hung from branches. They were outside, carefully spread, splayed as if to dry, on the outer leaves of the great oak's crown. Were there pillowcases, blankets? I can't remember. There was a gay assortment of cotton underwear, yellow dresses, children's green sweaters, plaid skirts. . . . You know roads. A bend comes and you take it, thoughtlessly, moving on. I looked behind me for another split second, astonished; both sides of the tree's canopy, clear to the top, bore clothes. Trompe!

But there is more to the present than a series of snapshots. We are not merely sensitized film; we have feelings, a memory for information, and an eidetic memory for the imagery of our own pasts.

Our layered consciousness is a tiered track for an unmatched assortment of concentrically wound reels. Each one plays out for all of life its dazzle and blur of translucent shadow pictures; each one hums at every moment its own secret melody in its own unique key. We tune in and out. But moments are not lost. Time out of mind is time nevertheless, cumulative, informing the present. From even the deepest slumber you wake with a jolt—older, closer to death, and wiser, grateful for breath. You quit your seat in a darkened movie theater, walk past the empty lobby, out the double glass doors, and step like Orpheus into the street. And the cumulative force of the present you've forgotten sets you reeling, staggering, as if you'd been struck broadside by a plank. It all floods back to you. Yes, you say, as if you'd been asleep a hundred years, this is it, this is the real weather, the lavender light fading, the full moisture in your lungs, the heat from the pavement on your lips and palms—not the dry orange dust from horses' hooves, the salt sea, the sour Coke, but this solid air, the blood pumping up your thighs again, your fingers alive. And on the way home you drive exhilarated, energized, under scented, silhouetted trees.

I am sitting under a sycamore by Tinker Creek. It is early spring, the day after I patted the puppy. I have come to the creek—the backyard stretch of the creek—in the middle of the day, to feel the delicate gathering of heat, real sun's heat, in the air, and to watch new water come down the creek. Don't expect more than this, and a mental ramble. I'm in the market for some present tense; I'm on the lookout, shopping around, more so every year. It's a seller's market—do you think I won't sell all that I have to buy it? Thomas Merton wrote, in a light passage in one of his Gethsemane journals: "Suggested emendation in the Lord's Prayer: Take out 'Thy Kingdom come' and substitute 'Give us time!'" But time is the one thing we have been given, and we have been given to time. Time gives us a whirl. We keep waking from a dream we can't recall, looking around in surprise, and lapsing back, for years on end. All I want to do is stay awake, keep my head up, prop my eyes open, with toothpicks, with trees.

Before me the creek is seventeen feet wide, splashing over random sandstone outcroppings and scattered rocks. I'm lucky; the creek is loud here, because of the rocks, and wild. In the low water of summer and fall I can cross to the opposite bank by leaping from stone to stone. Upstream is a wall of light split into planks by smooth sandstone ledges that cross the creek evenly, like steps. Downstream the live water before me stills, dies suddenly as if extinguished, and vanishes around a bend shaded summer and winter by overarching tulips, locusts, and Osage orange. Everywhere I look are creekside trees whose ascending boles against water and grass accent the vertical thrust of the land in this spot. The creek rests the eye, a haven, a breast; the two steep banks vault from the creek like wings. Not even the sycamore's crown can peek over the land in any direction.

My friend Rosanne Coggeshall, the poet, says that "sycamore" is the most intrinsically beautiful word in English. This sycamore is old; its lower bark is always dusty from years of floodwaters lapping up its trunk. Like many sycamores, too, it is quirky, given to flights and excursions. Its trunk lists over the creek at a dizzying angle, and from that trunk extends a long, skinny limb that spurts high over the opposite bank without branching. The creek reflects the speckled surface of this limb, pale even against the highest clouds, and that image pales whiter and thins as it crosses the creek, shatters in the riffles and melds together, quivering and mottled, like some enormous primeval reptile under the water.

I want to think about trees. Trees have a curious relationship to the subject of the present moment. There are many created things in the universe that outlive us, that outlive the sun, even, but I can't think about them. I live with trees. There are creatures under our feet, creatures that live over our heads, but trees live quite convincingly in the same filament of air we inhabit, and, in addition, they extend impressively in both directions, up and down, shearing rock and fanning air, doing their real business just out of reach. A blind man's idea of hugeness is a tree. They have their sturdy bodies and special skills; they garner fresh water; they abide. This sycamore above me, below me, by Tinker Creek, is a case in point; the sight of it crowds my brain with an assortment of diverting thoughts, all as present to me as these slivers of pressure from grass on my elbow's skin. I want to come at the subject of the present by showing how consciousness dashes and ambles around the labyrinthine tracks of the mind, returning again and again, however briefly, to the senses: "If there were but one erect and solid standing tree in the woods, all creatures would go to rub against it and make sure of their footing." But so long as I stay in my thoughts, my foot slides under trees; I fall, or I dance.

Sycamores are among the last trees to go into leaf; in the fall, they are the first to shed. They make sweet food in green broadleaves for a while—leaves wide as plates—and then go wild and wave their long white arms. In ancient Rome men honored the sycamore—in the form of its cousin the Oriental plane—by watering its roots with wine. Xerxes, I read, "halted his unwieldy army for days that he might contemplate to his satisfaction" the beauty of a single sycamore.

You are Xerxes in Persia. Your army spreads on a vast and arid peneplain. . . . You call to you all your sad captains, and give the order to halt. You have seen the tree with the lights in it, haven't you? You must have. Xerxes buffeted on a plain, ambition drained in a puff. That fusillade halts any army in its tracks. Your men are bewildered; they lean on their spears, sucking the rinds of gourds. There is nothing to catch the eye in this flatness, nothing but a hollow, hammering sky, a waste of sedge in the lee of windblown rocks, a meager ribbon of scrub willow tracing a slumbering watercourse . . . and that sycamore. You saw it; you still stand rapt and mute, exalted, remembering or not remembering over a period of days to shade your head with your robe.

"He had its form wrought upon a medal of gold to help him remember it the rest of his life." Your teeth are chattering; it is just before dawn and you have started briefly from your daze. "Goldsmith!" The goldsmith is sodden with sleep, surly. He lights his forge, he unrolls the dusty cotton wrapping from his half-forgotten stylus and tongs, he waits for the sun. We all ought to have a goldsmith following us around. But it goes without saying, doesn't it, Xerxes, that no gold medal worn around your neck will bring back the glad hour, keep those lights kindled so long as you live, forever present? Pascal saw it. He grabbed pen and paper; he managed to scrawl the one word, FEU; he wore that scrap of paper sewn in his shirt the rest of his life. I don't know what Pascal saw. I saw a cedar. Xerxes saw a sycamore.

These trees stir me. The past inserts a finger into a slit in the skin of the present, and pulls. I remember how sycamores grew—and presumably still grow—in the city, in Pittsburgh, even along the busiest streets. I used to spend hours in the backyard, thinking God knows what, and peeling the mottled bark of a sycamore, idly, littering the grass with dried lappets and strips, leaving the tree's trunk at eye level moist, thin-skinned, and yellow—until someone would catch me at it from the kitchen window, and I would awake, and look at my work in astonishment, and think: Oh, no, this time I've killed the sycamore for sure.

Here in Virginia the trees reach enormous proportions, especially in the lowlands on banksides. It is hard to understand how the same tree could thrive both choking along Pittsburgh's Penn Avenue and slogging knee-deep in Tinker Creek. Of course, come to think of it, I've done the same thing myself. Because a sycamore's primitive bark is not elastic but frangible, it sheds continuously as it grows; seen from a distance, a sycamore seems to grow in pallor and vulnerability as it grows in height; the bare uppermost branches are white against the sky.

The sky is deep and distant, laced with sycamore limbs like a hatching of crossed swords. I can scarcely see it; I'm not looking. I don't come to the creek for sky unmediated; I come for shelter. My back rests on a steep bank under the sycamore; before me shines the creek—the creek that is about all the light I can stand—and beyond it rises the other bank, also steep and planted in trees.

I have never understood why so many mystics of all creeds experience the presence of God on mountaintops. Aren't they afraid of being blown away? God said to Moses on Sinai that even the priests, who have access to the Lord, must hallow themselves, for fear that the Lord may break out against them. This is *the* fear. It often feels best to lie low, inconspicuous, instead of waving your spirit around from high places like a lightning rod. For if God is in one sense the igniter, a fireball that spins over the ground of continents, God is also, in another sense, the destroyer, lightning, blind power, impartial as the atmosphere. Or God is one "G." You get a comforting sense, in a curved, hollow place, of being vulnerable to only a relatively narrow column of God as air.

In the open, anything might happen. Dorothy Dunnett, the great medievalist, states categorically: "There is no reply, in clear terrain, to an archer in cover." Any copperhead anywhere is an archer in cover; how much more so is God! Invisibility is the all-time great "cover"; and that the one infinite power deals so extravagantly and unfathomably in death—death morning, noon, and night, all manner of death—makes that power an archer, there is no getting around it. And we the people are vulnerable. Our bodies are shot with mortality. Our legs are fear and our arms are time. These chill humors seep through our capillaries, weighting each cell with an icy dab of nonbeing, and that dab grows and swells and sucks the cell dry. That is why physical courage is so important—it fills, as it were, the holes— and why it is so invigorating. The least brave act, chance taken and passage won, makes you feel loud as a child.

But it gets harder. The courage of children and beasts is a function of innocence. We let our bodies go the way of our fears. A teenaged boy, king of the world, will spend weeks in front of a mirror perfecting some difficult trick with a lighter, a muscle, a tennis ball, a coin. Why do we lose interest in physical mastery? If I feel like turning cartwheels—and I do—why don't I learn to turn cartwheels, instead of regretting that I never learned as a child? We could all be aerialists like squirrels, divers like seals; we could be purely patient, perfectly fleet, walking on our hands even, if our living or stature required it. We can't even sit straight, or support our weary heads.

When we lose our innocence—when we start feeling the weight of the atmosphere and learn that there's death in the pot—we take leave of our senses. Only children can hear the song of the male house mouse. Only children keep their eyes open. The only thing they *have* got is sense; they have highly developed "input systems," admitting all data indiscriminately. Matt Spireng has collected thousands of arrowheads and spearheads; he says that if you really want to find arrowheads, you must walk with a child—a child will pick up *everything*. All my adult life I have wished to see the cemented case of a caddis fly larva. It took Sally Moore, the young daughter of friends, to find one on the pebbled bottom of a shallow stream on whose bank we sat side by side. "What's this?" she asked. That, I wanted to say as I recognized the prize she held, is a memento mori for people who read too much.

*   *   *

We found other caddis fly cases that day, Sally and I, after I had learned to focus so fine, and I saved one. It is a hollow cylinder three quarters of an inch long, a little masterpiece of masonry consisting entirely of cemented grains of coarse sand only one layer thick. Some of the sand grains are red, and it was by searching for this red that I learned to spot the cases. The caddis fly larva will use any bits it can find to fashion its house; in fact, entomologists have amused themselves by placing a naked larva in an aquarium furnished only with, say, red sand. When the larva has laid around its body several rows of red sand, the entomologist transfers it to another aquarium, in which only white bits are available. The larva busily adds rows of white to the red wall, and then here comes the entomologist again, with a third and final aquarium, full of blue sand. At any rate, the point I want to make is that this tiny immature creature responds to an instinct to put something between its flesh and a jagged world. If you give a "masonry mosaic" kind of caddis fly larva only large decayed leaves, that larva, confronted by some-thing utterly novel, will nevertheless bite the leaves into shreds and rig those shreds into a case.

The general rule in nature is that live things are soft within and rigid without. We vertebrates are living dangerously, and we vertebrates are positively piteous, like so many peeled trees. This oft was thought, but ne'er so well expressed as by Pliny, who writes of nature: "To all the rest, given she hath sufficient to clad them everyone according to their kind: as namely, shells, cods, hard hides, pricks, shags, bristles, hair, down feathers, quills, scales, and fleeces of wool. The very trunks and stems of trees and plants, she hath defended with bark and rind, yea and the same sometimes double, against the injuries both of heat and cold: man alone, poor wretch, she hath laid all naked upon the bare earth, even on his birthday, to cry and wraule presently from the very first hour that he is born into the world."

I am sitting under a sycamore tree: I am soft-shell and peeled to the least puff of wind or smack of grit. The present of our life looks different under trees. Trees have dominion. I never killed that backyard sycamore; even its frailest inner bark was a shield. Trees do not accumulate life, but deadwood, like a thickening coat of mail. Their odds actually improve as they age. Some trees, like giant sequoias, are, practically speaking, immortal, vulnerable only to another ice age. They are not even susceptible to fire. Sequoia wood barely burns, and the bark is "nearly as fireproof as asbestos. The top of one sequoia, struck by lightning a few years ago during a July thunderstorm, smoldered quietly, without apparently damaging the tree, until it was put out by a snowstorm in October." Some trees sink taproots to rock; some spread wide mats of roots clutching at acres. They will not be blown. We run around under these obelisk creatures, teetering on our soft, small feet. We are out on a jaunt, picnicking, fattening like puppies for our deaths. Shall I carve a name on this trunk? What if *I* fell in a forest: Would a tree hear?

I am sitting under a bankside sycamore; my mind is a slope. Arthur Koestler wrote, "In his review of the literature on the psychological present, Woodrow found that its maximum span is estimated to lie between 2.3 and 12 seconds." How did anyone measure that slide? As soon as you are conscious of it, it is gone. I repeat a phrase: the thin tops of mountains. Soon the thin tops of mountains erupt, as if volcanically, from my brain's core. I can see them; they are, surprisingly, serrate—scalloped like the blade of a kitchen knife—and brown as leaves. The serrated edges are so thin they are translucent; through the top of one side of the brown ridge I can see, in silhouette, a circling sharp-shinned hawk; through another, deep tenuous veins of metallic ore. This isn't Tinker Creek. Where do I live, anyway? I lose myself, I float. . . . I am in Persia, trying to order a watermelon in German. It's insane. The engineer has abandoned the control room, and an idiot is splicing the reels. What could I contribute to the "literature on the psychological present"? If I could remember to press the knob on the stopwatch, I wouldn't be in Persia. Before they invented the unit of the second, people used to time the lapse of short events on their pulses. Oh, but what about that heave in the wrist when I saw the tree with the lights in it, and my heart ceased, but I am still there?

Scenes drift across the screen from nowhere. I can never discover the connection between any one scene and what I am more consciously thinking, nor can I ever conjure the scene back in full vividness. It is like a ghost, in full-dress regalia, that wafts across the stage set unnoticed by the principal characters. It appears complete, in full color, wordless, though already receding: the tennis courts on Fifth Avenue in Pittsburgh, an equestrian statue in a Washington park, a basement dress shop in New York City—scenes that I thought meant nothing to me. These aren't still shots; the camera is always moving. And the scene is always just slipping out of sight, as if in spite of myself I were always just descending a hill, rounding a corner, stepping into the street with a companion who urges me on, while I look back over my shoulder at the sight that recedes, vanishes. The present of my consciousness is itself a mystery, which is also always just rounding a bend like a floating branch borne by a flood. Where am I? But I'm not. "I will overturn, overturn, over-turn it: and it shall be no more. . . ."

All right, then. Pull yourself together. Is this where I'm spending my life, in the "reptile brain," this lamp at the top of the spine like a lighthouse flipping mad beams indiscriminately into the darkness, into the furred thoraxes of moths, onto the backs of leaping fishes and the wrecks of schooners? Come up a level; surface.

I am sitting under a sycamore by Tinker Creek. I am really here, alive on the intricate earth under trees. But under me, directly under the weight of my body on the grass, are other creatures, just as real, for whom also this moment, this tree, is "it." Take just the top inch of soil, the world squirming right under my palms. In the top inch of forest soil, biologists found "an average of 1,356 living creatures present in each square foot, including 865 mites, 265 springtails, 22 millipedes, 19 adult bee-tles and various numbers of 12 other forms. . . . Had an estimate also been made of the microscopic population, it might have ranged up to two billion bacteria and many millions of fungi, protozoa and algae—in a mere *teaspoonful* of soil." The chrysalids of butterflies linger here too, folded, rigid, and dreamless. I might as well include these creatures in this moment, as best I can. My ignoring them won't strip them of their reality, and admitting them, one by one, into my consciousness might heighten mine, might add their dim awareness to my human consciousness, such as it is, and set up a buzz, a vibration like the beating ripples a submerged muskrat makes on the water, from this particular moment, this tree. Hasidism has a tradition that one of man's purposes is to assist God in the work of redemption by "hallowing" the things of creation. By a tremendous heave of his spirit, the devout man frees the divine sparks trapped in the mute things of time; he uplifts the forms and moments of creation, bearing them aloft into that rare air and hallowing fire in which all clays must shatter and burst. Keeping the subsoil world under trees in mind, in intelligence, is the *least* I can do.

Earthworms in staggering processions move through the grit underfoot, gobbling downed leaves and spewing forth castings by the ton. Moles mine intricate tunnels in networks; there are often so many of these mole tunnels here by the creek that when I walk, every step is a letdown. A mole is almost entirely loose inside its skin, and enormously mighty. If you can catch a mole, it will, in addition to biting you memorably, leap from your hand in a single convulsive contraction and be gone as soon as you have it. You are never really able to see it; you only feel its surge and thrust against your palm, as if you held a beating heart in a paper bag. What could I not do if I had the power and will of a mole! But the mole churns earth.

Last summer some muskrats had a den under this tree's roots on the bank; I think they are still there now. Muskrats' wet fur rounds the domed clay walls of the den and slicks them smooth as any igloo. They strew the floor with plant husks and seeds, rut in repeated bursts, and sleep humped and soaking, huddled in balls. These, too, are part of what Buber calls "the infinite ethos of the moment."

I am not here yet; I can't shake that day on the interstate. My mind branches and shoots like a tree.

Under my spine, the sycamore roots suck watery salts. Root tips thrust and squirm between particles of soil, probing

minutely; from their roving, burgeoning tissues spring infinitesimal root hairs, transparent and hollow, which affix themselves to
specks of grit and sip. These runnels run silent and deep; the
whole earth trembles, rent and fissured, hurled and drained. I
wonder what happens to root systems when trees die. Do those
spread blind networks starve, starve in the midst of plenty, and
desiccate, clawing at specks?

Under the world's conifers—under the creekside cedar
behind where I sit—a mantle of fungus wraps the soil in a weft,
shooting out blind thread after frail thread of palest dissolved
white. From root tip to root tip, root hair to root hair, these filaments loop and wind; the thought of them always reminds me
of Rimbaud's "I have stretched cords from steeple to steeple,
garlands from window to window, chains of gold from star to
star, and I dance." King David leaped and danced naked before
the ark of the Lord in a barren desert. Here the very looped soil
is an intricate throng of praise. Make connections; let rip; and
dance where you can.

The insects and earthworms, moles, muskrats, roots, and
fungal strands are not all. An even frailer, dimmer movement, a
pavane, is being performed deep under me now. The nymphs of
cicadas are alive. You see their split skins, an inch long, brown,
and translucent, curved and segmented like shrimp, stuck arching on the trunks of trees. And you see the adults occasionally,
large and sturdy, with glittering black-and-green bodies, veined
transparent wings folded over their backs, and artificial-looking
bright-red eyes. But you never see the living nymphs. They are
underground, clasping roots and sucking the sweet sap of trees.

In the South, the periodical cicada has a breeding cycle of
thirteen years, instead of seventeen years as in the North. That
a live creature spends thirteen consecutive years scrabbling
around in the root systems of trees in the dark and damp—thirteen years!—is amply boggling for me. Four more years—or
four less—wouldn't alter the picture a jot. In the dark of an
April night the nymphs emerge, all at once, as many as eighty-
four of them digging into the air from every square foot of
ground. They inch up trees and bushes, shed their skins, and
begin that hollow, shrill grind that lasts all summer. I guess as

nymphs they never see the sun. Adults lay eggs in slits along twig bark; the hatched nymphs drop to the ground and burrow, vanish from the face of the earth, biding their time, for thirteen years. How many are under me now, wishing what? What would I think about for thirteen years? They curl, crawl, clutch at roots and suck, suck blinded, suck trees, rain or shine, heat or frost, year after groping year.

And under the cicadas, deeper down than the longest tap-root, between and beneath the rounded black rocks and slanting slabs of sandstone in the earth, groundwater is creeping. Groundwater seeps and slides, across and down, across and down, leaking from here to there minutely, at the rate of a mile a year. What a tug of waters goes on! There are flings and pulls in every direction at every moment. The world is a wild wrestle under the grass: earth shall be moved.

What else is going on right this minute while groundwater creeps under my feet? The galaxy is careening in a slow, muf-fled widening. If a million solar systems are born every hour, then surely hundreds burst into being as I shift my weight to the other elbow. The sun's surface is now exploding; other stars implode and vanish, heavy and black, out of sight. Meteorites are arcing to earth invisibly all day long. On the planet the winds are blowing: the polar easterlies, the westerlies, the north-east and southeast trades. Somewhere, someone under full sail is becalmed, in the horse latitudes, in the doldrums; in the northland, a trapper is maddened, crazed, by the eerie scent of the chinook, the snow-eater, a wind that can melt two feet of snow in a day. The pampero blows, and the tramontane, and the boro, sirocco, levanter, mistral. Lick a finger: feel the now.

Spring is seeping north, toward me and away from me, at sixteen miles a day. Caribou straggle across the tundra from the spruce-fir forests of the south, first the pregnant does, hurried, then the old and unmated does, then suddenly a massing of bucks, and finally the diseased and injured, one by one. Somewhere, people in airplanes are watching the sun set and peering down at clustered house lights, stricken. In the montaña in Peru, on the rain-forested slopes of the Andes, a woman kneels in a dust clearing before a dark shelter of overlapping broadleaves; between her breasts hands a cross of smooth sticks she peeled with her teeth and lashed with twistings of vine. Along estuary banks of tidal rivers all over the world, snails in black clusters like currants are gliding up and down the stems of reed and sedge, migrating every moment with the dip and swing of tides. Behind me, Tinker Mountain, and to my left, Dead Man Mountain, are eroding one thousandth of an inch a year.

The tomcat that used to wake me is dead; he was long since grist for an earthworm's casting, and is now the clear sap of a Pittsburgh sycamore, or the honeydew of aphids sucked from that sycamore's high twigs and sprayed in sticky drops on a stranger's car. A steer across the road stumbles into the creek to drink; he blinks; he laps; a floating leaf in the current catches against his hock and wrenches away. The giant water bug I saw is dead, long dead, and its moist gut and rigid casing are both, like the empty skin of the frog it sucked, dissolved, spread, still spreading right now, in the steer's capillaries, in the windblown smatter of clouds overhead, in the Sargasso Sea. The mockingbird that dropped furled from a roof . . . But this is no time to count my dead. That is nightwork. The dead are staring, underground, their sleeping heels in the air.

The sharks I saw are roving up and down the coast. If the sharks cease roving, if they still their twist and rest for a moment, they die. They need new water pushed into their gills; they need dance. Somewhere east of me, on another continent, it is sunset, and starlings in breathtaking bands are winding high in the sky to their evening roost. Under the water just around the bend downstream, the coot feels with its foot in the creek, rolling its round red eyes. In the house, a spider slumbers at her wheel like a spinster curled in a corner all day long. The mantis egg cases are tied to the mock orange hedge; within each case, within each egg, cells elongate, narrow, and split; cells bubble and curve inward, align, harden or hollow or stretch. The Polyphemus moth, its wings crushed to its back, crawls down the driveway, crawls down the driveway, crawls. . . . The snake whose skin I tossed away, whose homemade, personal skin is now tangled at the county dump—that snake in the woods by the quarry stirs now, quickens now, prodded under the leaf mold by sunlight, by the probing root of May apple, the bud of blood-root. And where are you now?

I stand. All the blood in my body crashes to my feet and instantly heaves to my head, so I blind and blush, as a tree blasts into leaf spouting water hurled up from roots. What happens to me? I stand before the sycamore, dazed; I gaze at its giant trunk.

Big trees stir memories. You stand in their dimness, where the very light is blue, staring unfocused at the thickest part of the trunk as though it were a long, dim tunnel: the Squirrel Hill tunnel. You're gone. The egg-shaped patch of light at the end of the blackened tunnel swells and looms; the sing of tire tread over brick reaches an ear-splitting crescendo; the light breaks over the hood, smack, and full on your face. You have achieved the past.

Eskimo shamans bound with sealskin thongs on the igloo floor used to leave their bodies, their skins, and swim "muscle naked" like a flensed seal through the rock of continents, in order to placate an old woman who lived on the sea floor and sent or withheld game. When he fulfilled this excruciating mission, the Eskimo shaman would awake, return to his skin exhausted from the dark ardors of flailing peeled through rock, and find himself in a lighted igloo, at a sort of party, among dear faces.

In the same way, having bored through a sycamore trunk and tunneled beneath a Pennsylvania mountain, I blink, awed by the yellow light, and find myself in a shady side of town, in a stripped dining room, dancing, years ago. There is a din of trumpets, upbeat and indistinct, like some movie score for a love scene played on a city balcony; there is an immeasurably distant light glowing from half-remembered faces. . . . I stir. The heave of my shoulders returns me to the present, to the tree, the sycamore, and I yank myself away, shove off, and, moving, seek live water.

*   *   *

Live water heals memories. I look up the creek and here it comes, the future, being borne aloft as on a winding succession of laden trays. You may wake and look from the window and breathe the real air and say, with satisfaction or with longing, "This is it." But if you look up the creek, if you look up the creek in any weather, your spirit fills, and you are saying, with an exulting rise of the lungs, "Here it comes!"

Here it comes. In the far distance I can see the concrete bridge where the road crosses the creek. Under that bridge and beyond it the water is flat and silent, blued by distance and stilled by depth. It is so much sky, a fallen shred caught in the cleft of banks. But it pours. The channel here is straight as an arrow; grace itself is an archer. Between the dangling wands of bankside willows, beneath the overarching limbs of tulip, walnut, and Osage orange, I see the creek pour down. It spills toward me, streaming over a series of sandstone tiers, down, and down, and down. I feel as though I stand at the foot of an infinitely high staircase, down which some exuberant spirit is flinging tennis ball after tennis ball, eternally, and the one thing I want in the world is a tennis ball.

There must be something wrong with a creekside person who, all things being equal, chooses to face downstream. It's like fouling your own nest. For this and a leather couch they pay fifty dollars an hour? Tinker Creek doesn't back up, pushed up its own craw, from the Roanoke River; it flows down, easing, from the northern, unseen side of Tinker Mountain. "Gravity, to Copernicus, is the nostalgia of things to become spheres." This is a curious, tugged version of the great chain of being. Ease is the way of perfection, letting fall. But, as in the classic version of the great chain, the pure trickle that leaks from the unfathomable heart of Tinker Mountain, this Tinker Creek, widens, taking shape and cleaving banks, weighted with the live and intricate impurities of time, as it descends to me, to where I happen to find myself, in this intermediate spot, halfway between here and there. Look upstream. Just simply turn around; have you no will? The future is a spirit, or a distillation of *the* spirit, heading my way. It is north. The future is the light on the water; it comes, mediated, only on the skin of the real and present creek. My eyes can stand no brighter light than this; nor can they see without it, if only the undersides of leaves.

Trees are tough. They last, taproot and bark, and we soften at their feet. "For we are strangers before thee, and sojourners, as were all our fathers: our days on the earth are as a shadow, and there is none abiding." We can't take the lightning, the scourge of high places and rare airs. But we can take the light, the reflected light that shines up the valleys on creeks. Trees stir memories; live waters heal them. The creek is the mediator, benevolent, impartial, subsuming my shabbiest evils and dis-solving them, transforming them into live moles, and shiners, and sycamore leaves. It is a place even my faithlessness hasn't offended; it still flashes for me, now and tomorrow, that intri-cate, innocent face. It waters an undeserving world, saturating cells with lodes of light. I stand by the creek over rock under trees.

It is sheer coincidence that my hunk of the creek is strewn with boulders. I never merited this grace, that when I face upstream I scent the virgin breath of mountains, I feel a spray of mist on my cheeks and lips, I hear a ceaseless splash and susurrus, a sound of water not merely poured smoothly down air to fill a steady pool, but tumbling live about, over, under, around, between, through an intricate speckling of rock. It is sheer coincidence that upstream from me the creek's bed is ridged in horizontal croppings of sandstone. I never merited this grace, that when I face upstream I see the light on the water careening toward me, inevitably, freely, down a graded series of terraces like the balanced winged platforms on an infinite, inex-haustible font. "Ho, if you are thirsty, come down to the water; ho, if you are hungry, come and sit and eat." This is the present, at last. I can pat the puppy anytime I want. This is the now, this flickering, broken light, this air that the wind of the future presses down my throat, pumping me buoyant and giddy with praise.

My God, I look at the creek. It is the answer to Merton's prayer: "Give us time!" It never stops. If I seek the senses and skill of children, the information of a thousand books, the innocence of puppies, even the insights of my own city past, I do so only, solely, and entirely that I might look well at the creek. You don't run down the present, pursue it with baited hooks and nets. You wait for it, empty-handed, and you are filled. You'll have fish left over. The creek is the one great giver. It is, by definition, Christmas, the incarnation. This old rock planet gets the present for a present on its birthday every day.

Here is the word from a subatomic physicist: "Everything that has already happened is particles, everything in the future is waves." Let me twist his meaning. Here it comes. The particles are broken; the waves are translucent, laving, roiling with beauty like sharks. The present is the wave that explodes over my head, flinging the air with particles at the height of its breathless unroll; it is the live water and light that bear from undisclosed sources the freshest news, renewed and renewing, world without end.

A ROSY, COMPLEX LIGHT FILLS my kitchen at the end of these lengthening June days. From an explosion on a nearby star eight minutes ago, the light zips through space, particle-wave, strikes the planet, angles on the continent, and filters through a mesh of land dust: clay bits, sod bits, tiny windborne insects, bacteria, shreds of wing and leg, gravel dust, grits of carbon, and dried cells of grass, bark, and leaves. Reddened, the light inclines into this valley over the green western mountains; it sifts between pine needles on northern slopes, and through all the mountain blackjack oak and haw, whose leaves are unclenching, one by one, and making an intricate toothed and lobed haze. The light crosses the valley, threads through the screen on my open kitchen window, and gilds the painted wall. A plank of brightness bends from the wall and extends over the goldfish bowl on the table where I sit. The goldfish's side catches the light and bats it my way; I've an eyeful of fish scale and star.

This Ellery cost me twenty-five cents. He is a deep red orange, darker than most goldfish. He steers short distances mainly with his slender red lateral fins; they seem to provide impetus for going backward, up, or down. It took me a few days to discover his ventral fins; they are completely transparent and all but invisible—dream fins. He also has a short anal fin, and a tail that is deeply notched and perfectly transparent at the two tapered tips. He can extend his mouth, so that it looks like a length of pipe; he can shift the angle of his eyes in his head so he can look before and behind himself, instead of simply out to his sides. His belly, what there is of it, is white ventrally, and a patch of this white extends up his sides—the variegated Ellery. When he opens his gill slits he shows a thin crescent of silver where the flap overlapped—as though all his brightness were sunburn.

For this creature, as I said, I paid twenty-five cents. I had never bought an animal before. It was very simple; I went to a store in Roanoke called Wet Pets; I handed the man a quarter, and he handed me a knotted plastic bag bouncing with water in which a green plant floated and the goldfish swam. This fish, two bits' worth, has a coiled gut, a spine radiating fine bones, and a brain. Just before I sprinkle his food flakes into his bowl, I rap three times on the bowl's edge; now he is conditioned, and swims to the surface when I rap. And he has a heart.

Once, years ago, I saw red blood cells whip, one by one, through the capillaries in a goldfish's transparent tail. The goldfish was etherized. Its head lay in a wad of wet cotton wool; its tail lay on a tray under a dissecting microscope, one of those wonderful light-gathering microscopes with two eyepieces, like a stereoscope in which the world's fragments—even the skin on my finger—look brilliant with myriads of colored lights, and as deep as any alpine landscape. The red blood cells in the goldfish's tail streamed and coursed through narrow channels invisible save for glistening threads of thickness in the general translucency. They never wavered or slowed or ceased flowing, like the creek itself; they streamed redly around, up, and on, one by one, more, and more, without end. (The energy of that pulse reminds me of something about the human body: if you sit absolutely perfectly balanced on the end of your spine, with your legs either crossed tailor fashion or drawn up together, and your arms forward on your legs, then even if you hold your breath, your body will rock with the energy of your heartbeat, forward and back, effortlessly, for as long as you want to remain balanced.) Those red blood cells are coursing in Ellery's tail now, too, in just that way, and through his mouth and eyes as well, and through mine. I've never forgotten the sight of those cells; I think of it when I see the fish in his bowl; I think of it lying in bed at night, imagining that if I concentrate enough I might be able to feel in my fingers' capillaries the small knockings and flow of those circular dots, like a string of beads drawn through my hand.

Something else is happening in the goldfish bowl. There on the kitchen table, nourished by the simple plank of complex light, the plankton is blooming. The water yellows and clouds; a transparent slime coats the leaves of the water plant, elodea; a blue-green film of single-celled algae clings to the glass. And I have to clean the doggone bowl. I'll spare you the details: it's the plant I'm interested in. While Ellery swims in the stoppered sink, I rinse the algae down the drain of another sink, wash the gravel, and rub the elodea's many ferny leaves under running water until they feel clean.

The elodea is not considered much of a plant. Aquarists use it because it's available and it gives off oxygen completely submersed; laboratories use it because its leaves are only two cells thick. It's plentiful, easy to grow, and cheap—like the goldfish. And like the goldfish, its cells have unwittingly performed for me on a microscope's stage.

I was in a laboratory, using a very expensive microscope. I peered through the deep twin eyepieces and saw again that color-charged, glistening world. A thin, oblong leaf of elodea, a quarter of an inch long, lay on a glass slide sopping wet and floodlighted brilliantly from below. In the circle of light formed by the two eyepieces trained at the translucent leaf, I saw a clean mosaic of almost colorless cells. The cells were large— eight or nine of them, magnified four hundred fifty times, packed the circle—so that I could easily see what I had come to see: the streaming of chloroplasts.

Chloroplasts bear chlorophyll; they give the green world its color, and they carry out the business of photosynthesis. Around the inside perimeter of each gigantic cell trailed a continuous loop of these bright-green dots. They spun like paramecia; they pulsed, pressed, and thronged. A change of focus suddenly revealed the eddying currents of the river of transparent cytoplasm, a sort of "ether" to the chloroplasts, or "space-time," in which they have their tiny being. Back to the green dots: they shone, they swarmed in ever shifting files around and around the edge of the cell; they wandered, they charged, they milled, raced, and ran at the edge of apparent nothingness, the empty-looking inner cell; they flowed and trooped greenly, up against the vegetative wall.

All the green in the planted world consists of these whole,

rounded chloroplasts wending their ways in water. If you analyze a molecule of chlorophyll itself, what you get is one hundred thirty-six atoms of hydrogen, carbon, oxygen, and nitrogen arranged in an exact and complex relationship around a central ring. At the ring's center is a single atom of magnesium. Now: if you remove the atom of magnesium and in its exact place put an atom of iron, you get a molecule of hemoglobin. The iron atom combines with all the other atoms to make red blood, the streaming red dots in the goldfish's tail.

It is, then, a small world there in the goldfish bowl, and a very large one. Say the nucleus of any atom in the bowl were the size of a cherry pit: its nearest electron would revolve around it one hundred seventy-five yards away. A whirling air in his swim bladder balances the goldfish's weight in the water; his scales overlap, his feathery gills pump and filter; his eyes work, his heart beats, his liver absorbs, his muscles contract in a wave of extending ripples. The daphnias he eats have eyes and jointed legs. The algae the daphnias eat have green cells stacked like checkers or winding in narrow ribbons like spiral staircases up long columns of emptiness. And so on diminishingly down. We have not yet found the dot so small it is uncreated, as it were, like a metal blank, or merely roughed in—and we never shall. We go down landscape after mobile, sculpture after collage, down to molecular structures like a mob dance in Brueghel, down to atoms airy and balanced as a canvas by Klee, down to atomic particles, the heart of the matter, as spirited and wild as any El Greco saints. And it all works. "Nature," said Thoreau in his journal, "is mythical and mystical always, and spends her whole genius on the least work." The creator, I would add, churns out the intricate texture of least works that is the world with a spendthrift genius and an extravagance of care. This is the point.

I am sitting here looking at a goldfish bowl and busting my brain. *Ich kann nicht anders.* I am sitting here, you are sitting there. Say even that you are sitting across this kitchen table from me right now. Our eyes meet; a consciousness snaps back and forth. What we know, at least for starters, is: here we—so incontrovertibly—are. This is our life, these are our lighted seasons, and then we die. (You die, you die; first you go wet, and then you go dry.) In the meantime, in between time, we can see. The scales are fallen from our eyes, the cataracts are cut away, and we can work at making sense of the color patches we see in an effort to discover *where* we so incontrovertibly are. It's common sense: when you move in, you try to learn the neighborhood.

I am as passionately interested in where I am as is a lone sailor sans sextant in a ketch on the open ocean. What else is he supposed to be thinking about? Fortunately, like the sailor, I have at the moment a situation that allows me to devote considerable hunks of time to seeing what I can see, and trying to piece it together. I've learned the names of some color patches, but not the meanings. I've read books. I've gathered statistics feverishly: The average temperature of our planet is 57 degrees Fahrenheit. Of the 29 percent of all land that is above water, over a third is given to grazing. The average size of all living animals, including man, is almost that of a housefly. The earth is mostly granite, which in turn is mostly oxygen. The most numerous of animals big enough to see are the copepods, the mites, and the springtails; of plants, the algae, the sedge. In these Appalachians we have found a coal bed with one hundred twenty seams, meaning one hundred twenty forests that just happened to fall into water, heaped like corpses in drawers. And so on. These statistics, and all the various facts about subatomic particles, quanta, neutrinos, and so forth, constitute in effect the infrared and ultraviolet light at either end of the spectrum. They are too big and too small to see, to understand; they are more or less invisible to me though present, and peripheral to me in a real sense because I do not understand even what I can easily see. I would like to see it all, to understand it, but I must start somewhere, so I try to deal with the giant water bug in Tinker Creek and the flight of three hundred redwings from an Osage orange, with the goldfish bowl and the snakeskin, and let those who dare worry about the birthrate and population explosion among solar systems.

So I think about the valley. And it occurs to me more and more that everything I have seen is wholly gratuitous. The giant water bug's predations, the frog's croak, the tree with the lights in it, are not in any real sense necessary per se to the world or to its creator. Nor am I. The creation in the first place, being itself, is the only necessity, for which I would die, and I shall. The point about that being, as I know it here and see it, is that, as I think about it, it accumulates in my mind as an extravagance of minutiae. The sheer fringe and network of detail assumes primary importance. That there are so many details seems to be the most important and visible fact about the creation. If you can't see the forest for the trees, then look at the trees; when you've looked at enough trees, you've seen a forest: you've got it. If the world is gratuitous, then the fringe of a goldfish's fin is a million times more so. The first question—the one crucial one—of the creation of the universe and the existence of something as a sign and an affront to nothing, is a blank one. I can't think about it. So it is to the fringe of that question that I affix my attention, the fringe of the fish's fin, the intricacy of the world's spotted and speckled detail.

The old cabalistic phrase is "Mystery of the Splintering of the Vessels." The words refer to the shrinking or imprisonment of essences within the various husk-covered forms of emanation or time. The Vessels splintered and solar systems spun; ciliated rotifers whirled in still water, and newts with gills laid tracks in the silt-bottomed creek. Not only did the Vessels splinter: they splintered exceeding fine. Intricacy, then, is the subject, the intricacy of the created world.

You are God. You want to make a forest, something to hold the soil, lock up solar energy, and give off oxygen. Wouldn't it be simpler just to rough in a slab of chemicals, a green acre of goo?

You are a man, a retired railroad worker who makes replicas as a hobby. You decide to make a replica of one tree, the long-leaf pine your great-grandfather planted: just a replica—it doesn't have to work. How are you going to do it? How long do you think you might live, how good is your glue? For one thing, you are going to have to dig a hole and stick your replica trunk in the ground halfway to China if you want the thing to stand up. Because you will have to work fairly big; if your replica is too small, you'll be unable to handle the slender, three-sided needles, affix them in clusters of three in fascicles, and attach those laden fascicles to flexible twigs. The twigs themselves must be covered by "many silvery-white, fringed, long-spreading scales." Are your pine cones' scales "thin, flat, rounded at the apex, the exposed portions (closed cone) reddish brown, often wrinkled, armed on the back with a small, reflexed prickle, which curves toward the base of the scale"? When you loose the lashed copper wire trussing the replica limbs to the trunk, the whole tree collapses like an umbrella.

You are a starling. I've seen you fly through a longleaf pine without missing a beat.

You are a sculptor. You climb a great ladder; you pour grease all over a growing longleaf pine. Next, you build a hollow cylinder like a cofferdam around the entire pine, and grease its inside walls. You climb your ladder and spend the next week pouring wet plaster into the cofferdam, over and inside the pine. You wait; the plaster hardens. Now open the walls of the dam, split the plaster, saw down the tree, remove it, discard, and your intricate sculpture is ready: this is the shape of part of the air.

You are a chloroplast moving in water heaved one hundred feet above ground. Hydrogen, carbon, oxygen, nitrogen, in a ring around magnesium. . . . You are evolution; you have only begun to make trees. You are God—are you tired? finished?

Intricacy means that there is a fluted fringe to the something that exists over against nothing, a fringe that rises and spreads, burgeoning in detail. Mentally reverse positive and negative space, as in the plaster cast of the pine, and imagine emptiness as a sort of person, a boundless person consisting of an elastic, unformed clay. (For the moment forget that the air in our atmosphere is "something," and count it as "nothing," the sculptor's negative space.) The clay man completely surrounds the holes in him, which are galaxies and solar systems. The holes in him part, expand, shrink, veer, circle, spin. He gives like water, he spreads and fills unseeing. Here is a ragged hole, our earth, a hole that makes torn and frayed edges in his side, mountains and pines. And here is the shape of one swift, raveling edge, a feather hole on a flying goose's hollow wing extended over the planet. Five hundred barbs of emptiness prick into clay from either side of a central, flexible shaft. On each barb are two fringes of five hundred barbules apiece, making a million barbules on each feather, fluted and hooked in a matrix of clasped hollowness. Through the fabric of this form the clay man shuttles unerringly, and through the other feather holes, and the goose, the pine forest, the planet, and so on.

In other words, even on the perfectly ordinary and clearly visible level, creation carries on with an intricacy unfathomable and apparently uncalled for. The lone ping into being of the first hydrogen atom *ex nihilo* was so unthinkably, violently radical, that surely it ought to have been enough, more than enough. But look what happens. You open the door, and all heaven and hell break loose.

Evolution, of course, is the vehicle of intricacy. The stability of simple forms is the sturdy base from which more complex stable forms might arise, forming in turn more complex forms, and so on. The stratified nature of this stability, like a house built on rock on rock on rock, performs, in Jacob Bronowski's terms, as the "ratchet" that prevents the whole shebang from "slipping back." Bring a feather into the house, and a piano; put a sculpture on the roof, sure, and fly banners from the lintels—the house will hold.

There are, for instance, two hundred twenty-eight separate and distinct muscles in the head of an ordinary caterpillar. Again, of an ostracod, a common freshwater crustacean of the sort I crunch on by the thousands every time I set foot in Tinker Creek, I read: "There is one eye situated at the fore-end of the animal. The food canal lies just below the hinge, and around the mouth are the feathery feeding appendages which collect the food. . . . Behind them is a foot which is clawed and this is partly used for removing unwanted particles from the feeding appendages." Or again, there are, as I have said, six million leaves on a big elm. All right . . . but they are toothed, and the teeth themselves are toothed. How many notches and barbs is that to a world? In and out go the intricate leaf edges, and "don't nobody know why." All the theories botanists have devised to explain the functions of various leaf shapes tumble under an avalanche of inconsistencies. They simply don't know, can't imagine.

I have often noticed that these things, which obsess me, neither bother nor impress other people even slightly. I am horribly apt to approach some innocent at a gathering and, like the ancient mariner, fix him with a wild, glitt'ring eye and say, "Do you know that in the head of the caterpillar of the ordinary goat moth there are two hundred twenty-eight separate muscles?" The poor wretch flees. I am not making chatter; I mean to change his life. I seem to possess an organ that others lack, a sort of trivia machine.

When I was young I thought that all human beings had an organ inside each lower eyelid which caught things that got in the eye. I don't know where I imagined I'd learned this piece of anatomy. Things got in my eye, and then they went away, so I supposed that they had fallen into my eye pouch. This eye pouch was a slender, thin-walled purse, equipped with frail digestive powers that enabled it eventually to absorb eyelashes, strands of fabric, bits of grit, and anything else that might stray into the eye. Well, the existence of this eye pouch, it turned out, was all in my mind, and, it turns out, it is apparently there still, a brain pouch, catching and absorbing small bits that fall deeply into my open eye.

All I can remember from a required zoology course years ago, for instance, is a lasting impression that there is an item in the universe called a Henle's loop. Its terrestrial abode is in the human kidney. I just refreshed my memory on the subject. The Henle's loop is an attenuated oxbow or U-turn made by an incredibly tiny tube in the nephron of the kidney. The nephron in turn is a filtering structure that produces urine and reabsorbs nutrients. This business is so important that one-fifth of all the heart's pumped blood goes to the kidneys.

There is no way to describe a nephron; you might hazard into a fairly good approximation of its structure if you threw about fifteen yards of string on the floor. If half the string fell into a very narrow loop, that would be the Henle's loop. Two other bits of string that rumpled up and tangled would be the "proximal convoluted tubule" and the "distal convoluted tubule," shaped just so. But the heart of the matter would be a very snarled clump of string, "an almost spherical tuft of parallel capillaries," which is the glomerulus, or Malpighian body. This is the filter to end all filters, supplied with afferent and efferent arterioles and protected by a double-walled capsule. Compared to the glomerulus, the Henle's loop is rather unimportant. By going from here to there in such a roundabout way, the Henle's loop packs a great deal of filtering tubule into a very narrow space. But the delicate oxbow of tissue, looping down so far, and then up, is really a peripheral extravagance, which is why I remembered it, and a beautiful one, like a meander in a creek.

Now, the point of all this is that there are a million nephrons in each human kidney. I've got two million glomeruli, two million Henle's loops, and I made them all myself, without the least effort. They're undoubtedly my finest work. What an elaboration, what an extravagance! The proximal segment of the tubule, for instance, "is composed of irregular cuboidal cells with characteristic brushlike striations (brush border) at the internal, or luminal, border." Here are my own fringed necessities, a veritable forest of pines.

Van Gogh, you remember, called the world a study that didn't come off. Whether it did "come off" is a difficult question. The chloroplasts do stream in the leaf as if propelled by a mighty, invisible breath; but on the other hand, a certain sorrow arises, welling up in Shadow Creek, and from those lonely banks it appears that all our intricate fringes, however beautiful, are really the striations of a universal and undeserved flaying. But, van Gogh: a *study* it is not. This is the truth of the pervading intricacy of the world's detail: The creation is not a study, a roughed-in sketch; it is supremely, meticulously created, created abundantly, extravagantly, and in fine.

*   *   *

Along with intricacy, there is another aspect of the creation that has impressed me in the course of my wanderings. Look again at the horsehair worm, a yard long and thin as a thread, whipping through the duck pond, or tangled with others of its kind in a slithering Gordian knot. Look at an overwintering ball of buzzing bees, or a turtle under ice breathing through its pumping cloaca. Look at the fruit of the Osage orange tree, big as a grapefruit, green, convoluted as any human brain. Or look at a rotifer's translucent gut: something orange and powerful is surging up and down like a piston, and something small and round is spinning in place like a flywheel. Look, in short, at practically anything—the coot's feet, the mantis's face, a banana, the human ear—and see that not only did the creator create everything, but he is apt to create *anything*. He'll stop at nothing.

There is no one standing over evolution with a blue pencil to say, "Now, that one, there, is absolutely ridiculous, and I won't have it." If the creature makes it, it gets a "stet." Is our taste so much better than the creator's? Utility to the creature is evolution's only aesthetic consideration. Form follows function in the created world, so far as I know, and the creature that functions, however bizarre, survives to perpetuate its form. Of the intricacy of form, I know some answers and not others: I know why the barbules on a feather hook together, and why the Henle's loop loops, but not why the elm tree's leaves zigzag, or why butterfly scales and pollen are shaped just so. But of the *variety* of form itself, of the multiplicity of forms, I know nothing. Except that, apparently, anything goes. This holds for forms of behavior as well as design—the mantis munching her mate, the frog wintering in mud, the spider wrapping a hummingbird, the pine processionary straddling a thread. Welcome aboard. A generous spirit signs on this motley crew.

Take, for instance, the African Hercules beetle, which is so big, according to Edwin Way Teale, "it drones over the countryside at evening with a sound like an approaching airplane." Or, better, take to heart Teale's description of South American honey ants. These ants have abdomens that can stretch to enormous proportions. "Certain members of the colony act as storage vessels for the honeydew gathered by the workers. They never leave the nest. With abdomens so swollen they cannot walk, they cling to the roof of their underground chamber, regurgitating food to the workers when it is needed." I read these things, and those ants are as present to me as if they hung from my kitchen ceiling, or down the vaults of my skull, pulsing live jars, engorged vats, teats, with an eyed animal at the head thinking—what?

Blake said, "He who does not prefer Form to Colour is a Coward!" I often wish the creator had been more of a coward, giving us many fewer forms and many more colors. Here is an interesting form, one closer to home. This is the larva, or nymph, of an ordinary dragonfly. The wingless nymphs are an inch long and fat as earthworms. They stalk everywhere on the floors of valley ponds and creeks, sucking water into their gilled rectums. But it is their faces I'm interested in. According to Howard Ensign Evans, a dragonfly larva's "lower lip is enormously lengthened, and has a double hinge joint so that it can be pulled back beneath the body when not in use; the outer part is expanded and provided with stout hooks, and in resting position forms a 'mask' that covers much of the face of the larva. The lip is capable of being thrust forward suddenly, and the terminal hooks are capable of grasping prey well in front of the larva and pulling it back to the sharp, jagged mandibles. Dragonfly larvae prey on many kinds of small insects occurring in the water, and the larger ones are well able to handle small fish."

The world is full of creatures that for some reason seem stranger to us than others, and libraries are full of books describing them—hagfish, platypuses, lizardlike pangolins four feet long with bright-green, lapped scales like umbrella-tree leaves on a bush hut roof, butterflies emerging from anthills, spiderlings wafting through the air clutching tiny silken balloons, horseshoe crabs . . . the creator creates. Does he stoop, does he speak, does he save, succor, prevail? Maybe. But he creates; he creates everything and anything.

Of all known forms of life, only about ten percent are still living today. All other forms—fantastic plants, ordinary plants, living animals with unimaginably various wings, tails, teeth, brains—are utterly and forever gone. That is a great many forms that have been created. Multiplying ten times the number of living forms today yields a profusion that is quite beyond what I consider thinkable. Why so many forms? Why not just that one hydrogen atom? The creator goes off on one wild, specific tangent after another, or millions simultaneously, with an exuberance that would seem to be unwarranted, and with an abandoned energy sprung from an unfathomable font. What is going on here? The point of the dragonfly's terrible lip, the giant water bug, birdsong, the beautiful dazzle and flash of sunlighted minnows, is not that it all fits together like clockwork—for it doesn't particularly, not even inside the goldfish bowl—but that it all flows so freely wild, like the creek, that it all surges in such a free, fringed tangle. Freedom is the world's water and weather, the world's nourishment freely given, its soil and sap: and the creator loves exuberance.

What I aim to do is not so much learn the names of the shreds of creation that flourish in this valley, but to keep myself open to their meanings, which is to try to impress myself at all times with the fullest possible force of their very reality. I want to have things as multiply and intricately as possible present and visible in my mind. Then I might be able to sit on the hill by the burned books where the starlings fly over, and see not only the starlings, the grass field, the quarried rock, the viney woods, Hollins Pond, and the mountains beyond, but also, and simultaneously, feathers' barbs, springtails in the soil, crystal in rock, chloroplasts streaming, rotifers pulsing, and the shape of the air in the pines. And, if I try to keep my eye on quantum physics, if I try to keep up with astronomy and cosmology, and really believe it all, I might ultimately be able to make out the landscape of the universe. Why not?

Landscape consists in the multiple, overlapping intricacies and forms that exist in a given space at a moment in time. Landscape is the texture of intricacy, and texture is my present subject. Intricacies of detail and varieties of form build up into textures. A bird's feather is an intricacy; the bird is a form; the bird in space in relation to air, forest, continent, and so on, is a thread in a texture. The moon has its texture, too, its pitted and carved landscapes in even its flattest seas. The planets are more than smooth spheres; the galaxy itself is a fleck of texture, binding and bound. But here on earth texture interests us supremely. Wherever there is life, there is twist and mess: the frizz of an Arctic lichen, the tangle of brush along a bank, the dogleg of a dog's leg, the way a line has got to curve, split, or knob. The planet is characterized by its very jaggedness, its random heaps of mountains, its frayed fringes of shore.

Think of a globe, a revolving globe on a stand. Think of a contour globe, whose mountain ranges cast shadows, whose continents rise in bas-relief above the oceans. But then: think of how it *really* is. These heights aren't just suggested; they're there. Pliny, who knew the world was round, figured that when it was all surveyed, the earth would be seen to resemble in shape, not a sphere, but a pineapple, pricked by irregularities. When I think of walking across a continent I think of all the neighborhood hills, the tiny grades up which children drag their sleds. It is all so sculptured, three-dimensional, casting a shadow. What if you had an enormous globe in relief that was so huge it showed roads and houses—a geological survey globe, a quarter of a mile to an inch—of the whole world, and the ocean floor! Looking at it, you would know what had to be left out: the freestanding sculptural arrangement of furniture in rooms, the jumble of broken rocks in a creekbed, tools in a box, labyrinthine ocean liners, the shape of snapdragons, walrus. Where is the one thing you care about on earth, the molding of one face? The relief globe couldn't begin to show trees, between whose overlapping boughs birds raise broods, or the furrows in bark, where whole creatures, creatures easily visible, live out their lives and call it world enough.

What do I make of all this texture? What does it mean about the kind of world in which I have been set down? The texture of the world, its filigree and scrollwork, means that there is the possibility for beauty here, a beauty inexhaustible in its complexity, which opens to my knock, which answers in me a call I do not remember calling, and which trains me to the wild and extravagant nature of the spirit I seek.

In the eighteenth century, when educated European tourists

visited the Alps, they deliberately blindfolded their eyes to shield themselves from the evidence of the earth's horrid irregularity. It is hard to say if this was not merely affectation, for today, newborn infants, who have not yet been taught our ideas of beauty, repeatedly show in tests that they prefer complex to simple designs. At any rate, after the Romantic Revolution, and after Darwin, I might add, our conscious notions of beauty changed. Were the earth as smooth as a ball bearing, it might be beautiful seen from another planet, as the rings of Saturn are. But here we live and move; we wander up and down the banks of the creek, we ride a railway through the Alps, and the landscape shifts and changes. Were the earth smooth, our brains would be smooth as well; we would wake, blink, walk two steps to get the whole picture, and lapse into a dreamless sleep. Because we are living people, and because we are on the receiving end of beauty, another element necessarily enters the question. The texture of space is a condition of time. Time is the warp and matter the weft of the woven texture of beauty in space, and death is the hurtling shuttle. Did those eighteenth-century people think they were immortal? Or were their carriages stalled to rigidity, so that they knew they would never move again, and, panicked, they reached for their blindfolds?

What I want to do, then, is add time to the texture, paint the landscape on an unrolling scroll, and set the giant relief globe spinning on its stand.

Last year I had a very unusual experience. I was awake, with my eyes closed, when I had a dream. It was a small dream about time.

I was dead, I guess, in deep black space high up among many white stars. My own consciousness had been disclosed to me, and I was happy. Then I saw far below me a long, curved band of color. As I came closer, I saw that it stretched endlessly in either direction, and I understood that I was seeing all the time of the planet where I had lived. It looked like a woman's tweed scarf; the longer I studied any one spot, the more dots of color I saw. There was no end to the deepness and variety of the dots. At length I started to look for my time, but although more and more specks of color and deeper and more intricate textures appeared in the fabric, I couldn't find my time, or any time at all that I recognized as being near my time. I couldn't make out so much as a pyramid. Yet as I looked at the band of time, all the individual people, I understood with special clarity, were living at that very moment with great emotion, in intricate detail, in their individual times and places, and they were dying and being replaced by ever more people, one by one, like stitches in which whole worlds of feeling and energy were wrapped, in a never-ending cloth. I remembered suddenly the color and texture of our life as we knew it—these things had been utterly forgotten—and I thought as I searched for it on the limitless band, "That was a good time then, a good time to be living." And I began to remember our time.

I recalled green fields with carrots growing, one by one, in slender rows. Men and women in bright vests and scarves came and pulled the carrots out of the soil and carried them in baskets to shaded kitchens, where they scrubbed them with yellow brushes under running water. I saw white-faced cattle lowing and wading in creeks, with dust on the whorled and curly white hair between their ears. I saw May apples in forests, erupting through leaf-strewn paths. Cells on the root hairs of sycamores split and divided, and apples grew spotted and striped in the fall. Mountains kept their cool caves, and squirrels raced home to their nests through sunlight and shade.

I remembered the ocean, and I seemed to be in the ocean myself, swimming over orange crabs that looked like coral, or off the deep Atlantic banks where whitefish school. Or again I saw the tops of poplars, and the whole sky brushed with clouds in pallid streaks, under which wild ducks flew with outstretched necks, and called, one by one, and flew on.

All these things I saw. Scenes grew in depth and sunlit detail before my eyes, and were replaced by ever more scenes, as I remembered the life of my time with increasing feeling.

At last I saw the earth as a globe in space, and I recalled the ocean's shape and the form of continents, saying to myself with surprise as I looked at the planet, "Yes, that's how it was then; that part there we called ... 'France.'" I was filled with the deep affection of nostalgia—and then I opened my eyes.

*   *   *

We all ought to be able to conjure up sights like these at will, so that we can keep in mind the scope of texture's motion in time. It is a pity we can't watch it on a screen. John Dee, the Elizabethan geographer and mathematician, dreamed up a great idea, which is just what we need. You shoot a mirror up into space so that it is traveling faster than the speed of light (there's the rub). Then you can look in the mirror and watch all the earth's previous history unfolding as on a movie screen. Those people who shoot endless time-lapse films of unfurling roses and tulips have the wrong idea. They should train their cameras instead on the melting of pack ice, the green filling of ponds, the tidal swing of the Seven Bore. They should film the glaciers of Greenland, some of which creak along at such a fast clip that even the dogs bark at them. They should film the invasion of the southernmost Canadian tundra by the northernmost spruce-fir forest, which is happening right now at the rate of a mile every ten years. When the last ice sheet receded from the North American continent, the earth rebounded ten feet. Wouldn't that have been a sight to see?

People say that a good seat in the backyard affords as accurate and inspiring a vantage point on the planet Earth as any observation tower on Alpha Centauri. They are wrong. We see through a glass darkly. We find ourselves in the middle of a movie, or, God help us, a take for a movie, and we don't know what's on the rest of the film.

Say you could look through John Dee's mirror whizzing through space; say you could heave our relief globe into motion like a giant top and breathe life on its surface; say you could view a time-lapse film of our planet: What would you see? Transparent images moving through light, "an infinite storm of beauty."

The beginning is swaddled in mists, blasted by random blinding flashes. Lava pours and cools; seas boil and flood. Clouds materialize and shift; now you can see the earth's face through only random patches of clarity. The land shudders and splits, like pack ice rent by a widening lead. Mountains burst up, jutting, and dull and soften before your eyes, clothed in forests like felt. The ice rolls up, grinding green land under water forever; the ice rolls back. Forests erupt and disappear like fairy rings. The ice rolls up—mountains are mowed into lakes, land rises wet from the sea like a surfacing whale—the ice rolls back.

A blue green streaks the highest ridges, a yellow green spreads from the south like a wave up a strand. A red dye seems to leak from the north down the ridges and into the valleys, seeping south; a white follows the red, then yellow green washes north, then red spreads again, then white, over and over, making patterns of color too swift and intricate to follow. Slow the film. You see dust storms, locusts, floods, in dizzying flash-frames.

Zero in on a well-watered shore and see smoke from fires drifting. Stone cities rise, spread, and crumble, like patches of alpine blossoms that flourish for a day an inch above the permafrost, that iced earth no root can suck, and wither in an hour. New cities appear, and rivers sift silt onto their rooftops; more cities emerge and spread in lobes like lichen on rock. The great human figures of history, those intricate, spirited tissues that roamed the earth's surface, are a wavering blur whose split second in the light was too brief an exposure to yield any image but the hunched, shadowless figures of ghosts. The great herds of caribou pour into the valleys like slag, and trickle back, and pour, a brown fluid.

Slow it down more, come closer still. A dot appears, a flesh-flake. It swells like a balloon; it moves, circles, slows, and vanishes. This is your life.

Our life is a faint tracing on the surface of mystery. The surface of mystery is not smooth, any more than the planet is smooth; not even a single hydrogen atom is smooth, let alone a pine. Nor does it fit together; not even the chlorophyll and hemoglobin molecules are a perfect match, for even after the atom of iron replaces the magnesium, long streamers of disparate atoms trail disjointedly from the rims of the molecules' loops. Freedom cuts both ways. Mystery itself is as fringed and intricate as the shape of the air in time. Forays into mystery cut bays and fine fiords, but the forested mainland itself is implacable both in its bulk and in its most filigreed fringe of detail.

"Every religion that does not affirm that God is hidden," said Pascal flatly, "is not true."

What is man, that thou are mindful of him? This is where the great modern religions are so unthinkably radical: the love of God! For we can see that we are as many as the leaves of trees. But it could be that our faithlessness is a cowering cowardice born of our very smallness, a massive failure of imagination. Certainly nature seems to exult in abounding radicality, extremism, anarchy. If we were to judge nature by its common sense or likelihood, we wouldn't believe the world existed. In nature, improbabilities are the one stock-in-trade. The whole creation is one lunatic fringe. If creation had been left up to me, I'm sure I wouldn't have had the imagination or courage to do more than shape a single, reasonably sized atom, smooth as a snowball, and let it go at that. No claims of any and all revelations could be so far-fetched as a single giraffe.

The question from agnosticism is, Who turned on the lights? The question from faith is, Whatever for? Thoreau climbs Mount Katahdin and gives vent to an almost outraged sense of the reality of the things of this world: "I fear bodies, I tremble to meet them. What is this Titan that has possession of me? Talk of mysteries!—Think of our life in nature,—daily to be shown matter, to come in contact with it,—rocks, trees, wind on our cheeks! the *solid* earth! the *actual* world! the *common* sense! *Contact! Contact!* Who are we? *where* are we?" The Lord God of gods, the Lord God of gods, he knoweth. . . .

Sir James Jeans, British astronomer and physicist, suggested that the universe was beginning to look more like a great thought than a great machine. Humanists seized on the expression, but it was hardly news. We knew, looking around, that a thought branches and leafs, a tree comes to a conclusion. But the question of who is thinking the thought is more fruitful than the question of who made the machine, for a machinist can of course wipe his hands and leave, and his simple machine still hums; but if the thinker's attention strays for a minute, his simplest thought ceases altogether. And, as I have stressed, the place where we so incontrovertibly find ourselves, whether thought or machine, is at least not in any way simple.

Instead, the landscape of the world is "ring-streaked, speckled, and spotted," like Jacob's cattle culled from Laban's herd. Laban had been hard, making Jacob serve seven years in his fields for Rachel, and then giving him instead Rachel's sister, Leah, withholding Rachel until he had served another seven years. When Laban finally sent Jacob on his way, he agreed that Jacob could have all those cattle, sheep, and goats from the herd that were ring-streaked, speckled, and spotted. Jacob pulled some tricks of his own, and soon the strongest and hardiest of Laban's fecund flocks were born ring-streaked, speckled, and spotted. Jacob set out for Canaan with his wives and twelve sons, the fathers of the twelve tribes of Israel, and, with these cattle that are Israel's heritage, into Egypt and out of Egypt, just as the intricate speckled and spotted world is ours.

Intricacy is that which is given from the beginning, the birthright, and in intricacy is the hardiness of complexity that ensures against the failure of all life. This is our heritage, the piebald landscape of time. We walk around; we see a shred of the infinite possible combinations of an infinite variety of forms.

Anything can happen; any pattern of speckles may appear in a world ceaselessly bawling with newness. I see red blood stream in shimmering dots inside a goldfish's tail; I see the stout, extensible lip of a dragonfly nymph that can pierce and clasp a goldfish; and I see the clotted snarls of bright algae that snare and starve the nymph. I see engorged, motionless ants regurgitate pap to a colony of pawing workers, and I see sharks limned in light twist in a raised and emerald wave.

The wonder is—given the errant nature of freedom and the burgeoning of texture in time—the wonder is that all the forms are not monsters, that there is beauty at all, grace gratuitous, pennies found, like the mockingbird's free fall. Beauty itself is the fruit of the creator's exuberance that grew such a tangle, and the grotesques and horrors bloom from that same free growth, that intricate scramble and twine up and down the conditions of time.

This, then, is the extravagant landscape of the world, given, given with exuberance, given in good measure, pressed down, shaken together, and running over.

I WAKENED MYSELF LAST NIGHT with my own shouting. It must have been that terrible yellow plant I saw pushing through the flood-damp soil near the log by Tinker Creek, the plant as fleshy and featureless as a slug, which erupted through the floor of my brain as I slept, and burgeoned into the dream of fecundity that woke me up.

I was watching two huge luna moths mate. Luna moths are those fragile ghost moths, fairy moths, whose five-inch wings are swallow-tailed, a pastel green bordered in silken lavender. From the hairy head of the male sprouted two enormous, furry antennae that trailed down past his ethereal wings. He was on top of the female, hunching repeatedly with a horrible animal vigor.

It was the perfect picture of utter spirituality and utter degradation. I was fascinated and could not turn away my eyes. By watching them I in effect permitted their mating to take place and so committed myself to accepting the consequences—all because I wanted to see what would happen. I wanted in on a secret.

And then the eggs hatched and the bed was full of fish. I was standing across the room in the doorway, staring at the bed. The eggs hatched before my eyes, on my bed, and a thousand chunky fish swarmed there in a viscid slime. The fish were firm and fat, black and white, with triangular bodies and bulging eyes. I watched in horror as they squirmed three feet deep, swimming and oozing about in the glistening, transparent slime. Fish in the bed!—and I awoke. My ears still rang with the foreign cry that had been my own voice.

* * *

For nightmare you eat wild carrot, which is Queen Anne's lace, or you chew the black seeds of the male peony. But it was too late for prevention, and there is no cure. What root or seed will erase that scene from my mind? Fool, I thought: child, you child, you ignorant, innocent fool. What did you expect to see—angels? For it was understood in the dream that the bed full of fish was my own fault, that if I had turned away from the mating moths the hatching of their eggs wouldn't have happened, or at least would have happened in secret, elsewhere. I brought it upon myself, this slither, this swarm.

I don't know what it is about fecundity that so appalls. I suppose it is the teeming evidence that birth and growth, which we value, are ubiquitous and blind, that life itself is so astonishingly cheap, that nature is as careless as it is bountiful, and that with extravagance goes a crushing waste that will one day include our own cheap lives, Henle's loops and all. Every glistening egg is a memento mori.

After a natural disaster such as a flood, nature "stages a comeback." People use the optimistic expression without any real idea of the pressures and waste the comeback involves. Now, in late June, things are popping outside. Creatures extrude or vent eggs; larvae fatten, split their shells, and eat them; spores dissolve or explode; root hairs multiply, corn puffs on the stalk, grass yields seed, shoots erupt from the earth turgid and sheathed; wet muskrats, rabbits, and squirrels slide into the sunlight, mewling and blind; and everywhere watery cells divide and swell, swell and divide. I can like it and call it birth and regeneration, or I can play the devil's advocate and call it rank fecundity—and say that it's hell that's a-poppin'.

This is what I plan to do. Partly as a result of my terrible dream, I have been thinking that the landscape of the intricate world that I have painted is inaccurate and lopsided. It is too optimistic. For the notion of the infinite variety of detail and the multiplicity of forms is a pleasing one; in complexity are the fringes of beauty, and in variety are generosity and exuberance. But all this leaves something vital out of the picture. It is not one pine I see, but a thousand. I myself am not one, but legion. And we are all going to die.

In this repetition of individuals is a mindless stutter, an imbecilic fixedness that must be taken into account. The driving force behind all this fecundity is a terrible pressure I also must consider, the pressure of birth and growth, the pressure that splits the bark of trees and shoots out seeds, that squeezes out the egg and bursts the pupa, that hungers and lusts and drives the creature relentlessly toward its own death. Fecundity, then, is what I have been thinking about, fecundity and the pressure of growth. Fecundity is an ugly word for an ugly subject. It is ugly, at least, in the eggy animal world. I don't think it is for plants.

I never met a man who was shaken by a field of identical blades of grass. An acre of poppies and a forest of spruce boggle no one's mind. Even ten square miles of wheat gladdens the hearts of most people, although it is really as unnatural and freakish as the Frankenstein monster; if man were to die, I read, wheat wouldn't survive him more than three years. No, in the plant world, and especially among the flowering plants, fecundity is not an assault on human values. Plants are not our competitors; they are our prey and our nesting materials. We are no more distressed at their proliferation than an owl is at a population explosion among field mice.

After the flood last year I found a big tulip-tree limb that had been wind-thrown into Tinker Creek. The current dragged it up on some rocks on the bank, where receding waters stranded it. A month after the flood I discovered that it was growing new leaves. Both ends of the branch were completely exposed and dried. I was amazed. It was like the old fable about the corpse's growing a beard; it was as if the woodpile in my garage were suddenly to burst greenly into leaf. The way plants persevere in the bitterest of circumstances is utterly heartening. I can barely keep from unconsciously ascribing a will to these plants, a do-or-die courage, and I have to remind myself that coded cells and mute water pressure have no idea how grandly they are flying in the teeth of it all.

In the lower Bronx, for example, enthusiasts found an ailanthus tree that was fifteen feet long growing from the corner of a garage roof. It was rooted in and living on "dust and roofing cinders." Even more spectacular is a desert plant, *Ibervillea sonorae*—a member of the gourd family—that Joseph Wood Krutch describes. If you see this plant in the desert, you see only a dried chunk of loose wood. It has neither roots nor stems; it's like an old gray knothole. But it is alive. Each year before the rainy season comes, it sends out a few roots and shoots. If the rain arrives, it grows flowers and fruits; these soon wither away, and it reverts to a state as quiet as driftwood.

Well, the New York Botanical Garden put a dried *Ibervillea sonorae* on display in a glass case. "For seven years," says Joseph Wood Krutch, "without soil or water, simply lying in the case, it put forth a few anticipatory shoots and then, when no rainy season arrived, dried up again, hoping for better luck next year." That's what I call flying in the teeth of it all.

(It's hard to understand why no one at the New York Botanical Garden had the grace to splash a glass of water on the thing. Then they could say on their display case label, "This is a live plant." But by the eighth year what they had was a dead plant, which is precisely what it had looked like all along. The sight of it, reinforced by the label "Dead *Ibervillea sonorae*," would have been most melancholy to visitors to the botanical garden. I suppose they just threw it away.)

The growth pressure of plants can do an impressive variety of tricks. Bamboo can grow three feet in twenty-four hours, an accomplishment that is capitalized upon, legendarily, in that exquisite Asian torture in which a victim is strapped to a mesh bunk a mere foot above a bed of healthy bamboo plants whose woodlike tips have been sharpened. For the first eight hours he is fine, if jittery; then he starts turning into a colander, by degrees.

Down at the root end of things, blind growth reaches astonishing proportions. So far as I know, only one real experiment has ever been performed to determine the extent and rate of root growth, and when you read the figures, you see why. I have run into various accounts of this experiment, and the only thing they don't tell you is how many lab assistants were blinded for life.

The experimenters studied a single grass plant, winter rye.

They let it grow in a greenhouse for four months; then they gingerly spirited away the soil—under microscopes, I imagine—and counted and measured all the roots and root hairs. In four months the plant had set forth 378 miles of roots—that's about three miles a day—in 14 million distinct roots. This is mighty impressive, but when they get down to the root hairs, I boggle completely. In those same four months the rye plant created 14 *billion* root hairs, and those little strands placed end to end just about wouldn't quit. In a single *cubic inch* of soil, the length of the root hairs totaled 6,000 miles.

Other plants use the same water power to heave the rock earth around as though they were merely shrugging off a silken cape. Rutherford Platt tells about a larch tree whose root had cleft a one-and-one-half-ton boulder and hoisted it a foot into the air. Everyone knows how a sycamore root will buckle a sidewalk, a mushroom will shatter a cement basement floor. But when the first real measurements of this awesome pressure were taken, nobody could believe the figures.

Rutherford Platt tells the story in *The Great American Forest*, one of the most interesting books ever written: "In 1875, a Massachusetts farmer, curious about the growing power of expanding apples, melons and squashes, harnessed a squash to a weightlifting device which had a dial like a grocer's scale to indicate the pressure exerted by the expanding fruit. As the days passed, he kept piling on counterbalancing weight; he could hardly believe his eyes when he saw his vegetables quietly exerting a lifting force of 5 thousand pounds per square inch. When nobody believed him, he set up exhibits of harnessed squashes and invited the public to come and see. The *Annual Report of the Massachusetts Board of Agriculture*, 1875, reported: 'Many thousands of men, women, and children of all classes of society visited it. *Mr. Penlow* watched it day and night, making hourly observations; *Professor Parker* was moved to write a poem about it; *Professor Seelye* declared that he positively stood in awe of it.'"

All this is very jolly. Unless perhaps I were strapped down above a stand of growing, sharpened bamboo, I am unlikely to feel the faintest queasiness about either the growth pressure of plants, or their fecundity. Even when the plants get in the way of human "culture," I don't mind. When I read how many thousands of dollars a city like New York has to spend to keep underground water pipes free of ailanthus, ginkgo, and sycamore roots, I cannot help but give a little cheer. After all, water pipes are almost always an excellent source of water. In a town where resourcefulness and beating the system are highly prized, these primitive trees can fight city hall and win.

But in the animal world things are different, and human feelings are different. While we're in New York, consider the cockroaches under the bed and the rats in the early morning clustered on the porch stoop. Apartment houses are hives of swarming roaches. Or again, in one sense you could think of Manhattan's land as high-rent, high-rise real estate; in another sense you could see it as an enormous breeding ground for rats, acres and acres of rats. I suppose that the rats and the cockroaches don't do so much actual damage as the roots do; nevertheless, the prospect does not please. Fecundity is anathema only in the animal. "Acres and acres of rats" has a suitably chilling ring to it that is decidedly lacking if I say, instead, "acres and acres of tulips."

The landscape of earth is dotted and smeared with masses of apparently identical individual animals, from the great Pleistocene herds that blanketed grasslands to the gluey gobs of bacteria that clog the lobes of lungs. The oceanic breeding grounds of pelagic birds are as teeming and cluttered as any human Calcutta. Lemmings blacken the earth and locusts the air. Grunion run thick in the ocean, corals pile on pile, and protozoans explode in a red tide stain. Ants take to the skies in swarms, mayflies hatch by the millions, and molting cicadas coat the trunks of trees. Have you seen the rivers run red and lumpy with salmon?

Consider the ordinary barnacle, the rock barnacle. Inside everyone of those millions of hard white cones on the rocks— the kind that bruises your heel as you bruise its head—is of

course a creature as alive as you or I. Its business in life is this:
when a wave washes over it, it sticks out twelve feathery feeding appendages and filters the plankton for food. As it grows, it
sheds its skin like a lobster, enlarges its shell, and reproduces
itself without end. The larvae "hatch into the sea in milky
clouds." The barnacles encrusting a single half mile of shore can
leak into the water a million million larvae. How many is that to
a human mouthful? In sea water they grow, molt, change shape
wildly, and eventually, after several months, settle on the rocks,
turn into adults, and build shells. Inside the shells they have to
shed their skins. Rachel Carson was always finding the old
skins; she reported: "Almost every container of sea water that I
bring up from the shore is flecked with white, semitransparent
objects. . . . Seen under the microscope, every detail of structure
is perfectly represented. . . . In the little cellophane-like replicas
I can count the joints of the appendages; even the bristles,
growing at the bases of the joints, seem to have been slipped
intact out of their casings." All in all, rock barnacles may live
four years.

My point about rock barnacles is those million million larvae
"in milky clouds" and those shed flecks of skin. Sea water
seems suddenly to be but a broth of barnacle bits. Can I fancy
that a million million human infants are more real?

What if God has the same affectionate disregard for us that
we have for barnacles? I don't know if each barnacle larva is of
itself unique and special, or if we the people are essentially as
interchangeable as bricks. My brain is full of numbers; they
swell and would split my skull like a shell. I examine the trapezoids of skin covering the back of my hands like blown dust
motes moistened to clay. I have hatched, too, with millions of
my kind, into a milky way that spreads from an unknown shore.

I have seen the mantis's abdomen dribbling out eggs in wet
bubbles like tapioca pudding glued to a thorn. I have seen a
film of a termite queen as big as my face, dead white and featureless, glistening with slime, throbbing and pulsing out rivers
of globular eggs. Termite workers, who looked like tiny long-
shoremen unloading the *Queen Mary*, licked each egg as fast as it

was extruded to prevent mold. The whole world is an incubator for incalculable numbers of eggs, each one coded minutely and ready to burst.

The egg of a parasite chalcid wasp, a common small wasp, multiplies unassisted, making ever more identical eggs. The female lays a single fertilized egg in the flaccid tissues of its live prey, and that one egg divides and divides. As many as two thousand new parasitic wasps will hatch to feed on the host's body with identical hunger. Similarly—only more so—Edwin Way Teale reports that a lone aphid, without a partner, breeding "unmolested" for one year, would produce so many living aphids that, although they are only a tenth of an inch long, together they would extend into space twenty-five hundred *light-years*. Even the average goldfish lays five thousand eggs, which she will eat as fast as she lays, if permitted. The sales manager of Ozark Fisheries in Missouri, which raises commercial goldfish for the likes of me, said, "We produce, measure, and sell our product by the ton." The intricacy of Ellery and aphids multiplied mindlessly into tons and light-years is more than extravagance; it is holocaust, parody, glut.

The pressure of growth among animals is a kind of terrible hunger. These billions must eat in order to fuel their surge to sexual maturity so that they may pump out more billions of eggs. And what are the fish on the bed going to eat, or the hatched mantises in the mason jar going to eat, but each other? There is a terrible innocence in the benumbed world of the lower animals, reducing life there to a universal chomp. Edwin Way Teale, in *The Strange Lives of Familiar Insects*—a book I couldn't live without—describes several occasions of meals mouthed under the pressure of a hunger that knew no bounds.

You remember the dragonfly nymph, for instance, which stalks the bottom of the creek and the pond in search of live prey to snare with its hooked, unfolding lip. Dragonfly nymphs are insatiable and mighty. They clasp and devour whole minnows and fat tadpoles. Well, a dragonfly nymph, says Teale, "has even been seen climbing up out of the water on a plant to attack a helpless dragonfly emerging, soft and rumpled, from its nymphal skin." Is this where I draw the line?

It is between mothers and their offspring that these feedings have truly macabre overtones. Look at lacewings. Lacewings are those fragile green insects with large rounded transparent wings. The larvae eat enormous numbers of aphids, the adults mate in a fluttering rush of instinct, lay eggs, and die by the millions in the first cold snap of fall. Sometimes, when a female lays her fertile eggs on a green leaf atop a slender stalked thread, she is hungry. She pauses in her laying, turns around, and eats her eggs one by one, then lays some more, and eats them, too.

Anything can happen, and anything does; what's it all about? Valerie Eliot, T. S. Eliot's widow, wrote in a letter to the London *Times:* "My husband, T. S. Eliot, loved to recount how late one evening he stopped a taxi. As he got in the driver said: 'You're T. S. Eliot.' When asked how he knew, he replied: 'Ah, I've got an eye for a celebrity. Only the other evening I picked up Bertrand Russell, and I said to him, "Well, Lord Russell, what's it all about," and, do you know, he couldn't tell me.'" Well, Lord God, asks the delicate, dying lacewing whose mandibles are wet with the juice secreted by her own ovipositor, what's it all about? ("And, do you know . . . ")

Planarians, which live in the duck pond, behave similarly. They are those dark laboratory flatworms that can regenerate themselves from almost any severed part. Arthur Koestler writes: "during the mating season the worms become cannibals, devouring everything alive that comes their way, including their own previously discarded tails which were in the process of growing a new head." Even such sophisticated mammals as the great predator cats occasionally eat their cubs. A mother cat will be observed licking the area around the umbilical cord of the helpless newborn. She licks, she licks, she licks until something snaps in her brain, and she begins eating, starting there, at the vulnerable belly.

Although mothers devouring their own offspring is patently the more senseless, somehow the reverse behavior is the more appalling. In the death of the parent in the jaws of its offspring I recognize a universal drama that chance occurrence has merely telescoped, so that I can see all the players at once. Gall gnats, for instance, are common small flies. Sometimes, according to

Teale, a gall gnat larva, which does not resemble the adult in the least, and which has certainly not mated, nevertheless produces within its body eggs, live eggs, which then hatch within its soft tissues. Sometimes the eggs hatch alive even within the quiescent body of the pupa. The same incredible thing occasionally occurs within the fly genus *Miastor,* again to both larvae and pupae. "These eggs hatch within their bodies and the ravenous larvae which emerge immediately begin devouring their parents." In this case, I know what it's all about, and I wish I didn't. The parents die, the next generation lives, *ad majorem gloriam,* and so it goes. If the new generation hastens the death of the old, it scarcely matters; the old has served its one purpose, and the direct processing of proteins is tidily all in the family. But think of the invisible swelling of ripe eggs inside the pupa, as wrapped and rigid as a mummified Egyptian queen! The eggs burst, shatter her belly, and emerge alive, awake, and hungry from a mummy case, which they crawl over like worms and feed on till it's gone. And then they turn to the world.

"To prevent a like fate," Teale continues, "some of the ichneumon flies, those wasplike parasites which deposit their eggs in the body tissues of caterpillars, have to scatter their eggs while in flight at times when they are unable to find their prey and the eggs are ready to hatch within their bodies."

You are an ichneumon. You mated and your eggs are fertile. If you can't find a caterpillar on which to lay your eggs, your young will starve. When the eggs hatch, the young will eat any body in which they find themselves, so if you don't kill them by emitting them broadcast over the landscape, they'll eat you alive. But if you let them drop over the fields you will probably be dead yourself, of old age, before they even hatch to starve, and the whole show will be over and done, and a wretched one it was. You feel them coming, and coming, and you struggle to rise. . . .

Not that the ichneumon is making any conscious choice. If she were, her dilemma would be truly the stuff of tragedy; Aeschylus need have looked no further than the ichneumon. That is, it would be the stuff of real tragedy if only Aeschylus and I could convince you that the ichneumon is really and truly as alive as we are, and that what happens to it matters. Will you take it on faith?

Here is one last story. It shows that the pressures of growth gang aft agley. The clothes moth, whose caterpillar eats wool, sometimes goes into a molting frenzy that Teale blandly describes as "curious": "A curious paradox in molting is the action of a clothes-moth larva with insufficient food. It sometimes goes into a 'molting frenzy,' changing its skin repeatedly and getting smaller and smaller with each change." Smaller and smaller . . . can you imagine the frenzy? Where shall we send our sweaters? The diminution process could, in imagination, extend to infinity, as the creature frantically shrinks and shrinks and shrinks to the size of a molecule, then an electron, but never can shrink to absolute nothing and end its terrible hunger. I feel like Ezra: "And when I heard this thing, I rent my garment and my mantle, and plucked off the hair of my head and of my beard, and sat down astonished."

I am not kidding anyone if I pretend that these awesome pressures to eat and breed are wholly mystifying. The million million barnacle larvae in a half mile of shore water, the rivers of termite eggs, and the light-years of aphids ensure the living presence, in a scarcely concerned world, of ever more rock barnacles, termites, and aphids.

It's chancy out there. Dog whelks eat rock barnacles, worms invade their shells, shore ice razes them from the rocks and grinds them to a powder. Can you lay aphid eggs faster than chickadees can eat them? Can you find a caterpillar, can you beat the killing frost?

As far as lower animals go, if you lead a simple life you probably face a boring death. Some animals, however, lead such complicated lives that not only do the chances for any one animal's death at any minute multiply greatly, but so also do the *varieties* of the deaths it might die. The ordained paths of some animals are so rocky they are preposterous. The horsehair worm in the duck pond, for instance, wriggling so serenely near the surface, is the survivor of an impossible series of squeaky escapes. I did a bit of research into the life cycles of these worms, which are shaped exactly like hairs from a horse's tail, and learned that although scientists are not exactly sure what happens to any one species of them, they think it might go something like this:

You start with long strands of eggs wrapped around vegetation in the duck pond. The eggs hatch, the larvae emerge, and each seeks an aquatic host, say a dragonfly nymph. The larva bores into the nymph's body, where it feeds and grows and somehow escapes. Then if it doesn't get eaten it swims over to the shore, where it encysts on submersed plants. This is all fairly improbable, but not impossibly so.

Now the coincidences begin. First, presumably, the water level of the duck pond has to drop. This exposes the vegetation so that the land host organism can get at it without drowning. Horsehair worms have various land hosts, such as crickets, beetles, and grasshoppers. Let's say ours can only make it if a grasshopper comes along. Fine. But the grasshopper had best hurry, for there is only so much fat stored in the encysted worm, and it might starve. Well, here comes just the right species of grasshopper, and it is obligingly feeding on shore vegetation. Now, I have not observed any extensive grazing of grasshoppers on any grassy shores, but obviously it must occur. Bingo, then, the grasshopper just happens to eat the encysted worm.

The cyst bursts. The worm emerges in all its hideous length, up to thirty-six inches, inside the body of the grasshopper, on which it feeds. I presume that the worm must eat enough of its host to stay alive, but not so much that the grasshopper will keel over dead far from water. Entomologists have found tiger beetles dead and dying on the water whose insides were almost perfectly empty except for the white coiled bodies of horsehair worms. At any rate, now the worm is almost an adult, ready to reproduce. But first it's got to get out of this grasshopper.

Biologists don't know what happens next. If at the critical stage the grasshopper is hopping in a sunny meadow away from a duck pond or ditch, which is entirely likely, then the story is over. But say it happens to be feeding near the duck pond. The worm perhaps bores its way out of the grasshopper's body, or perhaps it is excreted. At any rate, there it is on the grass, drying out. Now the biologists have to go so far as to invoke a "heavy rain," falling from heaven at this fortuitous moment, in order to get the horsehair worm back into the water, where it can mate and lay more seemingly doomed eggs. You'd be thin, too.

Other creatures have it just about as easy. A blood fluke starts out as an egg in human feces. If it happens to fall into fresh water, it will live only if it happens to encounter a certain species of snail. It changes in the snail, swims out, and now needs to find a human being in the water in order to bore through his skin. It travels around in the man's blood, settles down in the blood vessels of his intestine, and turns into a sexually mature blood fluke, either male or female. Now it has to find another fluke, of the opposite sex, who also just happens to have traveled the same circuitous route and landed in the same unfortunate man's intestinal blood vessels. Other flukes lead similarly improbable lives, some passing through as many as four hosts.

But it is for gooseneck barnacles that I reserve the largest measure of awe. Recently I saw photographs taken by members of the *Ra* expedition. One showed a glob of tar as big as a softball, jetsam from a larger craft, which Heyerdahl and his crew spotted in the middle of the Atlantic Ocean. The tar had been in the sea for a long time; it was overgrown with gooseneck barnacles. The gooseneck barnacles were entirely incidental, but for me they were the most interesting thing about the whole expedition. How many gooseneck barnacle larvae must be dying out there in the middle of vast oceans for every one that finds a glob of tar to fasten to? You've seen gooseneck barnacles washed up on the beach; they grow on old ship's timber, driftwood, strips of rubber—anything that's been afloat in the sea long enough. They do not resemble rock barnacles in the least, although the two are closely related. They have pinkish shells extending in a flattened oval from a flexible bit of "gooseneck" tissue that secures them to the substratum.

I have always had a fancy for these creatures, but I'd always assumed that they lived near shores, where chance floating holdfasts are more likely to occur. What are they doing—what are the larvae doing—out there in the middle of the ocean? They drift and perish, or by some freak accident in a world where anything can happen, they latch and flourish. If I dangled my hand from the deck of the *Ra* into the sea, could a gooseneck barnacle fasten there? If I gathered a cup of ocean water, would I be holding a score of dying and dead barnacle larvae? Should I throw them a chip? What kind of a world is this, anyway? Why not make fewer barnacle larvae and give them a decent chance? Are we dealing in life, or in death?

I have to look at the landscape of the blue-green world again. Just think: In all the clean beautiful reaches of the solar system, our planet alone is a blot; our planet alone has death. I have to acknowledge that the sea is a cup of death and the land is a stained altar stone. We the living are survivors huddled on flotsam, living on jetsam. We are escapees. We wake in terror, eat in hunger, sleep with a mouthful of blood.

Death: W. C. Fields called death "the Fellow in the Bright Nightgown." He shuffles around the house in all the corners I've forgotten, all the halls I dare not call to mind or visit for fear I'll glimpse the hem of his shabby, dazzling gown disappearing around a turn. This is the monster evolution loves. How could it be?

The faster death goes, the faster evolution goes. If an aphid lays a million eggs, several might survive. Now, my right hand, in all its human cunning, could not make one aphid in a thousand years. But these aphid eggs—which run less than a dime a dozen, which run absolutely free—can make aphids as effortlessly as the sea makes waves. Wonderful things, wasted. It's a wretched system. Arthur Stanley Eddington, the British physicist and astronomer, who died in 1944, suggested that all of "Nature" could conceivably run on the same deranged scheme. "If indeed she has no greater aim than to provide a home for her greatest experiment, Man, it would be just like her methods to scatter a million stars whereof one might haply achieve her purpose." I doubt very much that this is the aim, but it seems clear on all fronts that this is the method.

Say you are the manager of the Southern Railroad. You figure that you need three engines for a stretch of track between Lynchburg and Danville. It's a mighty steep grade. So at fantastic effort and expense you have your shops make nine thousand engines. Each engine must be fashioned just so, every rivet and bolt secure, every wire twisted and wrapped, every needle on every indicator sensitive and accurate.

You send all nine thousand of them out on the runs. Although there are engineers at the throttles, no one is manning the switches. The engines crash, collide, derail, jump, jam, burn. . . . At the end of the massacre you have three engines, which is what the run could support in the first place. There are few enough of them that they can stay out of one another's paths.

You go to your board of directors and show them what you've done. And what are they going to say? You know what they're going to say. They're going to say: It's a hell of a way to run a railroad.

Is it a better way to run a universe?

Evolution loves death more than it loves you or me. This is easy to write, easy to read, and hard to believe. The words are simple, the concept clear—but you don't believe it, do you? Nor do I. How could I, when we're both so lovable? Are my values then so diametrically opposed to those that nature preserves? This is the key point.

Must I then part ways with the only world I know? I had thought to live by the side of the creek in order to shape my life to its free flow. But I seem to have reached a point where I must draw the line. It looks as though the creek is not buoying me up but dragging me down. Look: Cock Robin may die the most gruesome of slow deaths, and nature is no less pleased; the sun comes up, the creek rolls on, the survivors still sing. I cannot feel that way about your death, nor you about mine, nor either of us about the robin's—or even the barnacles'. We value the individual supremely, and nature values him not a whit. It looks for the moment as though I might have to reject this creek life unless I want to be utterly brutalized. Is human culture with its values my only real home after all? Can it possibly be that I should move my anchor hold to the side of a library? This direction of thought brings me abruptly to a fork in the road, where I stand paralyzed, unwilling to go on, for both ways lead to madness.

Either this world, my mother, is a monster, or I myself am a freak.

Consider the former: the world is a monster. Any three-year-old can see how unsatisfactory and clumsy is this whole business of reproducing and dying by the billions. We have not yet encountered any god who is as merciful as a man who flicks a beetle over on its feet. There is not a people in the world who behaves as badly as praying mantises. But wait, you say, there is no right and wrong in nature; right and wrong is a human concept. Precisely: we are moral creatures, then, in an amoral world. The universe that suckled us is a monster that does not care if we live or die—does not care if it itself grinds to a halt. It is fixed and blind, a robot programmed to kill. We are free and seeing; we can only try to outwit it at every turn to save our skins.

This view requires that a monstrous world running on chance and death, careening blindly from nowhere to nowhere, somehow produced wonderful us. I came from the world, I crawled out of a sea of amino acids, and now I must whirl around and shake my fist at that sea and cry Shame! If I value anything at all, then I must blindfold my eyes when I near the Swiss Alps. We must as a culture disassemble our telescopes and settle down to backslapping. We little blobs of soft tissue crawling around on this one planet's skin are right, and the whole universe is wrong.

Or consider the alternative.

Julian of Norwich, the great English anchorite and theologian, cited, in the manner of the prophets, these words from God: "See, I am God: see, I am in all things: see, I never lift my hands off my works, nor ever shall, without end. . . . How should anything be amiss?" But now not even the simplest and best of us sees things the way Julian did. It seems to us that plenty is amiss. So much is amiss that I must consider the second fork in the road, that creation itself is blamelessly, benevolently askew by its very free nature, and that it is only human feeling that is freakishly amiss. The frog that the giant water bug sucked had, presumably, a rush of pure feeling for about a second, before its brain turned to broth. I, however, have been sapped by various strong feelings about the incident almost daily for several years.

Do the barnacle larvae care? Does the lacewing who eats her eggs care? If they do not care, then why am I making all this fuss? If I am a freak, then why don't I hush?

Our excessive emotions are so patently painful and harmful to us as a species that I can hardly believe that they evolved. Other creatures manage to have effective matings and even stable societies without great emotions, and they have a bonus in that they need not ever mourn. (But some higher animals have emotions that we think are similar to ours: dogs, elephants, otters, and the sea mammals mourn their dead. Why do that to an otter? What creator could be so cruel, not to kill otters, but to let them care?) It would seem that emotions are the curse, not death—emotions that appear to have devolved upon a few freaks as a special curse from Malevolence.

All right, then. It is our emotions that are amiss. We are freaks, the world is fine, and let us all go have lobotomies to restore us to a natural state. We can leave the library then, go back to the creek lobotomized, and live on its banks as untroubled as any muskrat or reed. You first.

Of the two ridiculous alternatives, I rather favor the second. Although it is true that we are moral creatures in an amoral world, the world's amorality does not make it a monster. Rather, I am the freak. Perhaps I don't need a lobotomy, but I could use some calming down, and the creek is just the place for it. I must go down to the creek again. It is where I belong, although as I become closer to it, my fellows appear more and more freakish, and my home in the library more and more limited. Imperceptibly at first, and now consciously, I shy away from the arts, from the human emotional stew. I read what the men with telescopes and microscopes have to say about the landscape. I read about the polar ice, and I drive myself deeper and deeper into exile from my own kind. But since I cannot avoid the library altogether—the human culture that taught me to speak in its tongue—I bring human values to the creek, and so save myself from being brutalized.

What I have been after all along is not an explanation but a picture. This is the way the world is, altar and cup, lit by the fire from a star that has only begun to die. My rage and shock at the pain and death of individuals of my kind is the old, old mystery, as old as man, but forever fresh, and completely unanswerable. My reservations about the fecundity and waste of life among other creatures is, however, mere squeamishness. After all, I'm the one having the nightmares. It is true that many of the creatures live and die abominably, but I am not called upon to pass judgment. Nor am I called upon to live in that same way, and those creatures who must are mercifully unconscious.

I don't want to cut this too short. Let me pull the camera back and look at that fork in the road from a distance, in the larger context of the speckled and twining world. It could be that the fork will disappear, or that I will see it to be but one of many interstices in a network, so that it is impossible to say which line is the main part and which is the fork.

The picture of fecundity and its excesses and of the pressures of growth and its accidents is of course no different from the picture I painted before of the world as an intricate texture of a bizarre variety of forms. Only now the shadows are deeper. Extravagance takes on a sinister, wastrel air, and exuberance blithers. When I added the dimension of time to the landscape of the world, I saw how freedom grew the beauties and horrors from the same live branch. This landscape is the same as that one, with a few more details added, and a different emphasis. I see squashes expanding with pressure and a hunk of wood rapt on the desert floor. The rye plant and the Bronx ailanthus are literally killing themselves to make seeds, and the animals to lay eggs. Instead of one goldfish swimming in its intricate bowl, I see tons and tons of goldfish laying and eating billions and billions of eggs. The point of all the eggs is of course to make goldfish one by one—nature loves the *idea* of the individual, if not the individual himself—and the point of a goldfish is exuberance. This is familiar ground. I merely failed to mention that it is death that is spinning the globe.

It is harder to take, but surely it's been thought about. I cannot really get very exercised over the hideous appearance and habits of some deep-sea jellies and fishes, and I exercise easy. But about the topic of my own death I am decidedly touchy. Nevertheless, the two phenomena are two branches of the same creek, the creek that waters the world. Its source is freedom, and its network of branches is infinite. The graceful mockingbird that falls drinks there and sips in the same drop a beauty that waters its eyes and a death that fledges and flies. The petals of tulips are flaps of the same doomed water that swells and hatches in the ichneumon's gut.

That something is everywhere and always amiss is part of the very stuff of creation. It is as though each clay form had baked into it, fired into it, a blue streak of nonbeing, a shaded emptiness like a bubble that not only shapes its very structure but also causes it to list and ultimately explode. We could have planned things more mercifully, perhaps, but our plan would never get off the drawing board until we agreed to the very compromising terms that are the only ones that being offers.

The world has signed a pact with the devil; it had to. It is a covenant to which every thing, even every hydrogen atom, is bound. The terms are clear: if you want to live, you have to die; you cannot have mountains and creeks without space, and space is a beauty married to a blind man. The blind man is Freedom, or Time, and he does not go anywhere without his great dog Death. The world came into being with the signing of the contract. A scientist calls it the Second Law of Thermodynamics. A poet says, "The force that through the green fuse drives the flower/Drives my green age." This is what we know. The rest is gravy.

LEARNING TO STALK MUSKRATS TOOK me several years.

I've always known there were muskrats in the creek. Sometimes when I drove late at night my headlights' beam on the water would catch the broad lines of ripples made by a swimming muskrat, a bow wave, converging across the water at the raised dark vee of its head. I would stop the car and get out: nothing. They eat corn and tomatoes from my neighbors' gardens, too, by night, so that my neighbors were always telling me that the creek was full of them. Around here, people call them "mushrats"; Thoreau called them "musquashes." They are not of course rats at all (let alone squashes). They are more like diminutive beavers, and like beavers, they exude a scented oil from musk glands under the base of the tail—hence the name. I had read in several respectable sources that muskrats are so wary they are almost impossible to observe. One expert who made a full-time study of large populations, mainly by examining "sign" and performing autopsies on corpses, said he often went for weeks at a time without seeing a single living muskrat.

One hot evening three years ago, I was standing more or less *in* a bush. I was stock-still, looking deep into Tinker Creek from a spot on the bank opposite the house, watching a group of bluegills stare and hang motionless near the bottom of a deep, sunlit pool. I was focused for depth. I had long since lost myself, lost the creek, the day, lost everything but still amber depth. All at once I couldn't see. And then I could: a young muskrat had appeared on top of the water, floating on its back. Its forelegs were folded languorously across its chest; the sun shone on its upturned belly. Its youthfulness and rodent grin, coupled with its ridiculous method of locomotion, which consisted of a lazy wag of the tail assisted by an occasional dabble of a webbed hind foot, made it an enchanting picture of decadence, dissipation, and summer sloth. I forgot all about the fish.

But in my surprise at having the light come on so suddenly, and at having my consciousness returned to me all at once, bearing an inverted muskrat, I must have moved and betrayed myself. The kit—for I know now it was just a young kit—righted itself so that only its head was visible above water, and swam downstream, away from me. I extricated myself from the bush and foolishly pursued it. It dove sleekly, reemerged, and glided for the opposite bank. I ran along the bankside brush, trying to keep it in sight. It kept casting an alarmed look over its shoulder at me. Once again it dove, under a floating mat of brush lodged in the bank, and disappeared. I never saw it again. (Nor have I ever, despite all the muskrats I have seen, again seen a muskrat floating on its back.) But I did not know muskrats then; I waited, panting, and watched the shadowed bank. Now I know that I cannot outwait a muskrat who knows I am there. The most I can do is get "there" quietly, while it is still in its hole, so that it never knows, and wait there until it emerges. But then all I knew was that I wanted to see more muskrats.

I began to look for them day and night. Sometimes I would see ripples suddenly start beating from the creek's side, but as I crouched to watch, the ripples would die. Now I know what this means, and have learned to stand perfectly still to make out the muskrat's small, pointed face hidden under overhanging bank vegetation, watching me. That summer I haunted the bridges, I walked up creeks and down, but no muskrats ever appeared. You must just have to be there, I thought. You must have to spend the rest of your life standing in bushes. It was a once-in-a-lifetime thing, and you've had your once.

Then one night I saw another, and my life changed. After that I knew where they were in numbers, and I knew when to look. It was late dusk; I was driving home from a visit with friends. Just on the off chance, I parked quietly by the creek, walked out on the narrow bridge over the shallows, and looked upstream. Someday, I had been telling myself for weeks, someday a muskrat is going to swim right through that channel in the cattails, and I am going to see it. That is precisely what happened. I looked up into the channel for a muskrat, and there it came, swimming right toward me. Knock; see; ask. It seemed to swim with a side-to-side, sculling motion of its vertically flattened tail. It looked bigger than the upside-down muskrat, and its face more reddish. In its mouth it clasped a twig of tulip tree. One thing amazed me: it swam right down the middle of the creek. I thought it would hide in the brush along the edge; instead it plied the waters as obviously as an aquaplane. I could just look and look.

But I was standing on the bridge, not sitting, and it saw me. It changed its course, veered toward the bank, and disappeared behind an indentation in the rushy shoreline. I felt a rush of such pure energy I thought I would not need to breathe for days.

That innocence of mine is mostly gone now, although I felt almost the same pure rush last night. I have seen many muskrats since I learned to look for them in that part of the creek. But still I seek them out in the cool of the evening, and still I hold my breath when rising ripples surge from under the creek's bank. The great hurrah about wild animals is that they exist at all, and the greater hurrah is the actual moment of seeing them. Because they have a nice dignity, and prefer to have nothing to do with me, not even as the simple objects of my vision. They show me by their very wariness what a prize it is simply to open my eyes and behold.

Muskrats are the bread and butter of the carnivorous food chain. They are like rabbits and mice: if you are big enough to eat mammals, you eat them. Hawks and owls prey on them, and foxes; so do otters. Minks are their special enemies; minks live near large muskrat populations, slinking in and out of their dens and generally hanging around like mantises outside a beehive. Muskrats are also subject to a contagious blood disease that wipes out whole colonies. Sometimes, however, their whole populations explode, like that of lemmings, which are their near kin; and they either die by the hundreds or fan out across the land, migrating to new creeks and ponds.

Men kill them, too. One Eskimo who hunted muskrats for a few weeks each year strictly as a sideline says that in fourteen years he killed 30,739 muskrats. The pelts sell, but the price is falling. Muskrats are the most important fur animal on the North American continent. I don't know what they bring on the Mackenzie River delta these days, but around here, fur dealers who paid $2.90 in 1971 now, in 1994, pay $2.50 a pelt. They make the pelts into coats, calling the fur anything but muskrat: "Hudson seal" is typical. In the old days, after they had sold the skins, trappers would sell the meat, too, calling it "marsh rabbit." Many people still stew muskrat.

Keeping ahead of all this slaughter, a female might have as many as five litters a year, and each litter contains six or seven or more muskrats. The nest is high and dry under the bank; only the entrance is under water, usually by several feet, to foil enemies. Here the nests are marked by simple holes in a creek's clay bank; in other parts of the country, muskrats build floating conical winter lodges that not only are watertight but are edible to muskrats.

The very young have a risky life. For one thing, even snakes and raccoons eat them. For another, their mother is easily confused, and may abandon one or two of a big litter here or there, forgetting as it were to count noses. The newborn hanging on their mother's teats may drop off if the mother has to make a sudden dive into the water, and sometimes these drown. The just-weaned young have a rough time, too, because new litters are coming along so hard and fast that they have to be weaned before they really know how to survive. And if the just-weaned young are near starving, they might eat the newborn—if they can get to them. Adult muskrats, including their own mothers, often kill them if they approach too closely. But if they live through all these hazards, they can begin a life of swimming at twilight and munching cattail roots, clover, and an occasional crayfish. Paul Errington, a usually solemn authority, writes: "The muskrat nearing the end of its first month may be thought of as an independent enterprise in a very modest way."

The wonderful thing about muskrats in my book is that they cannot see very well, and are rather dim to boot. They are extremely wary if they know I am there, and will outwait me every time. But with a modicum of skill and a minimum loss of human dignity, such as it is, I can be right "there," and the breathing fact of my presence will never penetrate their narrow skulls.

What happened last night was not only the ultimate in muskrat dimness; it was also the ultimate in human intrusion, the limit beyond which I am certain I cannot go. I would never have imagined I could go that far, actually to sit beside a feeding muskrat as beside a dinner partner at a crowded table.

What happened was this. Just in the past week I have been frequenting a different place, one of the creek's nameless feeder streams. It is mostly a shallow trickle joining several pools up to three feet deep. Over one of these pools is a tiny pedestrian bridge known locally, if at all, as the troll bridge. I was sitting on the troll bridge about an hour before sunset, looking upstream about eight feet to my right, where I know the muskrats have a den. I had just lighted a cigarette when a pulse of ripples appeared at the mouth of the den, and a muskrat emerged. He swam straight toward me and headed under the bridge.

Now, the moment a muskrat's eyes disappear from view under a bridge, I go into action. I have about five seconds to switch myself around so that I will be able to see him very well when he emerges on the other side of the bridge. I can easily hang my head over the other side of the bridge, so that when he appears from under me, I will be able to count his eyelashes if I want. The trouble with this maneuver is that once his beady eyes appear again on the other side, I am stuck. If I move again, the show is over for the evening. I have to remain in whatever insane position I happen to be caught, for as long as I am in his sight, so that I stiffen all my muscles, bruise my ankles on the concrete, and burn my fingers on the cigarette. And if the muskrat goes out on a bank to feed, there I am with my face hanging a foot over the water, unable to see anything but crayfish. So I have learned to take it easy on these five-second flings.

When the muskrat went under the bridge, I moved so I could face downstream comfortably. He reappeared, and I had a good look at him. He was eight inches long in the body, and another six in the tail. Muskrat tails are black and scaled, flattened not horizontally, like beavers' tails, but vertically, like a belt stood on edge. In the winter, muskrats' tails sometimes freeze solid, and the animals chew off the frozen parts up to about an inch of the body. They must swim entirely with their hind feet, and must have a terrible time steering. This one used his tail as a rudder and only occasionally as a propeller; mostly he swam with a pedaling motion of his hind feet, held very straight and moving down and around, "toeing down" like a bicycle racer. The soles of his hind feet were strangely pale; his toenails were pointed in long cones. He kept his forelegs still, tucked up to his chest.

The muskrat clambered out on the bank across the stream from me and began feeding. He chomped down on a ten-inch weed, pushing it into his mouth steadily with both forepaws as a carpenter feeds a saw. I could hear his chewing; it sounded like somebody eating celery sticks. Then he slid back into the water with the weed still in his mouth, crossed under the bridge, and, instead of returning to his den, rose erect on a submerged rock and calmly polished off the rest of the weed. He was about four feet away from me. Immediately he swam under the bridge again, hauled himself out on the bank, and unerringly found the same spot on the grass, where he devoured the weed's stump.

All this time I was not only doing an elaborate about-face every time his eyes disappeared under the bridge, but I was also smoking a cigarette. He never noticed that the configuration of the bridge metamorphosed utterly every time he went under it. Many animals are the same way: they can't see a thing unless it's moving. Similarly, every time he turned his head away, I was free to smoke the cigarette, although of course I never knew when he would suddenly turn again and leave me caught in some wretched position. The galling thing was, he was downwind of me and my cigarette: was I really going through all this for a creature without any sense whatsoever?

After the weed stump was gone, the muskrat began ranging over the grass with a nervous motion, chewing off mouthfuls of grass and clover near the base. Soon he had gathered a huge, bushy mouthful; he pushed into the water, crossed under the bridge, swam toward his den, and dove.

When he launched himself again shortly, having apparently

cached the grass, he repeated the same routine in a businesslike fashion and returned with another shock of grass.

Out he came again. I lost him for a minute when he went under the bridge; he did not come out where I expected him. Suddenly, to my utter disbelief, he appeared on the bank next to me. The troll bridge itself is on a level with the low bank; there I was, and there he was, at my side. I could have touched him with the palm of my hand without straightening my elbow. He was ready to hand.

Foraging beside me, he walked very humped up, maybe to save heat loss through evaporation. Generally, whenever he was out of the water he assumed the shape of a shmoo; his shoulders were as slender as a kitten's. He used his forepaws to part clumps of grass extremely tidily; I could see the flex in his narrow wrists. He gathered mouthfuls of grass and clover less by actually gnawing than by biting hard near the ground, locking his neck muscles, and pushing up jerkily with his forelegs.

His jaw was underslung, his black eyes close set and glistening, his small ears pointed and furred. I will have to try and see if he can cock them. I could see the water-slicked long hairs of his coat, which gathered in rich brown strands that emphasized the smooth contours of his body, and which parted to reveal the paler, softer hair, like rabbit fur, underneath. Despite his closeness, I never saw his teeth or belly.

After several minutes of rummaging about in the grass at my side, he eased into the water under the bridge and paddled to his den with the jawful of grass held high, and that was the last I saw of him.

In the forty minutes I watched him, he never saw me, smelled me, or heard me at all. When he was in full view, of course, I never moved except to breathe. My eyes would move, too, following his, but he never noticed. I even swallowed a couple of times: nothing. The swallowing thing interested me because I had read that when you are trying to hand-tame wild birds, if you inadvertently swallow, you ruin everything. The bird, according to this theory, thinks you are swallowing in anticipation, and off it goes. The muskrat never twitched. Only once, when he was feeding from the opposite bank about eight feet away from me, did he suddenly rise upright, all alert—and then he immediately resumed foraging. But he never knew I was there.

I never knew I was there, either. For that forty minutes last night I was as purely sensitive and mute as a photographic plate; I received impressions, but I did not print out captions. My own self-awareness had disappeared; it seems now almost as though, had I been wired with electrodes, my EEG would have been flat. I have done this sort of thing so often that I have lost self-consciousness about moving slowly and halting suddenly; it is second nature to me now. And I have often noticed that even a few minutes of this self-forgetfulness is tremendously invigorating. I wonder if we do not waste most of our energy just by spending every waking minute saying hello to ourselves. Martin Buber quotes an old Hasid master who said, "When you walk across the fields with your mind pure and holy, then from all the stones, and all growing things, and all animals, the sparks of their soul come out and cling to you, and then they are purified and become a holy fire in you." This is one way of describing the energy that comes, using the specialized cabalistic vocabulary of Hasidism.

I have tried to show muskrats to other people, but it rarely works. No matter how quiet we are, the muskrats stay hidden. Maybe they sense the tense hum of consciousness, the buzz from two human beings who in the silence cannot help but be aware of each other, and so of themselves. Then, too, the other people invariably suffer from a self-consciousness that prevents their stalking well. It used to bother me, too: I just could not bear to lose so much dignity that I would completely alter my whole way of being for a muskrat. So I would move or look around or scratch my nose, and no muskrats would show, leaving me alone with my dignity for days on end, until I decided that it was worth my while to learn—from the muskrats themselves—how to stalk.

The old, classic rule for stalking is, "Stop often 'n' set frequent." The rule cannot be improved upon, but muskrats will permit a little more. If a muskrat's eyes are out of sight, I can practically do a buck-and-wing on his tail, and he'll never notice. A few days ago I approached a muskrat feeding on a bank by the troll bridge simply by taking as many gliding steps toward him as possible while his head was turned. I spread my weight as evenly as I could, so that he wouldn't feel my coming through the ground, and so that no matter when I became visible to him, I could pause motionless until he turned away again without having to balance too awkwardly on one leg.

When I got within ten feet of him, I was sure he would flee, but he continued to browse nearsightedly among the mown clovers and grass. Since I had seen just about everything I was ever going to see, I continued approaching just to see when he would break. To my utter bafflement, he never broke. I broke first. When one of my feet was six inches from his back, I refused to press on. He could see me perfectly well, of course, but I was stock-still except when he lowered his head. There was nothing left to do but kick him. Finally he returned to the water, dove, and vanished. I do not know to this day if he would have permitted me to keep on walking right up his back.

It is not always so easy. Other times I have learned that the only way to approach a feeding muskrat for a good look is to commit myself to a procedure so ridiculous that only a total unselfconsciousness will permit me to live with myself. I have to ditch my hat, line up behind a low boulder, and lay on my belly to inch snake-fashion across twenty feet of bare field until I am behind the boulder itself and able to hazard a slow peek around it. If my head moves from around the boulder when the muskrat's head happens to be turned, then all is well. I can be fixed into position and still by the time he looks around. But if he sees me move my head, then he dives into the water, and the whole belly-crawl routine was in vain. There is no way to tell ahead of time; I just have to chance it and see.

I have read that in the unlikely event that you are caught in a stare-down with a grizzly bear, the best thing to do is talk to him softly and pleasantly. Your voice is supposed to have a soothing effect. I have not yet had occasion to test this out on grizzly bears, but I can attest that it does not work on muskrats. It scares them witless. I have tried time and again. Once I watched a muskrat feeding on a bank ten feet away from me;

after I had looked my fill I had nothing to lose, so I offered a convivial greeting. Boom. The terrified muskrat flipped a hundred and eighty degrees in the air, nose-dived into the grass at his feet, and disappeared. The earth swallowed him; his tail shot straight up in the air and then vanished into the ground without a sound. Muskrats make several emergency escape holes along a bank for this very purpose, and they don't like to feed too far away from them. The entire event was most impressive, and illustrates the relative power in nature of the word and the sneak.

Stalking is a pure form of skill, like pitching or playing chess. Rarely is luck involved. I do it right or I do it wrong; the muskrat will tell me, and that right early. Even more than baseball, stalking is a game played in the actual present. At every second, the muskrat comes, or stays, or goes, depending on my skill.

Can I stay still? How still? It is astonishing how many people cannot, or will not, hold still. I could not, or would not, hold still for thirty minutes inside, but at the creek I slow down, center down, empty. I am not excited; my breathing is slow and regular. In my brain I am not saying, Muskrat! Muskrat! There! I am saying nothing. If I must hold a position, I do not "freeze." If I freeze, locking my muscles, I will tire and break. Instead of going rigid, I go calm. I center down wherever I am; I find a balance and repose. I retreat—not inside myself, but outside myself, so that I am a tissue of senses. Whatever I see is plenty, abundance. I am the skin of water the wind plays over; I am petal, feather, stone.

Living this way by the creek, where the light appears and vanishes on the water, where muskrats surface and dive, and redwings scatter, I have come to know a special side of nature. I look to the mountains, and the mountains still slumber, blue and mute and rapt. I say, It gathers; the world abides. But I look to the creek, and I say, It scatters, it comes and goes. When I leave the house the sparrows flee and hush; on the banks of the creek jays scream in alarm, squirrels race for cover, tadpoles dive, frogs leap, snakes freeze, warblers vanish. Why do they hide? I will not hurt them. They simply do not want to be seen. "Nature," said Heraclitus, "is wont to hide herself." A fleeing mockingbird unfurls for a second a dazzling array of white fans . . . and disappears in the leaves. Shane! . . . Shane! Nature flashes the old mighty glance—the come-hither look—drops the handkerchief, turns tail, and is gone. The nature I know is old touch-and-go.

I wonder whether what I see and seem to understand about nature is merely one of the accidents of freedom, repeated by chance before my eyes, or whether it has any counterpart in the worlds beyond Tinker Creek. I find in quantum mechanics a world symbolically similar to my world at the creek.

Many of us are still living in the universe of Newtonian physics, and fondly imagine that real, hard scientists have no use for these misty ramblings, dealing as scientists do with the measurable and known. We think that at least the physical causes of physical events are perfectly knowable, and that, as the results of various experiments keep coming in, we gradually roll back the cloud of unknowing. We remove the veils one by one, painstakingly, adding knowledge to knowledge and whisking away veil after veil, until at last we reveal the nub of things, the sparkling equation from whom all blessings flow. Even wildman Emerson accepted the truly pathetic fallacy of the old science when he wrote grudgingly toward the end of his life, "When the microscope is improved, we shall have the cells analysed, and all will be electricity, or somewhat else." All we need to do is perfect our instruments and our methods, and we can collect enough data like birds on a string to predict physical events from physical causes.

But in 1927 Werner Heisenberg pulled out the rug, and our whole understanding of the universe toppled and collapsed. For some reason it has not yet trickled down to the man on the street that some physicists now are a bunch of wild-eyed, raving mystics. For they have perfected their instruments and methods just enough to whisk away the crucial veil, and what stands revealed is the Cheshire cat's grin.

The Principle of Indeterminacy, which saw the light in the summer of 1927, says in effect that you cannot know both a particle's velocity and its position. You can guess statistically what any batch of electrons might do, but you cannot predict the career of any one particle. They seem to be as free as dragonflies. You can perfect your instruments and your methods till the cows come home, and you will never ever be able to measure this one basic thing. It cannot be done. The electron is a muskrat; it cannot be perfectly stalked. And nature is a fan dancer born with a fan; you can wrestle her down, throw her on the stage and grapple with her for the fan with all your might, but it will never quit her grip. She comes that way; the fan is attached.

It is not that we lack sufficient information to know both a particle's velocity and its position; that would have been a perfectly ordinary situation well within the understanding of classical physics. Rather, we know now for sure that there is no knowing. You can determine the position, and your figure for the velocity blurs into vagueness; or you can determine the velocity, but whoops, there goes the position. The use of instruments and the very fact of an observer seem to bollix the observations; as a consequence, physicists are saying that they cannot study nature per se, but can study only their own investigation of nature. And I can see bluegills only within my own blue shadow, from which they immediately flee.

The Principle of Indeterminacy turned science inside out. Suddenly determinism goes, causality goes, and we are left with a universe composed of what Eddington calls "mind-stuff." Listen to these physicists: Sir James Jeans, Eddington's successor, invokes "fate," saying that the future "may rest on the knees of whatever gods there be." Eddington says that "the physical world is entirely abstract and without 'actuality' apart from its linkage to consciousness." Heisenberg himself says: "method and object can no longer be separated. *The scientific world-view has ceased to be a scientific view in the true sense of the word.*" Jeans says that science can no longer remain opposed to the notion of free will. Heisenberg says: "there is a higher power, not influenced by our wishes, which finally decides and judges." Eddington says that our dropping causality as a result of the Principle of Indeterminacy "leaves us with no clear distinction between the Natural and the Supernatural." And so forth.

These physicists are once again mystics, as Kepler was, standing on a rarefied mountain pass, gazing transfixed into an abyss of freedom. And they got there by the experimental method and a few wild leaps such as Einstein made. What a pretty pass!

All this means is that the physical world as we understand it now is more like the touch-and-go creek world I see than it is like the abiding world of which the mountains seem to speak. The physicists' particles whiz and shift like rotifers in and out of my microscope's field, and that this valley's ring of granite mountains is an airy haze of those same particles I must believe. The whole universe is a swarm of those wild, wary energies, the sun that glistens from the wet hairs on a muskrat's back and the stars that the mountains obscure on the horizon but which catch from on high in Tinker Creek. It is all touch and go. The heron flaps away; the dragonfly departs at thirty miles an hour; the water strider vanishes under a screen of grass; the muskrat dives, and the ripples roll from the bank, and flatten, and cease altogether.

Moses said to God, "I beseech thee, shew me thy glory." And God said, "Thou canst not see my face: for there shall no man see me, and live." But he added, "There is a place by me, and thou shalt stand upon a rock: and it shall come to pass, while my glory passeth by, that I will put thee in a clift of the rock, and will cover thee with my hand while I pass by: And I will take away mine hand, and thou shalt see my back parts: but my face shall not be seen." So Moses went up on Mount Sinai, waited still in a clift of the rock, and saw the back parts of God. Forty years later he went up on Mount Pisgah, and saw the promised land across the Jordan, which he was to die without ever being permitted to enter.

Just a glimpse, Moses: a clift in the rock here, a mountaintop there, and the rest is denial and longing. You have to stalk everything. Everything scatters and gathers; everything comes and goes like fish under a bridge. You have to stalk the spirit, too. You can wait forgetful anywhere, for anywhere is the way of his fleet passage, and hope to catch him by the tail and shout something in his ear before he wrests away. Or you can pursue him wherever you dare, risking the shrunken sinew in the hollow of the thigh; you can bang at the door all night till the innkeeper relents, if he ever relents; and you can wail till you're hoarse or worse the cry for incarnation always in John Knoepfle's poem: "and christ is red rover ... and the children are calling/come over come over." I sit on a bridge as on Pisgah or Sinai, and I am both waiting becalmed in a clift of the rock and banging with all my will, calling like a child beating on a door: come on out! ... I know you're there.

And then occasionally the mountains part. The tree with the lights in it appears, the mockingbird falls, and time unfurls across space like an oriflamme. Now we rejoice. The news, after all, is not that muskrats are wary, but that they can be seen. The hem of the robe was a Nobel Prize to Heisenberg; he did not go home in disgust. I wait on the bridges and stalk along banks for those moments I cannot predict, when a wave begins to surge under the water, and ripples strengthen and pulse high across the creek and back again in a texture that throbs. It is like the surfacing of an impulse, like the materialization of fish, this rising, this coming to a head, like the ripening of nut meats still in their husks, ready to split open like buckeyes in a field, shining with newness. "Surely the Lord is in this place; and I knew it not." The fleeing shreds I see, the back parts, are a gift, an abundance. When Moses came down from the clift in Mount Sinai, the people were afraid of him: the very skin on his face shone.

Do the Eskimos' faces shine, too? I lie in bed alert: I am with the Eskimos on the tundra who are running after the click-footed caribou, running sleepless and dazed for days, running spread out in scraggling lines across the glacier-ground hummocks and reindeer moss, in sight of the ocean, under the long-shadowed pale sun, running silent all night long.

IN SEPTEMBER THE BIRDS WERE quiet. They were molting in the valley: the mockingbird in the spruce, the sparrow in the mock orange, the doves in the cedar by the creek. Everywhere I walked, the ground was littered with shed feathers, long, colorful primaries and shaftless white down. I garnered this weightless crop in pockets all month long and inserted the feathers one by one into the frame of a wall mirror. They're still there; I look in the mirror as though I'm wearing a ceremonial headdress, inside out.

In October the great restlessness came, the *Zugunruhe*, the restlessness of birds before migration. After a long, unseasonable hot spell, one morning dawned suddenly cold. The birds were excited, stammering new songs all day long. Titmice, which had hidden in the leafy shade of mountains all summer, perched on the gutter; chickadees staged a conventicle in the locusts, and a sparrow, acting very strange, hovered like a hummingbird inches above a roadside goldenrod.

I watched at the window; I watched at the creek. A new wind lifted the hair on my arms. The cold light was coming and going between oversize, careening clouds; patches of blue, like a ragged flock of protean birds, shifted and stretched, flapping and racing from one end of the sky to the other. Despite the wind, the air was moist; I smelled the rich vapor of loam around my face and wondered again why all that death—all those rotten leaves that one layer down are black sops roped in white webs of mold, all those millions of dead summer insects—didn't smell worse. When the wind quickened, a stranger, more subtle scent leaked from beyond the mountains, a disquieting fragrance of wet bark, salt marsh, and mud flat.

The creek's water was still warm from the hot spell. It bore floating tulip leaves as big as plates, and sinking tulip leaves downstream and out of sight. I watched the leaves fall on water, first on running water, and then on still. It was as different as visiting Cornwall, and visiting Corfu. But those winds and flickering lights and the mad cries of jays stirred me. I was wishing: Colder, colder than this, colder than anything, and let the year hurry down!

The day before, in a dry calm, all the summer's ants took wings and swarmed, shining at the front door, at the back door, all up and down the road. I tried in vain to induce them to light on my upraised arm. Now at the slow part of the creek I suddenly saw migrating goldfinches in flocks hurling themselves from willow to willow over the reeds. They ascended in a sudden puff and settled, spreading slowly, like a blanket shaken over a bed, till some impulse tossed them up again, twenty and thirty together in sprays, and they tilted their wings, veered, folded, and spattered down.

I followed the goldfinches downstream until the bank beside me rose to a cliff and blocked the light on the willows and water. Above the cliff rose the Adams' woods, and in the cliff nested—according not only to local observation but also to the testimony of the county agricultural agent—hundreds of the area's copperheads. This October restlessness was worse than any April's or May's. In the spring the wish to wander is partly composed of an unnamable irritation, born of long inactivity; in the fall the impulse is more pure, more inexplicable, and more urgent. I could use some danger, I suddenly thought, so I abruptly abandoned the creek to its banks and climbed the cliff. I wanted some height, and I wanted to see the woods.

The woods were as restless as birds.

I stood under tulips and ashes, maples, sourwood, sassafras, locusts, catalpas, and oaks. I let my eyes spread and unfix, screening out all that was not vertical motion, and I saw only leaves in the air—or rather, since my mind was also unfixed, vertical trails of yellow color patches falling from nowhere to nowhere. Mysterious streamers of color unrolled silently all about me, distant and near. Some color chips made the descent violently; they wrenched from side to side in a series of diminishing swings, as if willfully fighting the fall with all the tricks of keel and glide they could muster. Others spun straight down in tight, suicidal circles.

Tulips had cast their leaves on my path, flat and bright as doubloons. I passed under a sugar maple that stunned me by its elegant unselfconsciousness: it was as if a man on fire were to continue calmly sipping tea.

In the deepest part of the woods was a stand of ferns. I had just been reading in Donald Culross Peattie that the so-called seed of ferns was formerly thought to bestow the gift of invisibility on its bearer, and that Genghis Khan wore such a seed in his ring, "and by it understood the speech of birds." If I were invisible, might I also be small, so that I could be borne by winds, spreading my body like a sail, like a vaulted leaf, to anyplace at all? Mushrooms erupted through the forest mold, the fly amanita in various stages of thrust and spread, some big brown mushrooms rounded and smooth as loaves, and some eerie purple ones I'd never noticed before, the color of Portuguese men-of-war, murex, a deep-sea, pressurized color, as if the earth, heavy with trees and rocks, had pressed and leached all other hues away.

A squirrel suddenly appeared and, eyeing me over his shoulder, began eating a mushroom. Squirrels and box turtles are immune to the poison in mushrooms, so it is not safe to eat a mushroom just because squirrels eat it. This squirrel plucked the nibbled mushroom cap from its base and, holding it Ubangi-like in his mouth, raced up the trunk of an oak. Then I moved, and he went into his tail-furling threat. I can't imagine what predator this routine would frighten, or even slow. Or did he take me for another male squirrel? It was clear that, like a cat, he seemed always to present a large front. But he might have fooled me better by holding still and not letting me see what insubstantial stuff his tail was. He flattened his body against the tree trunk and stretched himself into the shape of a giant rectangle. By some trick his legs barely protuded at the corners, like a flying squirrel's. Then he made a wave run down his tail held low against the trunk, the same flicking wave, over and over, and he never took his eyes from mine. Next, frightened more—or emboldened?—he ran up to a limb, still mouthing his mushroom cap, and, crouching close to the trunk, presented a solid target, coiled. He bent his tail high and whipped it furiously, with repeated snaps, as if a piece of gluey tape were stuck to the tip.

When I left the squirrel to cache his mushroom in peace, I almost stepped on another squirrel, who was biting the base of his tail, his flank, and scratching his shoulder with a hind paw. A chipmunk was streaking around with the usual calamitous air. When he saw me he stood to investigate, tucking his front legs tightly against his breast, so that only his paws were visible, and he looked like a supplicant modestly holding his hat.

The woods were a rustle of affairs. Woolly bears, those orange-and-black-banded furry caterpillars of the Isabella moth, were on the move. They crossed my path in every direction; they would climb over my foot, my finger, urgently seeking shelter. If a skunk finds one, he rolls it over and over on the ground, very delicately, brushing off the long hairs before he eats it. There seemed to be a parade of walking sticks that day, too; I must have seen five or six of them, or the same one five or six times, which kept hitching a ride on my pants leg. One entomologist says that walking sticks, along with monarch butterflies, are able to feign death—although I don't know how you could determine if a walking stick was feigning death or twigginess. At any rate, the female walking stick is absolutely casual about her egg-laying, dribbling out her eggs "from wherever she happens to be, and they drop willy-nilly"—which I suppose might mean that my pants and I were suddenly in the walking-stick business.

I heard a clamor in the underbrush beside me, a rustle of an animal's approach. It sounded as though the animal was about the size of a bobcat, a small bear, or a large snake. The commotion stopped and started, coming ever nearer. The agent of all this ruckus proved to be, of course, a towhee.

The more I see of these bright birds—with black backs, white tail bars, and rufous patches on either side of their white breasts—the more I like them. They are not even faintly shy.

They are everywhere, in treetops and on the ground. Their song reminds me of a child's neighborhood rallying cry—ee-ockee—with a heartfelt warble at the end. But it is their call that is especially endearing. The towhee has the brass and grace to call, simply and clearly, "tweet." I know of no other bird that stoops to literal tweeting.

The towhee never saw me. It crossed the path and kicked its way back into the woods, cutting a wide swath in the leaf litter like a bulldozer and splashing the air with clods.

The bark of trees was cool to my palm. I saw a hairy woodpecker beating his skull on a pine, and a katydid dying on a stone.

I could go. I could simply angle off the path, take one step after another, and be on my way. I could walk to Point Barrow, Mount McKinley, Hudson's Bay. My summer jacket is put away; my winter jacket is warm.

In autumn the winding passage of ravens from the north heralds the great fall migration of caribou. The shaggy-necked birds spread their wing tips to the skin of convection currents rising, and hie them south. The great deer meet herd on herd in arctic and subarctic valleys, milling and massing and gathering force like a waterfall, till they pour across the barren grounds wide as a tidal wave. Their coats are new and fine. Their thin spring coats—which had been scraped off in great hunks by the southern forests and were riddled with blackfly and gadfly stings, warble and botfly maggots—are gone, and a lustrous new pelage has appeared, a luxurious brown fur backed by a plush layer of hollow hairs that insulate and waterproof. Four inches of creamy fat cover even their backs. A loose cartilage in their fetlocks makes their huge strides click, mile upon mile over the tundra south to the shelter of trees, and you can hear them before they've come and after they've gone, rumbling like rivers, ticking like clocks.

The Eskimos' major caribou hunt is in the fall, when the deer are fat and their hides thick. If some whim or weather shifts the northern caribou into another valley, some hidden, unexpected valley, then even to this day some inland Eskimo tribes may altogether starve.

Up on the Arctic Ocean coasts, Eskimos dry the late summer's fish on drying racks, to use throughout the winter as feed for dogs. The newly forming sea ice is elastic and flexible. It undulates without cracking as the roiling sea swells and subsides, and it bends and sags under the Eskimos' weight as they walk, spreading leviathan ripples out toward the horizon, so that they seem to be walking and bouncing on the fragile sheath of the world's balloon. During these autumn days Eskimo adults and children alike play at cat's cradle, a game they have always known. The intricate string patterns looped from their fingers were thought to "tangle the sun" and so "delay its disappearance." Later, when the sun sets for the winter, children will sled down any snowy slope, using as sleds frozen seal embryos pulled with thongs through the nose.

These northings drew me, present northings, past northings, the thought of northings. In the literature of Arctic exploration, the talk is of northing. An explorer might scrawl in his tattered journal, "Latitude 82° 15' N. We accomplished 20 miles of northing today, in spite of the shifting pack." Shall I go northing? My legs are long.

A skin-colored sandstone ledge beside me was stained with pokeberry juice, like an altar bloodied. The edges of the scarlet were dissolved, faded to lymph like small blood from a wound. As I looked, a maple leaf suddenly screeched across the rock, arched crabwise on its points, and a yellow-spotted dog appeared from no place, bearing in its jaws the leg of a deer. The hooves of the deer leg were pointed like a dancer's toes. I have felt dead deer legs; some local butchers keep them as weapons. They are greaseless and dry; I can feel the little bones. The dog was coming toward me on the path. I spoke to him and stepped aside; he loped past, looking neither to the right nor to the left.

In a final, higher part of the woods, some of the trees were black and gray, leafless, but wrapped in fresh green vines. The

path was a fairway of new gold leaves strewn at the edges with
bright vines and dotted with dark-green seedlings pushing up
through the leaf cover. One seedling spruce grew from a horse's
hoofmark deep in dried mud.

There was a little hollow in the woods, broad, like a flat
soup bowl, with grass on the ground. This was the forest pasture
of the white mare Itch. Water had collected in a small pool five
feet across, in which gold leaves floated, and the water reflected
the half-forgotten, cloud-whipped sky. To the right was a stand
of slender silver-barked tulip saplings with tall limbless trunks
leaning together, leafless. In the general litter and scramble of
these woods, the small grazed hollow looked very old, like the
site of druidical rites, or like a theatrical set, with the pool at
center stage, and the stand of silver saplings the audience in
thrall. There at the pool, lovers would meet in various guises,
and there Bottom in his ass's head would bleat at the reflection
of the moon.

I started home. And one more event occurred that day, one
more confrontation with restless life bearing past me.

I approached a long, slanting mown field near the house. A
flock of forty robins had commandeered the area, and I watched
them from a fringe of trees. I see robins in flocks only in the fall.
They were spaced evenly on the grass, ten yards apart. They
looked like a marching band with each member in place, but
facing in every direction. Distributed among them were the
fledglings from summer's last brood, young robins still mottled
on the breast, embarking on their first trip to unknown southern
fields. At any given moment as I watched, half of the robins
were on the move, sloping forward in a streamlined series of
hops.

I stepped into the field, and they all halted. They stopped
short, drew up, and looked at me, every one. I stopped, too,
suddenly as self-conscious as if I were before a firing squad.
What are you going to do? I looked over the field, at all those
cocked heads and black eyes. I'm staying here. You all go on.
I'm staying here.

*   *   *

A kind of northing is what I wish to accomplish, a single-minded trek toward that place where any shutter left open to the zenith at night will record the wheeling of all the sky's stars as a pattern of perfect, concentric circles. I seek a reduction, a shedding, a sloughing off.

At the seashore you often see a shell, or fragment of a shell, that sharp sands and surf have thinned to a wisp. There is no way you can tell what kind of shell it had been, what creature it had housed; it could have been a whelk or a scallop, a cowrie, limpet, or conch. The animal is long since dissolved, and its blood spread and thinned in the general sea. All you hold in your hand is a cool shred of shell, an inch long, pared so thin it passes a faint pink light, and almost as flexible as a straight razor. It is an essence, a smooth condensation of the air, a curve. I long for the north, where unimpeded winds would hone me to such a pure slip of bone. But I'll not go northing this year. I'll stalk that floating pole and frigid air by waiting here. I wait on bridges; I wait, struck, on forest paths and meadows' fringes, hilltops and banksides, day in and day out, and I receive a southing as a gift. The north washes down the mountains like a waterfall, like a tidal wave, and pours across the valley; it comes to me. It sweetens the persimmons and numbs the last of the crickets and hornets; it fans the flames of the forest maples, bows the meadow's seeded grasses, and pokes its chilling fingers under the leaf litter, thrusting the springtails and earthworms, the sowbugs and beetle grubs, deeper into the earth. The sun heaves to the south by day, and at night wild Orion emerges, looming like the specter of the Brocken over Dead Man Mountain. Something is already here, and more is coming.

A few days later the monarchs hit. I saw one, and then another, and then others all day long, before I consciously understood that I was witnessing a migration, and it wasn't until another two weeks had passed that I realized the enormousness of what I had seen.

Each of these butterflies, the fruit of two or three broods of this summer, had hatched successfully from one of those emerald cases that Teale's caterpillar had been about to form when the parasitic larvae snapped it limp, eating their way out of its side. They had hatched, many of them, just before a thunderstorm, when winds lifted the silver leaves of trees, and birds sought the shelter of shrubbery, uttering cries. They were butterflies, going south to the Gulf states or farther, and some of them had come from Hudson's Bay.

Monarchs were everywhere. They skittered and bobbed, rested in the air, lolled on the dust—but with none of their usual insouciance. They had but one unwearying thought: South. I watched from my study window: three, four . . . eighteen, nineteen, one every few seconds, and some in tandem. They came fanning straight toward my window from the northwest, and from the northeast, materializing from behind the tips of high hemlocks, where Polaris hangs by night. They appeared as Indian horsemen appear in movies: first dotted, then massed, silent, at the rim of a hill.

Each monarch butterfly had a brittle black body and deep-orange wings limned and looped in black bands. A monarch at rest looks like a fleck of tiger, stilled and wide-eyed. A monarch in flight looks like an autumn leaf with a will, vitalized and cast upon the air, from which it seems to suck some thin sugar of energy, some leaflike drop or sap. As each one climbed up the air outside my window, I could see the more delicate, ventral surfaces of its wings, and I had a sense of bunched legs and straining thorax, but I could never focus well into the flapping and jerking before it vaulted up past the window and out of sight over my head.

I walked out and saw a monarch do a wonderful thing: it climbed a hill without twitching a muscle. I was standing at the bridge over Tinker Creek, at the southern foot of a very steep hill. The monarch beat its way beside me over the bridge at eye level, and then, flailing its wings exhaustedly, ascended straight up in the air. It rose vertically to the enormous height of a bank-side sycamore's crown. Then, fixing its wings at a precise angle, it glided *up* the steep road, losing altitude extremely slowly, climbing by checking its fall, until it came to rest at a puddle in front of the house at the top of the hill.

I followed. It panted, skirmished briefly westward, and

then, returning to the puddle, began its assault on the house. It struggled almost straight up the air next to the two-story brick wall, and then scaled the roof. Wasting no effort, it followed the roof's own slope, from a distance of two inches. Puff, and it was out of sight. I wondered how many more hills and houses it would have to climb before it could rest. From the force of its will it would seem it could flutter through walls.

Monarchs are "tough and powerful, as butterflies go." They fly over Lake Superior without resting; in fact, observers there have discovered a curious thing. Instead of flying directly south, the monarchs crossing high over the water take an inexplicable turn toward the east. Then when they reach an invisible point, they all veer south again. Each successive swarm repeats this mysterious dogleg movement, year after year. Entomologists actually think that the butterflies might be "remembering" the position of a long-gone, looming glacier. In another book I read that geologists think that Lake Superior marks the site of the highest mountain that ever existed on this continent. I don't know. I'd like to see it. Or I'd like to be it, to feel when to turn. At night on land migrating monarchs slumber on certain trees, hung in festoons with wings folded together, thick on the trees and shaggy as bearskin.

Monarchs have always been assumed to taste terribly bitter, because of the acrid milkweed on which the caterpillars feed. You always run into monarchs and viceroys when you read about mimicry: viceroys look enough like monarchs that keen-eyed birds who have tasted monarchs once will avoid the viceroys as well. New studies indicate that milkweed-fed monarchs are not so much evil-tasting as literally nauseating, since milkweed contains "heart poisons similar to digitalis," which make the bird ill. Personally, I like an experiment performed by an entomologist with real spirit. He had heard all his life, as I have, that monarchs taste unforgettably bitter, so he tried some. "To conduct what was in fact a field experiment the doctor first went South, and he ate a number of monarchs in the field. . . . The monarch butterfly, Dr. Urquhart learned, has no more flavor than dried toast." Dried toast? It was hard for me, throughout the monarch migration, in the middle of all that beauty and real splendor, to fight down the thought that what I was really seeing in the air was a vast and fluttering tea tray for shut-ins.

It is easy to coax a dying or exhausted butterfly onto your finger. I saw a monarch walking across a gas station lot; it was walking south. I placed my index finger in its path, and it clambered aboard and let me lift it to my face. Its wings were faded but unmarked by hazard; a veneer of velvet caught the light and hinted at the frailest depth of lapped scales. It was a male; his legs clutching my finger were short and atrophied; they clasped my finger with a spread fragility, a fineness as of some low note of emotion or pure strain of spirit, scarcely perceived. And I knew that those feet were actually tasting me, sipping with sensitive organs the vapor of my finger's skin: butterflies taste with their feet. All the time he held me, he opened and closed his glorious wings, senselessly, as if sighing.

The closing of his wings fanned an almost imperceptible redolence at my face, and I leaned closer. I could barely scent a sweetness, I could almost name it . . . fireflies, sparkles—honeysuckle. He smelled like honeysuckle; I couldn't believe it. I knew that many male butterflies exuded distinctive odors from special scent glands, but I thought that only laboratory instruments could detect those odors, compounded of many, many butterflies. I had read a list of the improbable scents of butterflies: sandalwood, chocolate, heliotrope, sweet pea. Now this live creature here on my finger had an odor that even I could sense—this flap actually smelled, this chip that took its temperature from the air like any envelope or hammer, this programmed wisp of spread horn. And he smelled of honeysuckle. Why not caribou hoof or Labrador tea, tundra lichen or dwarf willow, the brine of Hudson's Bay or the vapor of rivers milky with fine-ground glacial silt? This honeysuckle was an odor already only half remembered, a breath of the summer past, the Lucas cliffs and overgrown fence by Tinker Creek, a drugged sweetness that had almost cloyed on those moisture-laden nights, now refined to a wary trickle in the air, a distillation pure and rare, scarcely known and mostly lost, and heading south.

I walked him across the gas station lot and lowered him into a field. He took to the air, pulsing and gliding; he lighted on sassafras, and I lost him.

For weeks I found paired monarch wings, bodiless, on the grass or on the road. I collected one such wing and freed it of its scales; first I rubbed it between my fingers, and then I stroked it gently with the tip of an infant's silver spoon. What I had at the end of this delicate labor is lying here on this study desk: a kind of resilient scaffolding, like the webbing over a hot-air balloon, black veins stretching the merest something across the nothingness it plies. The integument itself is perfectly transparent; through it I can read the smallest print. It is as thin as the skin peeled from sunburn, and as tough as a parchment of flensed buffalo hide. The butterflies that were eaten here in the valley, leaving us their wings, were, however, few: most lived to follow the valley south.

The migration lasted in full force for five days. For those five days I was inundated, drained. The air was alive and unwinding. Time itself was a scroll unraveled, curved and still quivering on a table or altar stone. The monarchs clattered in the air, burnished like throngs of pennies—here's one, and here's one, and more, and more. They flapped and floundered; they thrust, splitting the air like the keels of canoes, quickened and fleet. It looked as though the leaves of the autumn forest had taken flight, and were pouring down the valley like a waterfall, like a tidal wave, all the leaves of hardwoods from here to Hudson's Bay. It was as if the season's color were draining away like lifeblood, as if the year were molting and shedding. The year was rolling down, and a vital curve had been reached, the tilt that gives way to headlong rush. And when the monarchs had passed and were gone, the skies were vacant, the air poised. The dark night into which the year was plunging was not a sleep but an awakening, a new and necessary austerity, the sparer climate for which I longed. The shed trees were brittle and still, the creek light and cold, and my spirit holding its breath.

Before the aurora borealis appears, the sensitive needles of compasses all over the world are restless for hours, agitating on their pins in airplanes and ships, trembling in desk drawers, in attics, in boxes on shelves.

I had a curious dream last night that stirred me. I visited the house of my childhood, and the basement there was covered with a fine sifting of snow. I lifted a snow-covered rug and found underneath it a bound sheaf of ink drawings I had made when I was six. Next to the basement, but unattached to it, extended a prayer tunnel.

The prayer tunnel was a tunnel fully enclosed by solid snow. It was cylindrical, and its diameter was the height of a man. Only an Eskimo, and then only very rarely, could survive in the prayer tunnel. There was, however, no exit or entrance; but I nevertheless understood that if I—if almost anyone—volunteered to enter it, death would follow after a long and bitter struggle. Inside the tunnel it was killingly cold, and a hollow wind like broadswords never ceased to blow. But there was little breathable air, and that soon gone. It was utterly without light, and from all eternity it snowed the same fine, unmelting, wind-hurled snow.

I have been reading the apophthegmata, the sayings of fourth- and fifth-century Egyptian desert hermits. Abba Moses said to a disciple, "Go and sit in your cell, and your cell will teach you everything."

A few weeks before the monarch migration I visited Carvin's Cove, a reservoir in a gap between Tinker and Brushy mountains, and there beside the forest path I saw, it occurs to me now, Abba Moses, in the form of an acorn. The acorn was screwing itself into the soil. From a raw split in its husk burst a long white root that plunged like an arrow into the earth. The acorn itself was loose, but the root was fixed: I thought if I could lift the acorn and stand, I would heave the world. Beside the root erupted a greening shoot, and from the shoot spread two furred, serrated leaves, tiny leaves of chestnut oak, the size of two intricate grains of rice. That acorn was pressured, blown, driven down with force and up with furl, making at once a power dive to grit and *grand jeté en l'air.*

Since then the killing frost has struck. If I got lost now on the mountains or in the valley, and acted foolishly, I would be dead of hypothermia and my brain wiped smooth as a plate long before the water in my flesh elongated to crystal slivers that would pierce and shatter the walls of my cells. The harvest is in, the granaries full. The broadleaf trees of the world's forests have cast their various fruits: "Oak, a nut; Sycamore, achenes; California Laurel, a drupe; Maple, a samara; Locust, a legume; Pomegranate, a berry; Buckeye, a capsule; Apple, a pome." Now the twin leaves of the seedling chestnut oak on the Carvin's Cove path have dried, dropped, and blown; the acorn itself is shrunk and sere. But the sheath of the stem holds water and the white root still delicately sucks, porous and permeable, mute. The death of the self of which the great writers speak is no violent act. It is merely the joining of the great rock heart of the earth in its roll. It is merely the slow cessation of the will's sprints and the intellect's chatter: it is waiting like a hollow bell with stilled tongue. *Fuge, tace, quiesce.* The waiting itself is the thing.

Last year I saw three migrating Canada geese flying low over the frozen duck pond where I stood. I heard a heart-stopping blast of speed before I saw them; I felt the flayed air slap at my face. They thundered across the pond, and back, and back again: I swear I have never seen such speed, such single-mindedness, such flailing of wings. They froze the duck pond as they flew; they rang the air; they disappeared. I think of this now, and my brain vibrates to the blurred bastinado of feathered bone. "Our God shall come," it says in a psalm for Advent, "and shall not keep silence; there shall go before him a consuming fire, and a mighty tempest shall be stirred up round about him." It is the shock I remember. Not only does something come if you wait, but it pours over you like a waterfall, like a tidal wave. You wait in all naturalness without expectation or hope, emptied, translucent, and that which comes rocks and topples you; it will shear, loose, launch, winnow, grind.

I have glutted on richness and welcome hyssop. This distant silver November sky, these sere branches of trees, shed and bearing their pure and secret colors—this is the real world, not the world gilded and pearled. I stand under wiped skies directly, naked, without intercessors. Frost winds have lofted my body's bones with all their restless sprints to an airborne raven's glide. I am buoyed by a calm and effortless longing, an angled pitch of the will, like the set of the wings of the monarch that climbed a hill by falling still.

There is the wave breast of thanksgiving—a catching God's eye with the easy motions of praise—and a time for it. In ancient Israel's rites for a voluntary offering of thanksgiving, the priest comes before the altar in clean linen, empty-handed. Into his hands is placed the breast of the slain unblemished ram of consecration: and he waves it as a wave offering before the Lord. The wind's knife has done its work. Thanks be to God.

They will question thee concerning what they should expend. Say:
"The abundance."

—THE KORAN

"FAIR WEATHER COMETH OUT OF the north: with God is terrible majesty."

Today is the winter solstice. The planet tilts just so to its star, lists and holds circling in a fixed tension between veering and longing, and spins helpless, exalted, in and out of that fleet blazing touch. Last night Orion vaulted and spread all over the sky, pagan and lunatic, his shoulder and knee on fire, his sword three suns at the ready—for what?

And today was fair, hot, even; I woke and my fingers were hot and dry to their own touch, like the skin of a stranger. I stood at the window, the bay window on which one summer a waxen-looking grasshopper had breathed puff puff, and thought: I won't see this year again, not again so innocent; and longing wrapped round my throat like a scarf. "For the Heavenly Father desires that we should see," said Ruysbroeck, "and that is why He is ever saying to our inmost spirit one deep unfathomable word and nothing else." But what is that word? Is this mystery or coyness? A cast-iron bell hung from the arch of my rib cage; when I stirred it rang, or it tolled, a long syllable pulsing ripples up my lungs and down the gritty sap inside my bones, and I couldn't make it out; I felt the voiced vowel like a sigh or a note but I couldn't catch the consonant that shaped it into sense. I wrenched myself from the window. I stepped outside.

Here by the mock-orange hedge was a bee, a honeybee, sprung from its hive by the heat. Instantly I had a wonderful idea. I had recently read that ancient Romans thought bees were killed by echoes. It seemed a far-fetched and pleasing notion, that a spoken word or falling rock given back by cliffs— that airy nothing which nevertheless bore and spread the uncomprehended impact of something—should stun these sturdy creatures right out of the air. I could put it to the test. It was as good an excuse for a walk as any; it might still the bell, even, or temper it true.

I knew where I could find an echo; I'd have to take my chances on finding another December bee. I tied a sweater around my waist and headed for the quarry. The experiment didn't pan out, exactly, but the trip led on to other excursions and vigils up and down the landscape of this brief year's end day.

It was hot; I never needed the sweater. A great tall cloud moved elegantly across an invisible walkway in the upper air, sliding on its flat foot like an enormous proud snail. I smelled silt on the wind, turkey, laundry, leaves . . . my God, what a world. There is no accounting for one second of it. On the quarry path through the woods I saw again the discarded aquarium; now, almost a year later, still only one side of the aquarium's glass was shattered. I could plant a terrarium here, I thought; I could transfer the two square feet of forest floor *under* the glass to *above* the glass, framing it, hiding a penny, and saying to passersby: Look! look! here is two square feet of the world.

I waited for an hour at the quarry, roving, my eyes filtering the air for flecks, until at last I discovered a bee. It was wandering listlessly among dried weeds on the stony bank where I had sat months before and watched a mosquito pierce and suck a copperhead on a rock; beyond the bank, fingers of ice touched the green quarry pond in the shade of the sheared bare cliffs beyond. The setup was perfect. Hello! I tried tentatively: Hello! faltered the cliffs under the forest; and did the root tips quiver in the rock? But that is no way to kill a creature, saying hello. Good-bye! I shouted; Good-bye! came back, and the bee drifted unconcerned among the weeds.

It could be, I reasoned, that ancient Roman naturalists knew this fact that has escaped us because it works only in Latin. My Latin is sketchy. *Habeas corpus!* I cried; *Deus Absconditus! Veni!* And the rock cliff batted it back: *Veni!* and the bee droned on.

That was that. It was almost noon; the tall cloud was gone. To West Virginia, where it snubbed on a high ridge, snared by trees, and sifted in shards over the side? I watched the bee as long as I could, catching it with my eyes and losing it, until it rose suddenly in the air like a lost balloon and vanished into the forest. I stood alone. I still seemed to hear the unaccustomed sound of my own voice honed to a quaver by rock, thrown back down my throat and cast dying around me, lorn: Could that have been heard at Hollins Pond, or behind me, across the creek, up the hill the starlings fly over? Was anybody there to hear? I felt again the bell resounding faint under my ribs. I'm coming, when I can. I quit the quarry, my spurt of exuberance drained, my spirit edgy and taut.

The quarry path parallels Tinker Creek far upstream from my house, and when the woods broke into clearing and pasture, I followed the creek banks down. When I drew near the tear-shaped island, which I had never before approached from this side of the creek, a fence barred my way, a feeble wire horse fence that wobbled across the creek and served me as a sagging bridge to the island. I stood, panting, breathing the frail scent of fresh water and feeling the sun heat my hair.

The December grass on the island was blanched and sere, pale against the dusty boles of sycamores, noisy underfoot. Behind me, the way I had come, rose the pasture belonging to Twilight, a horse of a perpetually different color whose name was originally Midnight, and who one spring startled the neighborhood by becoming brown. Far before me Tinker Mountain glinted and pitched in the sunlight. The Lucas orchard spanned the middle distance, its wan peach limbs swept and poised just so, row upon row, like a stageful of thin innocent dancers who will never be asked to perform; below the orchard rolled the steers' pasture yielding to floodplain fields and finally the sycamore-log bridge to the island, where in horror I had watched a green frog sucked to a skin and sunk. A fugitive, empty sky vaulted overhead, apparently receding from me the harder I searched its dome for a measure of distance.

Downstream at the island's tip, where the giant water bug clasped and ate the living frog, I sat and sucked at my own dry knuckles. It was the way that frog's eyes crumpled. His mouth was a gash of terror; the shining skin of his breast and shoulder shivered once and sagged, reduced to an empty purse; but oh, those two snuffed eyes! They crinkled, the comprehension poured out of them as if sense and life had been a mere incidental addition to the idea of eyes, a filling like any jam in a jar that is soon and easily emptied; they flattened, lightless, opaque, and sank. Did the giant water bug have the frog by the back parts, or by the hollow of the thigh? Would I eat a frog's leg if offered? Yes.

In addition to the wave breast of thanksgiving, in which the wave breast is waved before the Lord, there is another voluntary offering, performed at the same time. In addition to the wave breast of thanksgiving, there is the heave shoulder. The wave breast is waved before the altar of the Lord; the heave shoulder is heaved. What I want to know is this: Does the priest heave it *at* the Lord? Does he *throw* the shoulder of the ram of consecration—a ram that, before the priest slew and chunked it, had been perfect and whole, not "Blind, or broken, or maimed, or having a wen, or scurvy, or scabbed . . . bruised, or crushed, or broken, or cut"—does he hurl it across the tabernacle, between the bloodied horns of the altar, at God? Now look what you made me do. And then he eats it. This heave is a violent, desperate way of catching God's eye. It is not inappropriate. We are people; we are permitted to have dealings with the creator and we must speak up for the creation. God *look* at what you've done to this creature, look at the sorrow, the cruelty, the long damned waste! Can it possibly, ludicrously, be for *this* that on this unconscious planet with my innocent kind I play softball all spring, to develop my throwing arm? How high, how far, could I heave a little shred of frog shoulder at the Lord? How high, how far, how long until I die?

*   *   *

I fingered the winter-killed grass, looping it round the tip of my finger like hair, ruffling its tips with my palms. Another year has twined away, unrolled and dropped across nowhere like a flung banner painted in gibberish. "The last act is bloody, however brave be all the rest of the play; at the end they throw a little earth upon your head, and it's all over forever." Somewhere, everywhere, there is a gap, like the shuddering chasm of Shadow Creek, which gapes open at my feet, like a sudden split in the window or hull of a high-altitude jet, into which things slip, or are blown, out of sight, vanished in a rush, blasted, gone, and can no more be found. For the living there is rending loss at each opening of the eye, each *Augenblick*, as a muskrat dives, a heron takes alarm, a leaf floats spinning away. There is death in the pot for the living's food, flyblown meat, muddy salt, and plucked herbs bitter as squill. If you can get it. How many people have prayed for their daily bread and famished? They die their daily death as utterly as did the frog, *people*, played with, dabbled upon, when God knows they loved their life. In a winter famine, desperate Algonquian Indians "ate broth made of smoke, snow, and buckskin, and the rash of pellagra appeared like tattooed flowers on their emaciated bodies—the roses of starvation, in a French physician's description; and those who starved died covered with roses." Is this beauty, these gratuitous roses, or a mere display of force?

Or is beauty itself an intricately fashioned lure, the cruelest hoax of all? There is a certain fragment of an ancient and involved Eskimo tale I read in Farley Mowat that for years has risen, unbidden, in my mind. The fragment is a short scenario, observing all the classical unities, simple and cruel, and performed by the light of a soapstone seal-oil lamp.

A young man in a strange land falls in love with a young woman and takes her to wife in her mother's tent. By day the women chew skins and boil meat while the young man hunts. But the old crone is jealous; she wants the boy. Calling her daughter to her one day, she offers to braid her hair; the girl sits pleased, proud, and soon is strangled by her own hair. One thing Eskimos know is skinning. The mother takes her curved hand knife shaped like a dancing skirt, skins her daughter's beautiful face, and presses that empty flap smooth on her own skull. When the boy returns that night he lies with her, in the tent on top of the world. But he is wet from hunting; the skin mask shrinks and slides, uncovering the shriveled face of the old mother, and the boy flees in horror, forever.

Could it be that if I climbed the dome of heaven and scrabbled and clutched at the beautiful cloth till I loaded my fists with a wrinkle to pull, the mask would rip away to reveal a toothless old ugly, eyes glazed with delight?

A wind rose, quickening; it seemed at the same instant to invade my nostrils and vibrate my gut. I stirred and lifted my head. No, I've gone through this a million times: beauty is not a hoax—how many days have I learned not to stare at the back of my hand when I could look out at the creek? Come on, I say to the creek, surprise me; and it does, with each new drop. Beauty is real. I would never deny it; the appalling thing is that I forget it. Waste and extravagance go together up and down the banks, all along the intricate fringe of spirit's free incursions into time. On either side of me the creek snared and kept the sky's distant lights, shaped them into shifting substance and bore them speckled down.

This Tinker Creek! It was low today, and clear. On the still side of the island the water held pellucid as a pane, a gloss on runes of sandstone, shale, and snail-inscribed clay silt; on the faster side it hosted a blinding profusion of curved and pitched surfaces, flecks of shadow and tatters of sky. These are the waters of beauty and mystery, issuing from a gap in the granite world; they fill the lodes in my cells with a light like petaled water, and they churn in my lungs mighty and frigid, like a big ship's screw. And these are also the waters of separation: they purify, acrid and laving, and they cut me off. I am spattered with a sop of ashes, burned bone knobs, and blood; I range wild-eyed, flying over fields and plundering the woods, no longer quite fit for company.

Bear with me one last time. In the old Hebrew ordinance for the waters of separation, the priest must find a red heifer, a red heifer unblemished, which has never known the yoke, and lead her outside the people's camp, and sacrifice her, burn her wholly, without looking away: "burn the heifer in his sight; her skin, and her flesh, and her blood, with her dung, shall he burn." Into the stinking flame the priest casts the wood of a cedar tree for longevity, hyssop for purgation, and a scarlet thread for a vein of living blood. It is from these innocent ashes that the waters of separation are made, anew each time, by steeping them in a vessel with fresh running water. This special water purifies. A man—any man—dips a sprig of hyssop into the vessel and sprinkles—merely sprinkles!—the water upon the unclean, "upon him that touched a bone, or one slain, or one dead." So. But I never signed up for this role. The bone touched me.

I stood, alone, and the world swayed. I am a fugitive and a vagabond, a sojourner seeking signs. Isak Dinesen in Kenya, her heart utterly broken by loss, stepped out of the house at sunrise, seeking a sign. She saw a rooster lunge and rip a chameleon's tongue from its root in the throat and gobble it down. And then Isak Dinesen had to pick up a stone and smash the chameleon. But I had seen that sign, more times than I had ever sought it; today I saw an inspiriting thing, a pretty thing, really, and small.

I was standing lost, sunk, my hands in my pockets, gazing toward Tinker Mountain and feeling the earth reel down. All at once I saw what looked like a Martian spaceship whirling toward me in the air. It flashed borrowed light like a propeller. Its forward motion greatly outran its fall. As I watched, transfixed, it rose, just before it would have touched a thistle, and hovered pirouetting in one spot, then twirled on and finally came to rest. I found it in the grass; it was a maple key, a single winged seed from a pair. Hullo. I threw it into the wind and it flew off again, bristling with animate purpose, not like a thing dropped or windblown, pushed by the witless winds of convection currents hauling round the world's rondure where they must, but like a creature muscled and vigorous, or a creature spread thin to that other wind, the wind of the spirit which bloweth where it listeth, lighting, and raising up, and easing down. O maple key, I thought, I must confess I thought, oh, welcome, cheers.

And the bell under my ribs rang a true note, a flourish as of blended horns, clarion, sweet, and making a long, dim sense I will try at length to explain. Flung is too harsh a word for the rush of the world. Blown is more like it, but blown by a generous, unending breath. That breath never ceases to kindle, exuberant, abandoned; frayed splinters spatter in every direction and burgeon into flame. And now when I sway to a fitful wind, alone and listing, I will think, maple key. When I see a photograph of earth from space, the planet so startlingly painterly and hung, I will think, maple key. When I shake your hand or meet your eyes I will think, two maple keys. If I am a maple key falling, at least I can twirl.

Thomas Merton wrote, "There is always a temptation to diddle around in the contemplative life, making itsy-bitsy statues." There is always an enormous temptation in all of life to diddle around making itsy-bitsy friends and meals and journeys for itsy-bitsy years on end. It is so self-conscious, so apparently moral, simply to step aside from the gaps where the creeks and winds pour down, saying, I never merited this grace, quite rightly, and then to sulk along the rest of your days on the edge of rage. I won't have it. The world is wilder than that in all directions, more dangerous and bitter, more extravagant and bright. We are making hay when we should be making whoopee; we are raising tomatoes when we should be raising Cain, or Lazarus.

Ezekiel excoriates false prophets as those who have "not gone up into the gaps." The gaps are the thing. The gaps are the spirit's one home, the altitudes and latitudes so dazzlingly spare and clean that the spirit can discover itself for the first time like a once-blind man unbound. The gaps are the clifts in the rock where you cower to see the back parts of God; they are the fissures between mountains and cells the wind lances through, the icy narrowing fjords splitting the cliffs of mystery. Go up into the gaps. If you can find them; they shift and vanish too. Stalk the gaps. Squeak into a gap in the soil, turn, and unlock—more than a maple—a universe. This is how you spend this afternoon, and tomorrow morning, and tomorrow afternoon. *Spend* the afternoon. You can't take it with you.

*   *   *

I live in tranquillity and trembling. Sometimes I dream. I am interested in Alice mainly when she eats the cookie that makes her smaller. I would pare myself or be pared that I, too, might pass through the merest crack, a gap I know is there in the sky. I am looking just now for the cookie. Sometimes I open, pried like a fruit. Or I am porous as old bone, or translucent, a tinted condensation of the air like a water color wash, and I gaze around me in bewilderment, fancying I cast no shadow. Sometimes I ride a bucking faith while one hand grips and the other flails the air, and like any daredevil I gouge with my heels for blood, for a wilder ride, for more.

There is not a guarantee in the world. Oh, your *needs* are guaranteed, your needs are absolutely guaranteed by the most stringent of warranties, in the plainest, truest words: knock; seek; ask. But you must read the fine print. "Not as the world giveth, give I unto you." That's the catch. If you can catch it, it will catch you up, aloft, up to any gap at all, and you'll come back, for you will come back, transformed in a way you may not have bargained for—dribbling and crazed. The waters of separation, however lightly sprinkled, leave indelible stains. Did you think, before you were caught, that you needed, say, life? Do you think you will keep your life, or anything else you love? But no. Your needs are all met. But not as the world giveth. You see the needs of your own spirit met whenever you have asked, and you have learned that the outrageous guarantee holds. You see the creatures die, and you know you will die, And one day it occurs to you that you must not need life. Obviously. And then you're gone. You have finally understood that you're dealing with a maniac.

I think that the dying pray at the last not "please" but "thank you," as a guest thanks his host at the door. Falling from airplanes, the people are crying thank you, thank you, all down the air; and the cold carriages draw up for them on the rocks. Divinity is not playful. The universe was not made in jest but in solemn incomprehensible earnest. By a power that is unfathomably secret, and holy, and fleet. There is nothing to be done about it but ignore it, or see. And then you walk fearlessly, eating what you must, growing wherever you can, like the monk on the road who knows precisely how vulnerable he is, who takes no comfort among death-forgetting men, and who carries his vision of vastness and might around in his tunic like a live coal that neither burns nor warms him, but with which he will not part.

I used to have a cat, an old fighting tom, who sprang through the open window by my bed and pummeled my chest, barely sheathing his claws. I've been bloodied and mauled, wrung, dazzled, drawn. I taste salt on my lips in the early morning; I surprise my eyes in the mirror and they are ashes, or fiery sprouts, and I gape appalled, or full of breath. The planet whirls alone and dreaming. Power broods, spins, and lurches down. The planet and the power meet with a shock. They fuse and tumble, lightning, ground fire; they part, mute, submitting, and touch again with hiss and cry. The tree with the lights in it buzzes into flame and the cast-rock mountains ring.

Emerson saw it. "I dreamed that I floated at will in the great Ether, and I saw this world floating also not far off, but diminished to the size of an apple. Then an angel took it in his hand and brought it to me and said, 'This must thou eat.' And I ate the world." All of it. All of it intricate, speckled, gnawed, fringed, and free. Israel's priests offered the wave breast and the heave shoulder together, freely, in full knowledge, for thanksgiving. They waved, they heaved, and neither gesture was whole without the other, and both meant a wide-eyed and keen-eyed thanks. Go your way, eat the fat, and drink the sweet, said the bell. A sixteenth-century alchemist wrote of the philosopher's stone, "One finds it in the open country, in the village and in the town. It is in everything which God created. Maids throw it on the street. Children play with it." The giant water bug ate the world. And like Billy Bray I go my way, and my left foot says "Glory," and my right foot says "Amen": in and out of Shadow Creek, upstream and down, exultant, in a daze, dancing, to the twin silver trumpets of praise.

1974

HOLY THE FIRM

*No one suspects the days
to be gods.*
—Emerson

I LIVE ON NORTHERN PUGET Sound, in Washington State, alone.

There is a spider in the bathroom with whom I keep a sort of company. Her little outfit always reminds me of a certain moth I helped to kill. The spider herself is of uncertain lineage, bulbous at the abdomen and drab. Her six-inch mess of a web works, works somehow, works miraculously, to keep her alive and me amazed. The web itself is in a corner behind the toilet, connecting tile wall to tile wall and floor, in a place where there is, I would have thought, scant traffic. Yet under the web are sixteen or so corpses she has tossed to the floor.

The corpses appear to be mostly sow bugs, those little armadillo creatures who live to travel flat out in houses, and die round. There is also a new shred of earwig, three old spider skins, crinkled and clenched, and two moth bodies, wingless and huge and empty, moth bodies I drop to my knees to see.

Today the earwig shines darkly and gleams, what there is of him: a dorsal curve of thorax and abdomen, and a smooth pair of cerci, by which I knew his name. Next week, if the other bodies are any indication, he will be shrunken and gray, webbed to the floor with dust. The sow bugs beside him are hollow and empty of color, fragile, a breath away from brittle fluff. The spider skins lie on their sides, translucent and ragged, their legs drying in knots. And the moths, the empty moths, stagger against each other, headless, in a confusion of arcing strips of chitin like peeling varnish, like a jumble of buttresses for cathedral domes, like nothing resembling moths, so that I should hesitate to call them moths, except that I have had some experience with the figure Moth reduced to a nub.

Two years ago I was camping alone in the Blue Ridge Mountains in Virginia. I had hauled myself and gear up there to read, among other things, James Ramsey Ullman's *The Day on Fire,* a novel about Rimbaud that had made me want to be a writer when I was sixteen; I was hoping it would do it again. So I read, lost, every day sitting under a tree by my tent, while warblers swung in the leaves overhead and bristle worms trailed their inches over the twiggy dirt at my feet; and I read every night by candlelight, while barred owls called in the forest and pale moths massed round my head in the clearing, where my light made a ring.

Moths kept flying into the candle. They hissed and recoiled, lost upside down in the shadows among my cooking pans. Or they singed their wings and fell, and their hot wings, as if melted, stuck to the first thing they touched—a pan, a lid, a spoon—so that the snagged moths could flutter only in tiny arcs, unable to struggle free. These I could release by a quick flip with a stick; in the morning I would find my cooking stuff gilded with torn flecks of moth wings, triangles of shiny dust here and there on the aluminum. So I read, and boiled water, and replenished candles, and read on.

One night a moth flew into the candle, was caught, burned dry, and held. I must have been staring at the candle, or maybe I looked up when a shadow crossed my page; at any rate, I saw it all. A golden female moth, a biggish one with a two-inch wingspan, flapped into the fire, dropped her abdomen into the wet wax, stuck, flamed, frazzled, and fried in a second. Her moving wings ignited like tissue paper, enlarging the circle of light in the clearing and creating out of the darkness the sudden blue sleeves of my sweater, the green leaves of jewelweed by my side, the ragged red trunk of a pine. At once the light contracted again and the moth's wings vanished in a fine, foul smoke. At the same time her six legs clawed, curled, blackened, and ceased, disappearing utterly. And her head jerked in spasms, making a spattering noise; her antennae crisped and burned away, and her heaving mouth parts crackled like pistol fire. When it was all over, her head was, so far as I could determine, gone, gone the long way of her wings and legs. Had she been new, or old? Had she mated and laid her eggs, had she done her work? All that was left was the glowing horn shell of her abdomen and thorax—a fraying, partially collapsed gold tube jammed upright in the candle's round pool.

And then this moth essence, this spectacular skeleton, began to act as a wick. She kept burning. The wax rose in the moth's body from her soaking abdomen to her thorax to the jagged hole where her head should be, and widened into flame, a saffron-yellow flame that robed her to the ground like any immolating monk. That candle had two wicks, two flames of identical height, side by side. The moth's head was fire. She burned for two hours, until I blew her out.

She burned for two hours without changing, without bending or leaning—only glowing within, like a building fire glimpsed through silhouetted walls, like a hollow saint, like a flame-faced virgin gone to God, while I read by her light, kindled, while Rimbaud in Paris burned out his brains in a thousand poems, while night pooled wetly at my feet.

And that is why I believe those hollow crisps on the bathroom floor are moths. I think I know moths, and fragments of moths, and chips and tatters of utterly empty moths, in any state. How many of you, I asked the people in my class, which of you want to give your lives and be writers? I was trembling from coffee, or cigarettes, or the closeness of faces all around me. (Is this what we live for? I thought; is this the only final beauty: the color of any skin in any light, and living, human eyes?) All hands rose to the question. (You, Nick? Will you? Margaret? Randy? Why do I want them to mean it?) And then I tried to tell them what the choice must mean: you can't be anything else. You must go at your life with a broadax. . . . They had no idea what I was saying. (I have two hands, don't I? And all this energy, for as long as I can remember. I'll do it in the evenings, after skiing, or on the way home from the bank, or after the children are asleep. . . .) They thought I was raving again. It's just as well.

There is a gold cat here, named Small, who sleeps on my legs. In the morning I joke to her blank face: Do you remember last night? Do you remember? I throw her out before breakfast.

I have three candles on the table, which I disentangle from

the plants and light when visitors come. Small usually avoids them, although once she came too close and her tail caught fire; I rubbed it out before she noticed. The flames move light over everyone's skin, draw light to the surface of the faces of my friends. When the people leave I never blow the candles out, and after I'm asleep they flame and burn.

The Cascade range, in these high latitudes, backs almost into the water. There is only a narrow strip, an afterthought of foothills and farms sixty miles wide, between the snowy mountains and the sea. The mountains wall well. The rest of the country—most of the rest of the planet, in some very real sense, excluding a shred of British Columbia's coastline and the Alaskan islands—is called, and profoundly felt to be, simply "East of the Mountains." I've been there.

I came here to study hard things—rock mountain and salt sea—and to temper my spirit on their edges. "Teach me thy ways, O Lord" is, like all prayers, a rash one, and one I cannot but recommend. These mountains—Mount Baker and the Sisters and Shuksan, the Canadian Coastal Range and the Olympics on the peninsula—are surely the edge of the known and comprehended world. They are high. That they bear their own unimaginable masses and weathers aloft, holding them up in the sky for anyone to see plain, makes them, as Chesterton said of the Eucharist, only the more mysterious by their very visibility and absence of secrecy. They are the western rim of the real, if not considerably beyond it. If the Greeks had looked at Mount Baker all day, their large and honest art would have broken, and they would have gone fishing, as these people do. And as perhaps I one day shall.

But the mountains are, incredibly, east. When I first came here I faced east and watched the mountains, thinking: These are the Ultima Thule, the final westering, the last serrate margin of time. Since they are, incredibly, east, I must be no place at all. But the sun rose over the snowfields and woke me where I lay, and I rose and cast a shadow over someplace, and thought: There is, God help us, more. So gathering my bowls and spoons, and turning my head, as it were, I moved to face west, relinquishing all hope of sanity, for what is more.

And what is more is islands: sea, and unimaginably solid islands, and sea, and a hundred rolling skies. You spill your breath. Nothing holds; the whole show rolls. I can imagine Virginias no less than Pacifics. Inland valley, pool, desert, plain—it's all a falling sheaf of edges, like a quick-flapped deck of cards, like a dory or a day launched all unchristened, lost at sea. Land is a poured thing and time a surface film lapping and fringeing at fastness, at a hundred hollow and receding blues. Breathe fast: we're backing off the rim.

Here is the fringey edge where elements meet and realms mingle, where time and eternity spatter each other with foam. The salt sea and the islands, molding and molding, row upon rolling row, don't quit; nor do winds end nor skies cease from spreading in curves. The actual percentage of landmass to sea in the Sound equals that of the rest of the planet: we have less time than we knew. Time is eternity's pale interlinear, as the islands are the sea's. We have less time than we knew and that time buoyant, and cloven, lucent, and missile, and wild.

The room where I live is plain as a skull, a firm setting for windows. A nun lives in the fires of the spirit, a thinker lives in the bright wick of the mind, an artist lives jammed in the pool of materials. (Or, a nun lives, thoughtful and tough, in the mind, a nun lives, with that special poignancy peculiar to religious, in the exile of materials; and a thinker, who would think of something, lives in the clash of materials, and in the world of spirit where all long thoughts must lead; and an artist lives in the mind, that warehouse of forms, and an artist lives, of course, in the spirit. So.) But this room is a skull, a fire tower, wooden, and empty. Of itself it is nothing, but the view, as they say, is good.

Since I live in one room, one long wall of which is glass, I am myself, at everything I do, a backdrop to all the landscape's occasions, to all its weathers, colors, and lights. From the kitchen sink, and from my bed, and from the table, the couch, the hearth, and the desk, I see land and water, islands, sky.

The land is complex and shifting: the eye leaves it. There is a white Congregationalist church among Douglas firs; there is a green pasture between two yellow fallow fields; there are sheep bent over beneath some alders, and beside them a yard of running brown hens. But everything in the landscape points to sea.

The land's progress of colors leads the eye up a distant hill, a sweeping big farm of a hill whose yellow pastures bounce light all day from a billion stems and blades; and down the hill's rim drops a dark slope of fir forest, a slant your eye rides down to the point, the dark sliver of land that holds the bay. From this angle you see the bay cut a crescent; your eye flies up the black beach to the point, or slides down the green firs to the point, and the point is an arrow pointing over and over, with its log-strewn beach, its gray singleness, and its recurved white edging of foam, to sea: to the bright sound, the bluing of water with distance at the world's rim, and on it the far blue islands, and over these lights the light clouds.

You can't picture it, can you? Neither can I. Oh, the desk is yellow, the oak table round, the ferns alive, the mirror cold, and I never have cared. I read. In the Middle Ages, I read, "the idea of a thing which a man framed for himself was always more real to him than the actual thing itself." Of course. I am in my Middle Ages; the world at my feet, the world through the window, is an illuminated manuscript whose leaves the wind takes, one by one, whose painted illuminations and halting words draw me, one by one, and I am dazzled in days and lost.

There is, in short, one country, one room, one enormous window, one cat, one spider, and one person: but I am hollow. And, for now, there are the many gods of mornings and the many things to give them for their work—lungs and heart, muscle, nerve, and bone—and there is the no-man's-land of many things wherein they dwell, and from which I seek to call them, in work that's mine.

Nothing is going to happen in this book. There is only a little violence here and there in the language, at the corner where eternity clips time.

DAY ONE

Every day is a god, each day is a god, and holiness holds forth in time. I worship each god, I praise each day splintered down, splintered down and wrapped in time like a husk, a husk of many colors spreading, at dawn fast over the mountains split.

I wake in a god. I wake in arms holding my quilt, holding me as best they can inside my quilt.

Someone is kissing me—already. I wake, I cry "Oh," I rise from the pillow. Why should I open my eyes?

I open my eyes. The god lifts from the water. His head fills the bay. He is Puget Sound, the Pacific; his breast rises from pastures; his fingers are firs; islands slide wet down his shoulders. Islands slip blue from his shoulders and glide over the water, the empty, lighted water like a stage.

Today's god rises, his long eyes flecked in clouds. He flings his arms, spreading colors; he arches, cupping sky in his belly; he vaults, vaulting and spread, holding all and spread on me like skin.

Under the quilt in my knees' crook is a cat. She wakes; she curls to bite her metal sutures. The day is real; already, I can feel it click, hear it clicking under my knees.

The day is real; the sky clicks securely in place over the mountains, locks round the islands, snaps slap on the bay. Air fits flush on farm roofs; it rises inside the doors of barns and rubs at yellow barn windows. Air clicks up my hand cloven into fingers and wells in my ears' holes, whole and entire. I call it simplicity, the way matter is smooth and alone.

I toss the cat. I stand and smooth the quilt. "Oh," I cry, "Oh!"

I read. Armenians, I read, salt their newborn babies. I check somewhere else: so did the Jews at the time of the prophets. They washed a baby in water, salted him, and wrapped him in cloths. When God promised to Aaron and all the Levites all the offerings Israel made to God, the firstfruits and the firstling livestock, "all the best of the oil, and all the best of the wine," he said of this promise, "It is a covenant of salt forever." In the Roman Church baptism, the priest places salt in the infant's mouth.

I salt my breakfast eggs. All day long I feel created. I can see the blown dust on the skin on the back of my hand, the tiny trapezoids of chipped clay, moistened and breathed alive. There are some created sheep in the pasture below me, sheep set down here precisely, just touching their blue shadows hoof to hoof on the grass. Created gulls pock the air, rip great curved seams in the settled air: I greet my created meal, amazed.

I have been drawing a key to the islands I see from my window. Everyone told me a different set of names for them, until one day a sailor came and named them all with such authority that I believed him. So I penciled an outline of the horizon on a sheet of paper and labeled the lobes: Skipjack, Sucia, Saturna, Salt Spring, Bare Island. . . .

Today, November 18 and no wind, today a veil of air has lifted that I didn't know was there. I see a new island, a new wrinkle, the deepening of wonder, behind the blue translucence the sailor said is Salt Spring Island. I have no way of learning its name. I bring the labeled map to the table and pencil a new line. Call that: Unknown Island North; Water-Statue; Sky-Ruck; Newborn and Salted; Waiting for Sailor.

Henry Miller relates that Knut Hamsun once said, in response to a questionnaire, that he wrote to kill time. This is funny in a number of ways. In a number of ways I kill myself laughing, looking out at islands. Startled, the yellow cat on the floor stares over her shoulder. She has carried in a wren, I suddenly see, a wren she has killed, whose dead wings point askew on the circular rug. It is time. Out with you both. I'm busy laughing, to kill time. I shoo the cat from the door, turn the wren over in my palm, and drop him from the porch, down to the winter-killed hair grass and sedge, where the cat may find him if she will, or crows, or beetles, or rain.

When I next look up from my coffee, there is a ruckus on the porch. The cat has dragged in a god, scorched. He is alive. I run outside. Save for his wings, he is a perfect, very small man. He is fair, thin-skinned in the cat's mouth, and kicking. His hair is on fire and stinks; his wingtips are blackened and seared. From the two soft flaps of the cat's tiger muzzle his body jerks, naked. One of his miniature hands pushes hard at her nose. He waves his thighs; he beats her face and the air with his smoking wings. I cannot breathe. I run at the cat to scare her; she drops him, casting at me an evil look, and runs from the porch.

The god lies gasping and perfect. He is no longer than my face. Quickly I snuff the smoldering fire in his yellow hair with a finger and thumb. In so doing I accidentally touch his skull, brush against his hot skull, which is the size of a hazelnut, as the saying goes, warm-skinned and alive.

He rolls his colorless eyes toward mine: his long wings catch strength from the sun, and heave.

Later I am walking in the day's last light. The god rides barefoot on my shoulder, or astride it, or tugging or swinging on loops of my hair.

He is whistling at my ear; he is blowing a huge tune in my ear, a myth about November. He is heaping a hot hurricane into my ear, into my hair, an ignorant ditty calling things real, calling islands out of the sea, calling solid moss from curling rock, and ducks down the sky for the winter.

I see it! I see it all! Two islands, twelve islands, worlds, gather substance, gather the blue contours of time, and array themselves down distance, mute and hard.

I seem to see a road; I seem to be on a road, walking. I seem to walk on a blacktop road that runs over a hill. The hill creates itself, a powerful suggestion. It creates itself, thickening with apparently solid earth and waving plants, with houses and browsing cattle, unrolling wherever my eyes go, as though my focus were a brush painting in a world. I cannot escape the illusion. The colorful thought persists, this world, a dream forced into my ear and sent round my body on ropes of hot blood. If I throw my eyes past the rim of the hill to see the real—stars, were they? something with wings, or loops?—I elaborate the illusion instead; I rough in a middle ground. I stitch the transparent curtain solid with bright phantom mountains, with thick clouds gliding just so over their shadows on green water, with blank, impenetrable sky. The dream fills in, like wind widening over a bay. Quickly I look to the flat dream's rim for a glimpse of that old deep . . . and, just as quickly, the blue slaps shut, the colors wrap everything out. There is not a chink. The sky is gagging on trees. I seem to be on a road, walking, greeting the hedgerows, the rose hips, apples, and thorn. I seem to be on a road walking, familiar with neighbors, high-handed with cattle, smelling the sea, and alone. Already, I know the names of things. I can kick a stone.

Time is enough, more than enough, and matter multiple and given. The god of today is a child, a baby new and filling the house, remarkably here in the flesh. He is day. He thrives in a cup of wind, landlocked and thrashing. He unrolls, revealing his shape an edge at a time, a smatter of content, footfirst: a word, a friend for coffee, a windshift, the shingling or coincidence of ideas. Today, November 18 and no wind, is clear. Terry Wean— who fishes, and takes my poetry course—could see Mount Rainier. He hauls his reef net gear from the bay; we talk on its deck while he hammers at shrunken knots. The Moores for dinner. In bed, I call to me my sad cat, I read.

The god of today is rampant and drenched. His arms spread, bearing moist pastures; his fingers spread, fingering the shore. He is time's live skin; he burgeons up from day like any tree. His legs spread crossing the heavens, flicking hugely, and flashing and arcing around the earth toward night.

This is the one world, bound to itself and exultant. It fizzes up in trees, trees heaving up streams of salt to their leaves. This is the one air, bitten by grackles; time is alone and in and out of mind. The god of today is a boy, pagan and fernfoot. His power is enthusiasm; his innocence is mystery. He sockets into everything that is, and that right holy. Loud as music, filling the grasses and skies, his day spreads rising at home in the hundred senses. He rises, new and surrounding; he *is* everything that is, wholly here and emptied—flung, and flowing, sowing, unseen, and flown.

DAY TWO

Into this world falls a plane.

The earth is a mineral speckle planted in trees. The plane snagged its wing on a tree, fluttered in a tiny arc, and struggled down.

I heard it go. The cat looked up. There was no reason: the plane's engine simply stilled after takeoff, and the light plane failed to clear the firs. It fell easily; one wing snagged on a fir top; the metal fell down the air and smashed in the thin woods where cattle browse; the fuel exploded; and Julie Norwich seven years old burned off her face.

Little Julie mute in some room at Saint Joe's now, drugs dissolving into the sheets. Little Julie with her eyes naked and spherical, baffled. Can you scream without lips? Yes. But do children in long pain scream?

It is November 19 and no wind, and no hope of heaven, and no wish for heaven, since the meanest of people show more mercy than hounding and terrorist gods.

The airstrip, a cleared washboard affair on the flat crest of a low hill, is a few long fields distant from my house—up the road and through the woods, or across the sheep pasture and through the woods. A flight instructor told me once that when his students get cocky, when they think they know how to fly a plane, he takes them out here and makes them land on that field. You go over the wires and down, and along the strip and up before the trees, or vice versa, vice versa, depending on the wind. But the airstrip is not unsafe. Jesse's engine failed. The FAA will cart the wreckage away, bit by bit, picking it out of the tree trunk, and try to discover just why that engine failed. In the meantime, the emergency siren has sounded, causing everyone who didn't see the plane go down to halt—Patty at her weaving, Jonathan slicing apples, Jan washing her baby's face—to halt, in pity and terror, wondering which among us got hit, by what bad accident, and why. The volunteer firemen have mustered; the fire trucks have come—stampeding

Shuller's sheep—and gone, bearing burned Julie and Jesse her father to the emergency room in town, leaving the rest of us to gossip, fight grass fires on the airstrip, and pray, or wander from window to window, fierce.

So she is burned on her face and neck, Julie Norwich. The one whose teeth are short in a row, Jesse and Ann's oldest, red-kneed, green-socked, carrying cats.

I saw her only once. It was two weeks ago, under an English hawthorn tree, at the farm.

There are many farms in this neck of the woods, but only one we call "the farm"—the old Corcoran place, where Gus grows hay and raises calves: the farm, whose abandoned frame chicken coops ply the fields like longboats, like floating war canoes; whose clay driveway and grass footpaths are a tangle of orange calendula blossoms, ropes, equipment, and seeding grasses; the farm, whose canny heifers and bull calves figure the fences, run amok to the garden, and plant themselves suddenly black and white, up to their necks in green peas.

Between the gray farmhouse and the barn is the green grass farmyard, suitable for all projects. That day, sixteen of us were making cider. It was cold. There were piles of apples everywhere. We had filled our trucks that morning, climbing trees and shaking their boughs, dragging tarps heavy with apples, hauling bushels and boxes and buckets of apples, and loading them all back to the farm. Jesse and Ann, who are in their thirties, with Julie and the baby, whose name I forget, had driven down from the mountains that morning with a truckload of apples, loose, to make cider with us, fill their jugs, and drive back. I had not met them before. We all drank coffee on the farmhouse porch to warm us; we hosed jugs in the yard. Now we were throwing apples into a shredder and wringing the mash through pillowcases, staining our palms and freezing our fingers, and decanting the pails into seventy one-gallon jugs. And all this long day, Julie Norwich chased my cat, Small, around the farmyard and played with her, manhandled her, next to the porch under the hawthorn tree.

* * *

She was a thin child, pointy-chinned, yellow bangs and braids. She squinted, and when you looked at her she sometimes started laughing, as if you had surprised her at using some power she wasn't yet ready to show. I kept my eye on her, wondering if she was cold with her sweater unbuttoned and bony knees bare.

She would hum up a little noise for half-hour stretches. In the intervals, for maybe five minutes each, she was trying, very quietly, to learn to whistle. I think. Or she was practicing a certain concentrated face. But I think she was trying to learn to whistle, because sometimes she would squeak a little falsetto note through an imitation whistle hole in her lips, as if that could fool anyone. And all day she was dressing and undressing the yellow cat, sticking it into a black dress, a black dress long and full as a nun's.

I was amazed at that dress. It must have been some sort of doll clothing she had dragged with her in the truck; I've never seen its kind before or since. A white collar bibbed the yoke of it like a guimpe. It had great black sleeves like wings. Julie scooped up the cat and rammed her into the cloth. I knew how she felt, exasperated, breaking her heart on a finger curl's width of skinny cat arm. I knew the many feelings she had sticking those furry arms through the sleeves. Small is not large: her limbs feel like bird bones strung in a sock. When Julie had the cat dressed in its curious habit, she would rock it like a baby doll. The cat blinked, upside down.

Once she whistled at it, or tried, blowing in its face; the cat poured from her arms and ran. It leapt across the driveway, lightfoot in its sleeves; its black dress pulled this way and that, dragging dust, bent up in back by its yellow tail. I was squeezing one end of a twisted pillowcase full of apple mash and looking over my shoulder. I watched the cat hurdle the driveway and vanish under the potting shed, cringing; I watched Julie dash after it without hesitation, seize it, hit its face, and drag it back to the tree, carrying it caught fast by either forepaw, so its body hung straight from its arms.

She saw me watching her and we exchanged a look, a very conscious and self-conscious look—because we look a bit alike and we both knew it; because she was still short and I grown; because I was stuck kneeling before the cider pail, looking at her sidewise over my shoulder; because she was carrying the cat so oddly, so that she had to walk with her long legs parted; because it was my cat, and she'd dressed it, and it looked like a nun; and because she knew I'd been watching her, and how fondly, all along. We were laughing.

We *looked* a bit alike. Her face is slaughtered now, and I don't remember mine. It is the best joke there is, that we are here, and fools—that we are sown into time like so much corn, that we are souls sprinkled at random like salt into time and dissolved here, spread into matter, connected by cells right down to our feet, and those feet likely to fell us over a tree root or jam us on a stone. The joke part is that we forget it. Give the mind two seconds alone, and it thinks it's Pythagoras. We wake up a hundred times a day and laugh.

The joke of the world is less like a banana peel than a rake, the old rake in the grass, the one you step on, foot to forehead. It all comes together. In a twinkling. You have to admire the gag for its symmetry, accomplishing all with one right angle, the same right angle that accomplishes all philosophy. One step on the rake, and it's mind under matter once again. You wake up with a piece of tree in your skull. You wake up with fruit on your hands. You wake up in a clearing and see yourself, ashamed. You see your own face and it's seven years old and there's no knowing why, or where you've been since. We're tossed broadcast into time like so much grass, some ravening god's sweet hay. You wake up and a plane falls out of the sky.

That day was a god, too, the day we made cider and Julie played under the hawthorn tree. He must have been a heyday sort of god, a husbandman. He was spread under gardens, sleeping in time, an innocent old man scratching his head, thinking of pruning the orchard, in love with families.

Has he no power? Can the other gods carry time and its loves upside down like a doll in their blundering arms? As though we the people were playing house—when we are serious and do love—and not the gods? No, that day's god has no power. No gods have power to save. There are only days. The one great god abandoned us to days, to time's tumult of occasions, abandoned us to the gods of days, each brute and amok in his hugeness and idiocy.

Jesse, her father, had grabbed her clear of the plane this morning, and was hauling her off when the fuel blew. A gob of flung ignited vapor hit her face, or something flaming from the plane or fir tree hit her face. No one else was burned, or hurt in any way.

So this is where we are. Ashes, ashes, all fall down. How could I have forgotten? Didn't I see the heavens wiped shut just yesterday, on the road walking? Didn't I fall from the dark of the stars to these senselit and noisome days? The great ridged granite millstone of time is illusion, for only the good is real; the great ridged granite millstone of space is illusion, for God is spirit and worlds his flimsiest dreams: but the illusions are almost perfect, are apparently perfect for generations on end, and the pain is also, and undeniably, real. The pain within the millstones' pitiless turning is real, for our love for each other—for world and all the products of extension—is real, vaulting, insofar as it is love, beyond the plane of the stones' sickening churn and arcing to the realm of spirit bare. And you can get caught holding one end of a love, when your father drops, and your mother; when a land is lost, or a time, and your friend blotted out, gone, your brother's body spoiled, and cold, your infant dead, and you dying: you reel out love's long line alone, stripped like a live wire loosing its sparks to a cloud, like a live wire loosed in space to longing and grief everlasting.

I sit at the window. It is a fool's lot, this sitting always at windows spoiling little blowy slips of paper and myself in the process. Shall I be old? Here comes Small, old sparrow-mouth, wanting my lap. Done. Do you have any earthly idea how young I am? Where's your dress, kitty? I suppose I'll outlive this wretched cat. Get another. Leave it my silver spoons, like old ladies you hear about. I prefer dogs.

*   *   *

So I read. Angels, I read, belong to nine different orders. Seraphs are the highest; they are aflame with love for God, and stand closer to him than the others. Seraphs love God; cherubs, who are second, possess perfect knowledge of him. So love is greater than knowledge; how could I have forgotten? The seraphs are born of a stream of fire issuing from under God's throne. They are, according to Dionysius the Areopagite, "all wings," having, as Isaiah noted, six wings apiece, two of which they fold over their eyes. Moving perpetually toward God, they perpetually praise him, crying Holy, Holy, Holy. . . . But, according to some rabbinic writings, they can sing only the first "Holy" before the intensity of their love ignites them again and dissolves them again, perpetually, into flames. "Abandon everything," Dionysius told his disciple. "God despises ideas."

God despises everything, apparently. If he abandoned us, slashing creation loose at its base from any roots in the real; and if we in turn abandon everything—all these illusions of time and space and lives—in order to love only the real: then where are we? Thought itself is impossible, for subject can have no guaranteed connection with object, nor any object with God. Knowledge is impossible. We are precisely nowhere, sinking on an entirely imaginary ice floe, into entirely imaginary seas themselves adrift. Then we reel out love's long line alone toward a God less lovable than a grasshead, who treats us less well than we treat our lawns.

Of faith I have nothing, only of truth: that this one God is a brute and traitor, abandoning us to time, to necessity and the engines of matter unhinged. This is no leap; this is evidence of things seen: one Julie, one sorrow, one sensation bewildering the heart, and enraging the mind, and causing me to look at the world stuff appalled, at the blithering rock of trees in a random wind, at my hand like some gibberish sprouted, my fist opening and closing, so that I think: Have I once turned my hand in this circus, have I ever called it home?

Faith would be that God is self-limited utterly by his creation—a contraction of the scope of his will; that he bound himself to time and its hazards and haps as a man would lash himself to a tree for love. That God's works are as good as we make them. That God is helpless, our baby to bear, self-abandoned on the doorstep of time, wondered at by cattle and oxen. Faith would be that God moved and moves once and for all and "down," so to speak, like a diver, like a man who eternally gathers himself for a dive and eternally is diving, and eternally splitting the spread of the water, and eternally drowned.

Faith would be, in short, that God has any willful connection with time whatsoever, and with us. For I know it as given that God is all good. And I take it also as given that whatever he touches has meaning, if only in his mysterious terms, the which I readily grant. The question is, then, whether God touches anything. Is anything firm, or is time on the loose? Did Christ descend once and for all to no purpose, in a kind of divine and kenotic suicide, or ascend once and for all, pulling his cross up after him like a rope ladder home? Is there—even if Christ holds the tip of things fast and stretches eternity clear to the dim souls of men—is there no link at the base of things, some kernel or air deep in the matrix of matter from which universe furls like a ribbon twined into time?

Has God a hand in this? Then it is a good hand. But has he a hand at all? Or is he a holy fire burning self-contained for power's sake alone? Then he knows himself blissfully as flame unconsuming, as all brilliance and beauty and power, and the rest of us can go hang. Then the accidental universe spins mute, obedient only to its own gross terms, meaningless, out of mind, and alone. The universe is neither contingent upon nor participant in the holy, in being itself, the real, the power play of fire. The universe is illusion merely, not one speck of it real, and we are not only its victims, falling always into or smashed by a planet slung by its sun, but also its captives, bound by the mineral-made ropes of our senses.

But how do we know—how could we know—that the real is there? By what freak chance does the skin of illusion ever split, and reveal to us the real, which seems to know us by name, and by what freak chance and why did the capacity to prehend it evolve?

I sit at the window, chewing the bones in my wrist. Pray for them: for Julie, for Jesse her father, for Ann her mother, pray. Who will teach us to pray? The god of today is a glacier. We live in his shifting crevasses, unheard. The god of today is delinquent, a barn-burner, a punk with a pittance of power in a match. It is late, a late time to be living. Now it is afternoon; the sky is appallingly clear. Everything in the landscape points to sea, and the sea is nothing; it is snipped from the real as a stuff without form, rising up the sides of islands and falling, mineral to mineral, salt.

Everything I see—the water, the log-wrecked beach, the farm on the hill, the bluff, the white church in the trees—looks overly distinct and shining. (What is the relationship of color to this sun, of sun to anything else?) It all looks staged. It all looks brittle and unreal, a skin of colors painted on glass, which if you prodded it with a finger would powder and fall. A blank sky, perfectly blended with all other sky, has sealed over the crack in the world where the plane fell, and the air has hushed the matter up.

If days are gods, then gods are dead, and artists pyrotechnic fools. Time is a hurdy-gurdy, a lampoon, and death's a bawd. We're beheaded by the nick of time. We're logrolling on a falling world, on time released from meaning and rolling loose, like one of Atalanta's golden apples, a bauble flung and forgotten, lapsed, and the gods on the lam.

And now outside the window, deep on the horizon, a new thing appears, as if we needed a new thing. It is a new land blue beyond islands, hitherto hidden by haze and now revealed, and as dumb as the rest. I check my chart, my amateur penciled sketch of the skyline. Yes, this land is new, this spread blue spark beyond yesterday's new wrinkled line, beyond the blue veil a sailor said was Salt Spring Island. How long can this go on? But let us by all means extend the scope of our charts.

I draw it as I seem to see it, a blue chunk fitted just so beyond islands, a wag of graphite rising just here above another anonymous line, and here meeting the slope of Salt Spring: though whether this be headland I see or heartland, or the distance-blurred bluffs of a hundred bays, I have no way of knowing, or if it be island or main. I call it Thule, O Julialand, Time's Bad News; I name it Terror, the Farthest Limb of the Day, God's Tooth.

DAY THREE

I know only enough of God to want to worship him, by any means ready to hand. There is an anomalous specificity to all our experience in space, a scandal of particularity, by which God burgeons up or showers down into the shabbiest of occasions, and leaves his creation's dealings with him in the hands of purblind and clumsy amateurs. This is all we are and all we ever were; God *kann nicht anders*. This process in time is history; in space, at such shocking random, it is mystery.

A blur of romance clings to notions of "publicans," "sinners," "the poor," "the people in the marketplace," "our neighbors," as though of course God should reveal himself, if at all, to these simple people, these Sunday school watercolor figures, who are so purely themselves in their tattered robes, who are single in themselves, while we now are various, complex, and full at heart. We are busy. So, I see now, were they. Who shall ascend into the hill of the Lord? or who shall stand in his holy place? There is no one but us. There is no one to send, nor a clean hand, nor a pure heart on the face of the earth, nor in the earth, but only us, a generation comforting ourselves with the notion that we have come at an awkward time, that our innocent fathers are all dead—as if innocence had ever been—and our children busy and troubled, and we ourselves unfit, not yet ready, having each of us chosen wrongly, made a false start, failed, yielded to impulse and the tangled comfort of pleasures, and grown exhausted, unable to seek the thread, weak, and involved. But there is no one but us. There never has been. There have been generations which remembered, and generations which forgot; there has never been a generation of whole men and women who lived well for even one day. Yet some have imagined well, with honesty and art, the detail of such a life, and have described it with such grace, that we mistake vision for history, dream for description, and fancy that life has devolved. So. You learn this studying any history at all, especially the lives of artists and visionaries; you learn it from Emerson, who noticed that the meanness of our days is itself worth our thought; and you learn it, fitful in your pew, at church.

There is one church here, so I go to it. On Sunday mornings I quit the house and wander down the hill to the white frame church in the firs. On a big Sunday there might be twenty of us there; often I am the only person under sixty, and feel as though I'm on an archaeological tour of Soviet Russia. The members are of mixed denominations; the minister is a Congregationalist, and wears a white shirt. The man knows God. Once, in the middle of the long pastoral prayer of intercession for the whole world—for the gift of wisdom to its leaders, for hope and mercy to the grieving and pained, succor to the oppressed, and God's grace to all—in the middle of this he stopped, and burst out, "Lord, we bring you these same petitions every week." After a shocked pause, he continued reading the prayer. Because of this, I like him very much. "Good morning!" he says after the first hymn and invocation, startling me witless every time, and we all shout back, "Good morning!"

The churchwomen all bring flowers for the altar; they haul in arrangements as big as hedges, of wayside herbs in season, and flowers from their gardens, huge bunches of foliage and blossoms as tall as I am, in vases the size of tubs, and the altar still looks empty, irredeemably linoleum, and beige. We had a wretched singer once, a guest from a Canadian congregation, a hulking blond girl with chopped hair and big shoulders, who wore tinted spectacles and a long lacy dress, and sang, grinning, to faltering accompaniment, an entirely secular song about mountains. Nothing could have been more apparent than that God loved this girl; nothing could more surely convince me of God's unending mercy than the continued existence on earth of the church.

The higher Christian churches—where, if anywhere, I belong—come at God with an unwarranted air of professionalism, with authority and pomp, as though they knew what they were doing, as though people in themselves were an appropriate set of creatures to have dealings with God. I often think of the set pieces of liturgy as certain words that people have successfully addressed to God without their getting killed. In the high churches they saunter through the liturgy like Mohawks along a strand of scaffolding who have long since forgotten their danger. If God were to blast such a service to bits, the congregation would be, I believe, genuinely shocked. But in the low churches you expect it any minute. This is the beginning of wisdom.

Today is Friday, November 20. Julie Norwich is in the hospital, burned; we can get no word of her condition. People released from burn wards, I read once, have a very high suicide rate. They had not realized, before they were burned, that life could include such suffering, nor that they personally could be permitted such pain. No drugs ease the pain of third-degree burns, because burns destroy skin: the drugs simply leak into the sheets. His disciples asked Christ about a roadside beggar who had been blind from birth, "Who did sin, this man or his parents, that he was born blind?" And Christ, who spat on the ground, made a mud of his spittle and clay, plastered the mud over the man's eyes, and gave him sight, answered, "Neither hath this man sinned, nor his parents: but that the works of God should be made manifest in him." Really? If we take this answer to refer to the affliction itself—and not the subsequent cure—as "God's works made manifest," then we have, along with "Not as the world gives do I give unto you," two meager, baffling, and infuriating answers to one of the few questions worth asking, to wit, What in the Sam Hill is going on here?

The works of God made manifest? Do we really need more victims to remind us that we're all victims? Is this some sort of parade for which a conquering army shines up its terrible guns and rolls them down the streets for the people to see? Do we need blind men stumbling about, and little flamefaced children, to remind us what God can—and will—do?

I am drinking boiled coffee and watching the bay from the window. Almost all of the people who reef net have hauled their gear for the winter; the salmon runs are over, days are short.

Still, boats come and go on the water—tankers, tugs and barges, rowboats and sails. There are killer whales if you're lucky, rafts of harlequin ducks if you're lucky, and every day the scoter and the solitary grebes. How many tons of sky can I see from the window? It is morning: morning! and the water clobbered with light. Yes, in fact, we do. We do need reminding, not of what God can do, but of what he cannot do, or will not, which is to catch time in its free fall and stick a nickel's worth of sense into our days. And we need reminding of what time can do, must only do: churn out enormities at random and beat them, with God's blessing, into our heads—that we are created, *created*, sojourners in a land we did not make, a land with no meaning of itself and no meaning we can make for it alone. Who are we to demand explanations of God? (And what monsters of perfection should we be if we did not?) We forget ourselves, picnicking; we forget where we are. There is no such thing as a freak accident. "God is at home," says Meister Eckhart, "We are in the far country."

We are most deeply asleep at the switch when we fancy we control any switches at all. We sleep to time's hurdy-gurdy; we wake, if we ever wake, to the silence of God. And then, when we wake to the deep shores of light uncreated, then when the dazzling dark breaks over the far slopes of time, then it's time to toss things, like our reason, and our will; then it's time to break our necks for home.

There are no events but thoughts and the heart's hard turning, the heart's slow learning where to love and whom. The rest is merely gossip, and tales for other times. The god of today is a tree. He is a forest of trees or a desert, or a wedge from wideness down to a scatter of stars, stars like salt, low and dumb and abiding. Today's god said: shed. He peels from eternity always, spread; he winds into time like a rind. I am or seem to be on a road, walking. The hedges are just where they were. There is a corner, and a long hill, a glimpse of snow on the mountains, a slope planted in apple trees, and a store next to a pasture, where I am going to buy the communion wine.

How can I buy the communion wine? Who am I to buy the

communion wine? Someone has to buy the communion wine. Having wine instead of grape juice was my idea, and of course I offered to buy it. Shouldn't I be wearing robes and, especially, a mask? Shouldn't I *make* the communion wine? Are there holy grapes, is there holy ground, is anything here holy? There are no holy grapes, there is no holy ground, nor is there anyone but us. I have an empty knapsack over my parka's shoulders; it is cold, and I'll want my hands in my pockets. According to the Rule of St. Benedict, I should say, Our hands in our pockets. "All things come of thee, O Lord, and of thine own have we given thee." There must be a rule for the purchase of communion wine. "Will that be cash, or charge?" All I know is that when I go to this store—to buy eggs, or sandpaper, broccoli, wood screws, milk—I like to tease a bit, if he'll let me, with the owners' son, two, whose name happens to be Chandler, and who himself likes to play in the big bins of nails.

And so, forgetting myself, thank God: Hullo. Hullo, short and relatively new. Welcome again to the land of the living, to time, this hill of beans. Chandler will have, as usual, none of it. He keeps his mysterious counsel. And I'm out on the road again, walking, my right hand forgetting my left. I'm out on the road again, walking, and toting a backload of God.

Here is a bottle of wine with a label, Christ with a cork. I bear holiness splintered into a vessel, very God of very God, the sempiternal silence personal and brooding, bright on the back of my ribs. I start up the hill.

The world is changing. The landscape begins to respond as a current upwells. It is starting to clack with itself, though nothing moves in space and there's no wind. It is starting to utter its infinite particulars, each overlapping and lone, like a hundred hills of hounds all giving tongue. The hedgerows are blackberry brambles, white snowberries, red rose hips, gaunt and clattering broom. Their leafless stems are starting to live visibly deep in their centers, as hidden as banked fires live, and as clearly as recognition, mute, shines forth from eyes. Above me the mountains are raw nerves, sensible and exultant; the trees, the grass, and the asphalt below me are living petals of mind, each sharp and invisible, held in a greeting or glance full perfectly formed. There is something stretched or jostling about the sky, which, when I study it, vanishes. Why are there all these apples in the world, and why so wet and transparent? Through all my clothing, through the pack on my back and through the bottle's glass, I feel the wine. Walking faster and faster, weightless, I feel the wine. It sheds light in slats through my rib cage, and fills the buttressed vaults of my ribs with light pooled and buoyant.

Each thing in the world is translucent, even the cattle, and moving, cell by cell. I remember this reality. Where has it been? I sail to the crest of the hill as if blown up the slope of a swell. I see, blasted, the bay transfigured below me, the saltwater bay, far down the hill past the road to my house, past the firs and the church and the sheep in the pasture: the bay and the islands on fire and boundless beyond it, catching alight the unraveling sky. Pieces of the sky are falling down. Everything, everything, is whole, and a parcel of everything else. I myself am falling down, slowly, or slowly lifting up. On the bay's stone shore are people among whom I float, real people, gathering of an afternoon, in the cells of whose skin stream thin colored waters in pieces, which give back the general flame.

Christ is being baptized. The one who is Christ is there, and the one who is John, and the dim other people standing on cobbles or sitting on beach logs back from the bay. These are ordinary people—if I am one now, if those are ordinary sheep singing a song in the pasture.

The two men are bare to the waist. The one walks him into the water, and holds him under. His hand is on his neck. Christ is coiled and white under the water, standing on stones.

He lifts from the water. Water beads on his shoulders. I see the water in balls as heavy as planets, a billion beads of water as weighty as worlds, and he lifts them up on his back as he rises. He stands wet in the water. Each one bead is transparent, and each has a world, or the same world, light and alive and apparent inside the drop: it is all there ever could be, moving at once, past and future, and all the people. I can look into any sphere and see people stream past me, and cool my eyes with colors and the sight of the world in spectacle perishing ever, and ever renewed. I do; I deepen into a drop and see all that time contains, all the faces and deeps of the worlds and all the earth's contents, every landscape and room, everything living or made or fashioned, all past and future stars, and especially faces, faces like the cells of everything, faces pouring past me talking, and going, and gone. And I am gone.

For outside it is bright. The surface of things outside the drops has fused. Christ himself and the others, and the brown warm wind, and hair, sky, the beach, the shattered water—all this has fused. It is the one glare of holiness; it is bare and unspeakable. There is no speech nor language; there is nothing, no one thing, nor motion, nor time. There is only this everything. There is only this, and its bright and multiple noise.

I seem to be on a road, standing still. It is the top of the hill. The hedges are here, subsiding. My hands are in my pockets. There is a bottle of wine on my back, a California red. I see my feet. I move down the hill toward home.

You must rest now. I cannot rest you. For me there is, I am trying to tell you, no time.

There are a thousand new islands today, uncharted. They are salt stones on fire and dimming; I read by their light. Small the cat lies on my neck. In the bathroom the spider is working on yesterday's moth.

Esoteric Christianity, I read, posits a substance. It is a created substance, lower than metals and minerals on a "spiritual scale," and lower than salts and earths, occurring beneath salts and earths in the waxy deepness of planets, but never on the surface of planets where men could discern it; and it is in touch with the Absolute, at base. In touch with the Absolute! At base. The name of this substance is: Holy the Firm.

Holy the Firm: and is Holy the Firm in touch with metals and minerals? With salts and earths? Of course, and straight on up, till "up" ends by curving back. Does something that touched something that touched Holy the Firm in touch with the Absolute at base seep into groundwater, into grain; are islands rooted in it, and trees? Of course.

Scholarship has long distinguished between two strains of thought that proceed in the West from human knowledge of God. In one, the ascetic's metaphysic, the world is far from God. Emanating from God, and linked to him by Christ, the world is yet infinitely other than God, furled away from him like the end of a long banner falling. This notion makes, to my mind, a vertical line of the world, a great chain of burning. The more accessible and universal view, held by Eckhart and by many peoples in various forms, is scarcely different from pantheism: that the world is immanation, that God is in the thing, and eternally present here, if nowhere else. By these lights the world is flattened on a horizontal plane, singular, all here, crammed with heaven, and alone. But I know that it is not alone, nor singular, nor all. The notion of immanence needs a handle, and the two ideas themselves need a link, so that life can mean aught to the one, and Christ to the other.

For to immanence, to the heart, Christ is redundant and all things are one. To emanance, to the mind, Christ touches only the top, skims off only the top, as it were, the souls of men, the wheat grains whole, and lets the chaff fall where? To the world flat and patently unredeemed; to the entire rest of the universe, which is irrelevant and nonparticipant; to time and matter unreal, and so unknowable, an illusory, absurd, accidental, and overelaborate stage.

But if Holy the Firm is "underneath salts," if Holy the Firm is matter at its dullest, Aristotle's *materia prima*, absolute zero, and since Holy the Firm is in touch with the Absolute at base, then the circle is unbroken. And it is. Thought advances, and the world creates itself, by the gradual positing of, and belief in, a series of bright ideas. Time and space are in touch with the Absolute at base. Eternity sockets twice into time and space curves, bound and bound by idea. Matter and spirit are of a piece but distinguishable; God has a stake guaranteed in all the world. And the universe is real and not a dream, not a manufacture of the senses; subject may know object, knowledge may proceed, and Holy the Firm is in short the philosopher's stone.

These are only ideas, by the single handful. Lines, lines, and their infinite points! Hold hands and crack the whip, and yank the Absolute out of there and into the light, God pale and astounded, spraying a spiral of salts and earths, God footloose and flung. And cry down the line to his passing white ear, "Old Sir! Do you hold space from buckling by a finger in its hole? O Old! Where is your other hand?" His right hand is clenching, calm, round the exploding left hand of Holy the Firm.

How can people think that artists seek a name? A name, like a face, is something you have when you're not alone. There is no such thing as an artist: there is only the world, lit or unlit as the light allows. When the candle is burning, who looks at the wick? When the candle is out, who needs it? But the world without light is wasteland and chaos, and a life without sacrifice is abomination.

What can any artist set on fire but his world? What can any people bring to the altar but all it has ever owned in the thin towns or over the desolate plains? What can an artist use but materials, such as they are? What can he light but the short string of his gut, and when that's burned out, any muck ready to hand?

His face is flame like a seraph's, lighting the kingdom of God for the people to see; his life goes up in the works; his feet are waxen and salt. He is holy and he is firm, spanning all the long gap with the length of his love, in flawed imitation of Christ on the cross stretched both ways unbroken and thorned. So must the work be also, in touch with, in touch with, in touch with; spanning the gap, from here to eternity, home.

Hoopla! All that I see arches, and light arches around it. The air churns out forces and lashes the marveling land. A hundred times through the fields and along the deep roads I've cried Holy. I see a hundred insects moving across the air, rising and falling. Chipped notes of birdsong descend from the trees, tuneful and broken; the notes pile about me like leaves. Why do these molded clouds make themselves overhead innocently changing, trailing their flat blue shadows up and down everything, and passing, and gone? Ladies and gentlemen! You are given insects, and birdsong, and a replenishing series of clouds. The air is buoyant and wholly transparent, scoured by grasses. The earth stuck through it is noisome, lighted, and salt. Who shall ascend into the hill of the Lord? or who shall stand in his holy place? "Whom shall I send," heard the first Isaiah, "and who will go for us?" And poor Isaiah, who happened to be standing there—and there was no one else—burst out, "Here am I; send me."

There is Julie Norwich. Julie Norwich is salted with fire. She is preserved like a salted fillet from all evil, baptized at birth into time and now into eternity, into the bladelike arms of God. For who will love her now, without a face, when women with faces abound, and people are so? People are reasoned, while God is mad. They love only beauty; who knows what God loves? Happy birthday, little one and wise: you got there early, the easy way. The world knew you before you knew the world. The gods in their boyish, brutal games bore you like a torch, a firebrand, recklessly over the heavens, to the glance of the one God, fathomless and mild, dissolving you into the sheets.

You might as well be a nun. You might as well be God's chaste bride, chased by plunderers to the high caves of solitude, to the heartless rooms empty of voices, and of warm limbs hooking your heart to the world. Look how he loves you! Are you bandaged now, or loose in a sterilized room? Wait till they hand you a mirror, if you can hold one, and know what it means. That skinlessness, that black shroud of flesh in strips on your skull, is your veil. There are two kinds of nun, out of the cloister or in. You can serve or you can sing, and wreck your heart in prayer, working the world's hard work. Forget whistling: you have no lips for that, or for kissing the face of a man or a child. Learn Latin, an it please my Lord, learn the foolish downward look called Custody of the Eyes.

And learn power, however sweet they call you, learn power, the smash of the holy once more, and signed by its name. Be victim to abruptness and seizures, events intercalated, swellings of heart. You'll climb trees. You won't be able to sleep, or need to, for the joy of it. Mornings, when light spreads over the pastures like wings, and fans a secret color into everything, and beats the trees senseless with beauty, so that you can't tell whether the beauty is *in* the trees—dazzling in cells like yellow sparks or green flashing waters—or *on* them—a transfiguring silver air charged with the wings' invisible motion; mornings, you won't be able to walk for the power of it: earth's too round. And by long and waking day—Sext, None, Vespers—when the grasses, living or dead, drowse while the sun reels, or lash in any wind, when sparrows hush and tides slack at the ebb, or flood up the beaches and cliffsides tangled with weed, and hay waits, and elsewhere people buy shoes—then you kneel, clattering with thoughts, ill, or some days erupting, some days holding the altar rail, gripping the brass-bolt altar rail, so you won't fly. Do you think I don't believe this? You have no idea, none. And nights? Nights after Compline under the ribs of Orion, nights in rooms at lamps or windows like moths? Nights you see Deneb, one-eyed over the trees; you vanish into the sheets, shrunken, your eyes bright as candles and as sightless, exhausted. Nights Murzim, Arcturus, Aldebaran in the Bull: You cry: My father, my father, the chariots of Israel, and the horsemen thereof! Held, held fast by love in the world like the moth in wax, your life a wick, your head on fire with prayer, held utterly, outside and in, you sleep alone, if you call that alone, you cry God.

Julie Norwich; I know. Surgeons will fix your face. This will all be a dream, an anecdote, something to tell your husband one night: I was burned. Or if you're scarred, you're scarred. People love the good not much less than the beautiful, and the happy as well, or even just the living, for the world of it all, and heart's home. You'll dress your own children, sticking their arms through the sleeves. Mornings you'll whistle, full of the pleasure of days, and afternoons this or that, and nights cry love. So live. I'll be the nun for you. I am now.

1977